THE AUTOBIOGRAPHY OF
JAMES T. KIRK

THE STORY OF STARFLEET'S GREATEST CAPTAIN

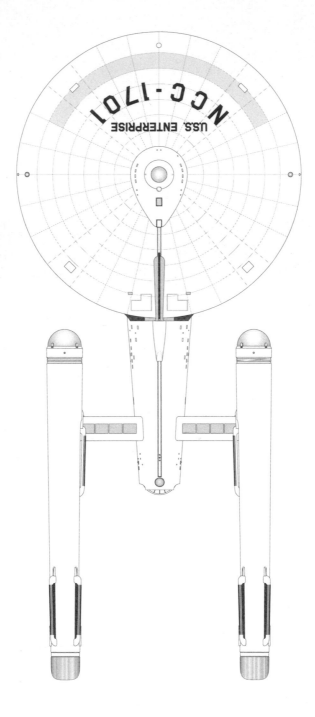

THE AUTOBIOGRAPHY OF
JAMES T. KIRK

THE STORY OF STARFLEET'S GREATEST CAPTAIN

BY
JAMES T. KIRK

EDITED BY DAVID A. GOODMAN

TITAN BOOKS

The Autobiography of James T. Kirk
Print Edition ISBN: 9781783297467
E-Book Edition ISBN: 9781783297474

Published by Titan Books
A division of Titan Publishing Group Ltd.
144 Southwark Street, London SE1 0UP

First edition: September 2015
10 9 8 7 6 5 4 3 2

The Autobiography of James T. Kirk is produced by becker&mayer! Book Producers,
Bellevue, Washington.
www.beckermayer.com

Jacket design: Julia Lloyd
Illustrations: Russell Walks
Editor: Dana Youlin
Interior design: Rosanna Brockley

A CIP catalogue record for this title is available from the British Library.

Printed and bound in the U.S.A.

Did you enjoy this book? We love to hear from our readers. Please e-mail us at:
readerfeedback@titanemail.com or write to Reader Feedback at the above address.

To receive advance information, news, competitions, and exclusive offers online,
please sign up for the Titan newsletter on our website: www.titanbooks.com.

CONTENTS

To Mom

THE AUTOBIOGRAPHY OF

JAMES T. KIRK

THE STORY OF STARFLEET'S GREATEST CAPTAIN

FOREWORD

BY LEONARD H. MCCOY, M.D.

FIRST LET ME JUST SAY, I'M A DOCTOR NOT A WRITER. But, having read this memoir, I've decided I do have something to add. For the most part, Jim Kirk said everything that needed to be said about himself. But he left out one important detail, for the obvious reason that he was too modest to think it, let alone say it, so I will:

He was the greatest hero who ever lived.

Now, before you assume I'm exaggerating, and before I tell you to go to hell, let's look at his life objectively. Who else in the last fifty years was at the center of so many critical events? Who else in that time made more decisions that affected the course of civilization? It seems unbelievable that so much history could be centered around one person, but the record is clear. And I don't know whether it was divine providence, luck, or the mythical Great Bird of the Galaxy that determined the man who would be in the center seat of the *Starship Enterprise*, I'm just thankful it was Jim Kirk.

Though he skips this description of himself, his memoir leaves out little else, and for that reason it is revelatory. The personal secrets in here paint an honest portrait of the man. In some ways, he was just like the rest of us: lonely, ambitious, a son, a father, a lover, never truly content. Where he set himself apart is in the way he took responsibility for his mistakes, embraced his weaknesses, and always strove to do better, to be better. It is in this way that he is a true hero; despite his successes, he knew there was always more work to be done, and he never shied away from the call of duty. His passing is a catastrophic loss; he looked after all of us.

For me, the loss is personal: I had no better friend, and I raise my glass to him one last time.

To James T. Kirk, captain of the *Enterprise*.

PROLOGUE

HIDING IN THE BASEMENT ON THE RUN FROM THE POLICE, it was difficult to see how I was going to save the Galaxy. But I had to work with what was at hand. Our hideout was neither well equipped nor comfortable. The brick room was cold and dark, smelled of ash and rodent urine, and its only source of heat against the bitter winter outside was a small coal-burning stove. All it provided in the way of equipment were thick cobwebs and a pile of damaged furniture. There were a few wooden storage boxes, stained presumably from exposed pipes that crisscrossed the low ceiling. Of course, the lack of the amenities was moot. This "headquarters" was only temporary, as it was doubtful the occupants of the building above would ignore us forever, especially if alerted by the local authorities.

And that was a concern, because though we'd been in the city, and the century, for less than ten minutes, I'd already managed to break the law. When we arrived through the time portal, I realized our uniforms made us stand out, so I stole some indigenous clothes hanging out to dry on the fire escape of a tenement building. Unfortunately, a policeman had observed my theft, so my companion had to momentarily disable him, allowing our escape. At the time, the crime didn't seem serious, but now I was having second thoughts; I had stolen the clothes from people living in poverty, who certainly couldn't afford to replace two sets of shirts and pants. This was further confirmed as I put the flannel shirt and cotton slacks on; though it presumably had been washed, the shirt still carried the strong odor of its owner's sweat. This smell was mixed with traces of diesel oil, tobacco smoke, and alcohol. The cloths' "bouquet" told a story: a primitive life of hard work, its stresses dulled by the use of cheap anesthetics. I found myself wishing for some.

"It's time we faced the unpleasant facts," I said. And they seemed endless. We didn't know where we were, only somewhere in the United States, and that we had arrived in the past *before* McCoy. That was crucial. We knew he would change the past, and thereby wipe out our future, but we didn't know exactly how. And we didn't know exactly *when* or *where* he would arrive.

"There is a theory," Spock said, when I voiced these concerns. "There could be some logic to the belief that time is fluid, like a river. With currents, eddies, backwash . . ."

So McCoy was going to surf a time current and wash up on our doorstep? If Spock hadn't been a Vulcan who had devoted his life to the pursuit of logic, I would've said it was wishful thinking. I had no choice, however, but to invest in this belief, because if McCoy were to show up somewhere else, how would we know? And even if by some miracle we found out, how would we get there? And even if we *could* get there, modes of travel were so primitive that we'd never reach another city in time to stop him. We didn't even know what he was going to do, so if any time passed before we found McCoy, he might have already changed the future. No, I was going to stick with Spock's river analogy. The alternative was too overwhelmingly bleak, and the fact that my unfailingly logical science officer believed it possible at least gave me hope.

"Frustrating," Spock said, referring to his tricorder. "Locked in here is the exact place and moment of his arrival. Even the images of what he did. If only I could tie this tricorder in with the ship's computer for just a few moments . . ."

"Couldn't you build some form of computer aid here?" I said.

"In this zinc-plated, vacuum-tubed culture?" Sometimes Spock spoke to me as though I was an idiot, and I knew most captains wouldn't put up with that from their first officers. But I accepted it as part of the package. And I had my own ways of torturing him.

"Well, it would prove to be an extremely complex problem in logic," I said, then turned to warm my hands in front of the stove. "Excuse me, I sometimes expect too much of you." The truth was, I did expect too much of him. Spock was right—the idea that he could construct a processing aid with technology 300 years out of date was ridiculous. Yet I fully expected that he'd be able to do it. And that expectation would motivate him to try. So I would leave that to him while I saw to our survival. Which seemed almost as impossible as building a computer from scratch.

We were stuck in an ancient capitalist-driven society where the *only* way to see to one's needs was by having money. We had none, and if we were going to survive, we were going to have to figure out how to earn some during a period where finding work was next to impossible. The more I thought about the situation, the more depressing it became. A lot of ancient religions relied on the concept of prayer, and in that moment I recognized the compelling power of superstition, to be able to silently ask for aid and comfort from a higher power. We would need help, and there was no one to ask, and I didn't believe in angels . . .

"Who's there?" A woman stood at the top of the stairs. I moved to intercept her to give Spock a moment to cover his ears with the wool hat I'd stolen for him. She stood in the light a few steps above me. She was in her thirties, wearing a plain blouse, skirt, and apron. Simple clothing, all somehow made elegant by its wearer.

"Excuse us, miss," I said, "we didn't mean to trespass. It's cold outside."

"A lie is a very poor way to say hello," she said. "It isn't that cold." Her light blue eyes carried a disdainful expression that immediately held sway over me. I knew at that moment either my lies were going to have to be a lot better, or that I was going to have to tell her the truth, as much of the truth as I could.

And I wanted to. I don't know why, but I didn't want to hide anything from her. And I would shortly learn that Spock's river analogy was true, and she was where it led. Because of her, I would literally save history. And I would also regret it for the rest of my life.

CHAPTER 1

WHEN MY MOTHER LEFT EARTH for a job on another planet, she said she'd be back often, and since I was nine, I took her at her word. The idea that a grown-up would not tell me the truth was beyond my experience.

I was with her and my dad on the front porch of our farm. The sun was setting and a few fireflies were out. You could see for miles; in the distance dark clouds let loose a bolt of lightning. My brother, Sam, was inside, lost in a book on his reader. Sam was twelve; he was always reading lately.

"I'm leaving in the morning," she said.

"Why do you have to go?"

My mother crouched down and met me eye-to-eye. She told me how important it was for her to go, and that it didn't mean she didn't love me. She had gotten a job as part of a colony on a planet called Tarsus IV. She said ships went back and forth all the time. I looked up at my dad, who was looking away. He watched the storm in the distance.

"When will you be back?"

"It'll be a few months," she said. "I'll definitely be back in time for your birthday."

"You don't know that," Dad snapped angrily. It was the first time he'd spoken since we had walked outside. I looked at him again, but he was still watching the storm.

"I'll be here," she said, still looking at me, determined to make it feel true. She then hugged me and lifted me up in her arms, making a big show of my weight. "God, you're so big. C'mon, let's get some dessert."

She looked over at Dad, then looked down. I desperately wanted him to make eye contact with her, and I could feel that Mom did too. But he wouldn't.

The next morning she was gone, taking my idea of home with her.

✦

Up to then I'd had a wonderful boyhood, filled with dogs, campfires, birthdays, horseback riding, snowball fights, and plenty of friends. Just like the Earth of today, there was no poverty or war or deprivation. My parents would talk about the problems in the Galaxy, but I wasn't really paying attention. Sometimes I'd look up in the sky and my brother would point out to me the satellites or a shuttle taking off, but that's as close as my mind got to outer space. Close to home felt perfect.

We lived on a farm near Riverside, Iowa, on a piece of property that had about 200 hectares of crops. We grew soybeans and corn, had chickens for eggs and cattle for milk and cheese. As far back as I can remember we were up at 4 a.m. every day to feed the chickens and milk the cows. Most of the caring of the crops was handled by automated machinery, but my father still insisted we get out in the fields for planting and harvesting. Though we were in no way dependent on the farm for our livelihood, my father still thought it important to understand the work involved in living off our land.

The house was four bedrooms, two floors, brick and wood. It was built using authentic materials and was a perfect copy of the house that had stood on the property for over 100 years in the 19th and 20th centuries. The property had belonged to seven generations of Kirks; it was family legend that my great-great-great-great-great-great-great-grandfather, Franklin Kirk, purchased the farm in 1843 from Isaac Cody, who was the father of William F. "Buffalo Bill" Cody.* My ancestors in the modern era let caretakers manage

---

*EDITOR'S NOTE: Though Isaac Cody was a well-known and successful developer in the region during the 19th century, there is no record of him selling a farm to Franklin Kirk.

it, until my grandparents moved back there when they retired. My father, George Kirk, also always had a strong desire to live there.

He had grown up as one of the original "Starfleet brats"; his father, Tiberius Kirk, was already in his twenties when Starfleet Academy was founded, and though he applied, he wasn't accepted. Still wanting to get out into space, Tiberius signed on in ordnance and supply, eventually serving on several of the then-new starbases. He met and married my paternal grandmother, Brunhilde Ann Milano, a nurse, on Starbase 8. My father was born there on December 13, 2206.

In those days, a child's life on a starbase was pretty spartan; there weren't a lot of families living on them, and the facilities were very limited. It was truly life on the frontier, and my father dreamed of getting back to see Earth, a dream that wouldn't be fulfilled until he arrived for his first day at Starfleet Academy. It was my grandfather's hope that his son would go to the academy, and admission had gotten even more competitive. But after rescuing five men after an explosion on the loading dock of Starbase 8, Tiberius was awarded the Starfleet Medal of Honor. And though my grandfather was still an enlisted man, the children of Medal of Honor winners are always given high priority during the admissions process.

My father graduated fifth in his class from the academy and, after serving a year as an instructor, was assigned to the *U.S.S. Los Angeles* (where he served with future captain Robert April). He was quickly promoted and eventually took the post of first officer aboard the *U.S.S. Kelvin*, when the previous first officer, Richard Robau, was promoted to captain. Over the course of six years he had moved up the ranks at record speed. If his career had continued, he might have been one of the youngest captains in the history of Starfleet, but his personal life led him in a different direction.

My mother, born Winona Davis, was also from a spacegoing family; her father, James Ogaleesha Davis (his middle name, as befit his heritage, was Native American Sioux, although I never did find out what it meant*), was in the first graduating class of Starfleet Academy; his wife, Wendy Felson, was in the third. My maternal grandfather was an engineer, my maternal grandmother a physician, and their daughter, my mother,

---

*EDITOR'S NOTE: The translation of the Sioux name "Ogaleesha" is "Wears a Red Shirt."

attended the academy and decided she wanted to be an astrobiologist. She was four years younger than my father, and had him as an instructor in her Introduction to Federation History class.

"There were strict rules about students 'fraternizing' with instructors," she told me, "and once I met your father, I wanted to break all of them."

It is hard to know how many of the rules they actually broke, as a son usually doesn't delve into those topics with his parents. However, when my father received his posting to the *Los Angeles*, the ship was still three months away from returning to Earth, so he asked for a short leave from his duties as an instructor, and immediately proposed to my mother.

"Most people assumed we'd made a terrible mistake," my mom said, "but it was impossible for us to see a possible downside then. We were crazy in love." And then, suddenly, the *Los Angeles* arrived, and my dad was off.

My mom was still in the academy and said she secretly hoped that they'd be posted together. It was over a year before she saw him next, and then almost two years after that, she graduated. She was not, however, posted to the same ship as Dad. Shortly after my mother was posted to the *U.S.S. Patton*, she discovered she was pregnant.

"Your father was aboard the *Los Angeles* then," she told me, "and by the time the subspace message reached him I was already in my second trimester."

Mom's Starfleet career came to an abrupt halt; she took a leave of absence, moving in with my dad's parents on Earth (her parents had passed away several years earlier) on the family farm. My brother, George Samuel, named for my father, was born on August 17, 2230.

The maximum amount of time my mother could stay away from Starfleet without resigning her commission was two years. For that period, she and my father were apart. She stayed on the farm and raised George with her in-laws, while she also continued her studies and completed a doctorate in astrobiology.

"It was a good time to be with George Jr.," she said, "but I missed George Sr. This was not what I expected my life to be. My own mother had resigned her commission when she had me. She had raised my brother and me by herself since Dad was off in space. I was determined not to be a single parent, yet here I found myself doing just that."

She told me she felt conflicted about leaving her two-year-old son. "Your grandparents were energetic and attentive, which made the decision a little easier, but I couldn't get past the idea that I was abandoning my baby."

Dad also missed Mom, and when the two years were up, he pulled whatever strings he could to get her posted to the *Kelvin*, where he was now the first officer. Unfortunately, soon after she arrived, she discovered she was pregnant again, this time with me.

My dad said Captain Robau was furious; even if regulations had allowed children aboard a ship, he wasn't a commander who would've wanted it. However, that wasn't really the impetus for Dad's impending decision. Shortly after determining that my mother was pregnant, Dad received word that his father, Tiberius, had passed away.

"It was a strange 'circle of life' kind of moment," my dad told me. "Though I'd grown up in space, my father had been with me the whole time. Now that he was gone, I realized I barely knew my first son, and I had a second child on the way. I wasn't going to let your mom go home and raise our children by herself." So he resigned his commission.

Over the years, I've thought a lot about the decision Dad made and how it affected me. I have told many people that my father leaving Starfleet inspired my own career, to complete the career he didn't get to finish. Though that is partially true, the rest of the story is a lot more complicated.

I was born on March 22, 2233, to a complete family: I grew up in a house with two parents, an older brother, and a grandmother. It was my own slice of heaven. I was protected, lived in a clean, safe world. But it was a façade; I just wasn't sophisticated enough to see through it.

As I look back now, I can see that my parents were not happy. They didn't fight, they didn't even disagree openly, but the moments of warmth between them were rare. Mom worked hard around the house, but the work itself wasn't what she wanted to do. I have a lot of memories of those times finding my mother off in a corner reading. My father was attentive to her, but not overly affectionate. He had strong ideas of what he wanted life on the farm to be like, and he got a lot of confirmation for this from his mother, Brunhilde, who still lived with us. Grandma Hilde had lived her whole life on the frontier of other worlds, and my memory of her was as a hardscrabble, somewhat unforgiving individual. My mother never saw herself as living on a farm, so she didn't argue with how they wanted to do things, but the situation took its toll. Eventually, she decided to pursue her career again.

"It wasn't what I wanted," my father told me much later, "but I wanted her to be happy."

✦

"Sam, can I come in?" I said. (I was the only one who called my brother by his middle name. I don't know how it started, but I kept calling him Sam well into adulthood.) I was standing outside of Sam's bedroom. He was lying on his stomach reading. It had been only a few weeks after my mother departed. It had been very quiet around the house. My father had kept up our routines of school, chores, homework. My grandmother was looking after our meals and clothing, and we were all pretending like nothing had changed.

"Yeah, you can come in," he said, without looking up. This was unusual for him to grant me permission to come into his room. It was also unusual for me to ask; normally I would just barrel in and wait for him to throw me out.

I took only a half step into the room and looked around. Sam had lots of trophies, some athletic, many academic. He always impressed me. In fact, from the minute I was aware, probably around two years old, all I wanted was my brother's approval and attention, and it seemed to me he took great pleasure in withholding both. Most of his energy directed at me went into putting up an emotional blockade to my devotion, though sometimes, if his friends weren't available, I was a stand-in playmate, or, more accurately, a fawning sidekick.

At five, I remember watching in fascination as he mixed homemade gunpowder and used it to make a cannon out of old tin cans with the bottoms cut out and soldered together. I shared the blame when his invention blew a hole in the side of the barn. Though we were given double chores for a week, I felt happy that somehow I'd been given credit for his rambunctious ingenuity. He, of course, was irritated by my delight at us being mistaken as a team.

He always seemed calm and logical, which led me to try to tease a reaction out of him with my big emotions. My dad would often have to intervene, but he seemed a little amused by my desire to get a rise out of Sam.

And as far as I could tell, both he and my father weren't the least bit affected by Mom's leaving. This didn't help me make sense of the confusion I felt. Dad was especially unapproachable; I felt an almost psychic fence around him. Sam, despite his "disdain" for me as the little brother, was somehow a little more accessible. Or maybe just a little less scary.

"What do you want?" he asked without looking up from his reader.

"Sam . . . do you know why Mom left?"

"It's because she got a job," Sam said.

"She didn't have a job before."

"She did, but she quit it to have kids," he said.

"Oh."

"She had work she always wanted to do," he said.

Sam stopped reading and looked at me. It seemed like he looked at me for a very long time. Then he spoke.

"Do you miss her?"

I don't remember if I answered; I just started crying.

Sam got off his bed and came over to me. He then awkwardly hugged me. I don't know if we'd ever hugged before that, and it didn't come naturally to him, but it was enough comfort for me. At that moment, my brother seemed like an adult, though he was only 12 years old and probably was feeling as lost as I was. I don't remember how long I cried, but eventually I stopped.

"You should probably go wash your face," he said. I left his room, but from that point on, Sam was no longer as cool to me, and eventually we became quite close.

✦

The weeks turned into months, and then years. Mom made a sincere, dogged effort to stay in touch with us over subspace, but there was no real-time communication over that distance, so we would record messages that she would watch, and then she would record responses that we'd watch. She kept her promise to be home for my next birthday, but it was the last birthday she'd celebrate with me for several years. Over time, the jealousy I had toward my friends whose families were still whole drove me into isolation. I spent my free time after school wandering our property, trying to get lost. I was starting to feel like I wanted to get away.

My dad still did his best to create the life he wanted us to have. We spent a lot of time together and took a lot of trips. He especially enjoyed camping, and during these excursions he would share with us his knowledge of the American frontier, which our ancestors helped settle. His interest became mine, one I pursue to this day.

We took advantage of the many national parks around the country, including Yosemite and Yellowstone. He had taught me horseback riding on our farm, and on these trips he'd let me go off on my own, as long as I was back in camp by sunset. I enjoyed the independence and the sense of adventure, though there was rarely any real danger.

However, during one of these solitary horseback rides, my horse was spooked by the sound of a loud boom. Once I'd gotten the animal under control, I looked up to find the source of the noise, and saw something high in the sky, falling fast. As it got closer, it looked like it was on fire. At first it was very distant, and then suddenly it wasn't; it was growing in size and seemed like it was headed directly toward me.

I grabbed the reins tight, tapped my heels against my horse, taking off at a fast gallop. I kept looking back over my shoulder, and my error became clear. I had misjudged the angle of the approaching object, and if I had just stayed still it would have flown over me. But by riding off, I was actually putting myself more directly in its path. My panic only led me to continue to try to outrun it.

I finally looked back and saw the large metal object now only a few hundred meters behind me, flames dancing off it. It looked like it was going to hit me, and in terror I leaped off my moving horse. I hit the ground and rolled, and as I looked up, I saw the flaming belly of the craft as it flew over me, then heard it crash. There was a blast of intense heat. I smelled smoke and could hear the crackling of fire. I stood up and saw the crash, only about 30 meters from me.

There was a gash in the forest; trees on either side of the wreck were broken away and charred black. The wreck was smoking and clearly not from this planet. It was small, a two-person shuttle of some kind. My horse was gone; I was momentarily scared that it had been hit, then saw its hoof-prints heading off from the wreck. The animal had had the good sense of how to get out of danger. But now I was stranded. I wasn't even sure how far away I was from our campsite, and it was getting dark.

"You! Get in here, now!"

The voice came from inside the ship. It was a scary, guttural, accented English. I started to back away.

"Stop, or you will regret it! Now get in here!"

I froze.

"Now!"

I slowly approached the craft. The front of the ship was firmly lodged in the ground, its back end pointed up toward the sky. There was an immense amount of steam emanating from the hull as the heat from its rapid reentry dissipated. There was an open hatch, but it was too dark inside to make anything out. I looked around for any sign of an adult. Spaceships couldn't just land on Earth without being noticed; somebody had to know about this. But I didn't see anyone. I knew, or hoped, help would be there soon.

"I said get in here!"

I climbed up inside the hatch. My eyes adjusted to the dim cabin light. The whole ship was on a severe tilt, and I held on to the hatch frame in order to maintain my footing. The cabin was small, jammed with control panels and storage lockers. There were two chairs in the front, and I could make out in the dim light two figures, both large, dark. One sat unmoving in the pilot's chair, the other in the passenger seat, wedged under a fallen piece of the ship's inner superstructure. He was the one who shouted orders at me. He was humanoid, but not a human. His features, dark eyes, prominent nose, and forehead were truly frightening. At first.

"You're a child!" He said it as if I'd committed a crime.

"I'm eleven," I said.

Trying to keep my balance in the tilted room, I moved carefully toward him. As I got closer, I became more fully aware that he wasn't tall, but just wide. And his face . . . once I got a look at it, I wasn't scared anymore. He looked to me like a giant pig.

"What are you waiting for? Get me out of here! Can't you see I'm injured?!"

This was the first time I'd met a Tellarite, and to this day I'm still impressed by the ease with which they can slide into argument. I've since learned that disagreeing is actually a societal and academic tradition in their culture, a challenging of the status quo that they see as crucial to their growth and prosperity as a society. At the time, however, I accepted his disdain as an accurate judgment of my abilities.

The metal girder pinning him down had cut into his leg. There was a thick, brown liquid on his pants, which I realized was his blood. I stepped in to try to lift the girder, but it was ridiculous to try; even a grown man wouldn't have been able to lift it.

"It's too heavy," I said. "I should go get help—"

"Ridiculous! You leave me and I will die!"

It was the first time I'd seen an adult of any kind more scared than I was. I turned and was startled at the other figure in the pilot's chair. There was a piece of shrapnel lodged in his forehead. His eyes and mouth were open as if in a silent scream. This was also the first time I had seen a dead body. I was shaking as the complainer grabbed me.

"What are you waiting for?!"

"Your leg doesn't look that bad. Are you sure I shouldn't just get—"

"Idiot! Do the humans teach their children nothing?! My leg isn't what's going to kill me! The ship's reactor is leaking radiation!"

I was old enough to know that "radiation" was bad. I suppose I should've run out of there to protect myself, but somehow I felt this pissed-off Tellarite was now my responsibility. I looked around the room for some kind of solution.

"Do you have a communicator or something?"

"You are an imbecile from a race of imbeciles! It's been damaged!"

"What about . . ." I said. "What about an engineer's tool kit?"

"Oh, so you think you're going to fix my broken ship? You, the idiot human? How did I get so lucky . . ."

"No, I thought if you had a laser torch, I could cut the metal piece that's holding—"

"Do I look like an engineer? Check those storage lockers," he said. "Hurry!" He obviously quickly changed his mind about my idea. I opened the storage lockers and finally found what looked like a tool kit. Inside, the tools were unfamiliar.

"Which one's—?"

"That one, you fool! We are going to die because you are such a fool!"

He indicated something that bore only a slight resemblance to my father's laser torch. I picked it up. It was bulky and heavy. I didn't know quite what do to with it, and felt a rising flood of frustration and anguish. I was going to cry. The Tellarite's histrionics, the dead body, the dark room, and now this tool I didn't know how to use. I wanted to leave, but I had to stay. Caught in an unresolvable conflict, I just tried to keep going.

I focused on the laser torch. It was designed for a hand with two thick fingers and a thumb. After a moment, I realized I could operate it if I used both of my hands, and quickly went back to the Tellarite. I aimed it at the girder just above his chest, when he grabbed my arm.

"What are you doing?! Trying to kill me? Is it revenge you want?"

"No," I said. "If I cut the piece here, I will be able to move it so you can slide out."

"Hurry up!" I guess he was on board.

I had seen my father use a torch to cut, but he used one designed for human hands. Still, I did what I could to imitate what I'd seen. I carefully aimed the torch and turned it on. A blue-white beam hit the girder. I slowly moved it up, away from the Tellarite, and I could see it was cutting through the thick metal. I took my time and sliced through the girder. I turned the torch off, carefully put it aside, then put both of my hands on the much smaller piece I'd cut and tried to move it. It initially wouldn't budge, and I was suddenly worried that I'd missed something. I looked it over, and decided I had no choice but to try again. I pushed, and this time it gave and slid away. I chuckled involuntarily, surprised at my success. But the Tellerite wasn't interested in congratulating me.

"Move!" He pushed me aside and slid from his chair. Screaming in pain, he fell to the tilted deck. He turned on his stomach, and I watched as he tried to scramble up to the hatch. But between his weight and his injury, and the severe angle of the deck, he was helpless. I stared at this pathetic sight, unsure of what to do, until he finally stopped struggling and turned to me, breathing heavily. He said nothing.

"Can . . . can I help you?" I asked.

He was silent. I took that as a yes.

It wasn't easy getting the Tellarite out of the ship, but once I did, I got under his left arm and helped him walk as far away from the wreck as we could. We'd only gotten a few steps when a Starfleet Fire and Rescue team landed in a medical shuttle. As the medics tended to their patient, it was satisfying to watch the Tellarite treat them with the same amount of disdain he had for me.

As one of the doctors gave me an examination, another shuttle arrived, and several Starfleet officers piled out, three in red shirts, one in gold. The one in gold was in his fifties, gray haired, had a natural sense of authority. He walked over to the Tellarite, spoke to him for a moment. The Tellarite indicated me, and the gold-shirted officer turned, looked at me with surprise, then came over. I was concerned that the Tellarite had somehow gotten me in trouble.

"What's your name, son?" he said.

"James Tiberius Kirk," I said.

"Nice to meet you. I'm Captain George Mallory." He shook my hand. "The Tellarite ambassador tells me you saved his life."

"He's . . . the ambassador?" I almost missed that part because I was so surprised that the Tellarite had given me credit for pulling him out of the ship.

"Yes," Mallory said. "He was heading to San Francisco, but his pilot refused to follow our landing procedures and got into some trouble. A few more minutes exposed to the radiation in that craft and he would've died. You helped prevent an intergalactic incident, son. You're a real hero."

"Thanks," I said. I couldn't hold back my smile.

✦

"You're going to go live with your mom for a little while," Dad said. It was June of 2245, I was 12, and Grandma Hilde had just passed away. Sam, at 15, had gained early acceptance to the University of Chicago and would be starting there in a few months. Mom had made the suggestion that I come to live with her, and though Dad resisted it, I was thrilled.

Since my encounter with the Tellarite ambassador, I had definitely become more interested with everything associated with other planets. I had started to ask my father if he thought I should join Starfleet, and was always surprised at how little enthusiasm he had for it. He would tell me how competitive gaining entrance to the academy was, even for the children of graduates, and he also constantly emphasized to me the careers available to people on Earth. I could tell that he was worried that my experience with the Tellarite had filled me with delusions of heroic grandeur; and at that point, he might have been right.

On top of the adventure of moving to a new planet, I was actually going to be traveling there by myself. Dad, however, was not ready to entrust me to the crew of a ship, so he made contact with a family that was moving to Tarsus IV, and they agreed to look after me for the two-month trip. Still, to be going somewhere without a parent at the age of 12 was exciting.

A couple of months later, I was packed and ready to go. Sam had already left for school, so it was just Dad taking me to the shuttle port in Riverside in his hover car. We drove in silence on the half-hour trip along the highway that connected our farm to the city.

The port was a small one; shuttles connected to the major cities of Earth, and one made the trip each day to Earth One, the orbital facility in space. When we arrived, Dad and I went to look for the family who I was going to be traveling with.

"George!" A big bearlike man with unkempt hair barreled toward us and warmly shook Dad's hand.

"Rod, this is my son Jim," Dad said. "Jim, this is Rod Leighton." The big man looked down at me and gave me a pat on the shoulder.

"Jim! Nice to meet you! Come meet the family!"

Rod led us over to the shuttle boarding entrance, where a diminutive woman and a boy about my age were waiting.

"Hello, Barbara," Dad said to the woman. She gave him a hug, then turned and looked at me.

"Jim, it's going to be a pleasure having you with us," she said. She gave me a warm smile.

"Are you kidding, we're lucky he's letting us come with him," Rod said. He then turned to the boy. "Tom, introduce yourself. You guys are going to be spending a lot of time together."

"I'm Tom," he said. There was a little bit of sarcasm in his voice, but he put his hand out and I shook it. This less-than-auspicious beginning to my relationship with Tom Leighton was interrupted by an announcement over the public address system.

"Attention, this is the final boarding call for Orbital Flight 37 . . ."

"That's us," Rod said.

I turned to look at my dad. This was the first moment in all the months leading up to this trip that I realized I'd be leaving him.

"Don't give the Leightons any trouble," he said.

"I won't."

"I'll see you soon," he said. "Take care of your mom. Be safe out there."

I thought he would give me a hug, but instead he held out his hand for me to shake. I shook it. We then all turned to board the shuttle. I turned back and saw him standing there. He smiled at me and waved me on. I was leaving him, without Mom or Sam in the house, all alone on the farm. And I was guilty, not because I wanted to stay, but because I really wanted to go. I felt I was finally getting to say goodbye to my childhood, and in truth I was, but not in the way that I thought.

We climbed aboard the shuttle, and Rod got us seats near one of the portholes. My face stayed plastered to the window as we took off. The gravity plating and inertial dampeners on the shuttle made it almost impossible to sense you were moving at all; it made the world outside look like a movie. As the shuttle banked before heading out into space, I caught sight of my dad, standing in the port alone, watching us go. I waved, but he couldn't see me.

✦

We cleared the atmosphere in less than five minutes and were suddenly in orbit. It was my first time in space, and it was stunning to see the big blue marble of Earth below, the sky filled with spaceships and satellites, and finally Earth One, the large orbital station that serviced and supplied the ships that came into orbit. We were flying to Tarsus on the *S.S. New Rochelle*, which was in a parking orbit away from the station. It was a supply ship, an old Class-J cargo tug with an updated engine. As we approached, the ship looked huge; it had a forward command section, and a long thin hull in the back that housed modular cargo holds. It looked like an ancient railroad train in space.

The shuttle docked at an airlock near the forward command section. I grabbed my duffel bag and followed the Leightons as we entered through a docking tunnel. A crewwoman holding a tablet checked us in, then directed us aft. We passed a few open hatchways to modular cargo pods, where we could see crewmen who worked busily in the cavernous holds, stacking crates and storage containers.

We reached a hatch to the rearmost cargo hold, and Rod led us inside. As we entered, we saw that it wasn't cavernous like the others. The interior had been redesigned; walls and corridors had been inserted to create several floors of passenger quarters. We found our stateroom.

"Here it is," Rod said. "Home sweet home." It was small, with two bunk beds, two closets, and four drawers for storage. But it was clean and spare, and I found its small size and efficiency somehow exciting. Rod went over to one of the bunk beds.

"I'm on top," he said, with a wink to his wife. She looked genuinely annoyed and slapped his shoulder. Rod then turned to me and Tom.

"What say you, boys? You want to go find a porthole and watch us leave orbit?" Rod didn't even wait for a response; he was out the door and Tom and I were on his heels. We headed forward and crossed through two cargo holds and reached the entrance to the command and drive section. There was a guard posted who stopped us.

"Sorry, authorized personnel only," he said.

"Oh, apologies, the captain's son wanted to see us leave orbit," Rod said, indicating me. "I figured it wouldn't be a problem. Come on, boys, let's—"

"Wait . . . whose son?" The guard looked worried. "He's Captain Mayweather's son?"

"Don't worry about it, I understand you've got orders. Come on, boys . . ."

Rod led us back the way we came, but the guard stopped us.

"I can let you into the command section, but you have to stay where I put you . . ."

"You sure? I don't want you to get in trouble."

"It's okay, but as soon as we go to warp, you have to come back."

"Sure, fine."

The guard led us into the command section; he indicated an access ladder, and we left him behind as we climbed it. The ladder led to a forward observation deck. It was cramped, barely enough room for the three of us, but the view port filled up the whole wall. It was like we were standing in outer space, looking out on Earth and all the spaceships in orbit.

"Mr. Leighton, how did you know the captain had a son?" I said.

"I didn't," Rod said, smiling. "And you can call me Rod."

I laughed. A bluff! And it was quite a big one we found out when we later met Captain Mayweather, whose dark skin indicated a pure African ancestry. He was also well over 100.

We were only on the observation deck for a few moments before we noticed Earth and the ships in orbit slipping away. As Earth moved behind us, I noticed off to the right in the distance a metal web surrounding a large space vehicle. It was a ship in dry dock. As we got closer, I could make out small repair craft buzzing about it. The superstructure of the dry dock kept me from getting a complete look at the ship, but it had the familiar saucer and two-engine nacelle design of many Starfleet vessels. Yet somehow it seemed larger and different than any ship I'd seen before.

"Dad, what ship is that?" Tom said. I was so intent on getting a better look at the ship I hadn't noticed Tom looking as well.

"One of the new *Constitution*-class ships," Rod said.

"What's the *Constitution* class?" Tom said.

"They say it's going to be faster than any ship ever built," he said. "It's going to be able to survive in space without maintenance and resupply the way most ships have to. They have high hopes for it."

We passed the dry dock and then it and the ship were gone. It would be a number of years before I got a better look at it.

CHAPTER 2

THE TWO-MONTH TRIP TO TARSUS IV was uneventful and eventually quite dull. Tom Leighton and I were the only two kids on the voyage, and by the time it was over we knew every detail of the ship and about each other. Tom reminded me a lot of Sam; he was smart and quiet, loved to read, and wanted to be a scientist. Once he got comfortable with me, I found him to be an engaging friend. He often pulled weird facts out of his head that were always interesting and entertaining.

One night, while everyone was asleep, he woke me up, excited.

"Come on, Jim, I found out where the artificial gravity generator is." I had no idea what he was talking about, but I got dressed and joined him as we headed out to the catwalk that led to the rest of the ship. Like most ships in Starfleet, the *New Rochelle* tried to imitate Earth's conditions of day and night, so this was the late shift and most of the crew were off duty and asleep.

Tom led me to a ladder that went down to the bottom of the main hull. When we reached the deck, he indicated a hatch.

"Right behind that is the artificial generator for the entire ship," he said. "It took me a while to figure out where it was."

"Congratulations," I said. I was really tired and not a little confused.

"Come on," he said, and immediately headed off.

"Where the hell are we going?"

"You'll see."

We headed back up the ladder, and then forward again. We then snuck into a cargo hold and stopped on the catwalk. We were about 100 feet off the floor of the hold, which was partially filled with storage containers.

"According to my measurements, we're about halfway between the artificial gravity generator and the bow plate." Tom put his hands on the railing of the catwalk.

"So?"

"Watch." Tom pushed hard on the railing and suddenly was rising off the deck. He flipped over and landed, feetfirst on the ceiling. It looked like he was standing upside down.

"Holy crap," I said. "What the hell is going on?"

"I read about it," Tom said. "These cargo ships used to be run by families who learned all sorts of facts about these ships. Some of them called this 'the sweet spot.' Try it!"

I grasped the railing and pushed. At first I was just pushing up my own weight, and then suddenly I was weightless and moving through the air. I tumbled end over end. I actually hit Tom and we fell to the "floor," which was actually the ceiling. It was amazing.

"Let's do it again!"

Both of us lost in laughter, we then pushed off together and landed on the catwalk. We kept going back and forth, laughing, yelling, almost missing the catwalk a couple of times, until finally a security guard found us and dragged us back to our quarters. We spent a lot of the next two months sneaking off to this area. Eventually, I became interested in why it was happening, and I sought out a crew member who explained it to me. It was my first experience trying to understand life in outer space, and the relationship between humans and their spacecraft. It also taught me a valuable lesson on the inherent risks involved in space travel, as on one of these excursions I got careless; I missed the catwalk and landed on the cargo bay floor, breaking my wrist.

While my wrist healed, I ended up spending a lot of time with Tom's parents. They were very loving and attentive to him, and treated me like I was a member of their family. They made sure I was taken care of, and that I kept up with my studies. Barbara, a physician, always asked me lots of questions about my interests and was on me constantly about whether I was getting enough to eat. She was small, probably just over five feet tall, but she had a quiet intensity that somehow gave her authority over the three larger males in her care. She stood in great contrast to her husband, a boisterous raconteur who thrived on attention. (Rod, much to his wife's chagrin, taught Tom and me poker on that trip, where I learned more about his ability to bluff. No real money exchanged hands, but it was still instructive.) Rod was skilled in modern construction and was very excited about joining the colony, and though my mother had been on Tarsus IV for years, it wasn't until this trip that I learned about its history.

Humans settled Tarsus IV in the 22nd century after the Romulan War. Most of the settlers were veterans of the conflict who, with their families, purposely picked a planet on the other side of the Galaxy from the Romulans and the Klingons. Their goal was a society devoted to peace. So, although many of them had served on ships as soldiers, they devoted themselves to a scientifically constructed technocracy. The government was built on completely practical notions of what the individuals in the society needed and what they in turn could provide. For a century the colony had flourished as one of the most successful examples of human achievement in the Galaxy. At 13 I don't know if I fully understood the accomplishment of the people who built this world, but looking back it makes what would happen there that much more tragic.

We arrived at Tarsus IV on schedule, and the Leightons and I were among the first people to be taken down to the planet. As the pilot took the shuttle below the cloud cover, I could see huge tracts of barren, rocky land. Then in the distance there was a strip of green, and we came in on a landing field outside a small city. When we stepped off the shuttle onto my first foreign planet, I was surprised at what I saw: blue skies, rolling hills, grass, and trees. My first exposure to a Class-M planet; it wasn't foreign at all. It could easily have been mistaken for Southern California.

The spaceport was only a few kilometers outside the main town. I could see the dense sprawl of buildings, none higher than four stories. It had the feel of a late-19th-century European city, dense but not quite modern. I was trying to take it all in, when I was startled by someone calling my name.

"Jim!" I turned. It was my mother. Because of the limits of communication while in transit, I hadn't heard from her in the months since I left Earth. I had gotten so caught up with space travel and landing on a new world I'd actually forgotten about her.

She ran toward me, a giant smile on her face. She'd gotten older since I'd seen her last; in my mind she was still the young, vibrant woman who lifted me up in her arms when I was little. Now, because I'd grown, she seemed small to me. It was a difficult adjustment; she strode like a beautiful colossus in my imagination and now she was only slightly taller than me. She squeezed me in a warm hug. I could feel her tremble as she fought back tears. I felt the eyes of everyone around us as she embraced me, and though as a child I'd missed this affection, in this moment I could not return it. She felt my awkwardness and stepped back. We were almost on the same eye level.

"You've gotten so big," she said. Whether intentionally or not, that was one of the last things she said to me before she left Earth. Now, unlike then, I heard the regret in her voice. We stood in uneasy silence for a long moment; then the Leightons stepped in and introduced themselves to her. Barbara said some things about what a nice young man I was. Mom wasn't particularly warm to them; she seemed uncomfortable, anxious to get me away.

"Come on, Jim, let's go home."

I could see Rod was a little put off by her attitude, but Barbara placed a gentle hand on his forearm. Barbara said they'd see me later, she was sure, and I said goodbye and thanked them. Mom helped me with my luggage, and we headed off to a waiting hover car, a simple vehicle with four seats and an open trunk. She drove it herself into the main city.

As we glided through the streets, Mom gave me a tour. She seemed very self-conscious talking to me, and I frankly wasn't doing anything to help put her at ease. She filled the time by explaining the colony to me.

"There are 12 boulevards that radiate out from the city center," she said, as we entered the outer perimeter. The boulevard we were on was surrounded on both sides by buildings no more than three stories in height, and they looked to be made of brick and stone. It all seemed very old to me.

"All the buildings except the ones of the original settlement are made of indigenous materials," she said. I sat there quietly. "You know what indigenous means?"

"Yes," I said. I was being purposely curt. Since seeing her, I had felt an unexpected surge of anger, and it was overwhelming me.

The boulevard, simply labeled 12th Street, converged with all the boulevards in the center square. This was the site of the original settlement, and the buildings here, while in fact the oldest, looked the newest. Arranged to establish a town square, they were made from prefabricated materials designed to weather harsh environments. The square was quite large, and we drove through it and continued on to the other side of town. My mother tried to fill in as much information as she could, then asked me for details of my trip. I gave her mostly one-word answers. She was struggling to connect, and I was making sure she failed.

She pulled the hover car over near a redbrick two-story building. We got out and she led me inside to a first-floor apartment. It was simple, clean, and quaint. She had indulged in the ancient tradition of putting photographs on the wall; Sam and I were everywhere I looked, at every age. I didn't even remember some of the pictures being taken. She showed me to my room, which had a small bed, dresser, and its own window that looked out onto the street.

"I know it's not much," she said.

"It's fine," I said.

"Let me help you unpack."

"I can handle it."

"Okay," she said. There was a chime that I assumed was a doorbell. Mom left my room to head to the front door. I didn't follow, but stood and watched as she opened it. On the other side was a short, bald man in some kind of uniform coveralls. He had a badge and held a tablet with a stylus. He had a friendly, open demeanor.

"Hey Winona," he said. "Just checking to make sure you got your son okay."

"Thanks, Peter," she said. "Yes, it went fine."

"So I'll change the occupancy on your unit," he said, marking the tablet. "Can I meet him?"

"Sure," she said. "Jim?"

I pretended I hadn't been listening and came out after she called a second time.

"Jim, this is Peter Osterlund. He's an officer in the colony's security section."

"Nice to meet you, son," he said. "Now, Winona, you'll have him examined by medical—"

"In less than 24 hours, yes," she said.

"Okay, great," he said, finishing on the tablet. "See you soon!" And with that he was gone.

"What was that all about?"

"The colony keeps highly detailed records of its inhabitants. It allows for very specific planning regarding the use of resources. There are computer models that use our genetic makeup to determine accurate predictions of our consumption of food, water, medicine, everything. Even down to the wear and tear on the pavement of the sidewalks."

"Why?"

"Well, Jim, we're pretty far away from Earth and the rest of the Federation," she said. "This planet doesn't have an abundant supply of resources, so careful planning is necessary. We're self-sustaining, but just barely."

"I don't understand," I said.

"What?"

"Why does anyone want to live here?" My tone reflected a harshness that was out of proportion to the question; it belied a subtext of resentment that I'm not sure even I was aware of.

"Well, one might see it as a challenge," she said. "You can have an impact out here that you can't on Earth. But that might not be a good enough reason." I may not have been aware of my resentment, but she certainly was.

✦

Despite the initial awkwardness with my mother, it didn't take me long before I felt at home on Tarsus IV. I went to school during the day, and afterward I usually hung around with Tom Leighton. Though we were quite different boys we had formed a bond during the journey that continued. I spent a lot of time at his dwelling, which my mother initially was reticent about. Even so, she still did her best to make a home for me; she cooked us dinner every night, and though she worked a five-day week, on her free days she would take me on excursions outside of the town. The planet's small strip of arable land had been part of a limited, primitive terraforming by the original settlers; the rest of the world was what I had seen when I first arrived—rocky, unforgiving terrain. Mom, however, was an avid rock climber, and it was during this period that she taught me how to do it. It's something I still indulge in even to this day.

Mom's job on Tarsus involved research on xenobiology, the various life that was indigenous to the planet, as well as those that may have been extraterrestrial in origin. These extraterrestrial forms found their way through meteorites and asteroids that entered the atmosphere. It was one of these forms of life that ended up causing all the difficulties.

One day I came home from school to find Mom hurriedly going through some files on her computer. She seemed distraught.

"Jim, I'm going to have to go back to the lab," she said. "I've called the Leightons. You can sleep there tonight." Mom was usually restrained about all the time I spent at the Leightons', so the fact that she was facilitating the sleepover told me something was seriously wrong.

"Is there anything the matter?"

She turned and looked at me. I could see her trying to figure out whether to tell me what she knew.

"It's nothing to worry about now," she said. She then got up and gave me a kiss. "Come on, pack an overnight bag and I'll take you over to the Leightons' while I head back to work."

As we drove to the Leightons' I noticed that there was a sense of panic in the people we passed: worried looks, alarmed conversations, many of them running. At the Leightons', Mom said goodbye and I went inside. Barbara wasn't home, but Rod was there, and he wasn't his usual jovial self. He told me where I could find Tom, who was in his room reading.

"You know what's going on?" I said.

"Yeah, something to do with the food," Tom said. "Dad knows someone in the agriculture department who said it's really bad."

As history would show, that turned out to be an understatement. An alien fungus had attacked the food supply. It wasn't indigenous to Tarsus IV; the fungi lay dormant in the planet's soil for thousands of years. When a species of Earth squash was introduced into the colony's crops, it somehow caused the fungi to become active. Spores were carried in the air to every food and water storage and production facility. By the time emergency procedures were implemented, all the planet's food production capability had been decimated; half the food and water supply had been wiped out. The officials estimated that the food would run out a full month before relief could arrive. Casualties were estimated at 60 percent of the planet's population.

Tarsus IV was populated by rational technocrats, so the initial reaction wasn't nearly as panicked as it might have been on other worlds. The government was not elected; the officials were chosen based on their specific skills to carry out specific duties. The governor at the time, Arnold Kodos, was selected for his abilities to deal with the bureaucratic management of the colony. His own personal views therefore were not required to carry out his work, as he made his judgments based on computer modeling, using the detailed information about the resources available to him. It was assumed by the population that the crisis they faced would be handled in a similar manner.

School was canceled the next day, and it was sometime late the next evening when my mother came to get me from the Leightons'. As I packed my things, I heard Mom talking quietly to them in the kitchen. I approached the doorway where they were seated around the table, to listen without being noticed.

". . . the council isn't giving us any instructions," Barbara said. "The hospital management has been waiting for word about supply distribution."

"They've got to have a plan," Rod said. "They'll figure it out."

"I think you've got too much faith in them," Barbara said. She turned to Mom. "Have you heard anything?"

"They're afraid to start food production," Mom said. "The spores are still in the air. We haven't figured out how to counteract them."

"If they can't start food production—" Rod said.

"Jim, ready to go?" It was Barbara, who caught sight of me near the doorway. Mom thanked the Leightons. As we were leaving, Barbara gave my mother a hug.

"It'll be okay," Barbara said. My mother, though six inches taller, looked like a young girl next to Barbara, who had a natural maternal air about her.

As we were leaving, two security officers drove up to us in a hover car. One of them was Osterlund, the man who came to our apartment the first day I arrived. He looked different, less friendly, and he and the other security man with him now wore sidearms. He sat in the front passenger seat.

"Winona," he said. "You shouldn't be out here. Get in, I'll drive you home."

"It's okay," she said. "I've got my car—"

"Get in," he said, placing his hand on his holster. "It's for your own protection. You shouldn't be out in your own vehicle. You can retrieve it tomorrow."

Mom instinctively put her arm around me.

"Peter, what the hell is—"

"I said get in!" He now withdrew his weapon, an old pre-Starfleet phase pistol.

Mom looked at the weapon, then nodded to me. We got in the back of the hover car, and the security men drove us in silence back to our apartment. After a long beat, my mother finally spoke.

"Peter, what's going on?"

Osterlund exchanged a look with his partner, who was driving.

"You might as well tell her," the partner said. "They're going to find out soon anyway."

"Find out what?" Mom said.

Osterlund turned to us in the back.

"Governor Kodos has declared martial law."

"That doesn't make any sense," Mom said. "Why would this crisis be handled any differently than anything else—"

"The governor doesn't agree with you," Osterlund said. I didn't know this security man well, but I could see that giving him a gun and the right to use it had granted him a kind of power he was enjoying.

"So he . . . he's overthrown the council?"

The security men didn't answer. The hover car pulled over in front of our building.

"Stay inside until you receive instructions."

We got out of the hover car and Mom took me inside. She looked ashen, a vacant look in her eyes.

"Mom," I said. "What's martial law?"

"It's . . . it's when there's no more democracy. When the military takes over the government, and one man at the top of the hierarchy is making all the decisions. It's usually only in an emergency."

"Tom told me about the food," I said. "So couldn't this be a good thing?"

"Come on, it's late, you should get ready for bed." She didn't answer my question.

A few moments later, there was an official announcement. It came over the emergency public address system that was installed in all the buildings in the colony. The message just said what Mom and I already knew, that martial law had been declared, and a curfew was now in effect. The announcer said that the food emergency was being handled and that everyone should stay in their homes and await specific instructions from the government. This news didn't seem to give my mother any comfort, but it confirmed for me my faith in adults to take care of things. I went to bed as I did every night.

Several hours later, I was jostled awake. I turned to see Tom Leighton standing over my bed.

"Come on," he said. "Something big is happening."

"Tom, how did you—"

"Shh . . ." he said. "Just come on, I'll explain on the way."

Waking up for another of his late-night adventures didn't take any convincing. I quickly got dressed and we climbed out of my first-floor window, which is how Tom got in. We quietly moved through the deserted streets, hiding in alleys and behind garbage cans when security patrols drove past. We noticed several of the cars had other colonists in the backseat, and they were all headed toward the center square of the colony.

"A couple of security guys came and got my parents," he told me. "They thought I was asleep when they left, but I followed them. People have been gathering there for almost an hour now."

We were a few buildings from the square when Tom stopped me. I could see the large square was almost full now; there had to be thousands of people in there. A barricade had been erected on the boulevard to the entrance to the square, where a security man stood guard. Tom indicated a door to a nearby building that bordered the square, and we quickly slipped inside.

"We'll have a better view of what's going on from the roof," he said, as we climbed the stairs.

We got to the roof and, crouching, moved toward the end that bordered the square. We hid behind the ledge. We could see security guards on some of the other roofs, but their focus was on the people down below; we were just lucky that one wasn't posted on ours. I noticed that all the entrances to the square had been barricaded. It looked like no one could get in or out without permission.

"You see my folks?" Tom said. We scanned the crowd for a long time. The square was well lit, and I was able to find Tom's parents at the far end. Rod held Barbara in his arms. Even from as far away as we were, I could see that they were scared. I started to wonder about my mother; I had just assumed when I left our apartment she was asleep in her room, but now I realized that she might be in the square as well. I started searching for her when everyone's attention was drawn to the building at the head of the square. It was the building next to us. Two guards flanked the entrance to the roof of that building as a slight, redheaded man with a beard stepped out onto that roof and approached a lectern at the roof's edge.

"I am Governor Kodos," he said. "The Tarsus Governing Council has been dissolved." He then took a pause. "The revolution is successful."

There were audible gasps in the crowd. People seemed confused and worried. Revolution?

"What does he mean—" Tom said. I shushed him as Kodos continued.

"But survival depends on drastic measures. Your continued existence represents a threat to the well-being of society. Your lives mean slow death to the more valued members of the colony. Therefore, I have no alternative but to sentence you to death." He took out a piece of paper.

"Your execution is so ordered, signed Kodos, governor of Tarsus IV."

There was numb silence.

"Execution . . . ?" Tom said. As he did, I saw all the security men, both those on the roofs and at the barricades, take out their weapons and fire. The silence was broken by screams as high-energy weapons burned the people. I frantically scanned the crowd looking for Mom when my gaze fell on Rod and Barbara. Rod tried to protect Barbara as a blue beam of light hit them both. They screamed in pain, then turned to blackened ash before falling to dust.

"No!" It was Tom; he'd seen it as well and was already standing up. I saw that Tom's scream had gotten the attention of one of the guards near Kodos. He brought up his weapon . . .

I grabbed Tom and tackled him. He was screaming as he fell to the roof.

"Tom, be quiet. We gotta . . ." I looked at him. Half his face seemed covered with dirt. He was screaming, and I tried to brush it off, when I realized it wasn't dirt; his skin was horribly burned. When I tackled him the beam must have still glanced off his face; the whole left side was charred, the skin flapping in seared pieces. His left eye socket was a blackened hole. He wailed in pain and I could do nothing.

A guard leaped over from the other roof and aimed his weapon at us. I looked up into the barrel of the pistol, disbelieving . . .

"Stop!" The voice was from behind the guard.

Kodos. He walked over to me.

"What's your name?" he said.

"J-James Tiberius . . . Kirk."

Kodos turned to the guard who was holding the gun on us. As if obeying a silent order, he put the weapon away and took out a reader. He checked a list, turned to Kodos, and nodded.

"And who's he?" Kodos was referencing Tom, whose screams had faded to crying.

"Tom Leighton," I said.

The guard checked the list again. Another guard came over from another roof.

"Rod Leighton?" the guard with the reader said. "Rod Leighton is here on the register . . ." He was about to raise his weapon.

"It's Tom!" I shouted it. "This is Tom Leighton!"

Kodos looked over the guard's shoulder and indicated something on the reader. The guard lowered his weapon.

"Get the boy to a hospital," Kodos said.

They took Tom, and Kodos then turned to me.

"You go home," he said. "You're in violation of curfew." He then walked away.

I stood up and got a view of the square. It was filled with blackened ash in the shape of human bodies. Security men entered with a large mobile cleaner. They carved a path through the ash, sucking it up inside the machine. The people were all gone.

I wandered home in a fog and climbed into my window. I stood for a very long time in my bedroom, unable to move. I wanted to know if Mom was in the square. Her room was only a few feet away. I was afraid that I would find her gone. I don't know how long I stood there, unable to make a decision. Finally, I took a step toward the doorway of my room, then another. I went out into the hallway. The door to her room was closed. I gently slid it open a crack. The sheets and blanket were crumpled at the edge of the bed. I slid the door open a little more: I saw the bottom hem of her nightgown and her feet. She was there. Asleep. I gently slid the door closed and went back into my room. I don't remember going to sleep that night, but I did eventually, because I was awakened the next morning by the sound of my mother's crying.

✦

I never told her what happened, and when Tom came to live with us, he didn't talk about it either. I don't know why I didn't want to tell my mother; most likely because I couldn't face reliving the tragedy of what I'd witnessed. Mom couldn't get any answers out of the security force about how Tom received his injuries, and she was reluctant to press Tom himself, who was traumatized for a long time. He wore a patch over the whole left side of his face; the surgeon who would've been able to reconstruct his face had been killed in the square. That surgeon was, ironically, his mother. As an adult, he could've had his face reconstructed, but he chose not to, and would wear that patch until the day he died, as a remembrance of his lost parents.

But shortly after the tragedy, Mom's attitude changed toward me. I don't know if she saw me more as an adult, or I was acting like one, but before, she had sought to protect me from information I might not be ready for; now she shared everything with me. Looking back, I now think she needed help getting through it. She'd lost a lot of friends in the massacre, and we only had each other.

The execution was made public, and it had the desired effect on the remaining populace. No one dared question Governor Kodos's orders. Life continued on Tarsus as the remaining food and water were rationed and we awaited the relief. There was a lot of quiet discussion among the survivors about how Kodos had made his decisions about who would live and who would die. It defied logic; in some cases, whole families were killed; in others, like Tom's, one or another would be spared.

Finally, Mom introduced me to a friend, Kotaro Kimura, who worked in data analysis for the hospital. Kotaro's parents, Hoshi and Takashi, had been among the first settlers of Tarsus IV, and they were among those massacred. He told Mom that Kodos had used the medical database, plugging an algorithm into it based on his own theories about who was most useful in the colony. None of the survivors knew exactly why they were valuable in his eyes, which made everyone feel that much more insecure about their status; he could always change his mind.

But two weeks after the executions, something very strange happened. Mom was waiting for me one day when Tom and I got out of school.

"Kodos is dead," Mom told us.

"What happened?" I said.

"No one knows," she said. "The security people found his body, burned in his quarters. The governing council is re-forming, and they're appointing a new governor."

"The bastard deserves it," Tom said. "I wish it was me who'd done it."

Mom put her hand on Tom's shoulder.

"I don't understand," I said. "Who killed him?"

"It looks like suicide," Mom said.

Suddenly, there was the tingling sound of what seemed like wind chimes. It was the first time I'd ever heard, and then seen, the effect of matter transportation. I turned and saw three Starfleet officers appear.

"Bob!" Mom said. She was shouting to the leader of the three, in a gold shirt and with the most braid on his cuff. He walked over to her, and they hugged.

"Winona, what the hell's been going on down here?" the man said, after they separated.

"How did you get here so fast? The relief wasn't supposed to be here for another three weeks."

"The *Enterprise*," he said, with obvious pride. "Fastest ship in the quadrant. It was supposed to be another month before she was ready to leave spacedock, but I rushed it through. We contacted Governor Kodos a week ago . . ." He then noticed me. "Is this Jim?"

"Yes," she said. "Jim, this is Robert April. He's here to save us." I could see she meant it. And I felt saved.

CHAPTER 3

"WELCOME, CADETS, TO YOUR FIRST DAY at Starfleet Academy."

Admiral Reed, old, British, commandant of the academy, stood in front of us. It was Induction Day, I was 18, it was 5 p.m., and I was already exhausted, but knew not to show it. I was at attention with all the other first-year cadets, buttoned up in our silver cadet dress tunics, our shined black boots reflecting in the sun like spilled crude oil. We were on the Great Lawn, once part of the ancient military installation called the Presidio. I had spent the last ten hours being run ragged, yelled at by any and every upperclassman who had laid eyes on me; and it was still the greatest day of my life. It had all started five years before, when a starship captain beamed down to Tarsus IV and I decided who I wanted to be.

After the death of Kodos, life on the colony would never fully return to normal. The trauma of what happened led many of the survivors to want to leave, and the news of the horror would keep new settlers away. Mom and I, however, stayed for another year; she wanted to complete her work before she left. (The results would lead to safeguards that prevented similar food disasters on other Federation colonies.) Eventually, however, it was time to go, and we were evacuated with the remainder of the population.*

---

*EDITOR'S NOTE: The colony on Tarsus IV would be reestablished 25 years after the Kodos incident, albeit under a different form of government.

Several months earlier I had said my goodbyes to Tom Leighton, whose relatives on the Earth colony Planet Q were going to take him in. Tom and I had lived through a trauma together; we shared a bond. Though our lives went down different roads, we stayed in regular contact for the rest of his life.

Mom and I returned to Earth, and my dad met us at the shuttle station in Riverside. I had been seeing him via subspace transmissions, but in person he was a bit of a shock. He had gained weight around the middle and gray around the temples. He greeted me with a handshake and a warm pat on the shoulder. He then turned and saw Mom. They gave each other a hello kiss and hug that somehow both conveyed affection and distance. The three of us returned home to live in the same house, but things were far from what they had been. Sam was off at school and seldom came home. Mom focused on her work, which sometimes took her away, but for only short periods. She never made another declaration about leaving or staying, and Dad seemed all right with that arrangement. But I suppose the biggest change was inside me.

I'd been hardened by the events on Tarsus and couldn't trust my parents, or any adults, to look after me anymore. I had been on my own; I was looking for some way to exert control over a world that could be cruel and merciless. Seeing how that starship captain and his crew had almost single-handedly restored civilization by their mere presence had made a strong impression. I wanted to be a part of that. Or maybe I needed to. So I focused on getting accepted into Starfleet Academy.

My first goal was academics. Up to that point in my life, I hadn't taken my studies all that seriously, but for the next two years I was determined to change. I had very good role models, my brother and mother were both academics, and they taught me a lot about focus and time management. My grades soon improved greatly.

I also knew that self-defense techniques were seen as an important part of Starfleet training, so I began my own study of martial arts, including among other things karate, judo, and the Vulcan discipline of *Suus Mahna*.

As my 17th birthday approached, I started thinking seriously about my application. The competition was fierce: Starfleet Academy had deservedly earned a reputation as one of the finest academic institutions in the Galaxy. The standards for acceptance were, excuse the phrase, astronomically high.

I wasn't just competing against humans; I was also competing with applicants from other planets, including Vulcans, who had received rigorous educations well beyond what humans considered normal. In 2251, the year I enrolled, Starfleet accepted fewer than 2 percent of its applicants.

This didn't deter me. I had the advantage that my parents were both graduates of the academy, and on my mother's side I would be third generation; my maternal grandfather had been in the first graduating class and rose to the rank of captain of engineering. But none of that made me a shoo-in, and the fact that both my parents had discontinued their Starfleet careers would work against me. What I considered the tipping point of my application was that I had been vital in preventing a diplomatic incident. I just had to figure out how to make use of it.

There was no notoriety for me in saving the Tellarite ambassador's life; Starfleet kept the incident quiet out of worries that the Tellarites would be embarrassed that an Earthling boy saved one of their most important diplomats. My parents and I had been told that the matter was confidential, and that if we told anyone, Starfleet would deny it happened. However, Captain Mallory's gratitude at the time led me to hope that he'd remember me and maybe help. All I had to do was track him down.

Starfleet Headquarters would only tell me he was now a commodore, but they would give me no information on his whereabouts. I thought about sending him an electronic letter, but I was worried it wouldn't find its way to him. So I embarked on what was, in hindsight, a ridiculously dangerous plan.

In our attic we had a storage container that was filled with my dad's belongings from his time in Starfleet: various pieces of equipment, tapes containing all his work, and, most important, his uniforms. When I was little, I would put them on and traipse around the house, always a little disappointed that no matter how "big" everybody said I was getting, they still didn't fit. However, it had been a few years, and now when I tried the uniforms on, they seemed almost tailored.

I made sure I wore the uniform with the rank of ensign, then found a recording disc with a Starfleet logo on it. I took it to my computer station and recorded a message for Mallory, reminding him who I was, and asking him to write me a recommendation.

The next morning I jammed the uniform and recorded message into a rucksack and snuck out early, borrowing Dad's hover car. I had told him that I was driving to Riverside to see friends and that I'd be back by noon, so I was on a tight schedule. I drove to the transportation station in Riverside and caught a Sub Shuttle to San Francisco.*

The trip took less than two hours, and I didn't want anyone on the Sub Shuttle to notice me in the uniform, so I stayed in my civilian clothes until about five minutes before we reached San Francisco. I then got up and changed in the bathroom, and waited until we pulled into the Starfleet Headquarters stop. I then quickly exited the bathroom and immediately got off the Sub Shuttle car.

I marched through the station, found a temporary locker to store my rucksack, then took the escalator to the street level. I found myself in a shuttle port and was stunned. Shuttles and flying trams flew in and out of the port, over the bay and the Golden Gate Bridge. People of all races and species in bright gold and blue uniforms walked with purpose to their destinations. I suddenly felt like a complete fraud, but I had committed to this course of action and had to see it through. I imitated the resoluteness of the people I saw around me and walked out of the spaceport.

I had studied the mall of structures that made up Starfleet Headquarters, and immediately recognized the main building, the Archer Building, named for Jonathan Archer.**

I walked into the large reception area, and where doubt had only crept into my mind when I entered the spaceport, it now completely consumed me. The lobby of the building was filled with officers, *adult* officers, of many different species and ages. The whole place had a sense of importance and dignity, and I was a kid playing dress-up. I was only a few steps inside when

---

*EDITOR'S NOTE: The Sub Shuttles were a subterranean rapid transit system, built in the early 22nd century, using tunnels that honeycombed the globe. They were taken out of operation in 2267 when they were made obsolete by the preponderance of matter/energy transporters.

**: Captain Kirk has made a common error: It is in fact named for Henry Archer, Jonathan's father and the inventor of the Warp Five engine. The building was constructed during Jonathan Archer's tenure as Federation president, and it was he who insisted it be named for his father.

I decided this wasn't going to work, and was about to turn around when someone blocked my way.

"May I help you?"

It was a young woman, not much older than me. She was petite, dressed in a blue uniform dress, had blond hair. Very beautiful.

"I have a message," I said, holding up the tape much too quickly. "It's for Commodore Mallory."

"Oh," she said. "Come with me."

I followed her to a reception desk, where she typed some information into the computer terminal.

"Commodore Mallory isn't here, Ensign," she said. "Were you under the impression he was?"

"Uh, no," I said. "I mean, yes, I thought he was here, but no, I didn't know for certain that he'd be here *right now*." She looked at me like she didn't know what I was talking about, which made two of us. "When do you think he'll be back?"

She laughed. "Not for several years," she said. "He's in command of Starbase 11, and they're in the middle of an extensive upgrade and remodel."

It was a testimony to the lack of forethought that went into this plan that it never occurred to me that Mallory, an officer in Starfleet, might not be on Earth anymore. My fantasy of walking into Starfleet and handing him the message had vaporized, and I just wanted to get out of there.

"Well, thanks for your help," I said, reaching for the tape.

"Don't you want to get the message to him?"

"Oh, um . . . I guess . . ."

"I'll have someone upload it to him," she said. "I'm just going to need your daily comm code."

I had no idea what that was. She was looking at me intently now.

"You know, I should double-check with my superior officer," I said. She nodded.

"Okay," she said, "and you might want to ask him what the penalty is for impersonating a Starfleet officer. I think it's five years on a penal colony." I felt all the blood drain out of my head. Up until that moment, I had no idea that what I was doing was indeed a crime. I was lucky that Mallory *wasn't* here; if he'd seen me in the uniform he probably would've made sure I never got near the academy. I was in a large amount of trouble. It was only her gentle hand on my arm that kept me from running.

"Don't worry," she said. "I'm just going to review it myself, and unless there's something objectionable, I'll make sure he gets it."

Though I'd been unaware I was holding my breath, I felt myself exhale.

"Thanks," I said. "I really appreciate it."

"Don't mention it," she said. "What's your name?"

"I'm Jim," I said, holding out my hand. She took it in both of hers. The gesture completely calmed me down.

"Nice to meet you. I'm Ruth." She looked me in the eye and I beamed like an idiot.

✦

Ruth later said she got the message to Mallory's chief of staff (and never mentioned my ludicrous "spy" mission), and since everyone I knew was pretty astounded when I was accepted to the academy, I assumed Mallory put in a good word, although at the time there was no way to know what exactly happened.

Nevertheless, a few months later, I was packed and ready to go. My parents took me to San Francisco. It was 6 a.m.; new cadets were lined up at the entry gates, waiting to go in. They were all saying goodbye to their parents, and I turned to mine. I looked at Mom and Dad. They'd both aged, but seemed happier, or at least more content than either had been in some time. Looking back, it was clear they'd found some kind of comfort in each other's presence. But I was ready to go. I took a hug from Mom and a hand-shake from Dad, and said I'd see them at the winter break.

"Get ready to suffer," Dad said, and Mom chuckled. I would shortly find out what he meant.

✦

There is only one military institution left in the Federation: Starfleet. Though its "brand" is one of exploration, diplomacy, and civilization, the security of the Federation and its citizens is still an important part of its charter, and to look after it requires a military chain of command. So the one not-so-secret secret of its academy is that it makes sure its graduates can be soldiers when they need to be. And that starts on Induction Day.

New cadets sign in, are handed a big empty red bag, and from that moment on they enter a maze of abuse. You're sent on an organized scavenger hunt to acquire your needed equipment in different buildings. And around every corner there's an angry upperclassman telling you *you're a stupid plebe who's walking too slow; you shouldn't be running, why aren't you at attention, why are you standing there, get moving you stupid plebe, put your bag down when I'm talking to you, who told you to drop your bag, look at me when I'm talking to you, why are you looking at me, don't you look at me!*

The bag gets heavier and heavier; you've got to carry it everywhere, and you very quickly have no idea where you're going or where you're supposed to be going, and that's the point. If you get through the day, it's because you finally realize you have no choice but to not think, just *do*, usually whatever the last thing the nearest upperclassman said. It's arduous, humiliating, and stressful, and more than a few cadets don't make it 'til sundown. I did, though just barely. I'd never been yelled at like this before, and it was only the beginning.

The first eight weeks of your first year are called "plebe summer," and they are designed to drive out those men and women who can't handle the physical and psychological stress. The survivors learn discipline and skills they need not only to get along at the academy, but more importantly in Starfleet. It is the one thing that separates it from the rest of the Federation: cadets, crewmen, and officers know the importance of following orders, because it saves lives.

At around noon, by which time I'd learned, among other things, to march in formation carrying a 50-pound bag, I was assigned to a company, the Second Cadet Corps, a barracks, and reported to my room. My section commander (there were eight of us in the section) was a cadet captain named Ben Finney. A few years older, big and fit, he commanded my attention immediately. He ordered me, two other humans, and an Andorian to stand at attention and hold our bags until further orders. We stood two on each side in front of our bunk beds for about an hour. My arms were shaking from the strain. I was looking straight ahead into the pale green eyes of the blue-skinned cadet. I'd never met an Andorian; I had dozens of questions for him, but one of the lessons I'd learned from that first day was not to speak until spoken to by an upperclassman.

"Drop your bags!" It was Finney, who finally came into our room. We dumped our bags on the floor, and before I could stop myself, I let out a "whew." Bad mistake. Finney went right up to me.

"You tired, plebe?"

"No sir!"

"Glad to hear it! Pick up your bag; you can hold on to it for a little while longer. The rest of you, unpack. I want this room shipshape." And with that, he left. While my roommates tried to navigate around me, I stood holding the bag. About an hour later, the roommates were now relaxing on their beds while I stood there, sweat pouring from me, my arms shaking.

"Atten-shun!" It was one of my roommates, who saw another upper-classman come into the room. He was a cadet lieutenant named Sean Finnegan—a big, blond, smiling Irishman.

"What's been going on in here, boyos?" I hadn't really heard an Irish accent as pronounced as this one, and felt it had to be somewhat affected. He looked at my three roommates. "You boyos should be getting down to lunch." They left, and he then turned to look at me.

"And what might you be doing?"

"Lieutenant sir, I've been ordered to hold my bag, sir!"

"What's your name, Cadet?"

"Lieutenant sir, Cadet James T. Kirk, sir!"

"Oh, well, Jimmy Boy," he said, pronouncing boy "bahy," "if you don't get unpacked, you're gonna miss chow. See you down there."

"Lieutenant sir, yes sir." I put the bag down, and Finnegan sauntered out, whistling "Danny Boy." I unpacked and made it down to lunch just in time. As I sat at the table, Finney looked up at me, stupefied.

"Kirk! You stupid plebe, what the hell do you think you're doing here?"

"Sir, I was ordered to lunch, sir!"

"Who ordered you?" Finney said, and he was bellowing. The whole room was quiet.

"Sir, Cadet Lieutenant Finney—" I said.

"There is no Cadet Lieutenant Finney!"

"Sir, sorry, sir, I meant Cadet Lieutenant Finnegan, sir." It wasn't the last time I would mix up their unfortunately similar names. Finnegan stood up.

"I gave no such order," Finnegan said. "I think the day has been too much for the boy."

I went over it in my head. He was right; Finnegan had not ordered me to put the bag down. I had read into it.

"What do you have to say to that?" Finney said.

"Sir, I was mistaken, sir!" I was also starving, but Finney sent me back up to my room and told me to repack my bag and hold it until he got there. I followed the order, and about 15 minutes later, my roommates returned from lunch, followed by Finney. My roommates stood tall as Finney inspected my living space to make sure that I'd put everything back in the bag. I felt like passing out, but held on. He smiled.

"Drop the bag, plebe." I slowly lowered the bag to the ground, then returned to attention. "Stow your gear," he said, and then left. As I started to put my gear away, I saw Finnegan standing in the doorway, smiling.

It was not a good start for me.

For the next two months we were put through a punishing regime of physical training: running with heavy packs, obstacle courses, battle simulations, survival training. The skills I had developed in my boyhood, considered primitive and unnecessary in our society, came in handy during this period: my mountain-climbing experience, my years camping with my father, and my knowledge of the Old West. Still, it was never easy, and there were always surprises.

Plebe summer was such a whirlwind that I really didn't get much downtime with my roommates. I never became close with the two humans, Jim Corrigan and Adam Castro; the Andorian, Thelin, was the first of his kind admitted to the academy, and did not always easily fit in. We shared the similarity that we tended to separate ourselves from the group.

The last weekend of plebe summer we got our first pass. I was thrilled; it was going to be my first chance to see Ruth in months. We'd seen each other several times, but not since I'd begun at the academy. The night before, as I came into my room from having washed up, I was lost in thought; she was the first girlfriend I'd ever had, and as the stress of my first few weeks at the academy relieved somewhat, she dominated my mind. I was so distracted I hadn't really noticed Castro, Corrigan, and Thelin's furtive glances to one aother as I hopped up on my bed on the top bunk. There was a splash; I'd landed in something that wasn't supposed to be there. I looked down and saw a soup bowl tipped over, my pants covered with thick, oily liquid.

"What the hell is this?" I said, totally confused, as the answer walked in.

"Atten-shun!" Finnegan said. We all leaped to our feet. In doing so, I made my situation worse as the bowl of soup followed me off the bed and spilled down my body. I now recognized the liquid as the corn chowder that had been served for lunch that day.

"Sneaking food, are we, Jimmy Boy?"

"No sir!" The congealed yellow liquid was dripping off me onto the floor.

"You know the regulations about eating in your rooms," he said. "This is a serious infraction. Twenty demerits."

"Yes sir!" I was furious. If a cadet got 100 demerits during his years at the academy, he was out. This man was carrying out some archaic practical joke that I couldn't imagine had ever been funny, *ever*, and it might cost me my future.

"Something you want to say to me, Jimmy Boy?" He was standing an inch in front of me. I held his stare.

"No sir!"

"Really? 'Cause you look like you want to lay one on me." He was right. I wanted to hit him. Which is what he wanted, because then I'd be out.

"No sir!"

"All right, then, clean up this mess, before I give you ten more demerits," Finnegan said as he swaggered through the doorway.

"Sorry, Jim," Castro said, handing me a towel. "We saw him come out of our room when we got back. He ordered us not to tell you what he'd done."

"If you report him," Thelin said, "it will be a mark on his record. If my testimony is necessary, I offer it."

The Andorian had a sense of honor, which I appreciated, but as I glanced over at Castro and Corrigan, I could see their reluctance, and I didn't blame them. Though I wanted to get Finnegan in trouble, I also knew what would happen if I went through channels. The story wouldn't be that Finnegan was abusing me unnecessarily; it would be that I couldn't take a joke.

"It's all right," I said, wiping the chowder off my pants. "I'll survive."

✦

Fortunately, I still had my pass and got to see Ruth. She still worked at Starfleet Headquarters. She had grown up in San Francisco, where Starfleet crewmen had been omnipresent, so once out of high school, looking to carve her own path, she'd enlisted, gone through the basic training in the noncommissioned officers' school, and became a clerk in the records department. She admitted to being a little lost in terms of her life goals, and she later told me that my confidence over what I wanted to do was part of what she found attractive. Though inside I was still very much a boy, I found her attention did a lot to assuage my insecurity.

We had seen each other a few times since we met the previous year, but I had had little experience with women, and the only physical contact we had up until that night was holding hands. We met in the Fisherman's Wharf section of San Francisco. It was a warm fall night, and she was wearing a lovely white-and-black lace dress. I wore my uniform, and like a crewman on a mission, I had gone into the evening having made the decision that I would kiss her. The question was when.

"Do you know why they call it Fisherman's Wharf?" she asked me as we walked along the landscaped shoreline.

"This whole area," I said, "used to be centered around the commerce of fishing. Fishermen moored their small vessels here, and early in the morning they'd leave to catch as much fish as they could, which they'd bring back here where they could sell . . ." I was about to continue when I could see she was smiling at me.

"Oh," I said, "you weren't asking. You were going to tell me . . ."

"Yeah," she said, laughing a little. "I grew up here. But you tell it well."

I laughed a little too. I felt like an idiot, but she held my arm tightly. I stopped and picked an orange and yellow sunflower and gave it to her.

"You're not supposed to pick the flowers," she said.

"I know. Let's break some rules."

I looked at her, not at all feeling the bravado I was expressing. I pushed through my fear and kissed her. She welcomed it. Mission accomplished. She parted from me and stared into my eyes. What happened next astounded me, but I tried not to show it.

"Why don't you take me home now?" she said, smiling.

✦

I had to be back at the academy by 24:00, and the guard on duty logged me in at 23:57. I was giddy, confused, happy, proud of myself at the same time I was certain I had nothing to do with causing what had just happened. So I was a little lost in my head, and I didn't notice the unusual way the door to my room was propped open. I could see the light on inside and could hear Castro and Thelin talking.

"You guys up, 'cause I got a story—" Before I could finish my sentence I was covered in ice-cold water, and a plastic bucket hit me in the head. I almost couldn't breathe the water was so frigid. I now saw Finnegan was in there talking to my roommates.

"Welcome home, Jimmy Boy," Finnegan said. "Looks like you made another mess. Twenty demerits." He strutted out. When he was gone, Castro headed toward the dresser and got me a towel.

"Th-th-anks," I said, shivering.

"How was your furlough?" Castro said.

"Great until a second ago . . ."

"This human type of humor is very confusing," Thelin said.

"I'm not laughing either," I said.

"Atten-shun!" Castro said as Ben Finney walked in. We all stood at attention. Finney took in the scene, then turned to me.

"Kirk, you want to explain this?" he said.

"Sir, I have no explanation, sir!"

Finney picked the bucket up off the floor, then went over to the door, which was dripping with water. He clearly put together what happened, and addressed my roommates.

"Did you men do this?"

"No sir!" Thelin and Castro said in unison. Undoubtedly, Finnegan had ordered them to not say anything, and Ben was smart enough to figure out that they weren't to blame. He could've asked if they knew who was responsible, but we'd been taught the academy honor code. If they said they didn't do it, Finney had to believe them. Whether he would ask them to inform on another cadet was another question, and would cause us all a lot of headaches. It was a tense moment.

"Clean this up," Finney said, "and get to bed. You have classes tomorrow." He left. Whatever we had thought about Finney up to that point, we now liked him.

✦

"So, Mr. Kirk," Professor Gill said, "your theory is Khan wasn't all that bad."

That I had expounded a theory at all was news to me. We were covering some very dense, confusing material in my History of the Federation class, and as far as I knew up to that moment, I didn't have a theory about any of it. Professor Gill was ascribing something to me I don't remember even saying. And this was the shallow end of the academic swamp I found myself in every day.

Now that plebe summer was officially over, the long slog of the academic year began, and it was much tougher than I imagined. Along with all the usual subjects of literature, history, physical sciences, there was a whole slew of other disciplines not covered in the usual college education: xenobiology, xenoanthropology, galactic law and institutions, planetary ecologies, interplanetary economics. This went hand in hand with semantics, language structure, comparative galactic ethics, epistemology, xenopsychology, and so on. And on top of all that, Starfleet Academy had to be an engineering school. Its graduates, no matter what they decided to concentrate in, needed to understand technology in a practical way for a whole slew of possible emergencies, because the situations Starfleet officers faced might require a physician to pilot a shuttlecraft or a historian to operate a transporter. The standards were rigorous because lives were at stake.

Contributing to the high standards, many of the professors were the foremost scholars in their fields, and their teaching would affect me for the rest of my life. John Gill, the professor of my history class, was no exception. The history he wrote on the Third World War won the Pulitzer and MacFarlane prizes, and was one of the texts we used in his class. It was the subject we were currently studying.

"Uh . . . I don't think I meant that," I said. "I just meant that it was amazing for one man to rule such a large part of the Earth—"

"So you admire him?" I had been in Gill's class long enough to know he was setting some kind of intellectual trap, but I couldn't figure out what.

"I guess I admire his ability, yes."

"His ability to enslave millions of people?"

"I wasn't judging the morality of what he did," I said. "Just his capacity to get it accomplished."

"But weren't his accomplishments as a leader," Gill said, "directly related to his own lack of morality? His own feeling of superiority that allowed him to oppress his subjects?"

"I guess so," I said.

"And you still admire him," Gill said. "How do you justify that?"

"I admire the railroad of the old American West," I said. "It was an amazing piece of engineering and planning for such a primitive time, and directly led to the future prosperity of the United States. Yet it could only be constructed using slave labor, and its importance to capitalists led to the near genocide of the Native Americans. But I still admire the railroad."

Gill looked at me and smiled.

"Perhaps you shouldn't. The cost sounds like it was too high." Gill was trying to make a point, one that I wouldn't fully understand until much later. Interestingly, this conversation would come back to haunt us both.

But at the time I was too under siege by work to stop to think about it. I was determined to be an academic success. I was seeing less of Ruth than I wanted; I turned down furlough passes on several weekends to focus on my studies.

On one of these nights, alone in the deserted barracks, I was so lost in trying to make sense of the Xindi Incident* that I didn't notice Ben Finney standing in my doorway.

"Sir, sorry, sir," I said, quickly standing to attention.

"At ease," he said. "No plans tonight, cadet?"

"No sir."

Finney came into my room and looked at what I was studying.

"Oh, this mess," he said. "I never could make head or tail of it. Do you want to take a break?"

Finney wasn't acting like the usual upperclassman. A few minutes later we were in his room; he gave me a chair and then pulled out a bottle. It had a long, slightly curved neck. He poured us drinks in a coffee mug and plastic cup.

"Ever tried Saurian brandy?" He gave me a wry smile. In truth, I had had little exposure to any kind of spirits and was flabbergasted that my instructor was introducing them to me now.

"Sir, isn't this against regulations?"

"It is indeed. You should report this infraction to your immediate superior." That was him.

"Sir . . ."

"Call me Ben," he said. "Anyone finds out about this and we're both done."

He handed me the cup, and I took a swig. That first taste was vile. It was like turpentine with a fruit taste, something like apples, and burned my throat going down. I coughed and Finney laughed.

"Give it a second," he said.

Its effects were almost immediate. A warm, relaxing cloud fell over me.

"That's amazing," I said. "Thanks."

"You're welcome. You looked like you could use it."

We spent the next couple of hours drinking and laughing, and found we had a lot in common. We were both from the American midwest, both

---

*EDITOR'S NOTE: The Xindi Incident began when that race attacked Earth in 2153 with a prototype weapon that killed seven million people. Starfleet foiled a further attack involving a much larger weapon.

our parents went to the academy, and we both had dreams of serving aboard starships. Ben asked if I had a girlfriend, then showed me a picture of his, a lovely woman named Naomi, whom he was about to marry.

"Marry?" I said. "You graduate this year. Isn't that going to be hard if you get posted to a ship?"

"I'm already an instructor in computers; they'll probably ask me to stay on at least another year after graduation," Ben said. "Then we'll just have to see what happens. Naomi understands."

Ben let on that he didn't like the role he had to play as an upperclassman. He was gregarious and friendly, and, as I would learn, had a deep-seated need to be liked. He was a popular cadet not only in his class but in the other classes as well. Looking back, I can now see that Ben's desire to not only be my friend but everybody's undermined his own ability to command respect as a senior officer. This aspect of his personality, I think, contributed to the difficulties he would face later. But at the time, I was thrilled to have a pal and confidant. It helped me get through the rest of my plebe year, which was no easy feat, as 23 percent of the first-years dropped out.

✦

A cadet's second summer was spent in outer space, at the academy Training Station in Earth orbit. There we learned zero gravity combat techniques and got our first taste of actual piloting. They were century-old shuttle pods, but to get behind the stick of any kind of spacecraft was a thrill.

When I returned to the academy for my second year, things felt very different. For one, Finnegan had graduated and been posted to a starbase. He'd been a constant irritant during my first year. The hazing was endless. His parting shot before graduating was to switch my dress pants with someone much larger than me, which led to an unfortunate incident on the final day of that year during a full-dress parade.

I've often wondered what it was that made me Finnegan's target. I think it goes back to that first day, when he saw me standing at attention in my room, holding all my belongings. In that moment, I thought he was being nice to me, telling me to go to lunch. Because of that, because of my ingenuousness, he saw me as weak, as a target. Like many bullies, he enjoyed the power he had over me. I was there to do the work, and my seriousness somehow provoked him. Ironically, his lack of seriousness led to an unremarkable Starfleet career; I never ran into him again after the academy.*

Suffice it to say, it relieved a lot of stress when he was finally gone (though it still took me a while before I would open a door or get into bed too quickly). But more important, I'd made it through my first year. Except for the demerits I'd received from Finnegan, I was near the top of my class, and I was determined to stay there.

The only thing that suffered was my relationship with Ruth. She was still in her job in the records department, her life a little bit on hold. As my workload increased, I had the sense she was always waiting for me to spare some time for her, and I didn't like the pressure. Ben Finney, now my best friend, encouraged me to not let her go. Ben had graduated, but as he predicted, was asked to stay on as an instructor in Advanced Computer Programming. He had married Naomi and moved into faculty quarters, and on our off days, they would seek Ruth and me out for dinners, drinks, and other socializing. I enjoyed these times, but I wondered whether Ben himself was getting restless waiting for a ship assignment. One day, Ruth and I were sitting at dinner with them at their home, and I asked him.

"My career can survive my staying an instructor a little longer," Ben said, turning to Naomi, who was smiling. "I want to see my son."

"Oh, that's wonderful," Ruth said. She gripped my hand under the table as she said it.

"Good job," I said, with a smile. I gently removed my hand from Ruth's to shake Ben's. Ruth got up and gave Naomi a hug.

We talked at length that night about raising a family, where they wanted to live, how Ben's career might still be flexible enough to make it possible. I did my best to be supportive, but something about the dinner made me angry. I tried not to show it, though I think Ruth could sense my distance.

---

*EDITOR'S NOTE: Kirk's assessment is somewhat inaccurate. Shortly before this book went to press, Sean Finnegan's "unremarkable" career led him to be appointed commandant of Starfleet Academy.

After a little while, she and I said our goodbyes to the Finneys, and I walked her home.

"You didn't seem happy for them," she said.

"No, I am," I said. "It's just . . . I don't know if they're being realistic."

"They're grown-ups; they can make their own decisions."

"They're making decisions that affect a child," I said, somewhat harshly. "Starfleet makes demands that can get in the way of a family. Both my parents had to give up their careers."

"And you think that was wrong, that they gave up their careers for the people they loved?" She was asking more than one question, and though I had known this conversation was coming, I didn't think it would come so soon.

"It's not wrong," I said. "It's just not for me."

We walked the rest of the way to Ruth's apartment in silence. Ruth loved me, and she was trying to make it easy for me, give me what I wanted. We kissed goodnight, and it was the last time I saw her. I often look back with regret on how I treated her. I did love Ruth; she was in fact my first love, and I don't know if I was being honest with myself about why I broke up with her. She was willing to commit to me, but for some reason I couldn't, or wouldn't, trust that. So I pushed her away.

✦

"Mr. Mitchell," I said, "next time, *think* before you throw a punch."

"Sir, yes sir," Mitchell said, with a smirk.

He was lying on the floor; I was standing over him, having just thrown him with a judo move called *koshi garuma.* I was serving as an instructor in Hand-to-Hand Combat, and Gary Mitchell, a first-year cadet, was my problem student. It didn't seem to bother him that he was going to wash out of my class. Probably because it wasn't the only class he was going to fail.

It was my third year, I'd been promoted to cadet lieutenant, and Mitchell was in my squad. He was everything I wasn't: charming, gregarious, rough, and a little reckless. I had been leaning into him, hoping to shake loose a little intellect, but I wasn't having much success. I had a feeling at that time that Mitchell wouldn't make it through.

I was at the Finneys' home one night and mentioned it to Ben.

"Let him wash out," Ben said. "Who needs another loser graduating?"

Ben was now in his second year as a postgraduate instructor, and the academy had just asked him to stay on for a third. Unlike Finney, many computer specialists could often be notoriously bad teachers, which is why he was so valuable to the academy. But he'd watched two graduating classes leave him behind, and now he would see a third; it was starting to get under his skin.

His baby, Jamie, however, seemed to do a lot to soften his mood. Ben had said he wanted a son, but didn't seem at all disappointed in having a daughter. It had come as quite a shock when he and Naomi told me that they were naming their first child after me, and it made me feel more attached to them as a family. I leaned on them during those years after I broke up with Ruth. Aside from a couple of casual relationships, Ben and Naomi became my one major social outlet, as I threw myself into my studies. (I found out later that some underclassman had dubbed me a "stack of books with legs," which I would only criticize as not being particularly clever.)

✦

In any event, it was soon time to submit Mitchell's grade. I spoke to his other instructors; though he was passing most of his classes, he was going to fail his Philosophy of Religion course. That and another failing grade from me would lead to expulsion. I weighed the decision seriously and finally decided to pass him. Maybe I had softened on him, maybe I just liked him, but whatever the reasons, I would not regret that decision.

The following summer, I was part of a flying exercise of two squadrons of five craft each; we were flying academy trainers, the century-old Starfleet surplus shuttle pods, with basic instrumentation and updated piloting software. I had rated high on piloting, so by my third year I had my own squadron, and Gary was in it. We were out near Earth's moon, learning to operate in its gravity well. I was in the second squadron; my old roommate Adam Castro led the first. Our job was to follow them, stay within ten kilometers, and imitate their maneuvers as closely as possible. Castro acted the role of hotshot pilot, so he wasn't making it easy. There was also a little bit of competition between the two squadrons, which I did my best to tamp down.

We were doing a fair job of following, until their final maneuver. They lined up wingtip to wingtip, forming a three-dimensional loop. We imitated the maneuver, when I noticed something on one of my scanners. Gary noticed it too.

"Cobra Five to Cobra Leader," he said, "they're opening their coolant interlocks. Do we follow suit?"

"Cobra Leader to Cobra Group, do not, I say again, do not follow suit," I said. I could see what Castro was up to and I didn't like it.

"But they're accelerating, pulling ahead," Gary said. "You know what they're doing, don't you?"

"Yes, I do," I said. "Cobra Leader to Cobra Group, I repeat, keep your coolant interlocks closed. Engines to all stop; we'll wait here until they finish."

The ships of the other squadron spun, moved inward on the circle, and vented plasma. As they passed each other inside the circle, the plasma ignited. The maneuver, called a Kolvoord Starburst, usually ended as the ships moved out in separate directions, creating an expanding five-point eruption of ignited plasma. It was a "top gun" piloting maneuver that cadets had been performing for decades. I, however, hadn't prepared my squadron for it, and it was too risky. My caution was justified.

As the ships moved past each other, one of them veered off its course and hit another one. It caused a domino effect; all the ships crashed into each other and were destroyed.

"Oh my god . . ." It was someone over the intercom, maybe Gary. I couldn't be sure.

"Cobra Leader to Cobra Group, stand by for rescue operations—" Before I could finish that order, however, it was rendered pointless.

There was an explosion, and not the one the pilots intended. All the ships were engulfed in the cascading conflagration, and a much more dangerous wave of energy, caused by the detonation of five engines, was heading right toward us.

"Cobra Leader to Cobra Group, 180 degrees about and scatter, go, go go!" I said, shouting. I banked my ship and watched to make sure all the shuttle pods came about. The old ships moved achingly slow, but they all turned away from the explosion and each other.

I checked my six and saw the wave about to hit . . .

"All ships, brace for impact!"

I was jolted forward by the impact of the force wave. An alarm sounded and my instrumentation panel shorted out. Smoke billowed, and coughing, I waved it away. I looked up through my view port. I'd lost sight of the other shuttle pods.

"Cobra Leader to Cobra Squadron, damage report," I said. I tried again; no answer. My communications panel was out. I then checked my helm and navigation panel; I had no instruments, no sensors. I looked up through the view ports. I still didn't see any of the shuttle pods.

I couldn't risk navigating by sight. Protocol in a situation like this was to prioritize communications and signal for help; ships flying blindly were a navigation hazard. And after witnessing the death of five cadets who weren't following the rules, I decided I had to. So I ripped open the communications panel and attempted to repair the circuits.

After about half an hour, I was having no luck and started to regret my decision. The course the shuttle pods had been on was taking us away from Earth, so it might be a while before search and rescue found us. I had a squadron out here, I didn't know their status, and because I had followed the rules, they might all be dead. I gave up on the communicator and took control of the helm. I was going to have to try to find them by sight. I started scanning the sky when I heard a loud thunk on my ceiling. I looked up as the upper hatch opened, and Gary Mitchell came through. He had docked his shuttle pod to mine.

"Permission to come aboard," he said with a smile.

"Granted," I said. "How did you find me?"

"I just started looking," he said. "I found the rest of the squadron first; everybody's alive."

"You have instrumentation?"

"Nope," he said. "I did it by sight, and when I got close to a ship, I used Morse code with my landing lights to tell them to fall behind me. Then I found you."

"You . . . that's . . ." I was dumbfounded. He'd taken so many risks, but he had brought the squadron together, and now we could safely navigate to the dock.

"I think I owe you one," I said.

"We owe you one," he said, "for not trying that maneuver."

It was a terrible day; we'd seen five comrades die needlessly. But it was not without its lessons. The academy banned the Kolvoord Starburst, which has not been performed to this day. And I learned that I could count on Gary Mitchell.

✦

"This was a labor camp," Lev said. He was a native of Axanar, humanoid, short and stout like most of his species, with reddish skin and ridges along his neck. It was the beginning of my last year at the academy. I was with a group of cadets, and we were standing in the central square of what had once been a midsize city on his planet. Some buildings had been destroyed to make room for stretches of farmland; others were converted to barracks and monstrous factories. A million Axanars had lived in this converted city, with dozens like it all over the planet, and spent a lifetime under the relentless rule of the Klingon Empire. As slaves they had no rights, and rebellion was not tolerated. Lev led us behind a wrecked building. I gagged at the sight; others gasped; a young cadet vomited.

Thousands of people, charred to their bones, in a pile two stories high. They hadn't just been burned; heads had been bashed in, arms and legs broken. The faces of the blackened skulls seemed to scream in agony. There were smaller skeletons. Children. Babies.

"What a shame," someone said. They had a mocking tone, and I turned, expecting to deliver a reprimand to one of my cadets. I was surprised, however, to see our party of had been joined by a group of Klingon soldiers, intimidating in their gold tunics with impressive sidearms packed to their waists. The one who'd spoken, their leader, wore a smile that could freeze an open flame.

"You don't sound sincere," I said.

"Oh, but I am," he said. "The rules were clearly posted. If only they'd followed them, they might still be alive." We were all about the same age, part of the same mission. A mission of peace that at the moment I wanted no part of.

Axanar was the site of a battle between the Federation starship *Constitution* and three Klingon ships. Captain Garth of the *Constitution*, in some brilliant maneuvers, defeated the Klingon birds-of-prey. (In one particular move that we would study in school, he took remote control of his enemy's weapons console. No one had thought to try that before, and it led to all Federation ships having their own combination code so no one would try it on *us*.)

Garth was a unique captain, and rather than suing for peace, he boldly claimed the system was under his protection. It was a big gamble; since the Klingons considered Axanar part of their empire, Garth's action could have started a war. But Garth knew the Klingons were embarrassed by the defeat. The Klingons relied on fear to maintain their empire, and if they took him on and he somehow defeated them again, it could undermine their authority in the entire quadrant. In addition, Axanar was no longer of value to the empire; most of its assets were depleted. For those reasons, the Klingons hesitated before taking further action.

This allowed the Federation Diplomatic Corps leverage to step in. They reached out to the Klingons, hoping for a negotiated peace. The Klingons, for the first time in history, agreed. In truth, the Klingons decided to use the negotiations as an opportunity to get more information on what they considered their greatest enemy.

Starfleet saw the same opportunity; this peace mission was a chance for our military minds to gather as much information as possible about our greatest adversary. So along with the diplomats, a contingency of Starfleet officers was selected. I was part of a group of academy cadets included since we might one day have to face the Klingons in war.

It was not out of the question; right now, I wanted to hit the one standing in front of me.

"I'm Jim Kirk," I said, extending my hand. The Klingon looked down at it with a mix of amusement and disdain. He didn't take it, so I withdrew it.

"Koloth," he said.

"A pleasure to meet you," I said.

"I don't think it will help our negotiations," Koloth said, "if we start out lying to each other." He wanted me to be open about hating him; I had no problem with it.

"You're right," I said. "Great things may come of this." Koloth ignored me and turned to Lev, who'd shrunk behind my group of cadets.

"You there," he said. "We're thirsty. Get us some wine."

"I'm sorry," I said. "He's giving us a tour. Maybe you could find your drinks on your own." Koloth looked at me. One of the men behind him reached for a knife, but Koloth noticed, and with a slight motion of his hand signaled him to stop. Koloth then turned back to me.

"Very well. I imagine this won't be the last time you and I meet," Koloth said.

"I look forward to it," I said. I gave him a smile that told him, this time, I wasn't lying. Koloth led his men away.

In the end, the mission led to negotiations with the Klingons that would keep the peace and prevent a full-scale war for 15 years. But what I saw on Axanar also cemented the negative impression I'd had about them since childhood, one that wouldn't change for another 40 years.

✦

Ben tried to talk me out of it, but I wasn't listening.

"Come on, I need you," I said. "I have to get into the program bank, and you know that computer system better than anyone . . ."

"You're spending too much time with Mitchell," Ben said. "Since when do you take this kind of risk?" Ben was right; we could get in a lot of trouble, but I could tell he was coming around.

I was a few months away from graduation and had recently been given the *Kobayashi Maru* test, relatively new to the academy at the time. We had no idea who devised it, but we'd heard rumors that a Vulcan had included the proposal for it in his application, and it was one of the reasons he was accepted. The details were a closely guarded secret, and the honor code of the academy stated that you couldn't discuss the test with anyone who hadn't taken it yet. But, as it turned out, many in the academy did not observe the honor code, and the details became public.

The test placed a cadet in command of a starship that received a distress call for a fuel ship, the *Kobayashi Maru*, which was in the Neutral Zone bordering the Klingon Empire. The cadet had to decide whether to try to rescue the ship violating the treaty and risking interplanetary war. If the cadet chose this route, his/her ship was destroyed by the Klingons. It was considered an important test of command character.

I thought the test was bullshit.

I had spent the past four years preparing to find answers to the questions I would face in the Galaxy, and up until this test, every question had an answer. There was always a way to successfully complete your mission. My old roommate Thelin agreed with me. He had taken the test multiple times; he had not even tried to rescue the ship, but instead had used it as bait to try to trap the Klingons. This agressive tactic kept him from graduating.

I decided that the central problem of *Kobayashi Maru* was really about figuring out how to beat the test. I took it very personally, felt it was an insult to all the work I'd done. I just couldn't live with the failure. So, with Ben's help, I would reprogram the simulation. Thus, the third time I took the test, I rescued the *Kobayashi Maru* and escaped the Klingons.

It caused quite a stir. I was able to keep Ben's name out of it (no one knew the reprogramming was beyond my ability), and I was called before an honor review board for cheating. It looked like I might be expelled.

"What justification can you possibly give for such duplicitousness?" Admiral Barnett said. He was the imposing head of the review board.

"Sir, with all due respect, it wasn't duplicitous. Nowhere in the rules did it state that we were not allowed to reprogram the computer."

"You violated the spirit of the test," Admiral Komack said. He was sitting next to Barnett and he was annoyed. Judging from the reaction of the admirals on the board, he wasn't alone. I didn't think I could change their minds, but I also knew that I was right. I'd been carrying a lot of demerits on my record since first year, thanks to Finnegan, and it wouldn't take much to keep me from graduating. Looking back, I don't know why I took such a risk, with all the work I'd done to get into the academy, and then all the work I did there to succeed. But I actually think all my experiences led me to make my decision, and I had to let them know.

"If I'm in command, aren't I supposed to use every scrap of knowledge and experience at my disposal to protect the lives of my crew?" Barnett smiled at this. I could see the outrage on a few of the other admirals' faces begin to flag. Except one.

"You broke the rules," Komack said.

"No, I didn't, sir," I said. "I took the test within its own parameters twice. You have those results to judge me on. By letting me take it a third time, you invalidated those parameters. So I used my experience with the test to beat it."

This argument visibly swayed Barnett and a few of the other board members. I decided to pursue my advantage.

"In fact, if I'd just let the test run its course a third time without trying to adjust its programming," I said, "I would have been guilty of negligence, as I would not have done everything in my power to save my hypothetical crew, and you would have to expel me on that basis."

"We may expel you anyway," Barnett said, though he didn't sound serious.

The admirals said they had to make a determination, and I went back to my room that night, not sure what my future was going to be.

CHAPTER 4

"THAT'S IT, THAT'S THE *REPUBLIC*," Ben Finney said.

We were in a shuttlecraft, two newly minted officers packed in with some enlisted crewmen, crammed up against the porthole trying to get a glimpse of our first assignment. Through my sliver of a window, I could see the *U.S.S. Republic*, an old *Baton Rouge*–class starship. As we passed its engines, we noticed mismatched paneling that indicated an extensive history of repair work. It was a beaten-up rust bucket, and as an ensign assigned to engineering, it was in no way a glamorous posting.

The review board had not only let me graduate, they'd given me a commendation for original thinking. Only one admiral had opposed: Komack. He stuck to his opinion that I'd violated the spirit of the test, but he'd been overruled. However, Komack had his own avenue for punishment. He was head of the committee in charge of posting cadets to their first assignments. Though I was near the top of my class and requested starship duty, he made sure I was not given an exploratory ship, which were considered the most desired postings. Instead, I was put on a 20-year-old ship that made "milk runs," delivering personnel, medicine, spare parts, other supplies from Earth to starbases and colonies and back again. I could have complained, but I felt that would be pushing my luck; I decided I was doing penance for the *Kobayashi Maru*.

I wasn't too disappointed. I was getting what I wanted: I was an officer aboard a starship. And now, as we approached the ship, I was overcome with excitement. I wish I could've said the same of my companion.

The *Republic* was not at all what Ben Finney wanted. He was hoping for a more glamorous assignment to jump-start a career that he felt had already been unfairly slowed down because he'd been an instructor for so long. However, since he was older than a lot of cadets, he was less attractive to some starship captains who wanted to mold their own kind of junior officers. His only choice was also the *Republic*. But Ben wasn't going to be passive; before we even docked, he was making plans to get himself off this ship and onto a better assignment.

The shuttle flew into the hangar, and we all stepped out into the cramped bay; it wasn't the clean, state-of-the-art facility we'd become used to at the academy. Paneling had been stripped away to make more room for shuttles, so the ship's superstructure was visible. Overhead the various small crafts were stacked in their docks, making use of all available space. Before we could take it all in, we were greeted by the ship's chief petty officer, a salt-and-pepper veteran named Tichenor.

"Welcome aboard, sirs," Tichenor said. Before we could introduce ourselves, he shouted, "Atten-shun!"

We stood at attention with the noncommissioned crew, as our new commanding officer, Captain Stephen Garrovick, entered the bay. He was stoic and imposing: well over six feet, a little gray at his temples, with a stern expression that, only with the gift of hindsight, hinted at a smile underneath. He looked us over with an air of amused disdain.

"Kirk and Finney," he said. "Chief will get you squared away." He then turned and walked off. I think I was hoping for more, maybe a "welcome to the team" speech. But we weren't getting one; we grabbed our duffels and followed Tichenor out.

The CPO led us to our "quarters." I didn't expect it to be luxurious; I figured I'd be on a quadruple bunk bed in an eight-by-eight cube, crewmen stacked like those shuttles I saw in the bay. I was overly optimistic.

We were in the primary hull's engineering deck, a crowded area packed with monitors, piping, and crewmen, many of whom were engaged in loud repair work. Tichenor pointed to a space on the floor underneath a staircase leading to the impulse engines. It had been curtained off.

"Sir, that's your berth," he said.

This had to be a joke, a hazing of the new officers. I looked at Tichenor, and then at Finney, who shrugged.

"You have a complaint, sir?" Tichenor had a smile on his face; it looked like he wanted me to complain.

"No, Chief, this'll be fine," I said.

"All right, sir, once you're squared away, regulations require you to report to sickbay for your physical," he said, then led Finney off, presumably to his makeshift quarters. I looked at the cramped space under the staircase. I wasn't even sure I could fit lying down. I tossed down my duffel, figured I was "squared away," and headed toward sickbay.

I was halfway through my physical when Finney joined me.

"They've got me sleeping in the photon torpedo bay," Ben said.

Dr. Piper, the ship's chief medical officer, stout, affable, and seasoned, chuckled.

"It won't be forever, gentlemen," he said. "Officers do their best to get off this ship."

When the *Republic* was first commissioned, it was the state of the art in exploration and research vessels. But it was a small design, and upon being superseded by the newer classes of ships, it was reclassified to tasks it wasn't initially designed for. As a result, it had to devote a large portion of what had been crew quarters to storage. Thus I would spend my first six months in Starfleet sleeping under a staircase and using the common bathroom off the engineering section.

After our physicals, we reported to our immediate commanding officer, Chief Engineer Howard Kaplan, a balding, flabby man in his fifties. I would soon discover his annoyed expression was his resting state.

"Finney, you get beta shift, Kirk, you're on gamma shift," he said. Since Starfleet ships try to duplicate Earth conditions of night and day as closely as possible, gamma shift was midnight to eight. This meant I would be trying to sleep under a staircase during the "daytime" shifts, which were always the busiest.

Kaplan checked a console chronometer.

"Finney, you're on duty in an hour, Kirk in nine. Use the time, learn the job. I don't want to be woken up unless the ship's about to blow up," he said, then turned to a member of his staff. "Lieutenant Scott! Give 'em the tour."

A lieutenant, a little older than Ben, came over and put out his hand.

"Montgomery Scott, call me Scotty," he said. He had a brogue to match his name.

"Finney, go with 'em," Kaplan said. "You'll be late to your shift, and this'll be the last time."

Scott turned quickly and we followed as he took us on a thorough tour fore and aft. It took hours and seemed like we climbed every ladder and opened every hatch on the ship. Through it all, it was hard not to become impressed with Mr. Scott. He had knowledge of engineering far beyond anything either Ben or I had experienced. He showed us repairs and make-shift constructs on everything from the transporters to the lights in the galley, all clearly completed by him. The *Republic* was held together by spit and baling wire, and Assistant Engineer Scott had provided most of the spit.

Five hours later, we had completed the tour and were well into Ben's shift. Kaplan then had me shadow Ben for his shift, since I'd be alone on gamma shift.

"And I don't want you waking me up unless the ship's about to blow up," Kaplan said again. By the time my first shift was over, I'd been up for almost 24 hours straight. My concern that I wouldn't be able to sleep under a busy staircase proved to be unfounded.

We left Earth with a cargo of supplies for the Benecia Colony, then we'd head for Starbase 9, Starbase 11, then back to Earth, to start the route again. Those first few weeks I became acquainted with one of the truths of space travel: it can be very dull. All of the major maintenance and repair operations were carried out during alpha shifts, a few minor ones and follow-ups on beta shift; the duty officer on gamma shift (me) worked alone, so it was only monitoring duty. It was crushingly tedious work, but on a ship of this age I recognized that I carried serious responsibility.

Ben, however, seemed like he was on vacation. His off-time corresponded with more of the other crew, so he quickly fell in to a social groove.

He made a lot of friends; very soon after we got there it appeared everyone knew who he was. It led to a few personal advantages; he managed to convince a personnel officer to get him an actual bed in an actual stateroom. He was sharing the room with seven other crewmen, but it was better than the staircase.

We would sometimes meet for my breakfast and his dinner (I was just waking up; he was about to go on duty for the afternoon–early evening shift). On one of these occasions, about two months into our service, he asked for my help.

"I've convinced Hardy in communications to let me call Earth," he said. This was quite an accomplishment. Use of the subspace communicator was very restricted.

"Why?"

"It's Jamie's third birthday," he said. "I don't want to miss it." I could see for the first time how heartsick Ben was. I remembered my own childhood birthdays, and my mother calling me from Tarsus. It meant a lot to me then, and I eventually grew resentful that she didn't call more often. Now that I was on a ship and understood the power involved in sending subspace communications, it's amazing to me that she called as much as she did.

"What do you need me for?"

"Hardy says she'll only do it at the end of her shift, when she's finished with the official traffic. It's also at the end of my shift, but I need you to relieve me a few minutes early so I can get over there."

"You better hope Kaplan doesn't catch you," I said.

"I don't think I have to worry. Kaplan sleeps through my shift and yours," he said, and I laughed. We'd both come to the conclusion that Montgomery Scott was the actual chief engineer, and Kaplan wasn't letting him transfer out because with Scott around, Kaplan didn't have to do any work.

A few days later, I came on shift ten minutes early. Ben was anxious to get going, and quickly brought me up to speed on the maintenance alpha and beta shifts had performed on the ship's fusion reactor.*

---

*EDITOR'S NOTE: Though the *Republic* had warp drive, its class of vessel still used a fusion reactor as an emergency backup for propulsion and internal ship's power.

After Ben left, I started my routine, which involved studying the engineering consoles and checking the status of the systems. I immediately found a vent circuit to the fusion chamber had been left open. It was contaminating the air in the engine room, and, more important, if the bridge had to shift to fusion power after another five minutes, it could've blown up the ship.

I immediately closed the circuit. Kaplan's words "I don't want you waking me up unless the ship's about to blow up" echoed in my head, so, since the ship was no longer in any danger, I decided not to alert him. But regulations stated that I had to log the incident.

I hesitated. This would get Ben in trouble; he should have noticed the open circuit during his watch. My guess was that he'd been too preoccupied about getting to speak with Jamie. I considered leaving it out of the log and just telling Finney privately what had happened. But though Finney had not noticed it being open, it wasn't necessarily his fault that it had been left open in the first place. If the responsible parties weren't found, mistakes like it could almost certainly happen again. I felt I had no choice but to log it. Looking back, I might have had a slight bit of resentment that I had had to do Finney's job for him, that he had put all our lives in danger because of his own personal needs, which may have led to my going to sleep at the end of my shift, rather than trying to find him to tell him what had happened. That was definitely a mistake.

"Wake up, you bastard!"

I'd probably been sleeping for three hours, and before I could fully register the voice that was yelling at me, I was yanked out of my makeshift quarters under the staircase. Shirtless, half-asleep, I stood in the middle of engineering as alpha shift watched in confusion. A furious Ben Finney confronted me.

"What the hell did you do?!"

"Ben, I had no choice . . ."

He wasn't interested in listening to me. Kaplan, as he did every morning, reviewed the engineering log from my shift and became furious. I hadn't calculated that Kaplan would be embarrassed too; the fact that one of his staff had been this negligent reflected poorly on him, and he brought the full weight of discipline down on Finney. Ben had been severely reprimanded and put at the bottom of the promotion list.

"I spent three extra years at the academy teaching idiots like you computers, and now thanks to you I'm going to stay an ensign forever!" I'd never seen him this angry.

"I did what I had to do—"

"You didn't have to do it. You could've looked after me the way I looked after you!"

"I'm sorry . . ."

"You're not sorry. You've been competing with me since the day we came on board, and now you've taken me down! Congratulations! Does it feel good?" He was ranting; it sounded almost paranoid. Everything I tried to say made him angrier, so I just stood quietly as he continued to yell at me. Finally, he stormed off.

I tried to process what had happened. I assumed that once some time passed, Ben would calm down and understand that, had he been in my position, he would've done the same thing. But I was wrong. In the days to come, when I would relieve him on engineering duty, he would give me a by-the-book rundown of the engineering situation. I tried on several occasions to engage him in conversation, but he wasn't interested. To make matters worse, Ben was poisoning my reputation with the rest of the crew. I never got the full story of what he said about me, but it was clear he was making a case among the other officers that the open circuit was my mistake, not his, and that I had conspired to place the blame on him. However, since no one would talk openly to me about it, there was no way for me to air my side of it.

The next few months were exceedingly lonely and depressing. The officers kept their distance from me; when I went for meals or to the few recreation areas of the ship, I could feel the coolness from the other crewmen. On top of that, Chief Engineer Kaplan wanted to make my life hell; my action had made him look bad to the captain, and though he could do nothing to reprimand me since I'd acted properly, it was also clear he wasn't going to take me off gamma shift.

One night, I was sitting alone in one of the rec rooms, a few minutes before my shift, eating dinner. Lieutenant Scott came in. I generally didn't see much of him; he was an all-work-and-no-play kind of officer, and on his off hours he spent his free time reading technical journals. He got his food from one of the dispensers and came over to me.

"Mind if I join you, Ensign?" he said.

"Not at all, sir." He sat down and immediately started eating. We both ate in silence for a moment, then he spoke.

"It might interest you to know, I told the chief engineer you might be better off in another department," he said.

"Really?" I had no idea what this was about.

"Feel free to tell me I'm wrong," he said. "I just don't know if engineering is your passion." This came as a shock to me. Scott and I hadn't spent that much time together; I wondered why he was forming this impression. I assumed it was because he bought into Ben's version of events and didn't want me around.

"I did what I had to do," I said.

"What are you talking about?" Scott said.

"When I put Ben on report," I said, "I know what the rumors are . . ."

"We're not having the same conversation," Scott said, and he looked legitimately bewildered.

"Well, I've done my work, I don't know why you'd want me transferred—"

"I don't *want* you transferred, lad. I'm thinking what's best for you. You do your work, sure," he said. "But an engineer doesn't stop there. He's always fixing, building . . . you're on a warp-driven starship, one o' the best workshops you could ever ask for. And now I hear you're sittin' around worrying about what people are saying about you." I looked at the man in awe.

"You're right, sir," I said.

"I told you the first day you got here," he said. "Call me Scotty."

It was a little better after that. During my free shifts, I decided to spend time with Scotty, helping him with repairs and upgrades. I learned more about the limits of a warp-driven ship during those months, knowledge that would come in handy in the years to come.

But the rest of the crew was still pretty unfriendly to me, and as we completed a leg of our run to Starbase 9, I was shaken awake by CPO Tichenor.

"Sir, Captain needs to see you in his quarters," Tichenor said.

I got dressed as quick as I could, and Tichenor led me to Garrovick's quarters. He was at his desk, writing something on a PADD. He dismissed Tichenor and looked up at me. I was very nervous. Except for a few brief hellos in the corridor, the only time the captain had spoken to me in the last six months was when I came on board, and this was the first time we'd ever been alone.

"Ensign Kirk," Garrovick said, "sorry we haven't had time to get to know each other, but I'm transferring you off the *Republic*."

So, even the captain wasn't immune to the rumor mill.

"Is there something you want to say, Ensign?" I felt some judgment in the question, but I wasn't going to let myself get caught up in it. If this captain had no use for my honesty, then I had no use for him.

"No sir," I said.

"All right," he said. "We'll be at Starbase 9 in a couple of hours. Be ready to leave as soon as we dock. I'll have your orders for you then. You're dismissed." He couldn't wait to be rid of me, I thought.

"Thank you, sir," I said.

I went back to my cubby and packed my things. As I did, I started to wonder, could I have been this wrong about Starfleet? I had done my duty, with honor as it was defined for me, and it had led to this. Maybe I had made a mistake.

Once I finished packing, I still had over an hour, so I thought I'd find Scotty and say goodbye. He at least had been a bright spot. I found him in the Jefferies tube leading to the port nacelle.

"You're leaving me? Who's gonna carry my toolbox?" he said with a smile.

"Thank you for all your help," I said.

"I should be thanking you," he said. "It's been a pleasure. Kind of funny, you and the captain leaving at the same time."

"The captain's leaving?" Not having many friends on the ship, I missed out on a lot of gossip.

"That's the word," he said. "Anyway, good luck to you, lad. Hope we can serve together again."

Now I was really confused. Why was the captain bothering to get rid of me if he was leaving? It didn't make any sense.

Shortly after we docked at Starbase 9, the crew was called to the shuttle bay. Garrovick was there with another captain, who I didn't recognize. I had brought my duffel with me and had it at my feet.

"Attention to orders!" Tichenor shouted, and we all stood at attention. He then handed a PADD to Captain Garrovick, who read from it.

"To Captain Stephen Garrovick, commander, *U.S.S. Republic*, you are hereby requested and required to relinquish command to Captain Ronald Tracy as of this date, and report to Captain L. T. Stone of the *U.S.S. Farragut* for duty on board as his relief in command . . ."

Wow, I thought, Garrovick was getting a *Constitution*-class ship. That was a big step up from the *Republic*. I watched as Captain Tracy, a middle-aged, fierce-looking man, relieved Captain Garrovick. I was a little anxious and confused as to what I was supposed to do; Garrovick had told me he would get me my orders, but now he looked like he was leaving right away. Tracy turned to address the crew.

"All standing orders to remain in force until further notice," he said. "The following officers will immediately depart *U.S.S. Republic*, for duty on board *U.S.S. Farragut*." There was a pause, as crewmen exchanged excited looks at the possibility of getting off this garbage scow. But Tracy only read two names.

"CMO Mark Piper, Ensign James T. Kirk," Tracy said. "Flight deck personnel, prepare shuttle bay for immediate launch. Crew dismissed." Everyone looked at me, and I couldn't believe it. I looked over at Captain Garrovick, who stood at a shuttlecraft with Dr. Piper. Piper exchanged a look with him and boarded the shuttle, and Garrovick looked at me. He was enjoying what he was seeing; he had planned this. I couldn't put it all together before he tilted his head toward the shuttle, indicating I'd better get a move on. I immediately picked up my duffel, ignoring the jealous stares of my crewmates. I passed Ben Finney on my way; I wanted to say goodbye, but his stare conveyed such a pureness of hatred it chilled me, and I just kept moving. I went over to Garrovick, who stood talking with Tracy.

"Good luck, Mr. Kirk," Tracy said. "Sorry to lose you." He shook my hand. I was in a fog; everything was moving so fast, but I followed Garrovick onto the shuttle.

Dr. Piper sat in one of the seats at the rear of the ship. I was about to sit next to him when he stopped me.

"Captain likes to have a copilot," he said, indicating the empty navigator's seat next to the captain, who was manning the helm. I hesitantly moved forward.

"Have a seat, Ensign," Garrovick said.

I put my duffel down and took the seat next to him. Through the porthole, I saw the *Republic*'s shuttle bay doors open, and Garrovick piloted the shuttle out of the bay. Out the view port I could see an orange planet blocking out the stars. We flew in silence for a long while.

"Sir," I said, finally breaking in. "May I ask you a question?"

"Yes, Ensign?"

"Why me?"

"I've read your service record. You were very close to Ensign Finney."

"Yes sir."

"Yet you logged an incident that you could've easily covered up. Why?"

"I was worried that if I didn't log it, something like it would happen again."

"Well, Ensign, I can always use a man who'd sacrifice his closest friendship for the safety of my ship," he said. "I can't control all the gossip, but I didn't appreciate how you were treated for doing the right thing."

That was what the ceremony was all about. He was taking me with him and was rubbing it in the noses of the officers who'd believed Finney.

I was both gratified and sad. Ben had once been my closest friend; he had looked after me at the academy. But as I left the *Republic*, any fond memory of him was eclipsed by his angry glare.

Garrovick switched on the communicator.

"Shuttlecraft *McAuliffe* to *Farragut*," Garrovick said. "Request permission to come aboard."

Through the view port, the *Constitution*-class ship loomed. We were approaching the underside of the saucer section. The letters spelling out the ship's name dwarfed our craft.

"Permission granted," a woman said over the communicator. "You are cleared for main hangar deck."

"No going back," Garrovick said.

"I hope not, sir," I said. And he laughed.

✦

"That, friend James," Tyree said, in a whisper, "is the scat of mugato."

We were in a small clearing in the forest, looking down at a pile of yellow dung. The primitive humanoid hunters I was with, all dressed in animal skins, put an arrow in their bows, and scanned our surroundings cautiously. I supposed the scat looked fresh to them, and that meant our prey was near. We'd been hunting the mugato for about three hours, following footprints and other spoors, but it was only now that things had become tense. I had a phaser pistol hidden in the pouch I was carrying, but I was under strict orders not to use it. These people were to have no knowledge that I was, in fact, not from their planet. And since this was my first planetary survey, violating the Prime Directive* was foremost on my mind.

At that point, I'd been on the *Farragut* about eight months, and life aboard a *Constitution*-class ship couldn't have been more different than the *Republic.* The big news for me was I had my own quarters. And another thing, I was no longer working gamma shift in engineering. I'd already been rotated through several different departments: security, a variety of the astrosciences, finally landing navigation. The ship itself was on a mission of exploration; we'd charted eleven solar systems since I came aboard, and within eight months I'd received my promotion to lieutenant.

I was at my post on the bridge when we entered the Zeta Boötis system. The third planet, designated Neural, had signs of intelligent life, and

*EDITOR'S NOTE: The Prime Directive is Starfleet General Order One. It prevents Starfleet officers from interfering with the societies of other worlds, whether it's the natural development of a primitive world, or the internal politics of an advanced society.

the captain put us in a standard orbit. He ordered the launch of suborbital probes and had them transmit to the bridge's main viewscreen. We got a look at the primitive structures the natives lived in, the population divided among small villages, farms, and tribes living in the wilderness.

"Technology report," Garrovick said.

"Primitive," Commander Coto said, from the science station. "Roughly corresponds to fifth-century Earth, agrarian society. Sensors detect heat signatures that suggest iron forges."

"Pretty barbaric," I said.

"Hmm," Garrovick said. "Not much we can learn from them, Mr. Kirk?"

"I'm not sure, sir," I said, though I was pretty sure.

"Well, let's be certain," Garrovick said. "Let's send a survey team. Mr. Kirk, you're in command."

"What . . . I mean, yes sir!" This was new; I'd been on a couple of surveys, but never as leader. Suddenly I had to make decisions that I had never faced before. How many people in the team? Who to take with me?

"Anytime you're ready, Mr. Kirk," the captain said. He seemed amused. I keyed the intercom.

"Uh, Ensign Black and the two on-duty security officers, report to ship's stores for landing party. Have historical computer correlate data from satellite images to determine appropriate clothing—"

"Only taking three crewmen with you?" Garrovick asked, as if it was a mistake.

"Yes sir," I said. "Population seems very sparse. A large group of new people suddenly showing up might cause undue attention." I searched his face for some clue that he agreed or disagreed with me, but got nothing. I kept going. "I thought Ensign Black could gather samples while I investigate the tribes in the mountains."

"Proceed," he said. I could see him exchange an amused look with Coto as I left the bridge.

Ensign Christine Black, the security officers Sussman and Strong, and I donned disguises that did a pretty good job of approximating the local clothing. We beamed down and found ourselves on a rocky hillside. There was plenty of green, with a warm, inviting breeze. It had an immediate soothing effect on all of us, but I tried to ignore it. I sent Black to gather biological samples with Strong, ordering her to return to the ship when she was done. Minka Sussman came with me. I was hoping to view the natives without having to make contact, but I was in for a quick disappointment, as we almost immediately found ourselves surrounded by a hunting party of Hill People.

They all carried either bows or spears. Sussman's hand moved to the pouch that held her phaser, but I gestured for her to stop. Their weapons weren't aimed at us. The leader of the hunting party came forward and spoke to me in an unknown language. The universal translators instantly deciphered the language, so we could communicate. The leader, who called himself Tyree, asked where we were from. I told him we were from another land far away (the Prime Directive prevented us from revealing our true origin to primitive people who had no knowledge of spaceflight or other worlds), and that we were only staying a short time. He indicated that we follow him. He took us back to his camp, a loose conglomeration of tents near caves and a spring.

He and his people were remarkably trusting. The leader of his tribe, an older man named Yitae, welcomed us to the village. He put Sussman in a tent with other women, me in a tent with Tyree, and welcomed us to eat and hunt with them.

I was worried about what I would see, living among these primitive people. There was certainly a chance that they believed in a superstitious religion and would engage in violent sacrifices. There was also great potential for accidentally causing an incident because we didn't understand their primitive ways. I had warned Sussman to be careful.

Over the next three days I learned that they hunted for food and clothing, and had a great knowledge of the wild roots. They had a good trade relationship with the villagers, who, more adept at forging iron, provided arrowheads and knives in exchange for food and skins. I did pick up their references to some beliefs in spirits and spells, but other than that the life they led was simple and peaceful. They killed only to feed themselves or for limited trade, and there seemed to be no conflicts or jealousies that were usually part of primitive human society. And the enthusiasm with which Tyree welcomed me into his life was affecting. One morning, he woke me up.

"Today, friend James," he said, "we hunt mugato."

The mugato were an ape-like carnivore, dangerous and deadly, that the natives hunted for food. Sussman and I joined a hunting party of four Hill People. Sussman was a tough security officer, but even she found herself relaxing while part of this community.

"The quickest way to kill it," Tyree said, "is in the eye."

I had some experience from childhood with a bow, and I gave Sussman a spear. We set out, and now that we'd found our prey's feces, the hunt was almost over. I looked over at Sussman; I could sense, as tough as she was, she was scared. Her hand was firmly in her pouch, presumably on her phaser. I had told her before that under no circumstances could we show these people our advanced technology, but the pressure of the current situation was clearly overriding my orders. I was going to move closer to her to have a quiet word when I heard the menacing shriek.

A white simian, large as a man, with a ridge of bone running along its head and down its back, leaped into the center of our party. With one arm, it knocked Tyree and one of his men aside. Two of the others, both with bows, fired arrows into the creature, hitting it squarely in the chest. They didn't slow it down.

The beast moved toward Sussman, who panicked, dropped her spear, and fumbled through her pouch for the phaser. The mugato reached her just as she got it out, but the animal knocked her down and the small phaser went flying. Tyree was now up again, joining his men in firing arrows into the creature, but it wouldn't let Sussman go. The mugato bit Sussman and she screamed.

I fired off an arrow, but I could see none were having an effect on the raging animal. I could take out my phaser and vaporize it, but my training told me to resist that urge, that it would contaminate this culture. The Prime Directive said we were expendable, but seeing Sussman in peril, I had to do something. Tyree had said hitting the eye was its weakness, but since it was bent over Sussman, we couldn't get a shot. I dropped my bow and arrow and went for a knife one of the Hill People had dropped.

"Tyree! Get ready!"

I leaped onto the mugato, wedged my foot into the bone ridge, and stabbed it in the side of the neck. I hung on to the knife as the mugato reared up, and, reaching back, tried to grab me. I saw Tyree taking aim. The creature bucked hard and I lost my grip. I flew to the ground, and the mugato quickly turned to me and roared.

And then an arrow pierced its left eye. The beast froze and fell backward, dead. Tyree had made the shot.

I got up immediately and went to Sussman. The mugato had bitten her in the neck, and she was shivering. There was some kind of poison I could see mixed in with her blood in the wound. My mind raced. I had medical supplies in my pouch, but bringing them out would expose me. I wasn't even sure any of them would help against the beast's venom. I needed help. I had to get her back to the ship. If I used my communicator, that could literally be the end of my career, but I had no choice. I couldn't let her die. As I reached into the pouch, Tyree touched my arm.

"Don't worry, friend James," Tyree said. "We will help her." I looked up at him. Could he save her? Could I trust this primitive? He seemed certain. He then turned to one of his men and told him to find a *Kahn-ut-tu*, which the universal translator didn't have a meaning for. He then quietly handed me Sussman's phaser, which one of his men had picked up from the ground.

"This was hers," he said.

"Yes," I said.

"What is it?"

"I . . . can't tell you," I said. Tyree accepted that. He ordered the remaining three men to take care of carrying the mugato back to camp, while he helped me with Sussman.

In a cave at the camp, we were met by Yitae and a young man dressed differently than any of the Hill People. He had a brownish complexion, jet-black hair, and wore different skins, from a much darker animal. Tyree had expected him; this was a *Kahn-ut-tu*. It looked like I was placing my crewman's fate in the hands of a witch doctor, and I didn't feel good about it. I longed to get her back to the ship under the care of an actual physician.

There was a beat of a drum. The *Kahn-ut-tu* man kneeled over Sussman and took out a black root. The root seemed to move like an animal. As

Yitae beat the drum, the witch doctor fell into a trance, and eventually slapped the root hard on Sussman's wound. They both heaved in pain, and then fell unconscious. I had never seen anything like it, and when I went to examine Sussman's wound, it was gone. Sussman stirred awake. She was tired but cured.

I realized that I was due to communicate with the ship, so I thanked the *Kahn-ut-tu*, who seemed completely indifferent. I then left the cave, found a private spot near the spring, and took out my communicator.

"Kirk to *Farragut*."

"Mr. Kirk, we were starting to worry." It was Garrovick. I filled him in on what had happened. I said I thought we needed another day for Sussman to recover before I could leave without raising suspicions. Garrovick agreed with my assessment, then said something I didn't expect.

"I guess you were lucky those barbarians could help you out."

"They're not barbarians, sir," I said. "This is an amazing species . . ."

"It's nice to know we're not the only worthwhile people in the Galaxy." Garrovick signed off, and I realized the lesson he'd taught me. I felt ashamed, embarrassed. I closed my communicator and turned to see Tyree had found me. He looked confused.

"Were you speaking to a god?"

"No," I said. I wanted to tell him the truth, but the Prime Directive was clear. Of course, if I didn't tell him the truth, his imagination might lead to a worse kind of contamination. I had gotten to know this man in the past few days, he had saved the life of my crewman, and he was my friend. I felt there was a third alternative.

"Tyree . . . can you keep a secret?"

It turns out he could.

✦

The experience with Tyree and the Hill People helped me grow as an officer. I had faced what was probably my most terrible experience in Starfleet up to that point—I'd almost lost someone under my command. I couldn't imagine anything worse. Fate would soon punish me for my lack of vision.

A few months later, I'd been rotated to weapons control. Though I'd been trained in space combat, in my year and a half of service in Starfleet, I'd seen none. We were in orbit around the fourth planet in the Tycho star system. A landing party had been sent to chart the planet's surface, which was devoid of life, or so we thought.

"Red alert!" The captain's voice came over the intercom. "Shields up, phaser control report status!" I was manning weapons control along with Chief Metlay and Crewman Press. They reported that all weapons were charged and ready.

"Bridge, this is phaser control. All weapons show ready." As I said this, the monitor in front of me displayed what was on the bridge viewscreen. I saw the planet, but couldn't make out anything else. Then I noticed what looked like one of the clouds in the atmosphere moving up into space. It was headed directly toward the ship. This was my target? A cloud? (I would find out later that this "cloud" had attacked and killed our landing party, but at this moment in time, I had no idea what I was even looking at.)

"Phasers, lock on target," Garrovick said. I immediately tied in the tracking system and brought the cloud into the center of my range finder. Sensors showed me the cloud was made out of dikironium. Its gaseous nature made it difficult for the computer to lock on it.

"Sir, I can't get a definite lock," I said. It was moving much faster now, growing on the screen.

"Fire phasers!" Garrovick said. I looked at the cloud. It now filled the viewscreen. It was at point-blank range. I paused for just a second, tried to figure out what the hell I was even looking at. And then it was gone. I pressed the fire button, but it was too late.

"Sir," Chief Metlay said, "something's entered the main phaser bank emitter . . ."

What he said was technically impossible; only forms of energy could pass through the emitter. But before I could figure out what was going on, Metlay and Press were surrounded by white gas, leaking out of their consoles. There was the distinct odor of something very sweet, like honey. And then Metlay and Press immediately fell to the floor choking.

I ran to my console.

"Weapons control to bridge! It's in the ship! Repeat, it's in the ship! I'm sealing this section."

Whatever this gas was, I knew I had to keep it from getting to the rest of the *Farragut*. I began to activate the locks on the emergency bulkheads to seal off the section. I was only about halfway done when the sweet odor got stronger.

And then it was on me. It was as though I was drowning in a vat of syrup. I couldn't breathe. I started to lose consciousness, and as I did, I heard something. It wasn't a voice. It was in my head.

"I will feed here . . ."

✦

I don't know how long I had been out. I had been vaguely aware of people talking, the red alert klaxon, and then quiet. But it was all distorted, a haze. And then I felt a hypo in my neck, and I slowly regained consciousness.

My vision focused, and I found I was in sickbay. First Officer Coto was standing over my bed, along with Dr. Piper. The lights were dim. There was a medical device on my arm.

"You're getting blood transfusions," Piper said to me. "But you'll be fine."

I tried to ask about the cloud, to explain what happened.

"It's off the ship," Coto said. His voice was heavy; there was no relief in it.

"It was . . . a creature," I said.

Coto and Piper exchanged a look.

"What do you mean?" Piper said.

"I could feel . . . it thinking," I said. "It wanted to feed off us . . ." From Coto's look, he didn't believe me. Piper, however, was considering it.

"It would explain some things," the doctor said. "It didn't just dissipate through the ship like an uncontrolled gas," he said. "It took only red corpuscles from its victims. First the landing party, then the two crewmen in weapons control, but Kirk was left alive. The attacks happened in spurts— a few people at a time were killed—for lack of a better analogy, its stomach got full."

"Wait . . . attacks?" I said. "How many people?"

Piper realized he had been talking too much. He gave Coto an apologetic look.

"Please tell me," I said.

"Over 200," Coto said. Half the crew.

"The captain?" I asked even though I knew the answer.

"He's dead," Coto said.

"I'm sorry . . ." I choked it out. "I'm so sorry . . ."

"It's not your fault," he said. "Staying in the weapons control room to seal off the section saved the ship . . ."

I couldn't hear him. All those people, and Captain Garrovick, dead because I didn't fire in time. I felt myself starting to cry and turned away.

"Get some rest, Lieutenant," Coto said, and he turned and left.

✦

The *Farragut* limped to Starbase 12 with half a crew for repairs, resupply, and restaffing. I spent two weeks in a rehabilitation facility. The creature had taken most of the red corpuscles from my body, and it took a long time before my body healed. Mental health was going to take a lot longer.

Commander Coto and Dr. Piper both came to see me during my rehabilitation. They hadn't given Coto the promotion to captain, but he was still in temporary command and, as such, was supervising the restaffing of the ship. He had gotten approval to offer me the position of chief navigator. I said yes, although I was unsure. He told me my duties would be very light for a long time; it would take weeks for such a large number of crew replacements to make their way to Starbase 12.

Once I was released from the hospital, rather than return to the ship, I took quarters on the base. It was the first time since the academy that I lived on a planet, and it was a welcome change. Starbase 12 was a state-of-the-art facility, providing storage and repair services, and surrounded by living and recreational accommodations. About 4,000 Starfleet personnel and their families lived there.

My room was in a bungalow in the single officers' living area, two-story buildings set on winding pathways among rolling grass and trees.

The apartment was efficient and clean, with its own kitchen, but I took most of my meals either in the officers' mess or one of the small restaurants and bars that civilians and interplanetary traders had set up on the base. I found myself imbibing a lot during this period; the only way I could go to sleep was drunk, and even so my sleep was fitful and disturbed by nightmares.

A particular favorite haunt of mine was called Feezal's. It was run by a friendly proprietor whose race I wasn't familiar with. He had a large skull with ridges on the sides of his cheeks and forehead, which might have seemed threatening, except for his constant joviality. He said his name was "Sim," but I suspected he wasn't telling the truth. He seemed very old and would gently deflect any attempt on my part to get him to divulge anything personal, including what planet he was from. The only thing he would tell me about himself was that the bar was named after one of his wives.

He, however, did show a lot of interest in me, asking me lots of questions about my life and history, and it was therapeutic to talk to someone. He had lost a close friend on Tarsus, which led to several discussions on whether Kodos was really dead. There were galactic rumors that he'd gotten away. Sim seemed to always know what I needed, and one evening, he amazed me by introducing me to a young woman, whom I immediately recognized.

"Hello, Jim!" she said.

I'd met Carol Marcus at the academy, where she worked as a lab assistant while she finished her doctorate in molecular biology. We had had a short, casual fling that came to an end when I graduated.

Upon seeing her I was immediately sorry it hadn't continued. She was very attractive, blond, petite—which I guess was my type—and very smart. In the intervening years, Carol had gotten her doctorate and was now part of a research project using Starfleet facilities at the base. I felt myself drawn to her immediately. She was warm and attentive, flattered by my renewed interest, and our relationship reignited.

The restaffing of the *Farragut* dragged on for weeks, and I didn't mind. I would serve a shift on the *Farragut* for eight hours a day, then return to the starbase, where Carol and I would spend the rest of our time. I moved into her apartment, and we had a rapport that was both passionate and easy. We'd spend our free time rock climbing and horseback riding, we'd cook together and read together. I stopped drinking as much, and the nightmares, though they didn't go away completely, faded. I was settled and happy. And I didn't want it to end.

"Will you marry me?" I said one morning while we were still in bed.

"Jim," she said. "Wait . . . what?"

"I want to marry you," I said. "I want to be with you."

"Jim . . . I love you . . . but I can't leave my work . . ."

"Then I'll leave mine," I said, and thought I meant it. "I'll ask for a base posting. We can make this work. I want to have a family with you."

"It's . . . what I want too," she said, and kissed me. I called the ship and asked one of the junior officers to cover my shift, and we stayed together all day.

The next morning, I arrived for my shift on the *Farragut*. The ship was busier now; as chief navigator, I also had crewmen who reported to me. I saw Commander Coto in his quarters, and told him I wanted reassignment to the starbase. He looked at me in weary acceptance. He'd known about my relationship with Carol and said he'd been expecting this.

"Look, Jim," he said, "I'm not going to try to talk you out of it. But you're an exceptional Starfleet officer. Assuming I get command, I'm going to need men like you I can rely on to help me protect the lives of this crew."

"I'm sorry, sir," I said. "I've made up my mind." But I hadn't. I had committed myself to Carol, and that's what drove me to say what I said. But Coto had an effect, and I felt a responsibility to help him and the crew. Coto asked me to at least delay my transfer until the final replacements arrived, which would still be a few weeks. I agreed.

As time went on, I became more conflicted about my decision. I was enjoying my time with Carol, but I felt the pull of life aboard the ship. And, as new crewmen reported to the *Farragut,* I became cognizant of my importance; a lot of them were fresh from the academy, and though I'd only been out less than two years, I was surprised that the experiences even in that short a time gave me a wealth of knowledge to share. I also found that, in grieving for the loss of Captain Garrovick and my shipmates, I had renewed my determination to serve, to correct the mistake I had made. I should've been talking about this to Carol, but I knew it would hurt her.

A few weeks later, *Farragut* was almost completely restaffed. As I finished up my shift, Commander Coto came over to me.

"I've received my promotion," he said. I congratulated him. He'd worked harder than anyone to get the ship back in shape, and I was glad he was rewarded. He then told me the ship would be leaving in two days, and he wondered if I'd reconsidered my decision, as he still had not filled the position of chief navigator. It was still mine if I wanted it. I said I did. I left the ship, my heart heavy with the fact that I now had to break this news to Carol. I decided I would tell her everything I'd been thinking, that I needed this to close out my grief. I knew she would be hurt, but I thought she would understand, knowing what I'd been through. I didn't get the chance; when I walked in, she met me with a smile.

"Jim, I'm pregnant," she said as she fell into my arms.

A child. I had not expected this. It was thrilling and confusing. Suddenly my self-centered arguments felt hollow. The idea of a baby was so overwhelming, so joyous, so intimidating, that I didn't know what to say. Carol, however, immediately sensed something was wrong. She stepped back and looked at me.

"I'll make it work," I said. "I promise—"

"This is exactly what you said you didn't want," she said, through tears.

"I know," I said. "But I love you—"

"You said you hated your mother going away; you didn't want that for your kids." She had been listening to me talk about the pain of my childhood. But in that moment, I thought I could do things differently. I believed I could be there as a father, and also do my job as a Starfleet officer. I would make it work. I loved her, and I wanted to have a family with her.

"Let's have this baby," I said. "I'll be there for you."

✦

"Clear the bridge!" I shouted too late. I'd been manning the *Hotspur*'s engineering station. We'd been hit several times, and the last one had shorted out the engineering console, electrocuting the crewman who was operating it. I was trying to reroute power to the shields but had been unsuccessful. Captain Sheridan took the helm and was trying to get us out of orbit.

We had been attacked by pirates on the way to deliver supplies and medicine to Altair IV, at the edge of the Federation. Aliens in unmarked ships would often attack lone Starfleet vessels in the region, in the hopes of stealing profitable cargo. We knew, in fact, that some of these ships were actually Klingon, under orders from their government to unofficially pilfer whatever they could from Federation shipping. If caught, they would deny their empire's involvement. We weren't a hundred percent sure that the ship we were currently engaged with was Klingon, but just the possibility that they were motivated me; every encounter I had with that species furthered my growing personal animosity. I watched as the stubby pirate vessel launched another torpedo, just as the captain laid in the course. The torpedo was on track to hit the primary hull and the bridge. I was a few feet from the turbolift, and just before we were hit, I shouted and leaped for it.

The torpedo obliterated what was left of our deflectors and blasted a ten-meter gaping wound in the primary hull; the bridge was open to space. I was at the door of the turbolift as the air and everything not tied down was blown out of the hole. In the millisecond before I was blown out with everything else I had grabbed the edge of the closing turbolift door. The tremendous force of the atmosphere departing the confines of the ship lifted me off the deck. I held the door with both hands; the rushing air and the sudden cold of space weakened my grip. I held my breath; I knew I wouldn't have much time.

And as suddenly as the wind started, it stopped.

I fell to the deck. The bridge was now an airless void, and I felt the unbearable cold slice through my uniform. I knew I had maybe ten seconds before I passed out. I looked up; my right hand still clutched the turbolift door. I couldn't feel it; my extremities had already gone completely numb. What had saved me so far was the ship's computer, locked in an unsolvable dilemma; it couldn't seal the turbolift as long as its sensor detected a human life-form holding the door open. As long as I didn't let go, the door wouldn't close.

I pulled myself toward the small opening and felt unbelievable pressure on my lungs. I had an overwhelming desire to exhale, but knew that would be the end of me. The lift seemed too far away. I stumbled, then dragged myself forward. Blackness surrounded me. I couldn't move anymore, tried to pull, and then had the sensation of rolling on the deck.

I'd made it into the lift and heard the doors close with a pneumatic whoosh; the sound told me there was air, so I exhaled and inhaled. I was on the floor, shivering, desperately trying to catch my breath. On the verge of blacking out, I rolled over, got to my knees, and reached for one of the lift's control handles. I grabbed it, trying to fight off the dark waiting to envelop me. I pulled myself to my feet and hit the comm panel.

"Kirk . . . to auxiliary control," I said.

"Yes sir," a voice responded.

"Captain Sheridan laid in a course—"

"I see it, sir, it's on the board—"

"Execute . . . immediately." Looking for shelter, Sheridan had set a course for a nearby gas giant. The pirate ship was too old and small to stand the pressure. The *Hotspur*, a *Baton Rouge*–class ship like the *Republic*, wouldn't be able to stand it for long either, but it would buy us some time.

I felt the deck plates shudder. The ship was moving. I turned the control handle of the turbolift, and as it moved toward auxiliary control, I took in the empty lift car and its implication: I was the only one who'd made it off the bridge. The captain and first officer were both dead. Sheridan had been a good commander. He was collaborative, encouraged my input. I learned a lot from him. I tried not to think about the fact that he was now gone.

I had only been aboard the *Hotspur* a month. It was not a desired posting because the ship was so old, but after two years of relative comfort as Captain Coto's navigator, I was looking for something different. When Coto told me his priority was protecting the lives of his crew, he wasn't exaggerating; he had become very risk averse. I really couldn't blame him given the trauma he'd been through, but the upshot was he made sure the *Farragut* always played it safe. So when the *Hotspur* needed a communications officer, who would also be fourth-in-command, I jumped at it. The ship was also on "milk runs," like the *Republic*, but in a sector of space much more dangerous.

The turbolift stopped; I got off and found my way to the auxiliary control room. It was manned by a few crewmen I didn't know well, and one that I did: the chief engineer and third-in-command, Howard Kaplan, my old superior officer from the *Republic*. He was moved to the *Hotspur* when the *Republic* was retired from service. Though he technically outranked me, I was a bridge officer, and he had not been happy to see me come aboard. The rest of the crewmen were among the least experienced on the ship; they were reserve crewmen sent to man the auxiliary control room during a red alert. When the bridge was declared uninhabitable, any and every senior officer available was supposed to report here and take over. Kaplan and I were the only ones who showed up.

"Are you all right, sir?" asked the crewman manning the helm. She was a beautiful young woman named Uhura who'd just gotten out of the academy.

"Report," I said, ignoring her question, because I was far from all right. I was freezing, my legs were weak, and my vision was blurry. But I wasn't going to let them know that, especially Kaplan.

"We're inside the gas giant, sir," Uhura said.

"Warp drive is out and we're not going to be able to stay here for long," Kaplan snapped.

He wasn't offering a solution; I looked around the room at the other faces, all of them younger than me, all of them looking for guidance. I wasn't going to get any ideas from them either, so I had to figure something out.

The pirates were better armed than we were and had caught us by surprise. I couldn't go back out there and engage in a conventional battle. They'd damaged our weapon targeting control—in a pounding match, they'd have a distinct advantage.

"Ensign," I said to Uhura, "bring up what we have on our opponent." Uhura threw a few switches, and a schematic of the pirate ship appeared on the viewscreen. I immediately looked at its mass; it was about a third of *Hotspur's*. I did a quick calculation in my head and smiled to myself. I had a plan, and I was sure it would work.

I glanced again at Kaplan. He was technically in command, so I should run my idea by him, but there was no use to that. He'd spent his career in engineering. He had no experience commanding a ship. He looked at me, worried, angry, scared. He wasn't in any position to judge my idea, and I was past hesitating where the safety of the ship was concerned.

"Stand by on tractor beam," I said. I had checked and it was still operational. "We're going to come out of the gas giant, lock on to that ship, then we're going to drag it back into the gas giant with us . . ."

"We won't have a lot of thrust—" Kaplan said.

"We won't need it," I said. "We're deeper in the gravity well than they are, and we're three times their mass. That'll do most of the work for us. They'll either overload their engines trying to pull away, or get crushed by the gas giant."

Uhura and the other crewmen look relieved, pleased by the confidence I had expressed. We might get out of this. Kaplan just scowled at me, embarrassed but contrite.

"Execute my orders," I said, then turned to Kaplan. "Start your repairs on the warp drive."

"Aye sir," Kaplan said, as he left.

I was 27, and I was now a captain.

And I hadn't seen my child in two years.

CHAPTER 5

"I'M A DOCTOR, NOT A BABYSITTER," McCoy said. I wanted to hit him.

I'd known Leonard McCoy for over a year, since I came aboard the *Hotspur.* We did not have a lot in common; he was older than me, and though he was at the academy for a short time when I was there, we hadn't met. On the ship, he seemed competent though always a little put out. Things only got worse when I took command; he made it clear on more than one occasion that he thought I wasn't ready for the job. I suppose I couldn't blame him; at 29 I was the youngest captain in the history of Starfleet. Usually, I'd ignore his attitude as long as he followed my orders. In this case, however, I needed his help.

"I'm not asking you to babysit," I said. "The boy is going to be on board for three weeks; we're cramped for space. I want to make sure it's safe."

"It'd be safer if he didn't come on board," McCoy said.

"McCoy—" I said. He could see that I was annoyed.

"Look, Commander, what do you want me to say? This ship is barely safe for adults, let alone a two-year-old. Why the hell are they coming aboard anyway?"

I wasn't going to let McCoy or anyone else know why we were transporting Carol and little David back to Earth, or their connection to me, at least not yet. When I came to see him in sickbay, I suppose I thought he might have sympathy for a mother and child being stuck on a starship, but I could see that was too much to hope for.

"First of all, he's three years old," I said, dodging his question. "And second of all, the health and well-being of everyone aboard is your responsibility. That goes for all our passengers. I want facilities set up for the care of a three-year-old. That's an order."

"Yes sir," he said, and as I left he gave me a curious look.

I headed back to the bridge. As I walked the corridors, I was reminded that McCoy was an exception; most of the crew went out of their way to show me deference and respect. But, paradoxically, this deference thrust me into a specific kind of loneliness. This was not the friendless solitude I'd faced on the *Republic*. My responsibility to the people I was now in command of was a burden; my actions could and would literally affect their lives. And I experienced a strange sensation as captain, a shrinking of my personal identity, as if my nerve endings had been extended to the physical limits of *Hotspur*. I never quite slept, not in the way I had before; I was like a young parent, my ears listening apprehensively even in my sleep. The crew were my children; I was looking after all of them, so I could be a friend to none of them.

And yet, ironically, I hadn't experienced that with my own child. I was going to try to change that. The last leg of our current run took us to Starbase 12, where Carol had been now for four years. I hadn't seen very much of her and David during that time. We had spoken frequently by subspace, and when David was a baby she would hold him up to the screen. However, recently, she would speak to me alone, always having a reason why David wasn't there. During our last conversation, she had told me her project was finished and she was heading back to Earth. Conventional transport wouldn't be able to take her for another month, so I arranged for a scheduled layover at Starbase 12 under the guise of some minor ship maintenance that I'd been putting off, and we would transport Carol and David home.

I was very excited about them coming on board. I knew that I'd been neglecting them because of my work, but now with my position I felt I could exert some control over my life. There were starship captains who were married and had children; why couldn't I be one of them? Which is why I had also decided to make it official and marry Carol on this voyage, although since I was in command, I wasn't sure who was going to perform the service.

I arrived on the bridge; my first officer turned and got out of the command chair.

"Captain on the bridge," Gary Mitchell said. Gary knew I hated this formality; though I was "captain of the ship," I had not received the official rank of captain.

"Status," I said, as Gary went back to the helm station.

"We've assumed standard orbit of Starbase 12," he said.

"Very well, begin transport of passengers and cargo," I said.

Gary had been serving on the *U.S.S. Constitution* as a relief helmsman when I was promoted. I immediately asked Starfleet personnel to transfer him as my first officer. He was probably a little young for the job too, which is one of the reasons why I wanted him. I was 27, and all of the senior officers on the ship were older than me; having a contemporary (and a friend) as my exec buttressed my confidence. My only criticism of him was he tended to be too loose regarding the rules of fraternization with the female crew members.

We began the complicated unloading of cargo from the ship. About two hours in, Ensign Uhura, the relief communications officer, relayed a message from ground control.

"Sir," Uhura said, "a request for permission for a Dr. Carol Marcus to beam up."

"Guess she can't wait," Gary said, a little too salaciously. Gary didn't know the full story; he knew Carol and I had been involved, but not how far it went. I gave him an annoyed look.

"Permission granted," I said. "I'll be in the transporter room."

As I left the bridge, I found myself smiling; my enthusiasm about seeing David began to overtake me. I remembered my own excitement to see my father or mother after any kind of absence, and also remembered fantasizing about what it must be like aboard a spaceship. Now I would be able to show my ship to my son, who I was sure had the same thoughts. I was indulging myself, looking forward to being proud, to walking down the corridor of my ship, while my crew showed deference to me in front of my child, and the pride he would feel at being my son. I was looking forward to that admiration and unconditional love.

I arrived in the transporter room. The technician on duty informed me that one person was standing by to beam up.

"One?" I didn't know what to make of it. "Very well, energize."

The image on the transporter pad shimmered into the recognizable form of Carol. She had no luggage. I could tell immediately she didn't want to be there.

"Hello, Carol," I said.

"Commander," she said. I realized she wasn't going to talk openly in front of a stranger. I turned to the transporter technician and relieved him of his post. Once he left, however, Carol showed no sign of being more comfortable.

"Where's David?" I said.

"With a sitter," she said.

"The ship needs to leave orbit in a few hours. I thought you'd want the time to settle him in on board—"

"We're not coming with you," she said. "I don't think it would be good for him."

"You don't think it would be good for him to see his father?" I was a little indignant.

"Right now, he doesn't know he has a father," she said.

I was stunned. I didn't know how to respond, so I got angry.

"Bring my son to me now," I said. It sounded ridiculous even to me, and Carol laughed, but without mirth.

"I'm not one of your crew," she said. "I'd like to go back now."

"No, wait," I said. "Carol, I'm sorry. I just—"

"He's a little boy," she said. "He wouldn't understand why his father doesn't love him enough to be with him."

"But I can now," I said. "Give me a chance—"

"I've given you several chances. Years of chances. I kept hoping . . ." She was welling up. I hadn't realized up to that moment just how much my absence had hurt Carol. I kept rationalizing that at some future date I would figure out how to be together, to be a family. But I'd taken too long. "So . . . I can't see him . . ."

"I think it would be better if you stayed away," Carol said. It was hard for me to hear, but I could also see it was hard for her to say. She took a pause, finally stepped down off the transporter pad. She took my hand. "Jim, there is no easy answer. Neither one of us is going to give up our work. And that means only one of us can be there for David, and it's going to be me."

I could see there was no changing her mind. And I knew, from my own history with my mother, that in one sense, she was right: David wouldn't understand.

"All right," I said. "But one day, when he's old enough . . ."

"One day," she said. She kissed me on the cheek, then turned and got back onto the transporter. I went to the controls, signaled the starbase, and, without another word, beamed her down. In a moment, she was gone, and I was alone.

✦

A short time later, I was on the bridge, making final preparations to leave orbit, when Dr. McCoy came to see me.

"Commander, I've got a play area set up," he said.

"What?"

"I had some crates moved out of a small storage locker off the gymnasium. I've put in some age-appropriate games, and taken out anything that might be harmful. I've also set up a schedule for the nursing staff to take turns—"

"We don't need it," I said, cutting him off. I'd completely forgotten about this task I'd given McCoy.

"What do you mean? What about the child?"

"There's no child on board," I said. "The passengers made other arrangements."

Gary looked back at me from the helm, surprised.

"Mind your helm, Mr. Mitchell," I said. My curtness told Gary I wasn't going to give him any information, at least not now, so he turned back to his console. McCoy, however, wasn't letting it go.

"I've spent the last three hours on this," he said.

"Look, Doctor—"

"I'm the chief medical officer aboard this ship. I'm responsible for the health of 300 crewmen, and you're wasting my time on some kind of horse-shit practical joke—"

"That's enough," I said.

"It's not enough—"

"Dismissed, Doctor," I said. McCoy still stood there, glaring at me, and I didn't like it. "Get the hell off the bridge."

"I'm putting this into my medical log," he said. "This isn't the end of it." He stormed off into the turbolift. I noticed the bridge crew glancing over at me, trying to figure what it was all about.

"Show's over, folks," I said. "Let's get out of here."

Leaving orbit and getting under way gave me a little while to cool down. I realized that I probably did owe McCoy an apology, but his attitude really didn't make me want to give him one. Still, I wasn't sure I wanted him entering this in his medical log either. I was already probably under scrutiny at Command because of my age, and I had a feeling it might not be the first time McCoy put something in his log that would undermine me in the eyes of Starfleet. Once we were under way, I left the bridge and went down to see him in his office.

"Captain," he said. "Please come in. I was just going to come see you . . ." His affect was much less confrontational than I expected. And he'd called me captain, as did many of the crew, in deference to naval tradition. But some of the older crewmen used my actual rank of com-mander, which I always took as a sign they didn't fully respect my posi-tion. Up until this moment, McCoy had been one of them.

"Look, McCoy, I owe you an apology . . ."

"No sir, it's unnecessary," he said. "I was way out of line." Any trace of his anger and resentment was gone.

"I'd still like to say I'm sorry," I said.

"Well, apology accepted," he said. We stood in awkward silence for a moment, and when I turned to leave, he stopped me and went over to a cabinet on the wall. "I was about to have a drink . . ."

He opened the cabinet and inside were a variety of bottles in different colors and shapes. His sudden cordiality didn't make any sense to me. He didn't seem like the same man.

"Quite a collection," I said.

"A doctor needs to be prepared for all medical contingencies." He took out a bottle of Saurian brandy and poured us two glasses. I sat down and took one.

"So, half an hour ago you were ready to rip my head off; now you're sharing the good liquor with me."

"Maybe I just realized we have more in common than I thought," he said, then activated his computer viewscreen, and turned it toward me. On it was a picture of a young girl, maybe eleven, dark hair, blue eyes. She was standing against the post of what I assumed was a porch, overlooking a grand green yard.

"She's lovely. Who is it?"

"My daughter, Joanna," McCoy said. "She lives with her mother." There was remorse in the way he said this.

This caught me by surprise. I hadn't told anyone, not even Gary, that David was my son. How could he have figured it out?

"They were coming aboard, and then suddenly they weren't," he said, obviously reading my bafflement. "It had a familiar emotional tinge to it."

It was my first exposure to McCoy's emotional perceptiveness, which I would eventually count on, but at the moment it caught me off guard. It took me a moment to realize that I also felt relief; someone knew the guilt I was carrying, someone who understood. I finished the drink in my glass, looked at the picture again.

"When was the last time you saw her?"

"It's been a while," he said, then held out the bottle. "Another?"

✦

"We're down to our last crystal," Kaplan said. "And it's fracturing. I don't know how much longer it's going to last." I had gathered my officers in the ship's small briefing room. McCoy, Kaplan, and Gary joined me at the table. Standing against the wall were Communications Officer Chen and Cargo Officer Griffin. I was very annoyed; Kaplan was a terrible choice for this ship. He went by the book, so I could never officially fault him, but the *Hotspur* was so old that it needed a lot more creative thinking than he was capable of. His regular maintenance schedule for the dilithium chamber was too lax, and had caused us to go through our crystals abnormally fast. Without them, we'd have no warp power, and he'd waited until the last minute to alert me to the situation. When the last crystal burned out, we could be stuck in the middle of nowhere.

I remember my years on the *Hotspur* with more nostalgia than they probably deserve. All we did was travel back and forth between the same planets, carrying the same supplies, and it didn't take long for me to figure out how to avoid the traps of the pirates who were looking to get our cargo. There was no real exploration, and the ship itself was never easy to run. But I often long for the simplicity of that period, my first command, when we were frequently risking our lives for no great cause other than cargo.

"Suggestions," I said. I looked at Kaplan, who sat quietly, scowling.

"I think we've got to find some dilithium," Gary said.

"That's a big help, Science Officer," I said. The ship did not have a crewman specifically trained as "science officer"; I had assigned it to Gary because he was the best choice of a bad lot.

"The Tellarites used to have a dilithium operation on Dimorous," Griffin said. "I remember the captain of my old ship, the *Rhode Island*, bought some crystals from them. Not cheap, is all I want to say, and those suckers love to argue . . ." Griffin, a breezy, rotund officer, had gotten a commission from my predecessor, for reasons that were never made clear to me.

Gary programmed some information on the computer console in front of him.

"He's right, sir," Gary said. "The Tellarites abandoned the mining facility about five years ago. It looks like they left a fair amount of gear."

"Don't expect me to operate Tellarite mining equipment," Kaplan said.

"Noted," I said. "Do we know why the Tellarites left?"

"They reported the operation was quote," Gary said, reading off his screen, "'No longer a profitable enterprise,' end quote."

"That sounds fishy," McCoy said, and I agreed with him. But I didn't see we had much of a choice.

"Any intelligent life on the planet?" I said.

"Various indigenous animals, but nothing to worry about . . ." Gary said.

✦

We achieved orbit of Dimorous and detected two compounds on the planet. One was clearly the dilithium mine, but the other, about 20 miles away, was a mystery. From orbit we detected what looked like some kind of laboratory facilities, as well as what appeared to be animal pens. There was also a large density of animal life surrounding that facility. It was tantalizingly peculiar, but there was no time to satisfy my curiosity.

I beamed down to the mining facility with Gary, McCoy, Assistant Engineer Lee Kelso, and Security Chief Christine Black. (I left Kaplan in command, since dragging him planetside was always an ordeal.) The Tellarite mining facility was housed in a bunker-like building, set in an arid area of rock and sand dunes. Inside the building, there was a control station set up next to a huge chasm, leading deep under the planet's surface. A mining laser hung over the chasm, set up to cut through the ground, down to the dilithium vein; the crystals would be brought up with tractor beams. It was state-of-the-art equipment, and the reactor that powered the station, though deactivated, was still nominal. It made little sense that the Tellarites would just leave it there, along with an abundantly rich vein of dilithium. The only explanation was that they left in a hurry.

"Jim," McCoy said, looking at his tricorder, "life-forms approaching. A lot of them." While Kelso quickly got to work, Gary, McCoy, Black, and I went outside. A wall, creating a fort-like structure, bordered the Tellarite facility. The four of us went up to the parapet and were unprepared for what we saw next.

"Jesus," McCoy said.

A moving mass of brown and gray rolled toward us. It was hard to make out distinct shapes in the mass, but there were hundreds, thousands of eyes and fangs. As it got closer, I could see the individual creatures moved on all fours, thick hind legs and small upper limbs, like rats. But huge; each was four or five feet long. They were scrambling over each other, biting, clawing, but moving fast over the terrain. As they approached, the cacophony of their piercing shrills grew in intensity.

"I think we know why the Tellarites left . . ." Gary said.

"There's no record of a life-form like this on Dimorous—" McCoy said.

"There is now," I said, taking out my communicator. "Kirk to Kelso, what's your status?"

"Kelso here. I'm bringing up the first sample now—"

"One sample's all you're going to get," I said. It would've been nice to have a little in reserve, but it was not to be. "On the double, we've got to get out of here." I then switched channels. "Kirk to *Hotspur*, stand by for emergency transport." I was prepared to leave even the one crystal behind, except I quickly found out that wasn't an option.

"Commander, this is *Hotspur*," Kaplan said. "Our power levels have dropped too low, transporter is out."

"Send a shuttle," I said. I looked out at the furry, noxious mass getting closer. I was angry; somehow I blamed this whole situation on Kaplan.

"Already launched, sir. They'll be there in minutes." At least he'd done that right.

The animals' shrieking was making it difficult to hear. I instinctively drew my phaser, but as Gary and Black followed suit, I was reminded of my responsibility.

"On stun," I said.

"Really?" Gary had already set his phaser to full power. "Is this the time to get sentimental?" I could see from Black's expression that she agreed with the first officer, but was respectful enough not to offer her opinion.

"Mr. Mitchell," McCoy said, "our mission is about the preservation of life."

"Yeah, I always figured that included us," Gary said.

"McCoy, go give Kelso a hand," I said. Having McCoy there harping on our duty to other life-forms wasn't helping; I knew the right thing to do, but I was also scared, and his somewhat self-righteous tone made me want to disagree with him.

"Let's see if we can scare them off," I said. "Take out a few in the front."

We fired and hit about a dozen of the creatures in front. It did not slow the mass down; the creatures climbed over their unconscious brethren without pause. The brown and gray wave now separated into more distinct shapes, spreading out in the plain surrounding the mining facility. They were moving on us from a broader front; their line was thinner, but we wouldn't be able to cover that wide an area.

"Sir, that was a tactical move," Black said. She was right; though fierce and relentless, it was a sign of intelligence. These were not wild animals. And then, just as I noticed something else, Gary did too.

"Jim, are some of them . . . armed?" Above their hind legs on a large portion of the creatures' backs were something that looked like bandoleers; each held several pointed projectiles.

"Gary, take the left wall, Black, the right. Don't let them flank us," I said.

"Can we kill them now?" Gary said.

"No, it'll drain our phasers too fast. And make your shots count. Short bursts." As Black and Gary moved to their positions, I fired my phaser. They soon joined me as our beams stunned creature after creature. It was only a temporary solution; the creatures didn't stay unconscious for very long. We weren't holding the line; there was just too many of them. Slowly they inched forward. As they did, some of the creatures gripped the dart-like projectiles strapped to their backs with one of their hind feet and threw them. They were thankfully still out of range, the darts falling a few feet short of the wall. I took out my communicator.

"Kirk to McCoy, status!" I said, now yelling to be heard over the din.

"Kelso's finished, we're on our way out," McCoy said. I then looked up and saw a shuttle break through an orange cloud. At the same time, I heard repeated thunks against the wall. The rodent creatures were in throwing range. I watched the shuttle approach. The landing pad was outside the walls of the mining facility, which, for obvious reasons, was not going to work, and there wasn't room inside the walls for the shuttle to land.

"Kirk to shuttle," I said.

"Uhura here, sir." I was pleased it was her. Uhura was a dedicated officer, and though she specialized in communications, she was a very good pilot.

"Uhura, we're not going to be able to make the landing pad—"

"I can see that, sir," she said. "I can land on the bunker, but I don't think it will hold the shuttle's weight for long . . ."

"Do it," I said.

I took a quick glance to my left. Gary was holding off his creatures' advance, but he was firing a little wildly, missing often; they were closing in. I then looked to my right and could see that Black's shooting was much more efficient; the creatures on that side were farther back. The shuttle zoomed over us, heading toward the bunker, where McCoy and Kelso were now waiting, holding a canister with the dilithium inside.

"Black, move back to the bunker," I said. I gambled that it would take a little longer for the creatures to reach her side of the wall. A few darts now hit just below where I was standing. "Stand by to give us cover."

Black leaped off the walkway of her wall and ran back to the bunker. The shuttle rested on the bunker, and I turned to Gary.

"Go!" We both turned and leaped. Darts cleared the wall just as we jumped. As I ran toward her, Black, having reached the bunker, aimed her phaser directly at me and fired. The beam missed me but presumably hit the creatures, which were now crawling up over the wall behind me.

"Get in the shuttle!" I yelled. McCoy and Kelso were already climbing up onto the roof of the bunker. Black then quickly scaled the wall, and immediately knelt and continued to fire. I turned and saw the horde of rodent-like monsters scramble over the barrier. I fired several shots as Gary reached the bunker with me. I continued to fire as he gave me a quick leg up onto the bunker. I then grabbed him and pulled him up. I looked down and saw cracks were spreading on the bunker's roof; the shuttle's weight was too much. We moved to the hatch and I motioned Black inside. I was following her in when I was suddenly shoved into the craft, onto its deck. I turned to see Gary was prone on the bunker. He'd pushed me inside and taken a dart in the upper right arm. The shuttle shifted; the roof of the bunker was giving way.

"Black, cover me!"

I dove out of the shuttle and saw the angry, empty eyes clear the roof. Black fired from the shuttle's entrance, shooting the creatures closest to me, giving me time to throw Gary over my shoulder and turn back to the shuttle. There were too many for Black to shoot, and she had to move back to let me on board. I could hear the skittering creatures inches behind me as I fell back into the shuttle. There was hot breath on my neck as the shuttle hatch slammed shut. Uhura, at the helm, screamed.

I turned; when the hatch closed, it had severed a creature's head and one of its paws. The face stared at us from the deck, its mouth open, revealing unnaturally sharp razor fangs, oozing yellow blood. I heard the thumping of the rodents outside against the hull.

The shuttle jarred, and we were all thrown against the starboard bulkhead; the roof was collapsing.

"Uhura!" I shouted, but she'd already regained her composure and grabbled the controls. She jammed the throttles forward, the engines groaned, and the shuttle righted itself as we lifted off.

McCoy had already moved to examine Gary. He ripped Gary's shirtsleeve to reveal the wound. A black stain was visibly spreading from the entry of the dart. McCoy took out his scanner. Gary looked up at me and forced a smile through his pain.

"What the hell were you thinking?" I said to him.

"Wasn't," Gary said, in pain. "Been . . . a problem . . . since the acad—"

"Gary, I have to knock you out," McCoy said. He took out the hypo from the medkit on his hip and injected it into Gary, who immediately passed out. McCoy turned to Black.

"Give me your phaser," McCoy said, as she handed him the weapon. "And everybody stand back."

"What are you doing?" I said. McCoy was adjusting the setting on the weapon.

"I don't know what this poison is. I need to buy some time." He moved Gary's injured arm out away from his body, carefully aimed the phaser, and *sliced off his arm* above the wound. The heat from the phaser cauterized the cut.

We all sat there in stunned silence for a moment. I looked around at my crew, scared, tired. There was the severed head and paw of a giant rat, as well as the amputated arm of my first officer and best friend.

"Well . . ." I said, "everybody, good work today." And after a moment, I laughed out of exhaustion. And everyone joined me.

✦

"The DNA is a 61 percent match to the animal native to Dimorous," McCoy said. "But someone made some additions."

On the viewscreen at McCoy's desk floated a double helix. Part of the strand was highlighted.

"Genetic engineering," I said. "Outlawed for a hundred years. You think the Tellarites—"

"I don't have any proof of who was doing what," McCoy said. "But someone was up to something. Even the poison on those darts wasn't completely indigenous."

An out-of-control genetic experiment would explain why the Tellarites had abandoned a rich dilithium vein as well as some state-of-the-art equipment. But it left a lot of unanswered questions. I wouldn't get the answers for a long time.

"How's Gary?" I said.

"Recovering," McCoy said. "I was able to clean out all the poison in his arm and reattach it. That poison was naturally occurring on the planet, but it had been weaponized. It was particularly malicious. Another few seconds would've been too late."

"Good job, Sawbones."

"What?" I was surprised that McCoy had never heard this piece of ancient Earth slang.

"It's what they called surgeons in the Old West," I said. "Often men of your profession only had one option to cure their patients. Cutting off limbs to prevent the spread of infection."

"I knew about the practice; never heard that nickname," McCoy said. "Gruesome. Please don't use it again."

He probably regretted saying that.

✦

After the incident on Dimorous, I was looking forward to my shore leave. I was still wounded by my experience with Carol, but I sought comfort with another woman. Janet Lebow was a young endocrinologist completing her doctorate on Benecia, one of the *Hotspur*'s stops, and she was part of a team that was tasked with examining the samples of the rodents from Dimorous. Janet seemed almost immediately familiar to me; in hindsight I can see that she reminded me of Carol: dedicated, beautiful, brilliant, a serious intellectual with a passionate devotion to her career. This devotion would allow me to rationalize my own emotional distance, and our fervent romance didn't last.*

But while there was a persistent emptiness in my personal life, my professional life was solidifying. I had dispensed with a lot of my early insecurities in managing a crew, and formed my command style. I knew, or thought I knew, what kind of captain I was. I was itching to get a step up, to gain more responsibility and respectability. As the years went by, I'd put together a good crew; I had a lot of bright young men and women who I thought would develop along with me and form a great team. I was counting on not losing them to better opportunities before I had a chance to take them with me wherever I would go. It was too much to hope for.

One night, I was awakened by the intercom. It was Uhura, who was on the bridge nightwatch.

"Sorry to wake you, sir," she said. "Priority message from Starfleet."

"Read it to me," I said, yawning, sitting up in bed.

"To Kirk, commanding *U.S.S. Hotspur*. From Komack, admiral, Starfleet Command. You are hereby ordered to make best possible speed to Utopia Planitia, Mars, Sol System, for decommissioning."

"Thank you, Ensign," I said. Now I was awake. "Have navigation alter our course for Sol System, best possible safe speed. Kirk out." I switched off the communicator. I'd heard that several of the *Baton Rouge*–class ships had already been decommissioned; they were all well out of their prime. Better-designed vessels specifically constructed for their tasks were taking their places. This was not good news.

I was losing my command, and since I hadn't received word of a transfer, it meant there were no other captaincies available. I could be sitting on

---

*EDITOR'S NOTE: Janet Lebow became Janet Wallace after marrying Dr. Theodore Wallace, also an endocrinologist, several decades her senior. They were only married a few years before he passed away. She continued her distinguished career until 2283, when she was on a mission aboard the *U.S.S. Vengeance*, which disappeared with all hands.

a shore posting for a long time waiting for a position to open up. It was risky; it was well-known the longer you were on a planet, the greater the chances Starfleet would leave you there. And since I had received a battle-field promotion to command of *Hotspur*, I was concerned I would be in competition with more senior commanders and captains for an open ship.

I informed the crew the next morning, but by then many had already heard. Over the next two weeks, most of them received their transfer orders; Starfleet was cannibalizing my crew, and it was painful. Many were given great opportunities: Kelso and Uhura were both posted to the *U.S.S. Enterprise*, though with no promotion. Black was made security chief of the *U.S.S. Excalibur*. I assumed McCoy would move up to a *Constitution* class as well, but no offer included a chief medical officer position, so he turned them all down. The biggest surprise, however, was Gary.

"Do you know Ron Tracy?" Gary said to me one day over breakfast.

"Met him for five seconds when he took over the *Republic*," I said.

"He's taking command of the *Exeter*. Offered me helmsman."

"I thought Mendez offered you exec on the *Astral Queen*."

"So?" Gary said.

"So the word is he's going to make commodore soon. You'd be in position to get command."

"No guarantee of that," Gary said, "and if you offer me exec somewhere, I can leave the *Exeter* without burning any bridges."

I was surprised and touched. Gary was putting his career on hold on the off chance we could continue to work together.

"Don't you want a ship of your own?"

"Me with absolute power?" he said, with a smirk. "Don't you think that'd be a little dangerous?"

✦

The Utopia Planitia shipyard, both on the surface and in orbit of Mars, was, even back then, a grand sight. There were ten dry dock superstructures that hung above the red planet, many filled with spaceships in various states of overhaul or construction, while repair crews in space suits and piloting small "worker bee" shuttles floated around them, building and mending.

We brought *Hotspur* into one of the dry docks in low orbit, and most of the crew disembarked, while a skeleton staff from engineering coordinated with the dock crews to begin shutting down the systems and inventorying what was salvageable. The day before we reached Mars, I was given my next assignment: department of strategic planning and studies, Starfleet Headquarters in San Francisco. It was the epitome of a desk job.

On the trip back, I had made sure to have a personal exit interview with every member of the crew. I told many I hoped I would serve with them again and meant it (except maybe when I said it to Kaplan). So when we docked at Mars, I didn't see any need to say goodbye to anyone again. I packed up my things in my duffel and headed for the shuttle bay; I had requisitioned one of the ship's shuttlecraft so I could pilot myself back to Earth.

As I walked through the corridors of the *Hotspur*, I was surprised at how deserted it already was. I realized that I had been looking forward to a few casual goodbyes on my way off the ship, and was disappointed that I passed literally *no one* on my way to the bay. I suppose that should've been a clue.

"Atten-shun!" I heard the words as the doors to the bay slid open, and tried to conceal my astonishment. It was Gary who shouted it, and 300 crew members immediately stood at attention. They formed up on both sides of the bay, with a clear path to the hatch of the shuttlecraft. I smiled and, duffel over my shoulder, walked by them. Kelso, Black, and Uhura (who had tears in her eyes) all stood at attention as I passed. Gary and McCoy waited at the end. McCoy was coming with me to Earth, but this was the last time I would be seeing Gary for a while. I turned and faced the crew. I looked at all the faces of my first command, many of whom I hadn't chosen, but to all of whom I'd felt connected.

"Dismiss all hands," I said.

"Company, dismissed!" Gary said, sounding as sincere as he ever had. "Prepare shuttle bay for immediate launch."

"Thanks for this," I said quietly to Gary, as I shook his hand.

"Stay in touch," he said, and followed the crew out of the bay. I then helped McCoy with his luggage onto the shuttle. He had a duffel as well as a very heavy crate.

"Are those your 'special contingencies'?" I said, as I heaved it onto the craft.

"They would be dangerous in the hands of someone less experienced," McCoy said. He sat down, and I took the helm controls. I could see through the view port that the bay had been cleared. I keyed the intercom.

"Shuttlecraft *Gates* to launch control," I said. "Request permission to depart."

"Launch control to shuttlecraft, permission granted," Gary said, now in the bay's launch center. "Uh, Jim, we're getting a request from traffic control for you to take another passenger to Earth with you. He's Starfleet."

"All right, transmit his coordinates," I said.

A moment later, I piloted the shuttle out of the bay, leaving *Hotspur* behind. I entered a maze of other ships in dock, old and new, and none of them were mine. I felt a longing to turn around, head back to *Hotspur*, but the ship wouldn't be there for much longer.

My extra passenger was in a dock in a higher orbit. As we moved toward it, we got a good look at the majestic craft inside it.

"What ship is that?" McCoy said.

"That's the *Enterprise*." Unlike the *Hotspur*, it was sleek and clean.

"She's a beauty," McCoy said. "Who's her captain?"

"Chris Pike," I said. Pike was well-known among Starfleet as a wildly successful officer. He'd been in command of a *Constitution*-class ship for ten years, made dozens of first contacts, and charted many new worlds. The sector of space he was assigned to explore also put him into several skirmishes with the Klingons. The rest of us were envious of his accomplishments.

The yard command directed me to a port not on the ship, but on the webbed superstructure surrounding it. I docked the shuttle, and the hatch opened. On the other side stood a Starfleet lieutenant commander from an immediately recognizable species.

"Request permission to come aboard," he said. I was surprised by his formality.

"Uh, permission granted, Mr. . . . ?"

"Lieutenant Commander Spock." He calmly came aboard the shuttle-craft with his small suitcase. He stood near the helm station and looked down at me. Though I'd seen plenty of Vulcans in my life, I'd never gotten used to their ominous, almost frightening, appearance. The pointed ears, slanted eyebrows, and yellowish skin, however, always stood in stark contrast to their ultra-civilized, stoic demeanor.

"Will you need any assistance in piloting? I am rated for this craft."

"Uh, no, thanks, have a seat." He quietly took the seat in the cabin next to McCoy, who rolled his eyes at me. Spock seemed quite comfortable not learning our names.

"I'm Jim Kirk," I said, then indicated McCoy. "This is Dr. Leonard McCoy."

"I was aware of your identities before I came aboard."

"Common courtesy would usually require asking our names anyway," McCoy said.

"I unfortunately have not made a study of the redundancies involved in human etiquette," Spock said. He said it very dryly; had he been human, I would've assumed he was being sarcastic, but in a Vulcan it was impossible to tell.

"Well, this is going to be a fun trip," McCoy said.

"No offense taken, Mr. Spock," I said, obviously not speaking for McCoy. "Strap yourselves in, we're leaving." I turned to the helm, and received clearance from the yard command as McCoy opened his crate.

"Anybody for a drink?"

"The consumption of inebriating beverages aboard shuttlecraft is forbidden under regulations," Spock said.

"I bet you're really good at making friends," McCoy said.

"Friendship is a classification humans use to define emotional relationships," Spock said. "It is not logical."

"Yeah, well, obviously not for you," McCoy said.

"Bones," I said, my tone telling him to cut it out. The shuttle pulled away from the dock, and I took it out of orbit. We left Mars behind and began our three-hour voyage to Earth. For a long while it was silent, until that was broken by the sound of McCoy pouring himself another drink.

"Mr. Spock, are you posted aboard the *Enterprise*?" I said.

"Yes sir," Spock said. "I am the science officer."

"I see. How long have you served with Captain Pike?"

"Nine years, ten months, sixteen days," Spock said. Vulcans didn't make it easy to carry on light conversation.

"What a coincidence," McCoy said. "That's going to be the same length as this shuttle ride."

"What brings you to Earth?" I said, ignoring McCoy. Whatever he was drinking was quickly making him impervious to authority.

"I'm visiting relatives on the North American continent, in a small town on the eastern coast called Grover's Mill," Spock said. That was strange; I wasn't aware of a Vulcan population center on Earth in that area.

"Oh. Are they stationed there?" I said.

"No, they're from there," Spock said. It was then that I remembered that I'd heard of a half-human, half-Vulcan at the academy; we'd overlapped but never met. He must have been quite a student; Spock had already distinguished himself serving aboard a *Constitution*-class ship for a decade.

"So, you're visiting your human relatives," I said.

"Yes. The *Enterprise* will be in dry dock for some time," Spock said. "It was at my mother's request I visit her sister and niece." He was a dutiful son. I wondered whether that was the Vulcan or human half.

"Wait," McCoy said, speech slightly slurring. "You've got human relatives?"

"As I implied previously," Spock said. "My mother is human."

"And yet you're still a rude son of a bitch," McCoy said.

"If I am, Doctor," Spock said, "it is a trait I share with billions of human beings."

I thought about putting a stop to it, but it seemed quite clear that Spock didn't need my help. And I was frankly starting to enjoy it.

They bickered for a while longer, but McCoy eventually settled into a nap, and Spock and I talked about the *Enterprise*'s refit. I was impressed by the amount of resources they were putting into the ship. The *Constitution*-class vessels got all the attention; ships like the *Hotspur* had to make do, until they were finally driven to the glue factory. I then asked the real question that was on my mind.

"Do you think Captain Pike is going to take her out for another five years?" An opening on a *Constitution*-class ship was rare.

"Such a mission would be beneficial to Starfleet and the Federation," he said.

He hadn't really answered my question. Maybe he knew something, maybe he didn't, but he wasn't going to help me. I had turned back to look at him for my next question, and thought I caught some emotion in his face, but it immediately evaporated.

"You like Captain Pike?"

"He's an efficient commander," he said. Served with him a decade, and showed no trace of any kind of sentiment. I moved back to the controls, suddenly jealous; Pike had been Spock's commanding officer since he got out of the academy. Garrovick had died within a couple of years.

I then started asking him about some of the scientific discoveries the *Enterprise* had been a part of, and I had the sense that he was downplaying his own role in many of the missions. It was talking about this that we stumbled upon a surprising mutual "acquaintance."

". . . but that was due mostly to what Dr. Marcus and her department had made in the area of subatomic engineering—"

"Wait," I said. "Carol Marcus? She was aboard the *Enterprise*?"

"For a short period," Spock said. "Are you familiar with her work?"

"Somewhat," I said.

I was almost unable to speak. Just the mention of Carol brought back the feelings for her and David. I was strangely jealous of this alien, just because he'd gotten to see her, to spend time with her.

"A capable scientist," Spock said. I nodded and focused on the controls. Since I was no longer keeping the conversation going, we both fell into silence. I silently castigated myself; it was ridiculous to be bitter because Spock had gotten to work with Carol.

Earth appeared in the center of my view port, and we received reentry instructions. I brought us into a landing at Starfleet Headquarters, and I shook McCoy awake. He had slept off some of the effects of his drinking.

Spock thanked me for the ride and said a curt goodbye to the two of us.

"There's a fun guy," McCoy said, as we watched him walk off. I didn't respond. I regretted my petulance over Carol, even though Spock hadn't picked up on it. I didn't know quite what to make of Spock then, but there was something compelling; he gave the impression of a man with a lot of character.

"Well, Jim," McCoy said, "hard to say when we may see each other again."

"It's been a pleasure, Bones," I said, as we shook hands. "Stay in touch." He smiled, yet also looked mildly irritated.

"You're determined to make that nickname stick, aren't you?"

I laughed. We promised to get together again while we were both on Earth, and then I headed to the Sub Shuttle station.

✦

I hadn't been home in quite some time. The house seemed very small to me; I guess it loomed large in my memory, even though I'd grown to my full height while still living there. I had decided to walk from the Riverside transportation station; they knew I was coming, but I hadn't given anyone a specific time when to expect me.

Sitting on the porch was a boy, about ten years old. He was the spitting image of my brother, Sam, at that age. He sat with his legs crossed, holding a magnifying glass. There were a couple of small insects on the porch in front of him.

"Any luck?" I said. He looked up at me.

"With what?"

"Burning them," I said. He looked annoyed.

"I wasn't burning them," he said. "I was examining them."

"I stand corrected," I said. A scientist, just like his father. "You must be Peter. I'm Jim."

"Oh, sorry," he said, standing up and holding out his hand. "Nice to meet you, Uncle Jim." The last time I'd seen Sam was shortly after he'd met Aurelan, whom he would marry. My missions in space had caused me to miss their wedding, as well as the birth of their son over ten years before. And now, here he was, in the flesh, healthy, curious. Before I could really take him in, everyone else was out on the porch, giving me warm hellos.

Sam was looking older, wearing a hearty mustache, though Aurelan was still stunning and youthful despite being the mother of a ten-year-old. But it was Dad and Mom that I really wasn't ready for. I'd really been gone a long time; they were both gray. Dad had put on more weight, and Mom had taken some off; she still looked energetic, though slightly frail. She gave me a fierce hug, and Dad grabbed my shoulder.

"Welcome home, Captain," he said, with a proud smile.

"Not a full captain yet, Dad," I said, somewhat self-consciously.

"It'll come," he said. They all but pulled me inside the house.

We sat down to dinner, and I was peppered with questions about my time on the *Hotspur*. I did my best to appear relaxed, but it was difficult; I'd spent the last several years in a command position, never fully letting my guard down, and now it wasn't coming easily. I had experienced a lot of stress that I hadn't quite worked through yet, and I wasn't willing to share stories that might bring it to the surface. I did my best to turn the attention to Sam and his family. Sam had continued work as a research biologist at the University of Chicago but was probably going to be transferred to a colony that specialized in research, either Earth Colony II or Deneva. Peter seemed excited about the idea of going into space. I found him the easiest to engage with for most of the evening.

"Do you stay in touch with Carol?" Mom said, later in the meal. She and Dad knew Carol and I had been serious, but I had never told them about David. Sam, however, did know, and I could feel him watching me as I answered. I'm sure he wasn't comfortable keeping a secret from them.

"Not really," I said. "I think we've both moved on." I could sense Mom's disappointment, though she didn't express it. She'd met Carol briefly when I was at the academy, and they'd hit it off. Coincidentally, their work paths had crossed later. They had a lot in common and I think Mom had some hopes for a lasting relationship for me. Peter then came over with a large box.

"Uncle Jim," Peter said, "Dad says you're good at three-dimensional chess. You want to play me?"

I looked at the young boy, the image of my brother. Peter was eager, pleasant, and solicitous of my attention. I thought of another boy, who I didn't know, who might by now be the image of me, and who would want the same things Peter wanted. I felt horrible, guilty.

"I'm sorry, pal," I said, "I'm really beat. We'll play tomorrow." I tousled his hair, said a quick goodnight to everyone, and headed off to my room.

✦

The next day I requisitioned quarters at Starfleet; I felt it would be too emotionally draining to stay at the farm, though I promised Mom and Dad I'd come back on the weekends, which I did.

The department of strategic planning and studies was housed, ironically, in the Archer Building, where about a decade before I'd impersonated a Starfleet officer. When I walked into the lobby now I was overcome with the feeling that I was still a fraud. I found my way to the offices on the tenth floor and reported to my commanding officer.

"Reporting for duty, Admiral," I said. Behind the desk was Heihachiro Nogura, a man of Japanese descent, white-haired, diminutive but with a quiet authority.

"At ease," Nogura said. "I hope you don't mind a little time at a desk, Commander. I like to have officers in the department who have extensive field experience."

"My pleasure, sir," I said, lying.

"We've got a lot going on here, Kirk. I'm afraid you're going to have to jump into the deep end." He indicated a small stack of tapes on his desk. "Take those. I'm going to need a report as soon as possible."

I was a little thrown. He wasn't telling me what he wanted the report *on*, and that was obviously on purpose. It felt like I was back in the academy again, being tested. I picked up the tapes.

"Yes sir," I said. "I'll need someplace to work."

Nogura had a yeoman show me to a cubicle with a desk, a simple setup with a computer and viewscreen. I sat down and started going through the tapes. They were excerpts from log entries of the commanders and officers on starships and starbases. A quick glance at the first few indicated encounters with Klingon ships and personnel. As I went through, I could see that the incidents were all in the past month. Not quite knowing what Nogura was looking for, I started collating the information, first on a graph of where the encounters took place, what the results of the encounters were, and what snippets of information the officers involved relayed about the Klingons' attitudes and intentions. A lot of the entries were from Christopher Pike's log; the sector of space the *Enterprise* was assigned covered a good portion of the border with the Klingons, and Pike had accumulated a lot of experience dealing with them. He had successfully survived several skirmishes with Klingon ships, but had lost multiple crew members in the battles.

The work was interesting enough that the days passed quickly. I got to know my colleagues in the department. Lance Cartwright, a few years my senior, was a full captain, having joined Nogura as his chief of staff after several years as captain of the *Exeter*. He was friendly and sharp, and was probably a few short years away from joining the Admiralty. Harry Morrow and William Smillie were commanders like me, and they considered this desk job one that they wanted. Though I was consumed with the assignment, I still felt the itch to get back on a bridge.

About a week in, I finished my report, and Nogura had me present it to the staff in his office. I went over the data that I pulled from the logs, and then summarized my conclusions.

"Within the time frame of the logs I reviewed, the Klingons appeared to be testing our response with aggressive moves in the disputed area of space that serves as the border between the Federation and their empire."

"Do you have any theories as to the purpose of these tests?" Nogura said. From the way he asked it, I felt that he thought there was only one possible answer.

"Without any actual proof," I said, "I would think it's a prelude to invasion."

"If that's the case," Cartwright said, "without the *Enterprise* on patrol in that sector, we are leaving ourselves wide open."

"The *Enterprise* is in desperate need of a refit that will take at least eight months," Morrow said. "The ship is 20 years old . . ."

"Then we need to reassign another starship to that sector," Cartwright said.

"Uh, sir," I said to Nogura, "I think there's another solution. I've examined the *Enterprise*'s refit schedule, and it could be split into a two-month period and a six-month period. The components necessary for the second period could be sent to Starbase 11."

"Why would we do that?" Cartwright said. "The *Enterprise* would still be out of action for those eight months."

"Yes, but if we are careful to keep the shipment of the upgrade components as well as the personnel transfers a secret, it would appear to the Klingons that Starfleet has a shipbuilding capacity well outside the Sol System. If they were planning to invade, it would give them pause, forcing them to take it into consideration as part of their strategy."

No one argued this point, which made me think it had landed. Nogura assigned me the task of determining how long it would take to ship the necessary components. I found out pretty quickly it was a much more difficult task than I originally thought; it would take over a year using the standard shipping routes to get all the material and personnel that far out. I presented my findings to Nogura but didn't think it would go any further.

As the days passed, it became clear to me that this department was doing a lot more than studying strategy. Nogura was an influential admiral, and he was using his department to gently guide Starfleet and Federation policy, to great effect. Resources were being moved around, officers transferred and promoted as a result of recommendations coming out of the department. One day, Nogura brought me into his office. There was a captain there and a younger man in a cadet uniform.

"Jim Kirk, this is Matt Decker," Nogura said, referencing the older man. I had heard of him; as a young lieutenant commander he'd fought a superior Klingon force to a standstill at Donatu V. Decker was shorter than me, but he had a rough presence, a force of personality that I felt immediately.

"Pleasure to meet you, Captain Decker," I said.

"It's commodore now," Decker said. "I haven't had a chance to change my braid." Decker's ship, the *Constellation*, had recently returned to Earth at the end of its five-year mission. I knew that Nogura had recommended Decker for promotion to commodore. He would keep command of his ship, but in case of a war with the Klingons, Decker's flag rank would put him in immediate command of all the ships in his sector. It was a strategic promotion where Nogura put a like-minded officer in charge of resources on the projected front lines.

Decker then indicated the younger man. "This is my son, Will." The young man seemed nothing like his father; where Matt was coarse and unrefined, Will appeared friendly and polished, although somewhat nervous around all the senior officers. I must have shown my surprise, because Decker added, "He takes after his mother."

"Cadet," I said, shaking his hand. "Fourth year?"

"Yes sir," Will said.

"Since he doesn't look like me, I want to make sure everyone knows he's my son," Decker said, then turned to Nogura. "Don't dump him on a starbase."

"I'll see what I can do," Nogura said, with a rare smile. Decker then turned to me.

"Wait, are you the Kirk who commanded the *Hotspur*?" he said.

"Yes sir," I said.

"I heard about that gas giant move," he said. "Well done. And call me Matt." Decker turned back to Nogura, referencing me. "Put this guy on a bridge too. He could come in handy." I was hopeful that Nogura would take Decker's suggestion, but I saw no sign of it.

A few days later, I walked into Cartwright's office, while he was meeting with another officer I didn't know.

"Jim, this is Major Oliver West," Cartwright said. We shook hands; he was much taller than me and had a stare that I could only describe as "mean." I noticed he had the rank of major and was part of the small contingent of Starfleet officers whose focus was infantry operations. Cartwright had brought me in because West wanted to ask me some questions about the incident on Dimorous. He seemed very familiar with my logs on the subject.

"How long do you think you could've held out?" he asked.

"Not very long," I said. "There were too many of them, and they were fearless."

"I was curious," West said, "why you didn't kill them, instead of using stun?"

"The Prime Directive," I said. "As far as I know, they were indigenous."

"Even though your lives were at stake?" West said.

"Isn't that the point?"

"So you can't imagine a situation where you'd violate the Prime Directive in order to protect the lives of Federation citizens?" West said. It felt like a trick question. Because in my mind, there was only one response.

"I think it's my duty not to," I said. West and Cartwright exchanged a look.

"Thanks for your time, Jim. I'll see you later," Cartwright said, getting up and leading me out.

I left feeling like I'd taken some kind of test and failed.

✦

"Pike is getting promoted to fleet captain," Nogura said. He had called me into his office, alone. Pike's promotion wasn't a complete surprise; our department had been discussing how his tactical knowledge of the Klingons was invaluable to Starfleet, and had to be part of overall mission planning. The revelation was what came next.

"You're receiving a promotion to full captain, and you're to assume command of the *Enterprise*," Nogura said.

"Thank you, sir," I said. I could barely get it out; I was thunderstruck.

"No need to thank me," he said. "You were on top of the promotion list. Your years on the *Hotspur* are well regarded by the Admiralty. You were assigned a dangerous area of space, completed all your missions without any loss of life." He made it sound very reasonable, but since joining the department, I had made a study of all the available command-grade officers. I was among the youngest, and there were several with years more experience than me as shipmasters.

"We are also implementing your plan to complete the *Enterprise*'s refit on Starbase 11," Nogura said.

"Sir, a conservative estimate has the components reaching Starbase 11 in ten months," I said.

"The ship should still function properly," Nogura said. "You're used to less-than-up-to-the-minute technology. Pike will bring the *Enterprise* to Earth tomorrow. We'll transfer command then. Start going over personnel; see what spots you can fill in 24 hours. I think, if my recollection's correct, you're going to need a first officer." He then stood up and shook my hand.

"Congratulations, Jim."

"Thank you, sir," I said. My head was mush; this was what I wanted, and yet I wasn't sure why at this moment I was getting it. I felt it was somehow connected to the conversation I had had with Cartwright and West the week before, but I couldn't figure out why.

Whatever doubts I had, I chose to put out of my mind. I went back to my desk, double-checked the *Enterprise*'s files to make sure the first officer position was open, and put a call in to Starfleet Personnel to requisition Gary Mitchell. His new captain wouldn't like it, but I would figure out some way to pay him back.

I then opened the rest of the personnel files and started scanning them, then decided to call my parents while I did it. I opened a call on the screen. Dad answered.

"Hey, Captain," he said. He took great pride in calling me that. "What's going on?"

"Dad," I said, "I really am a captain. I've got a ship. It's the *Enterprise*."

"Oh my god," he said. "Bob April's ship?"

"Yeah, but it hasn't been his in ten years," I said. "And anyway, it's Jim Kirk's ship now." My dad laughed, and I could see he was welling up.

"I'm so proud of you," he said. "You're 29, that's got to be some kind of record . . ." I hadn't realized it until Dad brought it up, but I did a quick record search, and he was right. I was the youngest person to receive the rank of full captain in Starfleet's history; the record, interestingly enough, had been held by Matt Decker, who achieved the rank at 31.

I'd been absently scrolling through the personnel records while we spoke, but stopped. I could see that Dad wanted to say something else to me, but I didn't know what. I felt like he needed me to either prod him or change the subject.

"Where's Mom?" I said. I chose the latter.

"She went to a conference this morning in London," he said. "She should be back a little later."

"Well, tell her the good news," I said. "I'll try to come home for a bit before I leave."

"Do what you need to; you've got a big job," he said. "Take care of yourself. I hope it's everything you want it to be."

"Thanks, Dad," I said. "I think it will be." We said goodbye and I shut off the communication. I could sense that he was proud, but there was something else, too. And then I thought about Carol and David. Dad didn't know about them specifically, but now, looking back, I think he wanted to tell me what I was giving up. He didn't know that I already knew.

I was soon distracted by all the work I had to do. I had to finish getting through the personnel records, to try to fill my open spots; I also had to see about a new uniform with the proper braid, and make any other last-minute arrangements before I shipped out. Busy with these tasks, I was happy. This was the fulfillment of my dreams. And just as I was thinking I was leaving all the struggles of my past behind, I noticed something in the personnel records that told me it wasn't going to be all that easy.

The *Enterprise*'s records officer was Ben Finney.

CHAPTER 6

"WELCOME TO THE *ENTERPRISE*, CAPTAIN," Christopher Pike said. I stepped off the transporter and shook his hand. I was struck by how tall he was, much taller than me. He greeted me with a friendly smile, and there was camaraderie about the way he said "Captain." I felt like I was joining a very exclusive club.

"I think you know our transporter operator," Pike said, and I saw a familiar face at the console.

"Mr. Scott," I said. "Need someone to carry your tool kit?" We shook hands warmly. I knew Scott had been transferred to the ship as an engineer, and I was thrilled. This was one bit of luck I would never take for granted, and I would make sure he was permanent.

"Thanks for the offer, sir," Scott said. "But I've got plenty of help here already." He gave me a weary smile. I noticed his eyes were a little bloodshot.

"Rough night?" I said.

"My going-away party," Pike said. "Come on, we've got a lot to cover."

Pike took me on a tour of the ship, giving me a rundown of the areas of the refit that weren't finished yet. It had been a while since I'd been on a *Constitution*-class ship, and its comfort was inviting. When we got to the bridge, it was twice the size of the *Hotspur*'s; it felt like a living room.

There were several familiar faces there: Lee Kelso was at navigation, Scotty had come up from the transporter room and was monitoring the engineering console. And Mr. Spock was at the science station, looking into his viewer. Pike took me over to him.

"Mr. Spock," Pike said, "this is Captain Kirk." Spock stood up from his viewer, at attention.

"We've had the pleasure. At ease," I said.

"He is," Pike said, smiling.

"Your record is very impressive, Mr. Spock," I said. "I look forward to serving with you."

"Thank you, Captain," Spock said. "Please let me know if there is any way I can be of service." It sounded as though he memorized it off a flash card. At that moment, I wasn't sure I was ever going to be completely comfortable with this guy.

Pike then continued on the tour; Scotty came with us to engineering. While down there, Pike took me over to a small hatch near the rear of the engineering section on the secondary hull. "The sensor pod?" I said. Pike nodded and opened the hatch. Inside was a plastic bubble, clear to space, crowded with various scientific instruments. One of the many scientific missions a ship has is to get radiation readings in abnormal conditions. Ion storms, quasars, etc. This can only be done by direct exposure of the necessary instruments in a plastic pod on the skin of the ship. It was particularly important if the ship was caught inside one of the phenomena; the borders and structures could change rapidly, so the sensor pod was often necessary to navigate out of it.

I climbed up inside the pod. There was only room for one person in the cramped space. But as I looked "up" it was as if I was standing on the outside of the ship; I could stare out at Earth and the various shuttles and ships in orbit. The pods were dangerous. In an ion storm, it picks up a charge of its own very quickly; since it's connected to the ship, if the charge is big enough, excess current could flow through whatever circuitry it could find, potentially blowing out vital ship's systems in the middle of an emergency. The captain has to make a determination how long to let that crewman stay in, acquiring as much information as he or she can without threatening the ship; if the crewman delays too long to get out, the captain might have to jettison the pod with the crewman still in it. On the *Hotspur*

I had a senior officer stand by at the hatch to jettison, but Pike told me he had the control moved up to his chair on the bridge.

"If someone has to die," Pike said, "I don't want anyone else to carry the burden."

As I stepped out of the pod, I saw that Pike had waved over another officer to introduce to me. I guess he didn't know we'd already met. It was Ben Finney. I politely cut off Pike's introduction by extending my hand to Finney.

"Good to see you, Ben," I said. I wasn't going to assume bad feeling. To my surprise, Ben smiled and shook my hand, albeit somewhat formally.

"Congratulations, sir," Ben said. "It's nice seeing you again."

We talked briefly about Jamie and then he excused himself to return to his post. It was difficult to tell how he was feeling about me; Ben had acted properly, was even friendly. I hoped this indicated my concern about serving with him was unfounded.

Pike and I continued on, finally ending in Pike's quarters, which it took me a minute to realize would soon be mine. I'd forgotten how much larger a captain's quarters were on a *Constitution*-class ship. I had gotten used to my stateroom on the *Hotspur*, which wasn't much more than a bed and a closet.

Pike and I sat on opposite sides of the desk and went over specific members of the crew. He had recommended Spock for my first officer, but I wasn't comfortable enough with him to give him that position. I wanted to keep him on as science officer, and asked Pike if Spock would care if someone was brought in over him.

"If he did," Pike said, "he'd rather die than let you know. He's all about the work." We then went through a few more. Pike's chief engineer was retiring, and I was determined to give Scotty that position. Mark Piper from the *Republic* had replaced Pike's chief medical officer, Philip Boyce, who died about a year before the end of Pike's mission. I could see that the loss had affected him. Pike said that the death of Boyce was the first sign that maybe he stayed in space too long. I changed the subject by congratulating Pike on the promotion, but he only laughed, somewhat derisively. I didn't realize until this moment how political promotions could be in Starfleet.

"Fleet captain is a desk job," Pike said. "They wanted me out of the way."

Decker and Pike were contemporaries and had different schools of thought about their roles as starship captains. Decker was more focused on defense and protection, while Pike saw himself as an explorer. Nogura favored Decker, who would now be in field command of all ships in the sector that bordered the Klingons if there was an incursion. Since Decker didn't like Pike, Pike felt he had played some role in getting the *Enterprise* away from him.

"I probably need a break," Pike said, although it sounded like a weak rationale. He started talking about the ship and how much it meant to him, but that the mission itself was much more trying than he ever expected. The *Constitution*-class ships were designed to operate without a net; you were really on your own. He'd lost a lot of friends during the ten years he'd been on the *Enterprise*.

"This job will rip the guts out of you," he said. "You have no choice but to lean on people. This crew will become your friends."

He took another long pause.

"And then they'll die."

We sat in silence for a long moment. I didn't quite know what to make of this advice. I'd faced the death of crewmen for my whole career, but I felt like answering would only make me appear weak, self-justifying. So I sat in silence until he was ready to move on. He then decided it was time to transfer command, and he ordered the ship's crew to report to the hangar deck.

A few minutes later, I was part of a ceremony I'd witnessed only once. Pike and I stood at a podium near the bay doors, facing the 400 faces of the crew. Spock stood by, and Pike gave him a nod.

"Attention to orders," Spock said, shouting. I'd never seen a Vulcan raise his voice; it was unnerving. But I supposed it was necessary serving aboard a starship. I stepped up to the podium, placed the tape of orders in the portable viewer that was set there, and read them.

"To Captain Christopher Pike, commander, *U.S.S. Enterprise*, you are hereby promoted to fleet captain, and requested and required to relinquish command to Captain James T. Kirk as of this date, signed Heihachiro Nogura, admiral, Starfleet Command." I then turned to Pike. "I relieve you, sir."

"I stand relieved," Pike said. We shook hands, and I turned and took in the faces; a familiar few: Scotty, Kelso, Mark Piper from the *Republic*, Uhura. But they were quickly lost in an ocean of strangers. I had never taken over a ship like this before; I had been serving on the *Hotspur* when I was given command, so I had already been working with everyone on that ship, and there had been no need for a ceremony. Now, I could see a lot of the crew members weren't looking at me; they looked at Pike. It was easy to read affection and admiration in their expressions.

I was envious; it was ridiculous for me to expect anything from these people. It would be the hardest job in my life to win them over, since being a good captain meant doing nothing that was designed to win them over. I had to count on them to do their jobs, and do my best to protect their lives, which, despite what Pike had said, meant I couldn't let anyone be my friend. Thrust into command of the *Hotspur*, I had felt alone, but not quite as alone as this.

And then I saw an unexpected face in the crowd. Gary Mitchell was in the back; he must have just come aboard, his duffel still over his shoulder. He gave me a conspiratorial grin and nodded. I smiled.

"All standing orders to remain in force until further notice," I said. "Crew dismissed." Captain Pike came over one last time and shook my hand.

"Hope to see you again," he said. "Good luck."

"To you too," I said.

I went back to the cabin, which only a little while ago had been Pike's. Now everything of his was gone; my clothing had arrived and had been magically put away. I decided to start going through the ship's status reports, which took me late into the evening, and fell asleep.

The next morning, I woke early, dressed, and left my cabin. As I walked along the corridors I received friendly but reserved hellos from the crew I passed. I reached the turbolift and noticed a lieutenant, who was obviously heading toward it, make a last-minute decision to turn in the other direction and take a ladder; whoever he was, he wasn't comfortable riding with his new captain. I didn't mind; I think I liked the fact that he was nervous.

I rode the lift alone and stepped out onto the bridge. The viewscreen was off; the night shift was still on duty. To my right, Uhura was at communications.

"Nice to see you again, Ensign," I said. "Have the department heads report to me on the bridge as soon as they come on duty."

"Yes sir," she said. "Oh, and congratulations." I smiled as I headed to the command chair, where Spock sat in command. He worked the night shift, Pike had told me, by his own request, as well as his day shift as science officer.

"You're relieved, Mr. Spock."

"You are 15 minutes and 44.3 seconds early for your shift, Captain," he said, as he got out of the chair.

"Captain's prerogative," I said. I sat down in the chair. It was a lot more comfortable than the one on the *Hotspur*. I took in the bridge, simultaneously busy and quiet. My nervousness was fading. I was now eager to get under way. I was lost in my reverie and didn't notice a zealous ensign in his twenties approach my chair. I was a little startled when he was suddenly standing beside it.

"Ensign Morgan Bateson reporting for duty," he said. I nodded. I had no idea who this kid was and what he was waiting for.

"Very well, Ensign," I said, "assume your post."

He looked at me, confused.

"Um, Captain Pike liked to have me on the bridge," he said. "If you prefer me to wait somewhere else . . ." I had no idea what he was talking about, and I guess he could tell from my expression.

"Sir," he said, in a low voice, "I'm your yeoman." I felt like an idiot, and somehow had forgotten that captains had yeomen; there wasn't room for that kind of luxury aboard the *Hotspur*. He must have been the one who magically put away all my clothes. I asked him for the morning status reports and a cup of coffee. He seemed pleased to be given something to do, and was off.

A few moments later, as I drank my coffee and scanned the reports, the day shift came onto the bridge. I caught the glances of a few officers who were somewhat worried that I made it there ahead of them. Lieutenant

Lloyd Alden relieved Uhura at communications; Gary took over the helm position and was joined by Kelso at navigation. After a few minutes, the department heads had gathered behind me.

Dr. Piper, chief medical officer, and Hikaru Sulu, the head of astrosciences, whom I had not met yet, stood with Scotty, who leaned forward as I joined them.

"Just want to thank you, sir," Scotty said. He'd gotten his official promotion to chief engineer. "I won't let you down."

"I'm sure you won't," I said. I then turned to the others and we had an impromptu conference. They all reported the status of their departments, and that they were ready for departure. I ordered communications to get clearance from the dockmaster for departure, and had Kelso plot a course for our patrol sector. Once we had clearance, I stepped back to my chair.

"Mr. Mitchell," I said, "take us out."

"Aye, sir." Gary keyed the console, and I watched the viewscreen as Earth quickly fell away.

As I think back on that moment, Pike's last advice would prove to be correct: everybody on that bridge would change or die. And I'd have the guts ripped out of me, a lot sooner than I could've imagined.

✦

"We're leaving the Galaxy, Mr. Mitchell. Ahead warp factor one," I said.

The *Enterprise* sat motionless, less than five light-minutes from the Galaxy's "edge." On my order, Gary keyed the controls, and I heard the now familiar rumble of the ship's engines. I'd been in the command chair of the *Enterprise* for almost two years and had done nothing of note. I had underestimated the *Enterprise's* need for a refit, and rather than risk the crew in an unreliable vessel, we spent most of our time waiting at Starbase 11 for the parts to arrive. Unfortunately, the wrong nacelle domes were delivered, and parts for the new internal communications system were somehow left off the manifest, so we would have to go back at some point. I then had a shakedown cruise that lasted another month. We finally began our patrol of the Earth colonies and starbases in the sector, over a year after we left Earth.

Despite the delays, my plan to refit the *Enterprise* seemed to have the desired effect; there wasn't a peep out of the Klingons, and in fact they'd agreed to negotiation regarding the disputed area between their territory and the Federation. Everything was peaceful enough that Starfleet gave us a mission of pure research, and all the scientists on board were as excited as I was. A true history-making venture; even if we discovered nothing, that too would be memorable. But that had changed just a few moments before.

We'd found an old-style ship recorder from the *S.S. Valiant*, a 200-year-old ship that had somehow also reached this far. The burnt-out tapes indicated the ship had encountered a "magnetic space storm"* that had thrown them out of the Galaxy, and in returning they'd encountered some unknown force that had caused the captain to order the destruction of his own ship.

Now, suddenly, our mission of pure research had a hint of danger. We were studying an area of space no one had ever been to before, and I was reminded that my responsibility included determining whether it was safe for future travel.

Suddenly, on the viewscreen ahead, a violent, crimson barrier appeared.

"Force field of some kind," Spock said. A force field? *There's a force field around the Galaxy?* It made no scientific sense.**

"Deflectors say there's something there, sensors say there isn't," Spock said. "Density, negative. Radiation, negative. Energy . . . negative." I looked over Kelso's shoulder and saw that our deflector screens were reading the wall of negative energy in infinite directions. There was no way around it. It literally surrounded the Galaxy, and we were heading right for it. This must have been the unknown force the *Valiant* encountered.

I watched the viewscreen as the force field grew, blocking out the rest of space. Just as I silently questioned whether our deflector shield would protect us from it, surges of energy went through the ship's instruments.

---

*EDITOR'S NOTE: It has been a generally accepted theory that the "magnetic space storm" the *Valiant* encountered was in fact an unstable wormhole that the scientists on the ship were unfamiliar with.

**To this day, there is no widely accepted scientific explanation for the origin of the field of negative energy that completely surrounds the Galaxy.

Control panels all over the bridge shorted out and exploded. Kelso frantically tried to fan out the smoke. We weren't going to make it through this thing. I ordered the helmsman, Gary, to turn us around.

But as Gary keyed the controls, his body suddenly flared with a torrent of energy. He fell to the deck. Spock took over the helm, navigating us out of that strange barrier.

Our engines were burnt out, and nine of my crew had been killed. I went over to Gary. He was okay. I was relieved, until I saw his eyes: they were silver orbs. Gary had been changed.

✦

About a week later, we were in orbit of Delta Vega. It had taken several days to get here without warp engines, and we then spent a few more days while the very talented engineering staff repaired the ship using components from an automated station on the planet's surface. We were finally ready to leave orbit. In that time, we'd lost three more crewmen. One of them was Gary Mitchell.

And I killed him.

It's hard to explain what happened, the series of events that led me to take the life of my first officer and best friend. That barrier at the edge of the Galaxy imbued Gary with a kind of almost magical power, giving him telepathy and telekinesis. As the ship moved away from the barrier, the powers grew, and as they did, Gary lost touch with the person he had been. He started using his abilities to adjust controls throughout the ship. He was making it very clear he could take over whenever he wanted. Spock was the only member of the crew trying to get me to face the truth that Gary would eventually destroy us without giving it a second thought.

"Kill Mitchell while you still can," he said to me.

I didn't want to hear it, so rather than kill him, I brought the ship to Delta Vega and had Gary imprisoned on the planet. My intention was to leave him there. But Gary was able to escape.

And then he killed Lee Kelso.

Kelso had been a good friend of Gary's, and Gary had killed him without blinking. Spock was right; I realized that this was a problem I couldn't just leave behind. It was impossible to know how powerful Gary would become. He had to be stopped.

I pursued Gary into the wilderness of Delta Vega. I didn't stand a chance against him. Either I got lucky or he was just too overconfident. He slipped, and I phasered a giant bolder that crushed him.

It was the first person I'd killed face-to-face. I never saw the faces of the beings who lost their lives battling me ship-to-ship. This face, Gary's face, is one I still see every day. He had been looking after me for almost ten years, and in a few short days he was turned into some kind of monster. Yet in my nightmares about that day I still see the face of the man who was my friend.

On the bridge, about to leave orbit, I recorded in my log that Gary had died in the line of duty. I noticed Spock listening in.

"He didn't ask for what happened to him," I said. Spock decided at that moment to surprise me.

"I felt for him too," he said. I didn't know what to make of that. Spock had never openly revealed an emotional side. But in that moment of despair, of loss, of losing the best friend I'd ever had, his decision to show me empathy was one I wouldn't forget.

"There may be hope for you yet, Mr. Spock," I said. It was probably the first time I'd smiled in a month.

✦

Though we'd been able to repair the warp drive on Delta Vega, the ship had still suffered extensive damage. We had to return to Starbase 11 for repairs. The final components for the refit had arrived by then, so the refit could finally be completed. It would also allow the crew a little time to recover from what we'd been through, and I could try to replace the people we'd lost. But in our damaged state, it would still take three weeks to get there.

A few days after Gary's death, I was sitting on the bridge, lost in thought, when Lieutenant Hong came off the turbolift and approached me.

"I'm sorry, sir," she said. "I know this has been a difficult period, but may I have a moment of your time, in private?" I nodded and led her off the bridge and to a conference room on Deck 5. She got right down to business.

"I'm sorry to bother you with this, sir," Lieutenant Hong said, "but we have to fill three positions immediately." Lieutenant Hong was the ship's personnel officer; one of her jobs was to make sure any open spots in the duty roster were filled appropriately, so as to prevent extra strain falling on any particular crewman. Given the deaths we'd had recently, this was a difficult subject to bring up, but necessary for her job. She put a tape in the slot and a list of available crewmen appeared on the viewscreen.

"There are three positions that need your immediate attention. We need a new chief navigator," she said.

"Bailey was on beta shift," I said. "Put him on alpha shift." Bailey was a competent young officer, a few years out of the academy. He'd served a few shifts with me on the bridge; he was a little eager to please, but he knew the job.

"Sir, Ensign Bailey is only two years out of the academy. Usually chief navigators have a minimum of four years shipboard service."

"He'll be fine. I'd been planning on promoting him," I said. It wasn't true; I was making a rash decision, I admit, partially because I found the process and Hong's officiousness at that moment annoying, and wanted to get it over with.

"Very well, sir. We also . . . need a new helmsman," she said. I could see that Hong had tears in her eyes. Gary as first officer had dealt with all the personnel issues; I'd seen him joke and flirt with Hong, as he did with most women. This was a loss for her too. I decided to cut her a little slack.

"What about Alden?" Alden was communications, but we had other officers qualified in that department, and Alden had often served as a helmsman when needed. Good, qualified officer.

"Mr. Alden has requested not to be considered for the position," she said. That was strange; I would have to look into it, but I wasn't going to assign Alden to a vital position if he didn't want it. Hong continued to scan through the files.

"Mr. Sulu has actually a lot of experience from his last assignment."

"Okay, I'll talk to him," I said. "And the third position?"

"First officer," she said. Gary again. Replacing the helmsman was one thing; a difficult job, but one that could be executed by someone with the proper training. First officer was something else; it was the person who took command when I wasn't available, whose advice I relied on the most. There wasn't anyone in the crew I had as much faith in as Gary.

"Who's next in line?" Since it was only three weeks to get to Starbase 11, maybe I could let whoever had the highest rank have the job, at least until then.

"Let's see . . ." she said, looking over the list. "Lieutenant Commander Benjamin Finney."

"No," I said, a little too quickly. I felt terrible, but that would never work. Finney, it turned out, still hated me. Gary had told me a few weeks before that he'd had a bit of a row with him when he'd heard Finney complaining to a few dinner companions that I had ruined his career, that I was holding him back. (Gary didn't specifically tell me what he'd done to get Finney to shut up, but I imagine it was more than just a stern talking-to.) Finney, early on, had requested transfer, but there were no open spots on other *Constitution*-class ships, and he didn't want a lesser class so he stayed on the *Enterprise*. And now, his one opportunity to move up, and I *was* holding him back.

No, I thought, it was his own fault; his attitude with me had affected my opinion of him. But I had to be careful; I couldn't pick someone obviously less qualified. Finney could complain about me, but I couldn't give the rest of the crew a reason to give his criticism legitimacy. And then I realized the answer was right in front of me.

"Spock," I said. "I'll give it to Spock." It made perfect sense; Spock was already a bridge officer, which, although not a requirement, was at least efficient. Pike had recommended him for the job; a lot of the crew would know that. They maybe weren't friends with him, but everybody respected him. Especially me; I'd just been through one of the toughest series of decisions I'd faced as a captain, and Spock's advice was correct at every stage. I was so lost in the satisfaction of my choice, I hadn't noticed Hong's expression. She didn't look happy.

"Yes sir," she said. "And I assume you would like me to continue regular personnel meetings with Mr. Spock, as I did with Mr. Mitchell?" There was a little subtext to her question, and I understood. Spock was not an easy person to deal with; his Vulcan demeanor could be very off-putting, if not a little scary. And he certainly wasn't going to try to make her laugh.

"Yes, Lieutenant," I said. We all had our assigned duties.

✦

"We've entered standard orbit," Sulu said, as the familiar image of Starbase 11 spun on our forward viewscreen. He, at least, was pleased to get the job of helmsman. When I spoke to him, he thought I was going to fire him; most ships needed a department head for astrosciences, but not the *Enterprise*. Spock, as science officer, was more than capable of handling that job as well, and Sulu had felt extraneous. He had ambition to command, and being a bridge officer was the faster route.

Spock had shown no emotion when he got the news that he was first officer. He said only that he would "endeavor to fulfill the job requirements satisfactorily." And Bailey was doing fine as navigator. Those positions were filled, but by the time we got to Starbase 11, there were two more openings.

Alden, my communications officer, was leaving the ship. He wasn't sleeping or eating, and Dr. Piper determined that he was suffering from a stress disorder caused by trauma. Gary had relieved him on the helm about ten minutes before we'd gone through the barrier. Piper thought that Alden somehow blamed himself for what happened to Gary, that if he'd stayed at the helm, it would've been him who'd been changed, even though there was no basis for believing that. I approved Piper's recommendation to give Alden a medical rest leave. It was a loss, but Uhura had already been filling a lot of Alden's shifts, and it was reasonable to promote her to the position. Alden's leave wasn't the only bad news Piper was going to give me.

"Jim, I've decided it's time to retire," he said. Piper was a veteran, which is what made him valuable in one sense, but was often at a disadvantage when dealing with the unknown. He said the experience with Gary had hit him hard; he had been focused on the physical health of his patient, but had offered no prognosis on his mental health. I'm not sure that any of us could've changed the outcome, but Piper especially felt that the situation had gotten away from him. I wished him the best, and felt a little bad about how quickly I moved to get his replacement.

As luck would have it, McCoy wasn't far away; he'd been posted to a planet, Capella IV. It was a primitive society that was, however, aware of the Federation. As such, under the Federation Charter, Starfleet was permitted to provide limited aid. McCoy had been stationed there to offer medical assistance. It wasn't long before I was facing his crabby expression on my viewscreen.

"I'll take it," he said. I laughed.

"I haven't offered anything yet," I said.

"I don't care. The Capellans are warriors, have very little technology, and even less medicine. They think the sick should die. They want nothing to do with doctors. So if you can get me out of here, I'll happily clean bedpans."

I was able to extricate McCoy from Capella, and he would end up joining us well before the refit was finished. I was thrilled; McCoy felt like a security blanket. Though I neglected to tell him that my new first officer was the Vulcan we had shared a ride to Earth with several years before. I knew he wouldn't like it, which is why I brought Spock with me to greet McCoy when he arrived on Starbase 11. Upon being reintroduced, McCoy turned to me and said:

"I should've stayed on Capella."

I laughed and took them both to a cafe on the base. I noticed in the same restaurant Ben Finney was sitting with a woman who I first took to be his wife, Naomi. I got up excitedly to go say hello to her, but as I approached, I realized the woman was far too young. I was a few feet away when she looked up at me and smiled in recognition.

"Uncle Jim!" She stood and hugged me.

"My god, Jamie," I said, "I didn't recognize you." I noticed that Ben had stood up too. He wore a smile that felt false and forced. I kept my focus on her. "What are you doing here? Shouldn't you be in school?"

"I graduated early," she said. "I'm taking a year off before I go to college. Dad arranged a job for me here so we could be a little closer." There was too much for me to process.

"You must be very proud of her," I said to Ben.

"Yes, Captain," he said, a little too formally. Jamie picked up on the awkwardness.

"I'm lucky the *Enterprise* is here for so long," she said. "I don't think Dad and I have had this much time together since he was at the academy."

"Well, I'll let you get back to your meal," I said. "It was great seeing you, Jamie." Upon saying her name, I could see Ben scowl; it hurt him that he'd named her after me. As I walked back to join Spock and McCoy, I realized that this was still an open wound.

✦

"The imposter's back where he belongs. Let's forget him," I said. But I couldn't forget him. He was back inside me, and I had all his memories. And they were monstrous. And I was beginning to understand what Pike had been talking about.

I'd been the victim of a transporter accident and been split into two people. But these weren't two evenly split halves. I had never ascribed human intelligence to a machine before, but I couldn't help but feel that the transporter itself decided to have some "fun" with the idea of good and evil. To use Freudian terminology, one half got both the id and the ego; he was brutal, savage, but also clever and resourceful. The other half had the morality, the superego. They were both me, and neither could live without the other.

We'd managed to keep what happened to me from most of the ship's population; Spock rightly pointed out that if the crew saw me as this vulnerable and human, I'd lose the almost inpenetrable image of perfection that allowed a captain to command. We just referred to the savage half as "the imposter," implying that some human or alien had taken on my form. The crew was familiar with the legend of the shape-shifting Chameloids, and now many believed they'd met one. But he was not an imposter. He was a part of myself.

Scotty and Spock had repaired the transporter, and my two halves were thrust back together. I was in command again, walking to my chair, when Yeoman Rand intercepted me.

My old yeoman, Bateson, had been promoted and transferred, and I hadn't been happy when I'd been assigned an attractive female yeoman; McCoy joked that I didn't trust myself. He was right; she was a compelling distraction. But whatever my personal attraction to her, I knew there was no hope for us; I was her commanding officer, and when one person wields that much power professionally over the other, it can't lead to a real relationship.

But my savage half had no need to abide by this wisdom, or show Janice any respect. He tried to use the power of his position, and when she refused, he'd assaulted her, or tried to. And his memories were now mine. As I stood looking at her, I remembered what he, or rather, what I, had done to her; her screams, struggling in my grip. I was nauseous, angry. I wanted to go back in time and stop that monster, but I was the monster.

"Sir, the imposter told me what happened," Rand said, quietly. I remember him telling her that I'd been split in half. She knew he *wasn't* an imposter. She knew.

"I just want to say . . ." she said. "Well, I just want you to know . . ." She didn't know what to say, but she wanted to make me feel better. I realized that she thought she understood, but she'd gotten it wrong; she thought the transporter *made* an evil Kirk. She really didn't understand that the evil Kirk was always there in me. It was making me feel worse; I could barely look at her. But I smiled.

"Thank you, Yeoman." I went to my command chair. I would try to face it, to accept it, but it was impossible.

✦

"Lieutenant Robert Tomlinson and Ensign Angela Martine have requested a marriage ceremony," Spock said, "and they would like you to perform it." I laughed reflexively, then remembered Spock wouldn't come all the way to my quarters to do a comedic bit. Once I realized he was serious, I had a different response.

"How wonderful," I said, unable to control my sarcasm. I suppose I should've been touched, but for reasons I couldn't quite identify, I found the whole thing annoying.

"We will have to schedule a time. Also, Ensign Martine is a Catholic," Spock said, "and she wishes to have the ceremony reflect the traditions of that religion." I knew nothing about the practices of ancient Earth religions.

"How different is Catholic than Christian?"

"They both come from the same root religion, but there are specific details of the wedding service—"

"Never mind," I said. "Just have somebody write up what I'm supposed to say, and I'll say it." Tomlinson was currently the officer in charge of weapons control, and Martine was doing a tour in that department. I had specifically recruited Martine less than two years before; she graduated second in her class at the academy, had a wide range of specialties. I saw a lot of potential for her as a member of my crew. I didn't initially understand why I had such a negative reaction to the idea of the two of them getting married, but I was silently determined to put a stop to it. "Have them report to me, immediately."

"Yes sir," Spock said, and left. A few minutes later, the door chime sounded, and Tomlinson and Martine came in. I had them sit opposite me on the other side of my desk. Tomlinson was boyish, friendly, and in my estimation wasn't Martine's equal. I wanted to talk them out of this.

"So, first, congratulations," I said.

"Thank you, sir," they both said, unintentionally in unison. Then they looked at each other and giggled.

"This is a big step. How long have you two . . ." I let the implication hang in the air for a moment. Tomlinson jumped right in.

"Not very long, sir," he said. "I've strictly obeyed the rules regarding fraternization with subordinates."

"Then forgive me, how do you know you want to get married?" It was a harsh thing to say, and Tomlinson wasn't ready for it. He looked like I'd just killed his pet dog.

"We're in love, sir," Martine said.

"You have no doubts," I said. "Because you will have to make sacrifices."

"That is what love is about," she said. And as a show of solidarity and love, she took Tomlinson's hand.

And I felt like a fool. What was I trying to do? Break up a couple, because I was unconvinced of their love? I looked at these two young people and remembered the intensity of affection and desire. I realized I was jealous; I was envious that they'd found each other.

"Yes," I said, chastised, "that is what love is about." I took a pause, then added that I was honored to perform the service. As they thanked me and left my quarters, hand in hand, these two people reminded me of my parents. They bore no physical resemblance, but something about their feeling for each other evoked Mom and Dad.

Six days later, the wedding ceremony was interrupted by the Romulans.

✦

A hundred years before, Earth engaged in a war with the enigmatic species. It was a war fought in space, on ships; no ground troops, no captives, against an enemy we never met face-to-face. The peace treaty was negotiated by subspace radio. Earth had defeated the Romulans and put them behind a Neutral Zone, cut off from the rest of the Galaxy. Outposts constructed on asteroids monitored the border, making sure the Romulans never crossed it. For a century we'd heard nothing from them, and then they came across with two new weapons: a working invisibility cloak for their ship and a catasrophically destructive plasma weapon, which they used to destroy our outposts. They were testing our resolve, looking for an easy victim. We'd engage them, and along the way, would discover a secret that would affect politics in the quadrant for decades to come.

"I believe I can get a look at their bridge," Spock said, early on in our engagement with the invisible ship. He had intercepted a communication and was using his creative technical wizardry to follow the transmission back to its source. On our viewscreen, we got a look at the cramped control room of the Romulan ship and the face of its commander.

Pointed ears, slanted eyebrows, he could've been Spock's father.

It was a revelation: the Vulcans and the Romulans were the same species—the Romulans an offshoot, a lost colony. It was fascinating to think about; when the war with the Romulans occurred, we had only known the Vulcans for a few decades. Would Earthmen and Vulcans been able to form a lasting friendship if this connection were known? It made me think that perhaps if it had been known, Starfleet Command might have kept it a secret all this time because of the negative connotations the war had for so many on Earth.*

I didn't think it would matter a century later, though I was quickly proven wrong. My navigator, Lieutenant Stiles, whose ancestors had fought

---

*EDITOR'S NOTE: Captain Kirk's instincts were correct. Shortly before publication of this work, Starfleet declassified a trove of documents from the Romulan War revealing, for the first time, that Starfleet Command and the leaders of Earth were aware of the Vulcan-Romulan connection during the war and kept it a secret to protect the Vulcan-Earth relationship.

in that war, immediately decided upon seeing the Romulans that Spock was a spy.

I wasn't having a lot of luck with navigators. Bailey had left after it became clear he wasn't ready for the position. I'd tried a few others who weren't up to snuff, and now here was Stiles, who showed the terrible judgment to openly insult his superior officer based on his looks. To Spock's credit, he didn't let it affect him. Or at least he said it didn't. But I wasn't going to have it; it was ridiculous, raw, and obvious bigotry, and as soon as I could replace Stiles, I would. But not in the middle of a crisis.

I was facing an invisible ship with a weapon that could pulverize large asteroids. I had to make sure the ship didn't get home, or we'd be facing an all-out war. But I couldn't cross the border without also risking a war that could be blamed on us. The *Enterprise* and the Romulan ship played a game of cat-and-mouse for hours. The commander of the enemy craft was clever, but his ship wasn't the juggernaut it pretended to be; we learned that its power was drained by its invisibility field, and its weapon had a limited range. The *Enterprise* could beat it: we could outrun its weapon. But during the engagement I'd failed to stop them before they returned to their space; they'd made it to the other side of the border, a border I'd been ordered not to cross. I had to draw them back.

I decided on a risky strategy. We'd suffered damage at the hands of the enemy ship, so it wasn't difficult to appear vulnerable. And though they'd made it into the Neutral Zone, I gambled that they wouldn't resist the opportunity to finish us off. So I ordered us to play dead.

If they fell for it, we'd have little time to fire. They couldn't fire their weapon while they were invisible, and we couldn't fire until we could see them. I had to make sure we fired before they got off a shot. As a precaution I sent Stiles to help Tomlinson, who was manning the forward phaser control room by himself.

I sat looking at the viewscreen, waiting for the ship to appear. My shields were down, engine power at minimum. If that ship fired first, we wouldn't be able to escape their plasma weapon. As I waited, I thought about the *Enterprise* and its 400 crewmen. They could all be dead in a moment, and it would be my fault. The seconds passed, and I became less sure of myself. I had a last-minute thought that maybe I should power up and warp away. That was the safer course. I was about to give that order when Sulu spoke up.

"Enemy vessel becoming visible," he said. I was committed. I told the phaser control room to fire.

And nothing happened.

The enemy ship was getting closer. For some reason, Stiles and Tomlinson weren't following my orders. I tamped down my panic, keyed in the public address system, and shouted for Stiles to fire. No response.

I looked up at the Romulan ship. It was so close now. I had the thought that I'd killed us all.

And then the phasers fired; the Romulan was hit.

What I didn't know at the time was there had been an accident in the phaser control room, reactor coolant was leaking in and suffocating Stiles and Tomlinson. Fortunately, Spock was nearby, went into the control room, and fired the phasers. He then pulled Stiles out in time to save his life. I'd always thought Spock might have been overcompensating by choosing to get Stiles first. His choice had further ramifications.

Because Spock chose Stiles first, Tomlison died.

I later found Angela Martine in the chapel, praying. It was surprising to me that in this day and age people still found comfort from this. But I was in no position to criticize how this woman chose to grieve. She turned and saw me, then came to embrace me.

"It never makes any sense," I said. "But you have to know there was a reason." This seemed empty; to appeal to her patriotism, her service, but I really didn't know what to say. Neither did she, and she soon left me alone in the chapel.

I looked up at the podium. I thought of the traditions of so many religions, where clergy, preaching from a similar podium, would offer comfort, protection, or motivation. And those clergy were required to sacrifice their personal lives to provide that comfort and motivation. They could help others achieve happiness and contentment, and the clergy's only reward was that service. There was really no rest for them.

I understood that job. I left the room and got back to work.

✦

"We have a request from Dr. Tom Leighton that we divert to Planet Q," Spock said, at our morning meeting. "He reports it's urgent."

I hadn't seen Tom since his wedding, five years before. He had grown into the image of his father, a bear of a man, but without the light touch. He still carried the burden of what had happened on Tarsus IV, even into adulthood. It had influenced his career path; he became an astroagricultural scientist, specifically devoting himself to the development of synthetic foods for Earth colonies. And he still wore the patch on half his face. But his career success and his marriage to a lovely, supportive woman had softened him somewhat. The wedding had been celebratory, and I saw some hope for happiness for my old friend.

"Planet Q is three light-years off our course," I said.

"He reports he has discovered the formula for a synthetic food that could avert famine on Cygnia Minor," Spock said.

This was a strange coincidence. Cygnia Minor was an Earth colony whose population growth had gone unchecked, and its arable land had been diminished because of uncontrolled development. It was off the major shipping routes, so a food crisis could develop there quickly, though it hadn't yet; Starfleet and Federation colonies had been placed on alert to the situation less than a month before. The fact that Leighton already had a solution to the problem was unbelievable. But I had to follow it up.

"Inform Starfleet Command, and set course for Planet Q," I said, and Spock left. I was always a little ambivalent about seeing Tom; it brought up a lot of memories that I'd pushed away, but I also felt a kinship and a responsibility to him.

When we arrived at the planet, I received a message for me to meet him at a theater in the capital city of Yu. I didn't know what to make of it, but I beamed down. The city was modern and sprawling, with a large distinctive arch at the city's entrance. I found my way to the theater, shaped like a giant silver chicken egg that lay on its side. There was a ticket waiting for me at the box office, and I went inside.

On the stage, the Acturian version of Shakespeare's *Macbeth* was being performed. As I found my way to the empty seat, I gathered I'd missed a good portion of it, as Macbeth was already about to kill King Duncan.

Tom was already there, sitting in the seat next to me. He did not give me a warm greeting; he was concentrating on the stage. This whole thing seemed very strange. I was here to get a food synthetic, but he was going to make me sit through a three-hour play.

And then he told me to pay attention to the voice of the actor playing Macbeth.

"That's Kodos the Executioner," he said, his voice intense and angry. I was baffled. Was he saying Macbeth reminded him of Kodos? I looked at the actor. It had been almost a quarter century, and the man playing the part did bear a small resemblance. But it was unbelievable that Tom thought it actually *was* him. I started to think Tom brought me here under false pretenses.

At the intermission, I told Tom I didn't have time to sit through a play. He took me back to his home where he told me the truth. There was no food synthetic; he had made it up to get me to Planet Q. Tom had seen this actor, Anton Karidian, and was sure he was Kodos. It made no sense. His theory was Governor Kodos had escaped death and was now traveling around the Galaxy acting in plays? My old friend, who I'd been through so much with, sounded insane.

Until Tom ended up dead. Murdered.

✦

"Are you Kodos?" I was a few feet from Anton Karidian. He did evoke Kodos in some way. But my memory still wasn't clear. I had only seen him the one time; he had towered over me, and I had been scared, in shock, crying. I didn't fully remember what he looked like. But Tom was dead, and Tom had been sure.

"Do you believe that I am?" he said. I said that I did, but I still wasn't sure. Circumstantial evidence had piled up. Karidian's history began almost to the day that Kodos's ended. And there had been deaths, seven people, all of whom had seen Kodos and knew what he looked like, each of whom died just when the Karidian players were nearby.

But I still wasn't sure.

If this was Kodos, I thought, what a monster; what an ego. He killed thousands of people, escaped punishment, but rather than going into hiding, he *performs on a stage*; his need for attention outweighed all other considerations.

Tom had been murdered after telling me he was sure Karidian was Kodos. I'd found him, stabbed to death out near his home. I'd felt guilty for not believing him immediately, and I had become obsessed. I engineered the situation so Karidian and his players would travel on the *Enterprise*. I was going to find out if Tom was right, and if this was his killer, and his parents' killer, and the killer of all those people I'd known as a child, I would have my revenge.

It was all coming back, the horror of Tarsus, of that night. I was confronted again with my helplessness in the face of evil.

So I became evil, and I went after Karidian in what I thought must be a weak spot.

I tried to seduce his 19-year-old daughter, Lenore.

She was lovely, smart, and she seemed easily dazzled by me. We had long walks together, both on Planet Q and then the ship. We talked about acting, Shakespeare, commanding a ship, her life in the space lanes. One night aboard the ship, I took her to the softly lit observation deck and kissed her. And then I took her back to my quarters.

She was lonely, as I was, and I began to feel guilty, because I felt a real connection to her. But my whole purpose had been to shake her father's identity from the shadows. She was of no help. She told me she'd never known her mother, who died in childbirth, so her father had been everything.

"He is a great man," she said that night we were together in my cabin. "He has given me so much, I'll never be able to repay him for this wonderful life and career he's given me." Though she was an adult, she was also a child, and I was trying to take away her only parent, as Tom's parents had been taken away. I decided I had to challenge him directly and leave this poor girl out of it.

So I went to see him in his quarters, and made him read the speech he gave when he killed all those people. I had written it out from memory, and made him record it.

"The revolution is successful . . ." I always remembered that phrase. He'd said it back then with confidence, with arrogance, as if the crazed rationale for killing all those people was somehow a cause. Now, an older man said it wearily, with some bitterness. He got through the whole speech.

I still didn't know.

✦

"I know how to use this, Captain," Lenore said, aiming a phaser at me.

She was an actress, and she had been acting, pretending to be enthralled by me. She was the one who had killed Tom, along with the six other people. The whole time, she wanted me dead, because I was one of the people who she thought could hurt her father. It was ironic that she wanted to kill me, because I still couldn't remember. I had to be told by Karidian that he was Kodos. I was a fool, almost as big a fool as Karidian, the narcissist, who didn't realize how he had damaged his daughter until it was far too late.

We were standing on the set of *Hamlet* in the *Enterprise*'s theater, where the Karidian players had been performing. Lenore raised the weapon and pulled the trigger.

And her father stepped in front of it, saving my life. It was again his own vanity that led him to do it. He'd destroyed so many lives, which mattered to him not at all, but when he'd discovered that his own daughter was a murderer, that moved him to regret, to self-sacrifice.

Kodos the Executioner was dead, by his own child, by his own actions. His whole life he had never taken responsibility for his crimes, and it killed him in the end. I was reminded of Shakespeare's King Lear: "We make guilty of our disasters the sun, the moon, and the stars: as if we were villains by necessity."

The quote also applied to me. Catching him had been my "necessity," and I became a villain.

✦

The *Enterprise* was falling into Psi 2000, an ancient, ice-covered planet in its death throes. We'd originally been sent to pick up a scientific party and watch the planet break up from a safe distance. Things didn't go according to plan. The scientific party had all succumbed to a strange disease that made them lose their self-control. One of them, a crewman named Rossi, had turned off the life-support system, and then gotten in the shower with his clothes on, while they'd all frozen to death. When we got there, everyone had been dead for over a day, and our landing party brought the disease back to the *Enterprise*.

The ship had quickly become, for lack of a better term, a nuthouse. A half-naked Sulu tried to stab me with a sword, and my new navigator, Kevin Reilly, literally turned off the engines. McCoy eventually found a cure, but not before we began to spiral into the planet's atmosphere. There wasn't enough time to turn the engines back on through the usual process. Our only hope was Spock: Could my brilliant science officer come up with a formula to "cold start" the engines? It was our last chance.

Spock, despite succumbing to the disease, came through. With Scotty's help, they manually combined matter and antimatter, creating a controlled implosion that jump-started our engines. We pulled away from the dying world.

And the immense power sent us into a time warp. We travelled backward in time over seventy hours.

The importance of the discovery was initially lost on me, because I had also succumbed to the disease. It was a little like being drunk—it removed the perimeter I kept around myself. It had also brought to the front of my mind just how attached I'd become to the *Enterprise*. I had found something I was willing to commit everything to, but because it was an inanimate object, the ship could give nothing in return. It was a dark psychological moment: I loved something that couldn't love me back. My science officer, however, was trying to make me see that we'd discovered something much more important than the heart of my relationship problems.

"This does open some intriguing prospects, Captain," Spock said. He pointed out we could go back in time to any planet in any era.

"We may risk it someday, Mr. Spock," I said, but I wasn't really processing it. I told Sulu to lay in the course for our next destination. As he did, however, I thought of something.

"Wait a minute," I said. "Spock, it's three days ago. That means Psi 2000 hasn't broken up yet."

"Yes," he said. And then he understood what I was getting at. "The scientific party might still be alive—"

"Mr. Sulu, reverse course! Get us back to Psi 2000, maximum warp!"

We made it back and beamed down. They were all succumbing to the disease, but we found Rossi as he was turning off the life-support systems. I had to stun him with my phaser, but we stopped him, and saved them all. McCoy gave them the cure, and we got them back up to the ship, where we watched the breakup of Psi 2000 again, this time from a safe distance.

Some days we'd had our losses, but some days we had our wins.

✦

The ship jerked violently. I checked the navigation sensors; we hadn't even reached the center of the ion storm; it was going to get much worse. I became concerned that the eddies of the storm would pull us off course if the helm didn't compensate.

"Hold on course, Mr. Hanson," I said.

"Aye sir," he said. "Natural vibration force two . . . force three . . ." Hanson, the beta shift helmsman, compensated for the force of the storm by reversing the starboard engine. He was not the man I wanted at the helm in the middle of an ion storm. He lacked confidence and experience, but I couldn't relieve him now.

No one fully understood what caused ion storms, the magnetic conflagrations of ionic particles traveling at thousands of kilometers an hour. Their mystery was part of their sway. They caused terror in a starship crew and its captain; they felt malevolent. You would move the ship, and it felt like the storm was countering your moves, trying to swallow you whole.

JAMES T. KIRK SC9370176CEC

STARFLEET ACADEMY
CLASS OF 2254

Kirk's graduation photo from the academy yearbook.

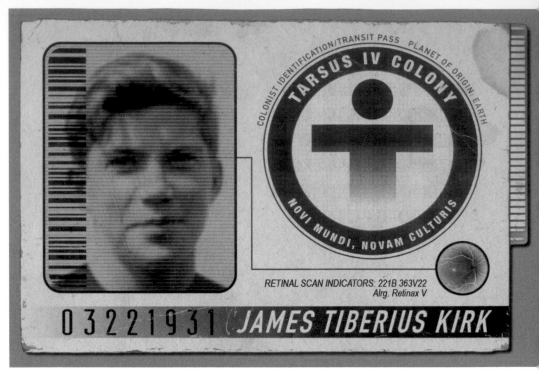

The travel pass issued to young Kirk for his journey to Tarsus IV.

James Kirk with his friend Gary Mitchell taken aboard the *U.S.S. Hotspur*.

STARFLEET ACADEMY

Be it known that **Cadet James Tiberius Kirk**
of the **Planet Earth**
having been carefully examined on all the Branches of the
Arts, Sciences, History, Literature and Engineering
taught at Starfleet Academy
has been judged worthy to graduate
with the rank of

ENSIGN

In testimony of and by virtue of authority vested in the
Academic Board
We confer upon him this rank.
This day,
The Eighteenth Day of June
Twenty-Two Hundred & Fifty-Four

Richard Barnett

Admiral, Chairman Academic Board of Starfleet Academy

Kirk's diploma from Starfleet Academy.

Kirk, Spock, and Yeoman Janice Rand taken around 2266.

A painting from the Starfleet Museum that commemorates the meeting of James Kirk and Christopher Pike. (The illustration favors Kirk; in reality, Pike was several inches taller.)

Photos and artifacts from Kirk's journey to the 1930s found among his belongings after his death.
Edith Keeler is seen in the photo strip, a common souvenir in 20th-century Earth.

Dear David,

How are you? I'm sorry I haven't ~~written to you in along~~ written until now, but I'm always thinking about you. If you get this letter and want to write back, I would love to hear from you. Tell me about where you live. Do you have a lot of friends? Where do you go to school? Do you like your teachers? Do you read a lot? I hope so—I read a lot when I was your age.

~~I don't know how much your mom has told you about me, but~~ I wanted to tell you a little bit about me and my work. I'm a starship captain. That means I'm in charge of a ship with a lot of people on it. I think it's a pretty important job, and I'm very proud ~~and happy~~ that I ~~have it~~ earned it. The ship is called the Enterprise, and it's part of Starfleet. Its job is to protect the people of the Federation, explore new planets and meet new people. Sometimes it's dangerous, but most of the time people are happy to meet me.

Yesterday I visited a planet where everybody acted like a gangster from ancient Earth. It was very strange because they weren't play acting. I met a little boy on that planet who was probably around your age. He helped me with my mission, and we had to pretend for a minute that I was his father. It made me think of you.

I hope I can see you one day soon, ask your mother if you can come visit me on my ship.

Hope to be in touch with you soon!

~~Love Best~~

~~Jim Dad~~ ~~your father,~~ ~~Dad~~ Jim

This handwritten draft of a message to his son David, whom he had not met, was among Kirk's effects. From the events described, it's estimated to have been written in 2268 when David Marcus was around seven. It appears the message was never sent.

Dr. Carol Marcus and her son David, at age two.

Kirk, Spock, and Dr. Leonard McCoy on a camping trip to Yosemite National Park in 2287.

Kirk and Spock during Kirk's first year as commander of the *U.S.S. Enterprise*.

And its greatest power was this fear it caused, fear that might lead a captain to make a wrong decision.

I checked the board, then ordered engineering to increase thrust, and called the ion pod.

"Ion pod," Ben Finney said. He sounded calm and confident. He'd been in the sensor pod during an ion storm before; he knew the orders were to gather as much sensor data as possible, but to get out before the pod itself gained a charge. It was a delicate balance, since navigating an ion storm without some data from the pod was almost impossible. Ion storms had been known to change their size by several million kilometers in a matter of minutes. The more data a ship had, the quicker it could find its way through.

"Stand by to get out of there, Ben," I said. I looked down at the panel by my right hand. The yellow alert light flashed; when I hit red alert, that would be Ben's signal to get out of the pod. I looked up, saw from the navigational sensors we were a third of the way through the storm.

"Steady as we go, Mr. Hanson," I said.

"Outer hull pressure increasing," Spock said.

"Natural vibration now force five," Hanson said. "Force six . . ." The ship could take this increased vibration, but the faster we could get through the storm, the better. I checked the telemetry from the sensor pod; it was giving me a three-dimensional view of the storm on the navigational console. The *Enterprise* was a little blip; the computer projected our course forward. I made a quick calculation; we'd be through in less than three minutes on our current heading, but it was going to be a rough ride.

The ship jolted; now the shuddering became continuous.

"Natural vibration now force seven," Hanson said, yelling above the din.

I looked down at my control pad and signaled red alert. Ben would know to get out of the pod.

The red alert klaxon was almost lost in the sound of the ship's vibrations; it was being buffeted now like an empty tin cup on a tidal wave, the inertial dampeners straining to keep us all upright. I watched the board near Hanson; he wasn't compensating enough.

"Helm, come right two degrees," I said.

"Aye sir," Hanson said. He initiated the change just before the ship was knocked hard. The inertial dampeners couldn't work fast enough, and the ship lurched to the starboard. I was thrown from my chair. I saw Spock had tumbled near the helm. He clawed his way up to the control, and diverted more power to the dampeners so that the ship turned upright again. I helped Hanson back to his chair, then checked our course: still a few minutes from the edge of the storm. The whole bridge was shuddering. I felt a tide of panic, but regained control; my decisions were the right ones.

And then my mind went back to the pod. In a storm of this magnitude, if we lost any of our control circuits to a burnout, the ship would be dead. Seconds had passed; Finney had had plenty of time to get out. Everyone on the bridge was caught up in their work, eyes on their consoles, doing their jobs to keep the ship safe. And I did mine. I went back to my chair and pressed the jettison button. It flashed green. The pod was away.

Soon, the vibration began to subside, and the ship began to calm.

"Natural vibration force five . . . force four . . ." Hanson said, his voice cooling with each lower number.

"Sir," Uhura said, "Mr. Finney has not reported in." It was standard procedure for the officer manning the pod to check in immediately after he'd gotten out.

"Inform security, he could be injured," I said, and got back to paying attention to getting the ship through the storm.

After a full day of searching, they didn't find Finney. It was determined that he must have still been on the pod when I jettisoned it. It made no sense; he knew the risks, he knew once the red alert had sounded, he had to get out of there.

The truth of what happened made even less sense. A few weeks later, I watched playback from the ship's log on a viewscreen. There was a close-up of my right hand, pressing the jettison button, but during the yellow alert, well before the ship was being torn apart.

And I was being court-martialed for it.

I sat facing Commodore Stone and three other command-grade officers in full dress, in the courtroom on Starbase 11. Their contention was that either I had some kind of mental lapse and panicked, jettisoning the pod earlier than I had to, or something far worse. The prosecution made the case that I'd grown to resent Ben Finney, and I used the opportunity to get rid of him.

But watching that viewscreen, looking at my hand jettisoning the pod much earlier than I remembered, I had to question my own memory. I knew how I felt about Ben: he was a pain in the ass, but he was also a good, reliable officer. The idea that I would kill him for such a petty reason was simply untrue and insulting. The theory that I had panicked was a little easier to take; I'd come close to panicking during the storm, but I held it together. I'd made the right decisions.

Except the playback of the log excerpt said otherwise. I looked guilty.

I wasn't alone; I had a lawyer named Samuel Cogley. He was an older man, tough and well-read. He was obsessed with books, the old, bound kind. He seemed quaint to me, and during the trial there wasn't much he could do in the face of the computer record. But it turned out his passion for the written word would end up saving my career.

Cogley had rested our case, just when Spock came into the courtroom with new evidence. Spock discovered that someone had tampered with the *Enterprise's* computer. But because we'd rested our case already, the court didn't have to hear it. That's when Cogley showed his true value.

He made an impassioned speech about man fading in the shadow of the machine, losing our individual rights as our computer technology takes over our way of life. It was a speech that I imagine was relevant to humans of many ages, going all the way back those people who succumbed to the primitive Internet of the early 21st century. And it moved the court to hear the evidence.

The court reconvened on the *Enterprise*. Spock testified that the modification made to the computer was so subtle, only a programming expert could pull it off. There were only three people qualified in Spock's view: him, me, and Ben Finney. It was then Cogley who made the seemingly outrageous assertion that Ben Finney had altered the log, after he supposedly died, to make it look like I'd killed him.

Which meant he had faked his death and was still hiding somewhere aboard the ship. With the ship's sensors, we were able to prove that he was still alive.

Finney had lost his senses. He'd become obsessed with taking revenge on me for ruining his career. He was truly sick, and I had to find him myself. He was hiding in the ship's engineering spaces. His twisted plan revealed, we fought, and he desperately tried to kill me, but was in no condition to take me on. In the end, he was on the deck, beaten and sobbing.

"Ben," I said. "Why? You have a daughter and wife who love you."

"No they don't," he said. "They don't."

He was ill, truly ill. I'd never seen it until now. I didn't know if he'd been born with it, or if the circumstances of his life had created it, but either way, Ben was lost.

✦

A young ensign had been recommended to me by the commandant of Starfleet Academy, and he joined the ship at Starbase 11. He had just graduated from the academy, and had exceptional grades in the sciences and navigation. I always introduced myself to new crewmen when they first came aboard; I remembered that Garrovick had done that for me, and I routinely followed his example. I also had established a practice of either Spock or myself mentoring the new crewmen, at least for a little while. So when the young man beamed aboard, I was in the transporter room.

"Ensign Chekov, reporting for duty, Keptin," he said, standing at attention upon seeing me. I was surprised at the thickness of his Russian accent; 23rd-century language education had for the most part done away with them. Except when the individual didn't want to get rid of it. I would quickly become convinced that Chekov fell into this category.

"At ease," I said. "Welcome aboard, Ensign." I shook his hand.

"A pleasure to meet you, sir," Chekov said. "I believe our ancestors are from the same region."

"I'm sorry?" I said, genuinely confused, but he kept going.

"Perhaps they served the now-forgotten Communist Party of the ancient USSR . . ."

"Ensign," I said. "What are you talking about?"

"Your ancestors were from Kirkovo, Bulgaria, yes? Though I was born in St. Petersburg, my mother's father was born in Odessa, which is just across the Black Sea . . ."

"Sorry to disappoint you, Ensign," I said, cutting him off, "but my ancestors are not from Bulgaria. And I don't believe any of them were ever communists." Chekov could not hide his disappointment, and I couldn't hide my amusement. I told him to report to sickbay for his physical. I decided I'd let Spock mentor this one.

✦

"Our last item, sir. Commodore Wesley has made a crew transfer request," Spock said. It was our morning briefing, in my quarters. McCoy was there, having stopped in for coffee before going on duty. "It struck me as rather odd."

"Who does he want?" I already knew the answer. Commodore Wesley was requesting Janice Rand be transferred to his ship, the *Lexington*, to fill an opening in his communications department. Bob Wesley had been an instructor for a short time when I was at the academy. We'd then met several times when I was captain of the *Hotspur*, and struck up a friendship. I asked him this favor, and he happily obliged me.

"He is offering her a promotion to lieutenant," Spock said.

"What's so odd about that?" McCoy said. "It sounds like a good opportunity."

"It is odd, Doctor, because Yeoman Rand has not requested a transfer," he said. There wasn't anything that got by Spock, which was usually a good thing. However, in this case, I'd hoped to keep anyone from being aware of my hand in this.

"Does Janice want to go?" I said, specifically avoiding the question Spock was implying. If he asked me directly, I wouldn't lie to him. He looked at me and seemed to sense I was avoiding the subject.

"I have kept Lieutenant Hong from presenting it to Yeoman Rand," he said, "awaiting your approval." I told him he should take it to her, and Spock nodded and left. Once he was gone, however, McCoy didn't waste any time getting to the heart of the matter.

"Commodore Wesley is a friend of yours, isn't he?" I nodded. "I don't think she wants to leave," McCoy said. "And as your doctor, I'm not sure this is the best way to deal with the situation." McCoy was the only one who knew about my guilt regarding Janice, and that it continued to afflict me. It had faded a little; I thought I could deal with it. But recent events made me reconsider.

"Bones, it's just better if she's not here. It's how I should've dealt with Finney. Maybe if I'd gotten him away from here, away from me—"

"It's not the same thing at all," McCoy said. "Ben Finney was sick. Paranoids are clever; they can seem normal most of the time. I gave him six quarterly physicals and I missed it."

"Maybe I should get you transferred," I said. McCoy could see that I was closing the subject.

"You can't transfer your troubles, Jim," McCoy said. "This is a personal problem, not a personnel problem." He was right, again, but I didn't have to listen.

✦

"This may be my last entry," I said into the recorder the Metrons had given me. I was on a bleak, hot, uninhabited planetoid, sitting on an outcropping of minerals, exhausted. The pain in my right leg was blinding. I thought I was done. I looked down at the minerals at my feet. There were diamonds and sulfur. Something lit in my memory, but it was faint. I was looking for weapons, something that could kill a formidable, deadly creature. I struggled to remember the connection between sulfur and weapons. I pulled myself up and kept going.

The Federation colony on Cestus III had been destroyed by a race known as the Gorn. The *Enterprise* had chased the culprits into an uncharted section of space. Another race, who called themselves the Metrons, had astonishingly reached out from their planet and stopped both vessels, plucked me and the Gorn captain off of our bridges, dropped us onto this desolate, rocky place, and told us to fight it out.

From the beginning, I'd underestimated my opponent. He was a seven-foot reptilian, dressed in a gold tunic, and despite his staggering strength, moved much slower than me; I misinterpreted this as an indication he might not be as clever. But he'd lured me into a trap, and I was barely able to slip away with an injured leg. I had no food, no water; in a short time I'd be too exhausted to stay ahead of him.

When the Metrons put us on the planet, they said there'd be weapons, yet I had not found any that could kill my opponent. But I couldn't give up. They had also said that if I lost the battle, my ship would be destroyed.

I stumbled onto a large rock and slipped to the ground. My hand landed in a white substance, a granular powder. It looked familiar. I tasted it. Salty. The memory connected to the sulfur now finally came forward.

Sam.

I'm five years old and watching my brother, Sam, build a cannon in our barn. He had soldered old tin cans with the bottoms cut out, and then he spread out three piles of chemicals onto an old table.

"What's that stuff?"

"That's sulfur," he said, pointing to a pile of yellow powder, "the black powder is charcoal, and the white is saltpeter." Before he could stop me, I had tasted the saltpeter.

"Spit that out!" I immediately did what he told me.

"You said it was salt."

"Salt*peter*. You don't eat it."

"What's it for?"

"Gunpowder."

I then watched as he confidently and carefully mixed the chemicals in the right amounts, then ground them together. I remembered that taste, and on Cestus III, I tasted the white powder on my hands and spit it out. It was the same. I smiled at the memory. Sam's cannon was going to save me.

History records that I defeated the Gorn with a bamboo cannon loaded with diamonds for cannonballs. Amazingly, the blast of diamonds coming out of a cannon only stunned the strange creature. But I had the advantage and could've killed him; I spared his life, however, and because of that the Gorn and the Federation now live in peace. I owed it all to Sam.

But I never got to tell him.

✦

Spock, McCoy, Scotty, and I sat across from Khan Noonien Singh. I had found him and his followers in suspended animation in an ancient spaceship. The product of controlled genetics, he was the superman whose rule of over a quarter of the planet Earth in the 1990s I'd studied at the academy in John Gill's class. And now, he was here in the present—the day before, he had taken over my ship and tried to kill me. He'd done this with the help of one of my officers, ship's historian Lieutenant Marla McGivers. She'd mutinied because she'd fallen in love with Khan. With her help, he'd revived the 72 followers still in suspended animation on his primitive ship. They quickly had taken over the *Enterprise*. But Khan couldn't run the ship without my crew, and they wouldn't follow him. When he tried to kill me, McGivers had a change of heart and intervened to save my life. I was able to retake the ship.

Now, we were all cleaned up in our dress uniforms at a hearing to determine what to do with Khan and McGivers. Despite her last-minute change of heart, I still couldn't forgive her act of mutiny. I looked at Khan, under guard, but still a leader. In that moment, I somehow forgot who he was, that he was a murderer, a dictator responsible for the death and oppression of millions. Instead, I fell in love with the idea that I would make a civilized decision.

"I declare all charges and specifications in this matter have been dropped," I said. McCoy was the only one who protested, but I cut him off and turned to Spock. He and I had already had a conversation regarding Ceti Alpha V, a planet that wasn't too far off our current course. It was a world of mostly jungle, with a variety of indigenous predators. The offer I made to Khan was he and his people could live there. It was arrogant on my part, but I didn't see it. I thought I was making the humane choice. These people had so much potential, it would be such a waste to confine them to a reorientation center, where they'd probably spend most of their time trying to escape. Instead, I gave Khan a world that was his to tame. He answered the offer with a smile.

"Have you ever read Milton, Captain?" He was referencing Lucifer's comment as he fell into the pit: better to rule in hell than serve in heaven.

His response was educated, rarefied, civilized. I was admiring him, and he was playing me for a fool.

I turned to my mutinous historian. Did she want a court-martial or a life on this unforgiving world with the man she loved? She of course chose the latter; no one was going to get in the way of the romantic, heroic ending to this story that I'd helped to engineer.

The prisoners left the room, and Spock ruminated on what we'd just done.

"It would be interesting, Captain, to return to that world in a hundred years and to learn what crop had sprung from the seed you planted today." It was a wonderful, hopeful thought, exactly what I was thinking when I'd proposed it.

Of course, we would be going back a lot sooner, to face the consequences of the biggest mistake of my career. But for the moment, I was confident and happy in my ignorant hubris.

It would take about a week to reach Ceti Alpha V. During the trip, I had confined Khan and his followers to one of the ship's cargo bays, and had a force field established around it. I had the bay filled with enough food and supplies so we wouldn't have need to bring the force field down; I didn't trust that they wouldn't try to take the ship again. When we reached Ceti Alpha V, I would have them beamed out of the cargo bay and directly down to the planet. During the trip, I had Scotty rig up some cargo carriers on the hangar deck to be used as temporary living quarters on the planet, which I would drop there once we arrived. I was inspecting his work when Spock came to see me.

"We've had another request for you to perform a marriage ceremony." I looked at him, incredulous. Why would he bring this up now?

"Can't it wait until after we drop Khan off?"

"I do not think so, sir. The request comes from Khan." I exchanged a look with Scotty.

"Here's one reason I never want to be captain . . ." Scotty said.

I told Spock we couldn't do it, that having 72 genetically engineered wedding guests was too big a risk. He countered that Khan had already offered to wait until we arrived at Ceti Alpha V, and that his followers could be beamed down to the planet. The only people required at the wedding were he and McGivers. I felt it had to be some sort of trick, but Spock didn't agree.

"I have given it a fair amount of consideration, Captain," he said. "Khan is a primitive man from a primitive time. He may take some comfort in ancient Sikh rituals."

"Wait," I said. "He wants a Sikh wedding?"

Spock was ready for this, too. He had assigned Ensign Chekov to research the customs for such a ritual, in the event I approved it. But the whole thing seemed unbelievable. I had to question Khan myself, so I went back to my quarters and communicated with him through the viewscreen on my desk.

"Khan, forgive me, but is this a joke?"

"I think you have known me long enough, Captain, to appreciate I have no sense of humor." He had me there. "I do not know what my situation will be once we arrive on that planet, and I want Marla to have the honor of being my wife from the moment we set foot on that new world. We are going to conquer it together."

"Then I guess . . . we're going to have a wedding."

We arrived at Ceti Alpha V. I had the cargo pods brought down to the surface, then had Khan's people beamed down, leaving only Khan and McGivers on board. I put on my dress uniform again and went to the chapel. Khan and McGivers sat on pillows that Ensign Chekov had procured from Lieutenant Uhura's quarters. The only guests, also on pillows, were Spock and McCoy. Five security guards lined the walls. I came in and sat on the one empty pillow, obviously reserved for me.

It was as close to a traditional Sikh wedding as we could approximate; Chekov gently prodded me through the ceremonies of the "Anand Karaj," which translates into "Blissful Union." The bride and groom announced their love for each other and detailed their roles in the equal partnership. It managed to be both quaint and progressive. The tradition ended with the groom taking the bride away from her own family, which in this situation had its own significance.

We escorted them to the transporter room, and as they stepped on the pad I saw a happy, contented, proud couple. Even Khan was not going to be denied marital bliss. I beamed them down.

✦

"So you're telling me," Matt Decker said, "it was all an illusion."

I was in the conference room aboard Decker's ship, the *U.S.S. Constellation.* A few days before, war had been declared between the Federation and the Klingon Empire. It had lasted for two days (and hence became known as the Two-Day War). I had been at the center of it, knew the most about it, so Commodore Decker, who was commander of the main force that was about to face off against the Klingons before the war was abruptly cut short, wanted a debrief. Admiral Nogura was also present via subspace and stared at us through the viewscreen in the center of the table.

"Not exactly an illusion," I said. "I should probably start from the beginning." I could see the doubt in Decker's expression, and I couldn't blame him. It had been a difficult truth to accept. When war had been declared the *Enterprise* had been sent to Organia, a centrally located Class-M world, to secure an agreement with the local populace for Starfleet to use the planet as a base of operations. We'd found a primitive people who didn't seem impressed with us, or the coming danger. They refused our help, and shortly thereafter the Klingons arrived.

Spock and I were stuck on the planet, in disguise, surrounded by hundreds of Klingon soldiers. All I could think about was Axanar. I was about to watch an innocent, peaceful society shattered by a Klingon occupation. The military governor, Kor, was everything I'd come to loathe about his species: arrogant, ruthless, proud of his society's glorification of war. It gave him a disgusting sense of entitlement that legitimized his atrocities on the weak.

But the Organians weren't powerless innocents. They only gave the illusion of being humanoid, and were in fact beings of pure energy, many millions of years more advanced than us. They put a stop to our war, deactivated our ships in space and our weapons on the ground. I was initially infuriated; I thought of myself as a man of peace, but my hatred for the Klingons had blinded me. I wanted a war, and the Organians weren't going to let me have my way. Because I had dealt directly with them, I had more time to accept the situation; after I finished my report to Decker, I could see he hadn't.

"We can't just let these beings tell us what to do," he said. Decker was having the struggle I'd just experienced, facing that humanity wasn't the most advanced civilization in the Galaxy, that we weren't even close. "We're not going to just sit by helplessly—"

"The Klingons are as helpless as we are," I said. They'd handed both the president of the Federation and the Klingon Chancellor a finished treaty, with an implied threat they'd disable our ships wherever they were if either side violated it.

"They'll figure some way out of this," Decker said. "We have to assume we're still at war and go forward with our plans. I could drop the bundle on Qo'noS* in two days . . ." This last comment was directed at Nogura, who held up his hand and shook his head. It was clear that Decker was referencing something that I wasn't cleared for. Nogura told Decker they had their orders, that the president of the Federation Council, the Andorian Bormenus, told Starfleet Command that we would abide by the treaty. Decker didn't look happy, and I wondered whether he would ever accept the situation.

And I also wondered what "the bundle" was.

But there would be no war, at least not for a while. It was the third war I'd been a part of stopping since taking command of the *Enterprise*. I felt I was making a difference; I was a part of history.

I was soon going to have to figure out how to save it.

---

*EDITOR'S NOTE: Pronounced like the English word "Kronos," this is the Klingon Homeworld.

CHAPTER 7

THE ANGEL WHO CAME DOWN THE STAIRS of the basement immediately saw to our needs and gave Spock and me a job.

"Fifteen cents an hour for ten hours a day," she said. "What are your names?"

"Mine's Jim Kirk," I said. "He's . . . Spock." What I knew of America in this period of the 1930s was a general lack in interest or education of the public in other cultures. I figured Spock would pass as some generalized Asian.

"I'm Edith Keeler. You can start by cleaning up down here," she said, and headed back upstairs. I really didn't want her to go.

"Miss," I said. "Where are we?"

"You're in the 21st Street Mission," she said. It had a religious ring to it. I found myself hoping she wasn't a nun.

"Do you run this place?"

"Indeed I do, Mr. Kirk." She left us to the messy basement. Spock and I immediately got to work cleaning it up. This is not where I expected to find myself a week ago, when the *Enterprise* was patrolling the [REDACTED] sector, and we'd started getting the strange readings on the chronometers. Spock had noticed that, every few hours, they were "skipping" a millisecond. He traced the source to an unknown particle wave, and the *Enterprise* tracked it back to its source: a planet, in the star system [REDACTED], over [REDACTED] light-years from the nearest world of the Federation.*

As we approached the strange old world, the particle wave's effect became much stronger, and the *Enterprise* was buffeted by what Spock described as "ripples in time." One of these ripples caused McCoy to accidentally inject himself with the dangerous stimulant Cordrazine. He left the ship a raving madman; Spock and I took a landing party down to the surface to find him.

On the world, a relic of a long-dead civilization, what could only be described as a glowing donut three meters in diameter announced:

"I am the Guardian of Forever."

A time portal. Without even asking, it showed us Earth's past in the hole of the donut. McCoy, before we could stop him, leaped into the portal.

We lost contact with the *Enterprise* immediately. McCoy had somehow changed the past. Spock and I then used the portal to follow him back in time in the hopes of stopping further damage. We couldn't be exact in our calculations; we only knew we arrived sometime before McCoy. We didn't know how much time we had.

For now, we had to clean a basement. The tools we had to work with were primitive and inefficient; the brooms were old and constructed of straw. They pushed the dirt on the floor around, but left residue behind. There was also a lot of irreparable furniture and other refuse that didn't look worth saving.

"Assuming a seven-day workweek," Spock said, "ten dollars and fifty cents a week for each of us in ancient U.S. currency." I had no idea how much money that was, relative to the time we were in. Spock pointed out

---

*EDITOR'S NOTE: Captain Kirk wanted to play a small trick on his readers; he told me that the star system he listed in his memoirs was not the true location, was in fact several thousand light-years from the actual world. He knew that news of this discovery he'd made had become public in the intervening decades, and he was doing his duty to try to keep its location a secret. After his death, Starfleet Command reviewed the manuscript, and discovered that Kirk had unwittingly left a subconscious clue to the location of the real place, so Starfleet redacted the false references. They would not tell me what the clue was, but had no problem with me revealing his original intentions.

that it wasn't necessarily the limit of our earning potential, as it left 14 hours in a 24-hour cycle to find other gainful employment. I was incredulous.

"We need to sleep," I said.

"I do not need to sleep," Spock said.

I couldn't argue with that, but said we wouldn't have time to find any work if we didn't figure out how to clean the basement. Spock suggested a phaser locked on a minimal disintegration setting would allow us to dispense with the dirt without harming the structure. This struck me as cheating.

"I was unaware that we were engaged in a competition," Spock said. I reconsidered all the work we had to do, and decided the time stream wouldn't mind if we took a shortcut.

"Set your phaser. I'll watch the door," I said.

Even with the help of our 23rd-century tools, it still took a couple of hours to clean the room. As we were finishing, the smell of cooking wafted down to us. It was a combination of meat and onions, which I found intoxicating. I realized we'd not eaten in hours, so I hurried us to finish, and we went upstairs to the mission.

It was a small place with a kitchen, a cafeteria-style eating area with an upright piano, another room with about 15 cots with a common bathroom and shower. The smell of the food became stronger, but it was now mixed with the other powerful scents of coffee, rotting wood, and body odor.

The dining area was filled with bearded, raggedy men in frayed, soiled clothes, many with a glassy-eyed hopelessness. They stood in line for a bowl of soup, a cup of coffee, and a hunk of bread. Spock and I did the same, and we sat down among them. I was starting to feel as hopeless as those around me. If I couldn't stop McCoy, would this world ever change? Is this where I would spend the rest of my days?

And then Edith Keeler got up to speak. She spoke of the years to come, weirdly prescient on the subject of space travel, and about the people of the future who would solve the problems of hunger and disease.

"Prepare for tomorrow," she said. "Get ready, don't give up. You can't control the hardship, but you can control its effect. The hunger might not abate, but the sadness is yours. The cold bites through your blanket, but you don't need to let the hopelessness in with it. It is your decision what kind of person you will be, how you will respond to the challenges you face.

Keep your promises, forgo your grudges, apologize when necessary, speak your love, and speak it again." It was as if she was talking to me, telling me to trust in myself. I found her calming and captivating. I looked around the room and could see I wasn't the only one. She was giving these people life. Afterward she came and found me.

"Mr. Kirk, you are uncommon workmen. That basement looks like it's been scrubbed and polished." I felt guilty getting this compliment, but I took it with a smile. She told us of a room in her building, which Spock and I could rent, that sounded affordable given our new wages. She walked us there.

It took us a long time to reach her apartment building, but not because it was far away. The streets of New York City were cold and unforgiving. As we walked, we came upon people huddled in doorways or on park benches, under tattered blankets and newspapers, trying to keep warm. Edith stopped at each one, told them where the mission was, that they could rest there and stay warm. Many were hostile to her, some intoxicated, but it didn't deter her; she knew many of them personally, and we helped some return to the mission. Her selflessness was astounding.

Finally, we made it back to her apartment, and she introduced us to her landlord, a hulking, wheezy man in a stained undershirt named Altman. He scowled at us.

"I'm not lettin' no slant eye live here," he said. I looked at him, confused. "The Chinaman's gotta go somewhere else." It took me a moment to understand what he was saying, and then I realized it was directed at Spock. I had never seen such unapologetic racism before. It was frightening in its casualness and acceptability. Edith, however, seemed ready for it.

"They're employees of mine," she said. "I'd consider it a personal favor."

"You're not the only one who lives in this building," Altman said. "People'll get upset."

"Father Cawley will also appreciate it, I'm sure." The mention of the clergy swayed him. She then pulled out two slips of paper that took me a moment to remember were money. She was paying him our rent a week in advance.

"He has to use the back entrance," he said. "And I catch him talking to any white women or kids, he's out."

"That sounds reasonable," Edith said. In fact, it sounded ridiculous, but it was clearly the practical course.

She left us with Altman, who took us to the room. Like everything else we'd seen so far, it was drab and depressing. A sagging bed, sooty curtains, and a wooden table and chair, scratched and stained. The room smelled of ashes; the habit of inhaling the smoke of burning tobacco was an epidemic in this world. I knew this was going to be a difficult time to navigate, but somehow this woman had given me hope.

The days filled up quickly. There was a lot of work to be done at the mission. Spock and I learned how to make coffee in a device called a "percolator," wash dishes, and cook food using other ancient appliances. We also went with Edith to scrounge food donations from the open markets all over the city. New York was in the grip of an economic downturn of massive proportions. People all over were in lines for soup or bread; despondent men stood on street corners, with wooden buckets filled with mostly rotten apples that they offered to sell for a penny. Yet Edith bullied her way into the kitchens of the upscale hotels and restaurants, getting discarded bones and bruised vegetables for soup, and three-day-old bread with mold that Spock and I would have to cut off.

I learned more about her. The daughter of a minister, she was raised in London, England. She came to America in the 1920s and worked in the church. She was doing the same work then she did now; there were always poor people who needed help, she said. Now there was just more of them, and some had once been rich.

We worked at the mission from 7 a.m. to 5 p.m. on that first day, and then we tried to find other work, which was very difficult. I found some day work at the loading docks. I also picked up ideas from the other men in the mission; you could go to one of the upscale parts of the city in the morning, gather up discarded newspapers, and resell them downtown. I was scrounging for pennies, but we needed whatever we could.

Spock discovered Chinatown in the lower part of the city. He passed for Chinese, and thanks to the universal translator in his pocket, it appeared that he could speak it. As such, he was able to acquire work, first washing dishes in the local restaurants, then repairing broken machinery.

Once our money started to come in, we began to acquire the bits of primitive electronic equipment Spock needed to build his memory circuit. He had to figure out some way to slow down the recording on his tricorder so we could see how history had been changed. We didn't know how much time we had; Spock estimated that McCoy might not arrive for a month.

Despite how hard I was working, I found myself more relaxed than I'd ever been. The work was physically exhausting, but all the responsibility for our mission lay with Spock; I could only wait for his machine to work. I began to feel differently; the emotional connection to the men and women of the future began to fade in my mind. I became this regular workingman on primitive Earth. It was a strange vacation: I was mistreated by employers, usually smelled terrible, and was always hungry.

And I was drawn to Edith, and she to me.

We'd take walks in the evening, I would talk honestly about the future, and she would laugh as if I was joking. But she was no primitive; she had an advanced view of people that would have made her quickly at home in the 23rd century. She seemed to know that rich industrialists were holding on to their money, and could end the suffering of the world in a heartbeat, but that they wouldn't.

"They'll only open their purses," she said, "to make some war."

She was disgusted by her era's priorities. I found her fervor appealing and enchanting. Our physical relationship was both passionate and chaste; she was a religious woman and this was a primitive time. But I spent many evenings in her apartment, where she would cook me something she called shepherd's pie and we'd talk and laugh and comfort each other. And I'd go back to my room in a bit of a romantic haze to find Spock, working on an ever-growing contraption of wires and radio tubes. One night, about a week and a half after we'd been there, I walked in, and he had something to show me. On the small screen of his tricorder, an image appeared of Edith in a newspaper article six years in the future. I read the opening sentence in proud astonishment.

"The president and Edith Keeler conferred for some time today—"

Suddenly, Spock's invention exploded in a shower of sparks and smoke.

"How bad?"

"Bad enough," Spock said. But I was lost in my delight in what I thought to be Edith's future.

"The president and Edith Keeler—"

"It would seem unlikely, Jim . . ." Spock said. "A few moments ago, I read a 1930 newspaper article . . ." I wasn't listening, or I would've heard that he called me "Jim," usually a bad sign.

"We know her future. In six years she'll be very important, nationally famous—"

"Or, Captain, Edith Keeler will die. This year. I saw her obituary. Some sort of traffic accident."

"They can't both be true," I said. It was stunning. What was he talking about? But even as I asked the question, I knew what the answer was.

"Edith Keeler is the focal point in time we've been looking for, the point both we and Dr. McCoy have been drawn to." Spock's theory about time rivers ended up being true. But it didn't seem possible that all of history could turn on one person. McCoy does something when he shows up.

"In his condition, what does he do? Does he kill her?" I felt terrible after I said it; I was actually *hoping* that McCoy had killed her, so that I could stop it, so that she could live.

"Or perhaps he prevents her from being killed, we don't know which."

I told him to fix his machine so we would. He then said it would take him weeks.

"We should stay as close to Miss Keeler as we possibly can," Spock said. "This will provide us with the best chance of stopping Dr. McCoy before he commits whatever act changes history."

"That shouldn't be a problem," I said.

"If you find it difficult, I will be willing—"

"I'll be all right, Spock." I then left the room and took a walk.

Days passed into weeks, and there was no sign of McCoy. I gave up my other jobs and escorted Edith to and from work. I spent every waking moment with her, and sometimes perched myself on the roof across the street from her apartment until she turned out the light and went to bed. Some nights she would let me stay in her apartment, as long as I slept on the floor. I was keeping her safe, but the truth was I felt safe next to her. I think, for the first time in years, free of the responsibilities of command, I let myself fall in love.

It was only bad luck that we missed McCoy arriving at the mission. He was exhausted and paranoid. Edith greeted him; he begged her not to tell anyone he was there. She took him to an upstairs room in the back, cared for him and kept the secret, even from me. Around this time, Spock completed the repairs to his machine. It told us that Edith started a pacifist movement that delayed the United States' entry into World War II, allowing Germany to win. It was clear how history was supposed to play out. Edith had to die.

But I wasn't going to let her. I didn't tell Spock, but I wouldn't let the woman I loved die. I couldn't. All those people whose lives would be changed weren't real to me anymore. I would stay in the past, live my life with Edith. I indulged in a delusion we could change the future together. With what I knew, with the knowledge I had, I could make sure Germany *didn't* win, and Edith could still live. I think Spock suspected my plan, but he said only that if I did what my heart told me to do, millions would die who didn't die before.

One night, I left work with Edith. I had a little money in my pocket now; we didn't need to spend it on radio tubes anymore. I was going to take her out to dinner; she, however, had a different suggestion.

"If we hurry, maybe we can catch the Clark Gable movie—"

"What?"

"You know, Dr. McCoy said the same thing . . ." I stopped and grabbed her.

"McCoy! Leonard McCoy?" McCoy was here . . .

"Yes, he's in the mission . . ." How long had he been here? Had he already saved her life? Had we missed it? I truly hoped that we had.

"Stay here. Stay right here," I said, then turned. "Spock!" I ran across the street. Spock was still working in the mission, and he heard my shouting. He came out, and seconds later, McCoy did too. I couldn't believe it. I grabbed him in a hug. And stepped back.

He was in his Starfleet uniform. I hadn't seen mine in over a month; it was in a bag at the bottom of the closet in our room. Suddenly I was back on the ship, back in my head as captain. I felt guilty at what I'd been doing, about what I'd been thinking. I turned and saw Edith. She was crossing the street. And a truck was barreling toward her.

"Go, Jim!" McCoy yelled. It almost drowned out Spock's shout.

"No, Jim!" I stared at Edith, frozen. The uniform blazed in my mind.

I felt McCoy try to push past me to grab her, so I grabbed him. I heard Edith's cry as the truck's horn honked and the terrible rending of metal and flesh. I held McCoy a long moment, as Edith's painful scream seemed to echo in my mind.

"Did you deliberately stop me, Jim?" McCoy was incredulous, angry. I pushed him away. And then we were soon back in the 23rd century, on that dead world.

After a week back on the *Enterprise*, I was more sure of my mistake. My mind wasn't on my job; I could only think of Edith. When I was in the past, the future faded in my mind. But now that I was back in my own time, Edith was right there. I should've saved her. I let her die. The millions that were saved still weren't real to me, even though they were with me every day. I didn't know how I was going to live with it. In some ways, her memory has faded now, but I find I still regret it emotionally. I was a content man; I discovered what life was without duty and honor—just a job and love. It is horrible and self-centered that I regret it, and I suppose I paid for that selfishness, because I would never experience that contentedness again.

✦

"I've got the receiver you requested, sir," Uhura said, over the intercom. I was in my quarters, lying down. I hadn't slept in days, but I couldn't put this off. I sat up on the bed and activated the small viewscreen.

"Thank you, Lieutenant, put it through." On the viewscreen, Uhura's face was replaced by Mom and Dad. They were looking particularly haggard.

"Jim, this is a nice surprise," Dad said, but Mom looked worried.

"I don't think it's a social call, George." Since she had seen through it so quickly, I knew there was no point holding off.

"Mom, Dad, Sam's dead." Mom immediately burst into tears. Dad put his arm around her. I had to keep going. "Aurelan too."

"What . . . about Peter?" It was Mom who asked. Though he wasn't crying, Dad stood in stunned silence.

"He's fine," I said. "I've got him here with me." That was only technically true; since his parents' death I'd had various members of the crew keep him occupied, though I made sure to see him for evening meals.

"What happened?" Mom asked.

"It was some kind of space parasite. It infected a lot of people on Deneva," I said. "A lot of people died."

"But you stopped it," Dad said, finally speaking.

"I stopped it," I said.

"Was it . . . painful?" Mom said. I had watched Aurelan die in unimaginable pain, and Sam had to have gone in much the same way.

"No," I said, "it was quick." The circumstances of what happened on Deneva would not become public, so I thought it was a useful lie. "How're the twins?"

"They keep us up a lot," Dad said, "but they're healthy." Aurelan had given birth to twins two months before Sam was transferred to Deneva. The babies were deemed too young for space travel, so Mom and Dad offered to care for them until they'd reached six months, when it was safe for them to go. Now, though . . .

"I'm going to take Peter to Starbase 10," I said. "He'll get quick passage back to Earth from there."

"You can't . . ." Mom said, pausing. "Can't you bring him—"

"I'm sorry, Mom," I said. I had known that the appropriate thing to do was to bring Peter home, but I just couldn't. First Edith, and now Sam. It was all I could do not to crumble. If I went home, I felt like I might not ever leave. But I could see the hurt in Mom's expression. She needed me.

"It'll be fine," Dad said. "How is he?"

"He's a trooper," I said. It was the truth. Peter, though sad, was holding up well. He seemed curious about the workings of a starship, and the crew had stepped in nicely as caregivers. While we talked, Sam's two babies, Joshua and Steven, woke up and began crying.

"You take care of yourself . . ." Dad said, his voice cracking. I could see he was about to cry. "We love you."

I smiled and turned off the viewer.

I felt guilty; I hadn't seen Peter all day. I left my quarters and went to the rec room. Peter was there, playing three-dimensional chess with Spock. The ship's quartermaster had fitted him into a gold command uniform. I went to the food dispenser, got a cup of coffee, and joined them. I asked how the game was going.

"Mr. Kirk has your predilection for unpredictability," Spock said.

"My dad taught me to play," Peter said.

"Then you and I had the same chess teacher," I said. "I hope he let you win every once in a while."

"Not really," Peter said. "Dad said I would never learn anything that way. I did beat him once, though." I watched them play for a little while. Spock eventually beat him, but it wasn't easy. Then Spock excused himself. I really didn't want him to leave; when I was alone with Peter, the pressure to connect with him was overwhelming.

"Should I set up another game?" he asked. I said sure. I watched Peter as he put the pieces in place. He reminded me of Sam; same color hair and eyes, same intensity. He was focused on setting up the game, but I could see the sadness. I didn't know what to do for him. And then I remembered when Mom had left, what Sam did for me.

"Peter, do you miss them?" He stopped putting the pieces on the board. "It's okay to miss them."

I hugged him for a while.

✦

"He's kind, and he wants what's best for us," Carolyn Palamas said. "And he's so lonely. What you ask would break his heart. Now how can I . . ."

I was on Pollux IV, otherwise known as planet Mount Olympus, and I was the prisoner of a man calling himself Apollo. This was one of my most fantastic encounters; a being who claimed to actually be a Greek god. He was from an advanced race who had visited Earth in the distant past and had seemed like gods to the primitive humans of prehistory. It wasn't hard to understand why, even to me: he controlled an incredible power source that he could channel through his body. When we first arrived, he had reached out with a force field like a giant hand that "grabbed" the *Enterprise*.

Spock stayed on the bridge, while I took a landing party down to meet him. He stood in front of his temple, the source of his power, and told us he expected we'd become his worshippers again. And then, like any accomplished Greek god, he seduced a human woman, who happened to be one of my crewmen.

Lieutenant Carolyn Palamas was an expert in archaeology, anthropology, and ancient civilizations. She was stunning, intelligent, and had fallen head over heels in love with a guy in a toga. He'd "magically" put her in a pink dress before taking her off alone. She had been a consummate professional for the year or so she'd been on the ship, but now she was willing to give it all up. And it was making me ill. Not because I looked down on it, but because I understood it.

The double tragedy of the deaths of both Edith and Sam in my own life forced me to retreat from the emotional world. I avoided connection with others, and I was critical of it in my crew. So now, I'd asked her to spurn him. My hope was that if he lost her, he'd be weakened and vulnerable. She initially refused. She'd forgotten her duty for love. I had to remind her.

"Give me your hand," I said. She gave it to me and I grasped it firmly. I appealed to her sense of loyalty. I gave her a long speech about how we were tied together beyond any untying, that all we had was humanity. She said she understood, and stood up. I wasn't sure I'd gotten through. I could tell her that I was speaking from experience, that I'd given up my love for duty. But I didn't want to. I wanted her to give me what I wanted without question.

She would. She walked off, and soon after, the storm clouds brewed, lightning cracked, and in the distance Carolyn screamed. Apollo had shown us that he had powers that conceivably could control the weather on this planet, and I had assumed this meant she'd done what I asked. Spock, still on the *Enterprise*, had figured out a way to penetrate the force field holding the ship, and fired phasers at Apollo's temple. The god alien returned, but too late; we'd destroyed the source of his power. We found Palamas bruised and beaten. He'd attacked her. Apollo, devastated, weakened, literally faded away. We'd won. But it didn't feel like a win.

Back on the ship a few days later, I was on the bridge. McCoy walked in. He told me that Carolyn Palamas had come to see him, not feeling well.

I asked if she brought some kind of infection back from the planet. McCoy smiled, ruefully.

"You could say that," McCoy said. "She's pregnant." I was stunned. I saw Spock turn from his scanner. It seemed impossible; they were different species.

"Interesting," Spock said. "There are many ramifications about having an infant born on the *Enterprise* who may have inherited some or all of his father's abilities." I was determined that this child was *not* going to be born on my ship. I told Chekov and Sulu to set course for Starbase 12 at our maximum safe speed, and then left the bridge for sickbay.

Palamas was in a diagnostic bed. Scotty stood by her; before Apollo had come into the picture, he had been pursuing a relationship with her, albeit unsuccessfully. He looked affectionate and concerned, and she seemed comforted by his presence.

"Mr. Scott, I believe it's still your shift," I said.

"Yes, Captain, I was just looking in on Carolyn."

"I believe the medical staff is well equipped for that," I said. Scotty nodded and repressed his annoyance before turning to Palamas.

"I'll stop in later," he said, then left us. She looked at me with a smile that I could only describe as chilly. I asked her how she was feeling, and she said she was experiencing a little nausea. I told her we were on our way to Starbase 12, which would have the necessary facilities to deal with the birth of a child with both human and alien blood, and that I would happily grant her the traditional two-year leave of absence.

"That won't be necessary," she said. "I'll be resigning my commission."

"You don't have to decide that now—"

"It had nothing to do with the pregnancy," she said. "I decided on Pollux IV." She didn't elaborate, and she didn't have to. I'd pushed her too hard. At the time, I didn't think I had a choice; in retrospect, however, once I found out Spock could destroy the temple, I probably didn't need her to spurn Apollo for the mission. Maybe just for myself.

"If you'll excuse me, Captain, I'm very tired," she said, as she turned away from me on the bed.

"Of course," I said. "Let me know if there's anything you need." She wouldn't; I lost touch with her as soon as she left the ship.[*]

✦

During this period, the only personal connections I relied on were with Spock and McCoy. McCoy and I went back far enough that our friendship was like old leather. Spock's friendship was different; because of his devotion to Vulcan principles, it never felt close, and he never required emotional support from me. But I could always count on him to be there. So the one time he was in emotional distress, I knew I had to be there for him.

Spock was the one member of the crew that I never had to worry about losing to romance. He didn't seem the least bit interested in women (despite the many romantic overtures made by the ship's head nurse, Christine Chapel). Which is why the events that transpired involving Spock's wedding came as a complete shock.

It began with Spock throwing a bowl of soup against a wall and heatedly asking for a shore leave to his home planet.

I had no idea what the hell was going on. I soon found out that if I didn't get Spock to Vulcan, he would die.

I learned something that, at that time, few other non-Vulcans knew. Spock was going through the "*Pon farr*," a kind of crazed sexual fever that men on his planet went through every seven years. The Vulcans were barbarians in the ancient past, and though they were among the most civilized races in the Galaxy now, their people had to let their inner barbarian out once in a while to allow them to mate. This mating rage was caused by a biochemical imbalance that, if not heeded, would eventually kill him. It explained a lot, and though in the last 20 years, the Vulcans have become more open about their mating practices, at the time, this was a well-guarded secret.

---

[*]**EDITOR'S NOTE:** Carolyn Palamas did have a child she named Troilus, and in 2271, she became part of an expedition that established a colony on Pollux IV.

So I had to get him to Vulcan, and I violated orders to do it. I wasn't going to let my friend die.

When we arrived, Spock asked me and McCoy to join him on the surface for a ceremony. I'd never been to Vulcan before; the sky was red, the breeze was hot, and the air was thin.

The ceremony was very primitive, held in an ancient outdoor stone arena with a gong in the center. It was astounding to find out how important Spock's family was. The wedding was officiated by T'Pau, who'd been a leader on Vulcan for over a century.

Spock's betrothed was a beautiful woman named T'Pring. The ceremony began; it was, to use Spock's favorite term, "fascinating."

And then everything went to hell. T'Pring referenced an ancient law that allowed her to choose a champion to fight for her. Spock was going to have to engage in a battle to win his bride. And no one, especially me, expected that the champion T'Pring chose would be *me*.

I would find out later that T'Pring had devised a strategy to get out of marrying Spock, as she had her eye on another Vulcan. By choosing me, she all but guaranteed that neither Spock nor her "champion" would want to marry her, thereby leaving her available.

I agreed to fight Spock, but I hadn't read the fine print; the battle was to the death. We were handed *lirpas,* ancient staffs with a blade on one end and a weighted cudgel on the other. Spock, lost in his fevered stupor, was clearly out to kill me, and he knew how to use the weapon. He sliced open my chest, knocked me on the ground. I was able to get a few shots in, but I was losing.

McCoy stepped in, told the Vulcans that the air was too thin for me, and said I needed a shot to help me breathe. He gave it to me, but it didn't feel like it was helping that much. We were given new weapons: *ahn woon,* similar to bolos. Spock had me on the ground right away; his *ahn woon* bands were tightly wrapped around my neck, and Spock wasn't letting up. Everything went black.

"How do you feel?" It was McCoy. He was standing over me in sickbay.

"My throat," I said. And then I remembered Spock choking me with the *ahn woon*. I put it all together. "That shot you gave me—"

"Neural paralyzer," McCoy said. "Very low dosage, so it took a minute to knock you out." I sat up in the bed.

"What about Spock?"

"He'll be beaming up soon," McCoy said. "His fever seemed to have broken. I think he wanted to say goodbye to everybody. So, am I going to get a thank-you?"

I told him it might have been simpler to let me die. He was confused, until I pointed out that it was a "battle to the death," and that we'd just committed fraud on Vulcan's most revered leader. Something that I didn't think the Vulcan government was going to appreciate.

"I have a solution," McCoy said. "Don't tell them."

"Bones, this isn't a joke—"

"I'm not joking," he said. "T'Pau's never going to see you again, and I don't think she's following the comings and goings of Starfleet captains." He made a fair point. It did seem unlikely that T'Pau would ever run into me again. At least at that moment. And there really wasn't anything I could do about it anyway.

Shortly, Spock came back aboard and couldn't control his emotions upon seeing me. He burst out with a big smile and bellowed "Jim!" as he grabbed me. He then immediately went back to his normal controlled self. It was a rare moment of affection that I will always remember.

✦

I watched Matt Decker die.

His murderer was a robot planet killer. It was several miles long, constructed of neutronium, with an anti-proton beam that allowed it to destroy planets and use the debris for fuel. It was an ancient machine from another galaxy, perhaps millions of years old. It had already destroyed three solar systems and was working on the fourth when Matt Decker's ship, the *Constellation*, tried to stop it. The result was a wrecked ship and a dead crew.

We found the *Constellation*, drifting, burnt, and broken. It was like looking at the *Enterprise* in a cracked mirror. Matt was the only one aboard; he had tried to save his crew by beaming them down to a planet, which the planet killer quickly destroyed. He was catatonic, weak, unshaven, on the verge of hysteria. He in no way resembled the confident, hardscrabble shipmaster I'd come to know. He was overcome with his failure. That would lead him to escape and commit suicide by taking a shuttlecraft into the maw of the machine.

His death was not completely in vain. The shuttle's explosion caused minor damage inside the planet killer, which I took advantage of and aimed the wrecked *Constellation* inside the giant construct. Once it entered the machine, I blew its engines up. The planet killer was defeated.

From the bridge of the *Enterprise*, I looked at the dead hulk of neutronium on the viewscreen. And I thought about the first time I'd met Matt Decker; he was with his son. When Matt decided to commit suicide, had he forgotten about him? But perhaps he didn't want to face his child after the disgrace of losing his ship. His son must now be serving on a starship somewhere. It made me think of my son, whom I hadn't spoken to in so many years. I hoped if he knew about me, I had been painted favorably. With that in mind, later that night I recorded my log.

"Captain's log, 4229.7, we have successfully deactivated the planet killer that destroyed the solar systems previously reported. Commodore Matt Decker was in the *Enterprise*'s shuttlecraft *Columbus* making his way back to the *Constellation* to lend me assistance when he was caught in the planet killer's tractor beam. Knowing he couldn't escape, he set his engines to overload. This selfless act provided necessary data on the possible weaknesses of the device that allowed me to use the *Constellation*'s engines in a similar way to deactivate the machine. Recommend highest posthumous honors for Commodore Decker."

It was the truth, with a sprinkling of fiction, for his son.*

---

*EDITOR'S NOTE: I questioned whether to include this, as Captain Kirk is admitting to falsifying records. His response to me: "They want to lock me up for that? Good luck to them." He seemed both determined to be as honest as possible in his account, as well as being confident that Starfleet wouldn't prosecute a hero whose success as an officer was often due to a loose interpretation of the regulations. In any event, the circumstances of the book's publication made the point moot.

✦

Dilithium crystals are a necessary component of warp engines. The unique properties of the crystals allow for precise control of the matter/antimatter reactions that propel starships faster than light. Unfortunately, the crystals don't exist everywhere, so when sensors detected them on the planet Halkan, the Federation dispatched the *Enterprise* to try to make a mining treaty.

The Halkans were a race that had already been to space and decided it wasn't for them. They had a peaceful, thriving society, and they greeted us with friendship. But they weren't interested in letting us mine dilithium on their planet. They had a dogmatic code and would prefer to die as a race than let their dilithium be used in the taking of one life. McCoy, Scotty, Uhura, and I did our best to make the case for the peacefulness of the Federation, but to no avail. And while we were on the planet, an ion storm moved in, engulfing the *Enterprise* as well. Since my ship was getting damaged, and I didn't seem to be getting anywhere with the Halkans, I called a temporary end to negotiations and had my landing party beamed up.

Like a hundred transports I'd been on, I started to see the *Enterprise*'s transporter fade in around me, but then it faded out again. I felt dizzy, and when we finally materialized, everything was different.

The room was darker. Spock and Transporter Chief Kyle gave us a strange salute. Their uniforms were more ornate.

And Spock had a beard.

I instinctively knew that we were in danger. I decided to play things close to my vest. (And I looked down and saw I was actually wearing a vest, a gold one.) I soon discovered that "standard procedure" was to destroy the Halkans if they didn't give us the dilithium crystals. I then watched as Spock *tortured* Lieutenant Kyle for some minor mistake during our beam-up with a small device called an agonizer. This was an insane world, and I had to get some time alone with the landing party to try to figure this out.

I made an excuse, and the four of us went to McCoy's lab for some privacy. I theorized that beaming up in an ion storm had disrupted the transporter circuits, and we were beamed to a parallel universe, transposing with our counterparts in this alternate reality. Another Kirk, McCoy, Scotty, and Uhura were now on our *Enterprise*. And where my mission had been to arrange a mining treaty with the Halkans, I now had to figure out how to save them, while also arranging to get back where we belonged.

We were in for quite an experience. The Chekov in this reality tried to kill me so he could move up in rank. I also discovered that the Captain Kirk on this ship had a "kept woman." She was a lieutenant, but it was clear that her duties on the ship weren't just in the service of Starfleet. (Since the woman's parallel counterpart in our universe is still a member of Starfleet, I have decided not to include her name.) This was a universe of ids, and since I'd previously seen my "id" in the flesh, I knew how to pass as one of them.

The parallel Spock was as clever as our own; he figured out who we were, and eventually helped us to return to our universe. He was also the only person on the ship with an ounce of integrity. I knew that as soon as I left, the Halkans would die. It seemed like such a waste, so I took a shot. I made a plea to Spock to get rid of the "me" in that universe, and save the Halkans, to change his world. As we beamed away, it sounded like he was going to try. I've never gone back, and I never want to, but my hope is that he made a difference.

✦

"I want more of these," Tyree said. He was holding a flintlock rifle. He was enraged, frightening. "Many more!"

I hadn't seen Tyree in thirteen years, and two days before, when I came back to his world on a routine survey, he had seemed the peaceful, friendly man who'd taken such good care of me when we were both much younger. But the Villagers, who'd lived in peace with the Hill People, now had weapons far too advanced for the technology of this world. I had discovered that the Klingons were providing these flintlock rifles to the Villagers in exchange for their obedience and access to the riches of the planet. They wanted to make it part of their empire, and the way they seduced the Villagers into being their slaves was by giving them their own slaves, in this case the Hill People.

Now, standing in a clearing, I was with Tyree as he saw his wife brutally attacked and killed in front of us by a group of Villagers. It changed him.

"I will kill them," he said to me, regarding the men who'd done it.

I couldn't let Tyree's people become slaves, so I'd decided to give them flintlocks as well with the idea that as the Klingons gave the Villagers improved weapons, the Federation would do the same for the Hill People, creating a balance of power. I went back to the ship, and contacted Admiral Nogura at Starfleet Headquarters. He didn't like my plan.

"It doesn't make sense," Nogura said. "For it to work, we'd have to know exactly what improvements the Klingons are giving the Villagers, and exactly when they were giving them." I suggested a Starfleet adviser be permanently posted on the planet to relay that information, to which Nogura laughed. That would be a flagrant violation of the Prime Directive.

"Admiral, if we don't do something, the Hill People will become subservient to the Villagers. And once the Hill People become conquered, there will be one government that will happily join the Klingon Empire. This will follow the letter of the Organian Peace Treaty, and the Klingons will have a planet well inside our borders." I could see this worried Nogura.

"You say you have the proof that the Klingons were providing the weapons? We will present it to the Klingons," Nogura said. "Under the terms of the treaty, they will have no choice but to withdraw." That had been my thinking when I acquired the proof, but now it wasn't what I wanted.

"But sir," I said, "the damage has been done. The Villagers will still have flintlocks."

"The damage was not done by *us*," Nogura said. "In fact, you may have violated the Prime Directive by getting us into this situation."

"The Klingons had already interfered," I said.

"They can't break the Prime Directive because they don't have one," he said, mockingly. "We do, so no matter what they've done, it's no excuse." Nogura felt with the evidence I'd gathered, the Klingons would no longer be providing upgrades and new materials. The cost to the planet would be temporary, and it would eventually find its own path again.

"The only victims will be the Hill People," I said.

Nogura wasn't interested in continuing the conversation, and signed off. Tyree would be on his own; the Villagers would continue to kill his people and take their land. It wouldn't go on forever, but I doubted my friend would survive it. At that moment, the door buzzed. Scotty entered, holding a flintlock rifle. I had forgotten that I'd already asked him to make some for the Hill People. He was very proud of his handiwork. I then had a thought.

"Scotty, did you log that you made them?"

"No sir. I was waiting for you to tell me what they were for."

"Well, it turns out you *didn't* make them," I said, and Scotty smiled. They wouldn't solve the problem that had been created down there, but I wouldn't be completely abandoning my friend either. The Admiralty was wrong, we can't be absolutists where the Prime Directive is concerned and stand by while the Klingons destroy something beautiful. Given what was to come, it would be ironic that the admiral I had this argument with was Nogura.

✦

About a week later, I was telling the whole story of Neural again. I was reminiscing, or more accurately orating, about life aboard the *Republic* and *Farragut* under the command of Stephen Garrovick. I was in my quarters, sharing a bottle of Saurian brandy, my drink of choice, and holding my audience of one in rapt attention; it was Captain Garrovick's son, David, who was now, coincidentally, my chief of security.

Garrovick was 12 years old when his father died, and he seemed hungry for information about his father. I told him everything I could remember, but most of the stories were from my point of view, and I really had not spent that much personal time with Captain Garrovick. Still, there seemed to be some entertainment value, especially the story of how I found out I was going over to the *Farragut*.

"He just waited until he was about to leave and told you to get on board the shuttle?" Garrovick was incredulous. It seemed almost impish to the young man, who thought of his father as serious and responsible.

I came to know the younger Garrovick during one of those freak coincidences that made primitive people believe in a higher power. The *Enterprise* accidentally stumbled on the cloud creature that had killed so many of the *Farragut*'s crew. It went on to kill some of mine, and in doing so, I discovered that Ensign Garrovick, the son of my former captain, was actually aboard my ship. We would eventually destroy the creature together, but not without cost.

Over the years, I'd had nightmares about the cloud creature. In the dream, I'm in phaser control, and I don't hesitate; I fire and the creature is destroyed. It was always a nightmare because I'd wake up to discover it wasn't true. Sometimes in the dream, Captain Garrovick is standing next to me.

I got to live the dream, because a few days earlier I was on the bridge, the creature was approaching the ship, and the image of Garrovick was standing next to me, in the form of his son. Like in the dream, I felt triumphant as I ordered Chekov to fire the phasers.

They did nothing.

And like the nightmare I'd already lived through, the creature came aboard my ship and started killing again. I was able to get it off the ship, and Garrovick and I had destroyed it using an antimatter bomb.

I had invited the young man for a drink. He evoked his father, and we had a far-ranging discussion. I learned that he had joined the academy searching for an identity, hoping to reconnect with his father by imitating his career. When I first met him, I was guilty over the fact that my own hesitancy had cost this son his father. I then learned my hesitancy made no difference; our phasers were useless against the creature, both now and eleven years ago.

It didn't make me feel better. As I talked to this young man, something about our discussion made me feel guilty. I didn't realize why until we finished our conversation and he got up to leave.

"Goodnight, David," I said. I had had a few drinks, but wasn't too drunk to realize he had the same name as my son.

✦

"Most efficient state Earth ever knew," John Gill said.

I was dressed as a Nazi, I was on a planet of Nazis, and I was staring at the Führer.

John Gill, my old academy history professor.

He was in a chair, drugged by a native named Melakon, his deputy Führer, who was now running the planet. Gill had come to Ekos, a world of unsophisticated, crude people as a cultural observer. They had a technology that corresponded with mid-20th-century Earth. Gill had stopped transmitting reports, so we'd been sent to find out what happened to him. Somewhere along the way, Gill had decided to start his own Nazi movement and take over the planet as the Führer. It made no sense.

"Perhaps Gill felt such a state," Spock said, "run benignly, could accomplish its efficiency without sadism." It was hard to take him seriously, since he too was dressed as a Nazi. Also, it didn't explain it.

John Gill was the greatest historian of his generation. He'd studied history his whole life and taught generations of students what he learned. He'd had a great effect on me as a student at the academy. He taught me to look at the causes and motivations of people to determine why history happens, and how to fight those trends that lead to large-scale suffering and conflict. I felt that any of the good I did in Starfleet was due in no small part to the teachings he gave me. I especially remembered my conversation with him about Khan, when he told me I couldn't separate admiration for accomplishments from the morals behind those accomplishments. It was a truth that would soon rear its head in my own life.

But I still didn't understand him, and what he had done on Ekos, and he would not survive to explain himself. After we corrected the damage he caused as best we could, we returned to the *Enterprise* without Gill, who'd been killed. McCoy and I talked at length about why a peaceful man would indulge himself in this way. As usual, McCoy was able to boil it down.

"All those years teaching history," McCoy said. "Maybe he just wanted to go out and make some."

✦

Something began to happen to me toward the end of my first five years on the *Enterprise*. I had many successes, made so many discoveries. I'd stopped wars, sometimes single-handedly; I had a record number of successful first contacts. I'd escaped death on numerous occasions, not just for myself but also for my crew.

I feel now that the problems began when I started to "believe my own press." I got arrogant, confident in the belief there was nothing I couldn't do. I was losing touch with who I was and buying into the prestige that went with being a starship captain. And since there was little else to my life than serving on the *Enterprise*, I began to think I needed more. I wanted promotion. I started taking unnecessary risks to get even more attention from my superiors.

One mission in particular comes to mind. I had received coded orders from Starfleet regarding intelligence on a new Romulan cloaking device. This new upgrade rendered our tracking sensors useless; the previous cloak was invisibility only and allowed Federation ships to detect movement. Now, however, the Romulans had solved that problem. It was a grave threat to our security; the Romulans had tried to start a war a couple of years before, and now, with this new weapon, they would do it again. It was too big an advantage, and we had to nullify it.

My orders were simply "acquire intelligence, specifications, and, if possible, procure a working example." That was it; whoever cut the orders knew that "procure a working example" was basically asking the impossible. At that time, however, I was convinced I could *do* the impossible. I came up with a plan and presented it to Spock, who would be the only crew member I would initially include. I briefed him on the intelligence, and then told him my intention.

"We're going to steal one," I said. I was looking for a reaction, and Spock gave me none.

"Indeed," Spock said. "That will prove difficult."

"I have a couple of ideas," I said. My plan involved both of us getting aboard a Romulan ship. For this to work, I needed to speak fluent Romulan. The shortcut I had in mind for this language course was for Spock to mind-meld with me.

I had had the experience of a mind-meld before with him. It is difficult to describe what it's like. It was a stripping away of all my mental armor. Your thoughts are there for the Vulcan to peruse; Spock picks up my memories and thoughts like they are books on the shelves of a library. You try to protect the secrets, but the Vulcan is in there and pushes you aside. Your most embarrassing memories and thoughts are his; yet his logical demeanor makes you trust him as he reads your intimate desires and fears. I was willing to go through it, however, because it could efficiently teach me a language that Spock already knew.

"How do you propose, Captain," Spock said, "that we then get aboard a Romulan ship?"

This part was far riskier. I was going to spend several weeks as a difficult captain on my own ship, convincing the crew I'd become irrational, someone who was craving success. Ironically, I was playing only a less affable version of the person I was turning into. This glory hound captain would take the *Enterprise* across the Neutral Zone into Romulan space.

"It is likely we will be captured relatively quickly," Spock said.

"Yes," I said, "and when we do, you're going to say it's my fault and defect to your Romulan brothers. And to prove your loyalty, you're going to kill me. Then, after I'm dead, I'm going to disguise myself as a Romulan, beam back aboard the Romulan ship, and steal the device. Then the *Enterprise* will beam us both back, and we'll get away."

Spock raised an eyebrow. *There* was my reaction.

The plan was audacious, dangerous, and in hindsight, ridiculous. And it also happened to work. Upon reflection, the only reason we succeeded was we encountered a Romulan commander who was so blinded by the possibility of capturing a functioning starship, she ignored some pretty obvious warning signs she was being manipulated. In any event, I delivered a new cloaking device to the Admiralty, and, in doing so, prevented another war. And in less than a year, it got me what I thought I wanted.

CHAPTER 8

"NOGURA SAYS THEY'RE GOING TO MAKE ME AN ADMIRAL," I said. I was sitting with McCoy and Spock in my quarters. McCoy had a drink and sat across from me; Spock stood by the door. He carried a data pad, clearly expecting this was a work meeting.

There were about six months left in our five-year mission. I should've had the meeting with Spock alone, but I'd become so used to the three of us together that I broke protocol. Upon hearing the news, they congratulated me, though McCoy said it wasn't really news; there'd been subspace chatter about it for weeks.

"It is, however, a logical choice, Captain," Spock said. "A gratifying recognition of your service and abilities."

"Don't get all mushy on us, Spock," McCoy said.

I brought up the fact that it left open the question of who would replace me. I let the implication hang there for a moment and looked at Spock with a smile.

"Captain Spock," McCoy said. "That's going to take some getting used to."

Spock didn't seem to take the bait, so I explicitly told him that Nogura said the "big chair" was his if he wanted it.

"I am honored by your faith in me," Spock said, "but I must respectfully decline."

I was somewhat taken aback. I wanted Spock to take over; it was a way for me to maintain connection with the ship and the crew. I found myself getting annoyed; this had hurt my feelings. I asked him why. He told me he had decided to resign his commission and return to Vulcan at the end of our tour.

It was really too much for me to take. I asked him to reconsider. He thanked me and said he appreciated it, but that his decision had been made. We hung in the awkward silence for a few moments, and then he excused himself. After he left I turned to McCoy.

"Did you know that was coming?"

"No idea," McCoy said. "But I'm not surprised."

"Why not?" I said. McCoy laughed and took another sip of his drink. He reminded me of how much Spock had changed in the years since we served together.

"Would you have ever thought that stick-in-the-mud we took that shuttle ride with would become your best friend?" I had to laugh at that too. When Spock first began serving with me, he'd been cold, distant, and harsh. As time went on, he seemed more confident revealing his human side; he once said prolonged exposure to humans caused "contamination," which had to be a joke, further proof he was okay with letting his human half peek through. I take some credit for this since I spent a lot of time teasing it out of him. Over time, however, I began to feel his friendship even though he couldn't express it. And though I was his commander, we were equals, partners.

"Friendship was the furthest thing from my mind," I said.

"Well, imagine how *he* feels," McCoy said. "He probably never thought he'd ever have *any* friends. Then scuttlebutt starts that the person he's closest to in the world is leaving him. How does he deal with that pain? The way his forefathers did, with logic."

This was insight that was exceptional, even by McCoy's standards. It never would have occurred to me that Spock would be hurt.

"He'll become the president of logic, if there is such a thing," McCoy said.

I suppose I understood. When I'd received news of the promotion I was ambivalent. I wanted to be an admiral; I wanted to get involved in Starfleet policy on a macro level. But I also didn't want to leave the *Enterprise*.

Two months later, we'd received orders to move our patrol. Starfleet wanted to bring the *Enterprise* to Earth when we were done with our mission, so the Admiralty put us on a leg that brought us closer to the inner systems of the Federation. There had been twelve *Constitution*-class ships in the fleet, and half of them had been lost.* It meant something to the Admiralty to bring the *Enterprise* home intact. The plan, as I understood it, would be for the ship then to undergo a major refit, much larger than it had undergone before. They wanted essentially a new ship, but still make it seem like it was connected to the *Enterprise*; the survival and continuity of this vessel was in Starfleet's view a powerful piece of propaganda.

So we would finish our five years, but maybe in less wild territory and on less hazardous duty. As it happened, our new patrol course put us only a few days away from Vulcan, and Spock came to me with a request.

"I would like to return to Vulcan," he said. "And use my accumulated leave." This was unusual; as far as I could remember, Spock had only asked for a leave once. As a result he had accumulated over four months of leave time. It didn't take me long to figure out what he was doing. The leave period would end just around the time he would be mustering out of the service. When we returned the ship to Earth, there would be wide-ranging ceremonies and baldly emotional goodbyes. He was trying to avoid it all by essentially going on vacation until the end of his term of enlistment.

"You're a complicated person, Spock," I said. I was torn. I wanted Spock at my side when we brought the *Enterprise* home, not only was he my friend; he was objectively responsible for so much of the success of this mission. But I also respected his wishes. I granted his leave. We set course for Vulcan.

When we arrived, McCoy and I waited for Spock in the transporter room. Spock entered, carrying his own duffel. I relieved the technician on duty.

"Well, Spock," McCoy said. "This is it."

"What 'is it,' Doctor?"

"It's goodbye," McCoy said.

"Goodbye," Spock said. McCoy shook his head.

---

*EDITOR'S NOTE: *U.S.S. Constellation, U.S.S. Defiant, U.S.S. Excalibur, U.S.S. Exeter, U.S.S. Intrepid,* and *U.S.S. Valiant.*

"The least you can do is shake my damn hand," McCoy said. He extended his hand and Spock took it. "I'm going to miss you."

"Yes," Spock said.

"You just can't make it easy," McCoy said.

"As I have perceived that you enjoy complaining," Spock said, "that is undoubtedly what you will miss about me." I laughed, and McCoy joined in. Spock turned to me. I took his hand. There was a lot to say. Too much, in fact, so we said nothing.

"Request permission to disembark," Spock said.

"Permission granted," I said. Spock stepped up onto the transporter pad. I moved to the control panel.

"Say hello to T'Pau," McCoy said.

"If you wish, Doctor," Spock said.

"Not for me," I said. "She thinks I'm dead."

And as I energized the transporter, I watched Spock dematerialize. And as he disappeared, I thought I caught the hint of a smile.

✦

About a month later we were on Delta IV. I had never been to the planet before; Starfleet maintained a base there, and the world itself was a curiosity to many of the other species of the Federation. The Deltans, humanoid but all bald, had a "sexually advanced" society, but what that meant hardly anyone knew, since they had strict rules about who they mingled with.

Will Decker, who was stationed there, looked very much the same as I remembered him; lanky and boyish, he was pleasant and friendly. We shared a bottle of Tellarite beer at a bar situated on a cliff, below us, the starbase, three-quarters surrounded by blue mountain foothills and facing a green sea. In the distance, the shiny metal spires of a city on an island (which the Deltans simply called "City Island"). The air was filled with the scent of flowers I didn't recognize but that was nevertheless very soothing.

Will seemed happy that I'd looked him up. We'd only met that one time, now over five years before. Since his father's death about a year ago, I had started to keep tabs on him. He had served on several ships, eventually on the scout ship *Revere*, where he rose to the rank of commander. He then stepped down from the center seat to join a program he had had a hand in devising.

"Emergency transporters for shuttlecraft," he said, after I'd asked what led him to give up his command. "I coauthored the proposal with several engineers I'd gone to the academy with. Delta IV was the natural place to experiment because the Deltans have designed and manufactured small transporters for replicating plants from stored patterns."

"How's it been going?" I said.

"Well, if failure is the mother of innovation," Will said, "then I guess we're innovators." I smiled at his little joke, as he continued. "We're definitely a few decades away from them being standard equipment, but if at some point in the future we can save the life of someone in Dad's situation, it'll be worth it." I nodded, trying to disguise my discomfort at the mention of Matt Decker's death. He was doing work that, if successful, would be an incredible boon for Starfleet and possibly save hundreds of lives.

All inspired by a lie I had recorded in my log. I hoped he'd never find out that Matt Decker would not have used an emergency transporter to beam out of his shuttlecraft, even if he'd had one. I decided to change the conversation to the topic I'd made the trip to discuss.

"You've had a taste of command, don't you miss it?"

"I don't know," Decker said. "I'm a scientist first, an officer second. And I'm pretty happy here." I read something into this and took a gamble.

"What's her name?" I said. In my experience the only thing that competes with commanding a ship is a woman. Decker smiled, and I knew I was right. He told me about a Deltan woman named Ilia who he'd started a relationship with.

"There's a lot of misconceptions about them," Decker said, a little defensively.

"I make no judgments," I said. That was a bit of a lie; I was judging him, but not in the way he thought. He was choosing a settled life, and I had other plans for him. "To get to the point, Will, I need a new first officer, and I think you're the man for the job."

"Um . . . what?" Will said. I could understand his surprise. He didn't know that I'd lost Spock, and that Scotty, who I'd made first officer, didn't enjoy many of the administrative requirements of the job. I had looked at other members of my command crew: Sulu, Chekov, Uhura, all great offi-cers, but I thought there was something missing with all of them. In truth, I now think any of them would've been a terrific choice in their own way, but I wasn't just choosing my first officer for the next four months.

"It's a great opportunity, sir," Decker said, "but you're almost done with your tour. I don't know that I'd want to leave this project just for a few months as your exec."

"I understand. I'm taking the *Enterprise* back to Earth, where it's going to undergo a major refit," I said. "I think it would be good if the next captain spent a little time on her with me."

Decker was momentarily staggered, for good reason. I'd gone from offering him executive officer for a few months to offering him a *Constitution*-class ship for however long he could succeed at the job. Finally, he opened his mouth.

"Why me?"

"It's a special ship," I said. "It needs a captain with a solid background in engineering to supervise the refit. I've looked at your record; I want it to be you." This explanation sounded a little thin, even to me. And I was being a little arrogant; I was going to have to convince the rest of the Admiralty of it, but since I was going to be one of them, I was confident I'd get my way.

"Captain Kirk," Decker said, "I'm floored. It's just so sudden."

"Opportunities like this come along once in a lifetime," I said. "Don't let it pass you by." I finished my beer and got up from the table, which I think startled him even more. I told him I'd be in orbit for two more days. The implication was clear; he had that time to decide whether to take the job. It was a brutal negotiating move, but it worked.

Decker showed up on the *Enterprise* the next day and accepted. He seemed a little discombobulated; I wondered if he had difficulty wrapping up his personal life that quickly. We left orbit, and I have to admit the next few weeks on the *Enterprise* were a little strange. The crew was guarded with the new first officer; I think many of them had hurt feelings that I didn't choose them (although Scotty was relieved to wash his hands of the cleri-cal duties). But Will worked hard to win them over. He was initially nervous and a little taciturn, but we soon developed an easy friendship and he fell into the role quickly. It was McCoy who decided, however, that I wasn't seeing the truth in the relationship.

"Are you going to stay aboard?" I asked while we were having drinks. I was curious what McCoy's plans were.

"I'm going to move on," he said. "I've got a lot of medical experience that I can share with a new generation of doctors. It's time to pass the torch. Besides, I can't take orders from Decker." That caught me off guard. He had given me no clue before then that he didn't think Decker was up to the job. More important, I thought Decker was working out nicely. I asked him what his problem was.

"I don't have a problem with Decker," McCoy said. "I have a problem with how he got the job. You picked him because you felt guilty."

"Guilty? What am I guilty about? I barely knew Decker when I gave him the job."

"You've defined yourself by this job, and now that it's coming to an end and you're going home, you're trying to fill a hole in your life you've been ignoring." We sat there in silence for a while. I didn't want to hear what he was saying, but I couldn't ignore it.

"Go on," I said.

"You picked a man like yourself, who doesn't have a father, who you could mentor, help in his career," McCoy said. "Do I have to spell it out? You don't want a replacement; you want your son."

"I don't know if I agree with you," I said. "But if you're right, what's the harm?"

"The harm is, there's no real relationship there," he said. "Someone could end up being very disappointed." We finished our drink in silence. What McCoy said cut deep, but I didn't let it get in the way of my plans. In hindsight, he of course was completely right; I was using Decker, and though he went on to something truly extraordinary, to this day I'm ashamed of the life I deprived him of because of my actions.

✦

The rest of our tour of duty was routine; with Sulu's and Chekov's help, I was able to time our return to Earth five years to the second after we left.

Admiral Nogura, now commander in chief of Starfleet, came aboard with Federation president Bormenus. In a grand ceremony, the entire crew was given medals, I was promoted to admiral, and Decker promoted to captain. We then had a reception on the shuttle bay hangar deck.

My parents were there, too. Both in their seventies now, they were fit, energetic, and happy to see me. They brought with them Sam's sons, Peter, now fifteen, and his twin brothers, Joshua and Steven, now three. The young boys all seemed awed by what they saw; Peter was friendly to the crew and delighted that they all remembered him. During the reception, I was surprised to find my father talking with Admiral Nogura very casually; I didn't know they'd served together. The three of us chatted for a while, and then Nogura made his excuses and left.

"Heihachiro was Robau's yeoman on the *Kelvin*," Dad said.

"Was he good at it?" I asked. It was hard to picture Nogura getting coffee.

"Depends how you define the job," Dad said. "He was ruthless. Unusual in a yeoman."

I left the party before it began to break up. I realized that I understood why Spock had not wanted to be here; saying goodbye to this crew was too much for me to handle. I think, also, I was sure I would be back in one way or another.

The next day, I put on my new admiral's uniform and reported for duty.

It was in the penthouse of the Archer Building, and I was greeted by a yeoman who showed me to my office. It was along a hallway with several other admirals, all of whom I knew: Cartwright, Harry Morrow, and Bill Smillie, and at the end of the hall was Nogura. He had successfully transferred his department of strategic planning and studies to the Admiralty, and had a group of relatively young admirals to help him make policy.

I reported to Nogura, who gave me my assignment: I was chief of Starfleet Operations. It sounded like a more important title than it was. I was responsible for a lot of the scut work of maintenance and supply the other more senior admirals didn't want to deal with. However, I was still in their ranks and would participate in the daily meetings of the Admiralty to decide on policy and planning. But on that first day there was a lot to catch up on, so I went back to my office to dive in.

I sat at my desk; behind me, the wall was transparent, and I had a view of the Golden Gate Bridge. In the distance, I could see the old prison island of Alcatraz.

I was 36, I was an admiral, and this lovely office would also turn out to be a prison cell.

I'm not sure I fully comprehended the endless but efficient bureaucracy I was a part of before becoming an admiral. Starfleet Command had the herculean task of maintaining its fleet, training its personnel, supplying and protecting the starbases and Earth colonies, monitoring trade between Federation members and nonmembers, law enforcement, emergency medical and disaster assistance, as well as implementing the political policies of the Federation Council. And that was when there wasn't even a war on.

And as a member of the Admiralty, every day was a pile of orders I had to cut so that tasks big and small could be completed across Federation space. On just one day: the starship *Obama* was running behind schedule and over budget at Utopia Planitia, so I had to call of meeting of the yard's officers to try to get them back on schedule; Starbase 10's commander, Commodore Colt, died unexpectedly, so I had to find her replacement; an intelligence report came across my desk that indicated increased activity of Tholian ships along their border with the Gorn, so I ordered a freighter, equipped with the latest surveillance equipment, to move near that area of space to surreptitiously gather more information; and I approved the budget for the building of three new cargo vessels, the *Waldron*, the *Kuhlman*, and the *Aurod*.

And then there was the politics. It seemed all the admirals had their own priorities and pet projects that they lobbied for. Everyone got along, though I sensed there was a subgroup who saw the Klingons as a growing threat. Diplomatic efforts with the Klingons had fallen away in recent years; admirals, especially Cartwright, were pushing for increased expenditures on defenses along the border. It was a two-tiered strategy: it guaranteed a little more security, but it also had the effect of pushing the Klingons to do the same, with the intent of straining their resources to defend the border. The theory was this would weaken them over time; it might also provoke an attack, which Cartwright felt we'd be ready for. This was obviously a continuation of the work Nogura had been pushing in the department of strategic planning and studies, though then it was much more discreet.

I had help in my new job; Uhura became my chief of staff, and I brought on Sulu and Chekov as well. This had the double advantage of keeping them from getting new assignments on other ships so I could put them back on the *Enterprise* when the time came, as well as providing me with a group of officers I was already comfortable with.

Even though I was busy, I found myself looking inward, trying to figure out if this was what I wanted. My last few years on the *Enterprise* had begun to feel empty, and I thought a promotion would be the solution; I found, however, it just left me with more questions about who I was and who I wanted to be. I began this self-examination during one of my first meetings of the Admiralty. I was approached by a colleague, one who I hadn't seen in over 20 years.

"Admiral Mallory," I said.

"Captain," he said. "I just wanted to thank you for that lovely note." This was the man who I'd met as a child when I saved the Tellarite ambassador, and who'd recommended me for entrance to the academy. But now he was a reminder that, though people considered my mission a success, a lot of good people lost their lives because of my decisions. I came to the *Enterprise* having never lost a crewman under my command; soon, I was responsible for eleven deaths on average for every year for my five years. This wasn't even counting Gary, whose death I thought about almost every day. This was what Pike had been talking about all those years ago—it had ripped the guts out of me, and left me now a little hollow. One of these losses was the son of Admiral Mallory, this man who'd changed my life by getting me into the academy.

"It was the least I could do," I said, referring to the note. "He was a fine crewman. And I felt I owed you." I smiled, but he looked confused.

"Have we met before?" Now I was confused. He wasn't that old. I reminded him about the incident with the Tellarite when I was a child. He laughed delightedly at the story.

"That was you?" he said. "I'm sorry I didn't remember, it was so long ago . . ."

"But," I said, "you helped me get into the academy." I then told him the story, that Ruth sent my message asking for his help.

"I'm sorry," he said. "I never got it." Ruth said she had given it to his chief of staff, and I was sure she hadn't lied. The only conclusion was the chief of staff hadn't passed it on, and that I somehow got into the academy on my own merits. It left me a little confused.

✦

"There's a planet called Dimorous, which has been off-limits for a number of years," I said. I had gathered Sulu, Chekov, and Uhura in my office. I had resources at my command, and I decided to make use of them. I showed them my log entries from the *Hotspur*, specifically the details of the attack of those mysterious rodent-like creatures. I then told them to see what they could find out about the Tellarite facilities on the planet. They were an efficient group; they had a report for me later that week. Uhura was convinced that, though the dilithium mining facility belonged to the Tellarites, the other facility did not. Sulu had contacts in the Tellarite embassy, and though they had very detailed records of the dilithium facility, they had no records of the other one.

"If it involved illegal genetic experiments, they might have kept them a secret," I said.

"Yes," Chekov said, "except their records clearly state that the dilithium facility had to be abandoned when they also were attacked by the creatures. If they were keeping the genetic experiments a secret, would they be so open about this fact?" That was a good point. I asked if they found any indication of who the facility belonged to.

"In one entry of the Tellarite manager's record," Uhura said, "he details an accident that led to some of his workers being severely injured. He reports receiving medical aid, but doesn't say from where." They had already personally tracked down the manager, who said he remembered that the aid was provided by the Federation starship *Constellation*. Even back then, it was Matt Decker's ship, and Nogura was his immediate superior.

They had checked the logs, which showed no record of the ship visiting Dimorous during that period, though there were gaps where the ship could have. It was starting to look like a conspiracy. Uhura asked if they should keep investigating, but I told them not to, at least not yet. It felt like a hornet's nest in our own backyard, and I wasn't sure how to proceed. But I thanked them and pointed out that they were fortunate the Tellarite manager they tracked down was so forthcoming. Uhura, Sulu, and Chekov exchanged looks that were simultaneously guilty, pleased, and conspiratorial.

"Well, sir," Chekov said, "I may have not been completely honest about who I worked for." Then he added, "Or what my rank was . . ."

"I think I've heard enough," I said.

✦

I did my work, and the time passed, but I never fully invested in the world of the Admiralty; I spent a disproportionate amount of time focused on the *Enterprise*'s refit. I consulted for a year with Decker and Scotty and all the designers and technicians who were working on the new *Enterprise*. The designs used for the refit were based on technologies and construction techniques of the many new classes of ships that were now flying. Scotty and I would help vet and refine the designs based on our practical experience from our five-year mission. Then it was another 15 months as they oversaw all the engineering work. I had a feeling they thought I was getting in the way. At the time I didn't care; the ship was somehow still mine. A few months before her scheduled launch, I became very hands-on in helping find the new crew.

One of my main focuses was trying to find a science officer. My experience told me that, no matter how brilliant or well trained a human officer was, there was no comparison with a Vulcan. The rigorous education and training they received from the time they were children made them invaluable in that position; it was like having a living computer with you at all times. I had to find one for the *Enterprise*.

My first thought was to go to Spock. Not to offer him the job, but to see if he had any recommendations. Of course, it was all an excuse to talk to him again; I hadn't seen him in over two years, and I missed him. I had

Uhura patch me through to his home on Vulcan. He wasn't there, but his mother took my call.

"Admiral Kirk," Amanda said. "It's a pleasure to see you again." I had met Spock's mother several years before on the *Enterprise*. She was human, and like many human mothers, completely maternal, protective, and loving of her son.

"The pleasure is mine, Amanda," I said. "I was hoping to talk to Spock."

"He's not here. In fact, he hasn't been for over a year," she said. "He's undergoing the *Kolinahr*." Her expression saddened a little. I didn't know what she was referring to.

"What is the *Kolinahr*?"

"It's the discipline where a Vulcan sheds his emotions completely. It is rigorous and unforgiving." I could see now why she was sad. The big misconception about Vulcans was that they didn't have emotions. That wasn't true; they just chose not to listen to them, to instead obey the philosophy of logic. But the emotions were still there, and a human mother like Amanda could still believe her son loved her, even if he couldn't show it. However, this was different.

"So, he will actually have *no* emotions?"

"That's his intention," she said. "He's in seclusion, at the *Kolinahr* temple, where he will stay."

"For how long?"

"Captain, *Kolinahr* is a . . ." Amanda said. She got choked up at the thought, then forced her way through. "He will be there for the rest of his life. Communication with the individual members of the temple is forbidden." It seemed that the practitioners of the *Kolinahr* acted as a kind of logic "think tank," working with each other, providing help to the Vulcan society through only occasional contact.

I thanked her and ended the communication. I now understood. She had lost her son completely. She would never see him again, and neither would I.

✦

"There was a Vulcan in my graduating class at the academy," Chekov said later, while we were going over candidates. "His name is Sonak. He's currently second-in-command of the science vessel *Okuda*." I looked at his record; it was impressive. I then looked at his photo. He even looked a little like Spock.

A week later, the young Vulcan was sitting across from me in my office.

"Do you like serving aboard the *Okuda*?" I said.

"The question, sir," Sonak said, "is irrelevant."

"So serving aboard the *Enterprise* as science officer is something you're interested in?"

"Again, sir, that is irrelevant," Sonak said. "I am interested in serving in Starfleet. Where I should serve is up to you and those in command." I smiled. I think one of the things I like about Vulcans is their lack of fear when addressing superior officers. After he left, I convened my staff and told them to pass him along to Decker with my highest recommendation. It was at this meeting that Uhura asked for special consideration of a "friend of hers" for transporter chief. She showed me the file on the viewscreen.

It was Janice Rand.

I hadn't seen her in four years, and as I looked over her record, she'd accomplished a lot. She'd aged a little, lovely but now a mature woman. I guess enough time had passed that the guilt and discomfort over what had happened had faded. And I wasn't going to be aboard the ship anyway. I told Uhura to make sure Will knew about her.

I also informed them that I wanted them to return to the *Enterprise*. Chekov requested to be put in charge of security; I wasn't completely comfortable with this, as I had hoped to have everyone back in his or her old jobs. (The fact was, this was really Decker's call, and I had no rational explanation for this desire. In a few weeks I would figure out what was behind it.) Chekov had also broken my bad luck streak with navigators, excelling in the position. But I didn't want to hold him back, so I recommended it. Uhura wondered if I didn't want to keep one of them around to help train whoever my new staff would be, but I told her I felt the *Enterprise* wouldn't be the same without them.

"It won't be the same without *you*, sir," she said. I appreciated the compliment, and I realized what was behind all my efforts regarding crewing the ship; I was literally trying to re-create a moment in time, the high point of my career, of my life. But I was re-creating it without me.

As the day approached for the refitted *Enterprise*'s launch, I found myself growing despondent. I'd look out and see the shuttle and trams flying everywhere, and I felt trapped, cheated that I wasn't on my old ship. Finally, three days before she was to begin her shakedown cruise, I decided to take a vacation.

My mother's brother had a farm in Idaho. He'd passed away several years before and left it to Mom. She didn't have any use for it, but hadn't gotten around to selling it either. Caretakers looked after it; my uncle had had a couple of horses and a fair amount of land. I decided this was the perfect chance to take a family vacation. I invited Mom and Dad to join me, and they brought my nephews. I thought a little time with my family might just be what I needed, since my other family was about to leave the Solar System without me.

It was a lovely couple of days and brought back some fond memories of childhood to be out with the boys and my parents. I had the sense right away upon seeing Mom that there was something on her mind, but she wanted to talk about it in private. When Dad had taken the boys off to fish in the creek, Mom stayed to talk to me alone.

"I ran into Carol Marcus," she said.

"Oh?" When I had returned to Earth, I had thought of looking up Carol. Something always prevented me from following through.

"It was at a conference in Bejing," she said. "Did you know she had a son?"

My mother was clever. She either knew or had guessed. I wasn't going to make it easy. I said I had heard she had a child.

"Cute kid," she said. "Reminded me of you when you were little." She wanted me to tell her. But I couldn't. I was a little raw now; the *Enterprise* was leaving without me, and the idea of facing the son I hadn't seen since he was a toddler was too much for me to handle. At first, I thought she understood, since she seemingly changed the subject.

"Are you sorry not to be on board the *Enterprise*?"

"Yes," I said. "I didn't think it would be this hard to let it go."

"Sometimes we think we know what we want, and we ignore other possibilities around us," she said. "I regret the time I missed as your mother . . ."

"I know how hard you tried to make up for it," I said. "But don't you wish you'd had a little more time in Starfleet?" She laughed.

"What I wish is that we'd been more careful," she said. "But I know now a few more years in Starfleet wouldn't have satisfied me. I was a little lost, never really clear on what I wanted to do, who I wanted to be. I blamed your father because I was envious at the clarity of his decision making. I compounded one bad decision with another, and missed some wonderful years with my sons that I'll never get back." She teared up at this; she was thinking of Sam. I took her hand. She smiled and went on.

"There's no rule book on how to be a parent and have a career. Man or woman, you end up sacrificing something. But whatever age your child is, there's always time to fix things."

She was telling me to try. She made me remember that I was a father. David would be ten. I could try now. I could reach out to him. Maybe Carol would be open to that, especially since I wasn't tethered to a ship. I had stability, I was only 38. But what if Carol had moved on? What if she was with someone else? The thoughts flew through my head. Whatever her situation, there was still David, my son. Mom wanted me to see it wasn't too late. I could reach out to them. I would reach out to them.

As I decided that this is what I needed to do, my wrist communicator suddenly signaled.

"Kirk here." It was my new chief of staff on the other end, Morgan Bateson, my first yeoman all those years ago. He informed me there was a Code One Emergency, which signaled a possible invasion or disaster code. He told me he'd already sent a tram to my location. I signed off.

"What is it?" Mom asked.

"I don't know," I said. I saw the white tram in the sky coming toward us. "Please make my apologies to Dad and the boys." I gave her a hug. "And thank you for giving me so much to think about."

Once I was aboard the tram, a yeoman provided me with a clean uniform, and I then watched a recording from the Epsilon IX Station, located near the Neutral Zone with the Klingon Empire. Commander Branch, the station's commander, dictated a report.

On my screen, a luminescent cloud of energy, immense, moving at warp speed through the Galaxy. Since nothing organic could move faster than the speed of light, this meant it was not a natural phenomenon. I watched as the cloud destroyed three Klingon *K'Tinga*-class cruisers and kept on coming. Branch then closed his report.

"The cloud, whatever it is, is on a precise path heading for Earth."

I immediately checked on the availability of starships that could intercept it. Given the speed it was traveling, and the course it was on, only one starship was in interception range. And it had a new captain who'd never dealt with a crisis like this before.

I don't know exactly at what point I decided I had to be the one to take over. I think my certainty might have come from the thoughts I had been having about David. Figuring out how to get back the *Enterprise* was a simpler task than figuring out how to be a father after all these years. Racing off to deal with a threat that had erased three powerful Klingon warships without slowing down was easier for me than facing possible rejection from Carol.

By the time I landed in San Francisco, I was determined to take over command of the *Enterprise* for this mission. I ran into Commander Sonak and was so sure of myself that I told him to report to *me* on the ship. Nogura, however, wasn't going to make that easy.

"Out of the question," he said, sitting at his desk. "I need you here." He raised a good point that if I felt Decker wasn't ready, why did I recommend him so enthusiastically? He also said I'd stacked the ship with the most experienced crew on any starship, many of whom could be captains themselves. The only argument I could make was that, as good as Decker was, I'd be better.

"Admirals don't command starships," Nogura said.

"Then make me a captain," I said.

"You're being ridiculous," Nogura said. "Request denied." Nogura wanted to go through a list of crew positions that hadn't been filled to make sure the ship was as fully staffed as possible before it left, but I wasn't listening. I couldn't let this go. It was too important; couldn't he see that he was putting Earth in danger? I had inflated my own abilities to such a degree that I was under the delusion that I alone could save the situation. I decided to play a card he didn't know I had.

"Admiral," I said, "before we continue, there is another matter I wanted to bring to your attention. It's regarding the planet Dimorous. I've uncovered some disturbing information about it."

Nogura looked at me. A heavy silence followed. He had no idea what I knew, and in fact I didn't really know what I was implying, but from his reaction, it was something dangerous to him and his reputation.

"I see," he said. "Well, whatever it is, can it wait until after the current crisis has passed?"

"I think so, sir," I said. "I can put it on the agenda for the next meeting of the Admiralty Operations Committee." Nogura knew what I was doing. If I were no longer in the Admiralty at the next meeting, it wouldn't be on the agenda.

"Very well." Nogura went on to say he had reconsidered my recommendation regarding command of the *Enterprise*. I'd made a bargain with the devil; whatever Dimourous was really about, it was serious, and I'd just blackmailed not only an admiral, but the man who was probably the biggest supporter of my career. There would be payment for this. But right now, I had the *Enterprise*.

✦

"You're what?" Will said. A second before, he'd been his usual affable self, but his demeanor transformed as soon as I told him I was taking over, and that he would stay on as my first officer.

We were standing in the *Enterprise*'s new engineering section. Crewmen buzzed about, hurrying to get the *Enterprise* ready to leave orbit in 12 hours. I'd found Decker with Scotty working on a problem with the transporter system. I looked at him; he was too young, and it was a mistake putting him in command. He wasn't ready. This was for the best, I thought. I was very convincing, to myself at least.

Will was furious, and I couldn't really blame him. He'd been working for two and a half years as captain of the *Enterprise*, yet had not spent one day in actual command of the ship. All his work had been in rebuilding it, almost from the ground up. And now, hours away from reaping the rewards of his hard work, I was taking it away from him.

"I'm sorry, Will," I said.

"No, Admiral, I don't think you're sorry," he said. "Not one damn bit." He knew me better than I thought. He was right; I wasn't sorry. I was getting exactly what I wanted. I'd given him the impression of being his mentor, that I would look after him. So he dismantled his life to take this job, putting his trust in me, and now I'd betrayed him. Will left, and I got an admonishing look from Scotty.

And then a console blew up.

The transporter system was malfunctioning, right in the middle of a beam-up. Scotty and I ran to the transporter room. Rand was on duty; she was trying to fix the problem, but it was out of her control. The faulty circuit was in engineering. Scotty and I took over the console.

On the transporter pad, two figures started to materialize. And then started to deform. I tried my best to pull them through, but it was too late. The figures on the pad screamed in agony. I recognized one of them; it was Sonak. The images faded from the pad, their screams with them. We would find out shortly that both died as a result.

I then noticed Rand. I hadn't seen her since she'd received her posting on the ship. This was one of her first days on duty, and these were the *first people she tried to beam up.* And they were dead.

"There was nothing you could've done, Rand," I said. "It wasn't your fault." I may not have sounded that comforting, as I was devastated myself. Because I'd been in command for five minutes and already lost two of my crew. The faces of the 55 who'd died when I last commanded this ship started to flood back. Had I done the right thing? Was I really the right man for the job? Doubt crept in.

✦

"That's all we know about it, except that it is 53.4 hours away from Earth."

I stood in front of the crew on the recreation deck, who I'd gathered to show the transmission I had received from Epsilon IX. I knew they needed to see that, despite the destructive power of that cloud, I was still confident. In the middle of my laying out our orders to intercept it, we received another communication from Epsilon IX. I had it relayed to the viewscreen, and the crew watched with me as Commander Branch appeared.

It was not a good idea. Commander Branch did his best to hold it together as the cloud, an advanced energy field, attacked his station. We went to an external view, saw the power field engulf it. Then suddenly the station was gone, and all that remained was the cloud.

I looked at the crew. Whatever confidence I had instilled in them was spent; we were going out to face something that would probably kill us. I tried to redirect their focus on their work.

"Prelaunch countdown will commence in 40 minutes," I said, and then left. I went to my quarters. It was clean and large, much larger than my old quarters on this ship. I changed out of my admiral's uniform and into one of the captain's uniforms hanging in the closet. I looked at myself in the mirror. I felt younger, better. And then again I thought of the two dead crewmen, one of them Commander Sonak, whom I'd just spoken to an hour ago. I tried to push the guilt away as I strode from my quarters and headed for the turbolift.

I walked onto the bridge and sat in the command seat. The bridge was different; darker, not as warm as it used to be. But the chair felt good; I'd missed it.

"Transporter personnel reports the navigator, Lieutenant Ilia, is already aboard and en route to the bridge," Uhura said. This was the last-minute replacement for the navigator who died in the transporter accident. I'd sent word to Nogura to get me someone as soon as possible who could fly this ship, so I assumed this must be the most qualified person available. The name sounded familiar to me, and I suddenly remembered where I'd heard it, as Uhura continued. "She's a Deltan captain."

The turbolift doors opened, and a bald woman stepped onto the bridge.

"Lieutenant Ilia, reporting for duty, sir," she said. She had a heavy Deltan accent. Despite her baldness, or perhaps because of it, she was exquisite.

I welcomed her aboard and saw Will Decker get up from his chair. They exchanged a greeting that immediately told me that this was the Ilia that Decker had left to join me on the *Enterprise*. He'd abandoned a comfortable life with her for the promise of command, which I'd just stolen. I could feel the resentment in both their tones as she realized what had happened.

"Captain Kirk has the utmost confidence in me," Decker said. Earth was in danger; I would have to live with the sarcasm.

✦

"In simpler language, Captain, they drafted me!" McCoy said, as he stepped off the transporter pad. He'd grown a thick beard and seemed even more cantankerous than I'd remembered. But I was thrilled. I'd seen very little of him over the past few years. He'd gone on a one-man medical teaching crusade, sharing his knowledge of "frontier medicine" with any doctors who'd listen. I'd arranged for Nogura to implement his reserve activation clause, forcing him to join me; McCoy quickly picked up on the fact that I didn't share his indignation about being brought back against his will.

I told him I needed him. He stared at me, surprised at the vulnerability I was showing. But I was alone; I'd forced my way back onto the ship, convinced everybody I was the person for the job, and I'd already presided over the death of two crewmen. The ship itself wasn't dependable, had a lot of new, untested equipment, and my first officer hated me. I needed the pieces of the *Enterprise* that I knew I could depend on, like my old crew. And now I needed the emotional support of a friend who I could count on to be honest, to tell me when I was wrong. I threw my hand out, silently begging McCoy to take it; it was a lifeline, not for him, but for me. He took it and smiled.

✦

"Wormhole! Get us back on impulse, full reverse!" I had pushed Scotty and the crew to get the warp engines operational too quickly; as a result, an imbalance had thrown us into an artificially created wormhole. Now we were spinning through a tunnel in the fabric of space, out of control, headed toward an asteroid. There was no way to stop, and at our speed if we hit it, we'd literally disintegrate.

I ordered Chekov to destroy it with phasers, but Decker counter-manded me. We had no time, so I couldn't stop to have an argument with Decker; he had to have his reason for belaying my order. He helped Chekov fire a photon torpedo, which vaporized the asteroid before we hit it. We were soon out of the wormhole, a fair distance from where we started.

I was embarrassed; it was my fault that we'd just gone through that ordeal. On top of that, Decker had made it worse by countermanding my order. I asked to see him in my quarters and found out just how badly I screwed up. Engine power had been cut off when we entered the wormhole, and the phasers with it. If Decker hadn't intervened, the ship would've been destroyed. I suddenly started to doubt the confidence that had gotten me here. Decker left me alone with McCoy, who decided he'd had enough.

"You rammed getting this command down Starfleet's throat. You've used this emergency to get the *Enterprise* back." I was aware of this before, but only when McCoy brought it up did the plan come to the surface of my conscious mind. I intended to keep her. That's why I wanted my old crew in their old jobs; I had always planned on getting her back and keeping her.

I went back to the bridge. I felt disconnected, self-conscious, and scared. I was now fully doubting myself. In the interim, Mr. Chekov had informed me that a warp-drive shuttlecraft had wanted to rendezvous with us, but I was so lost in my own emotional state that I'd forgotten about it.

So I was shocked when, like magic, Spock walked onto the bridge.

He was dressed in black robes and looked as severe as I'd ever seen him. The shuttlecraft had delivered him from Vulcan. He was back, just when I needed him most.

He stated that he'd been monitoring our communications, and thought he could help with the engines. I immediately reinstated him as science officer. I watched as several of his old comrades reached out to him, wel-coming him back, but he gave them nothing. He was different. I was ini-tially touched upon seeing him; now I was confused.

But his help was invaluable; in no time at all, the ship was at warp. I remembered what his mother had told me about the *Kolinahr*; it was a life-long discipline. That meant he broke it to join the *Enterprise* on this mission.

I had Spock join me and McCoy in the officers' lounge to find out what was going on. For a brief moment, it felt like old times, thanks to McCoy.

"Spock, you haven't changed a bit," McCoy said, obviously looking to restart their old relationship. "You're just as warm and sociable as ever." In falling back into old patterns, Spock obliged him.

"Nor have you, Doctor, as your continued predilection for irrelevancy demonstrates."

I pressed Spock on why he was there.

"On Vulcan I began to sense a consciousness from a source more powerful than any I had ever encountered," Spock said. It was remarkable; he had been in telepathic contact with whatever was in that cloud. He would be an amazing resource. But Spock made it clear that he was looking for personal answers, and, for the first time, I wondered if I could trust him to look after the ship's needs over his own.

I was disappointed, maybe a little hurt. Spock hadn't come back to participate in the mission and walk down memory lane with me. He had entered the *Kolinahr* discipline to purge his emotions, yet he broke that discipline to use the *Enterprise* to pursue his own self-centered goals. It was uncharacteristically *human*.

Despite my disappointment, I couldn't blame him. I was doing the same thing.

We were able to intercept the cloud a full day before it reached the Solar System. It filled the viewscreen; its deep blue plumes of energy were arresting, incomprehensible in size and power. Spock theorized that there was an object in the heart of it generating the field, so I ordered a course to take us inside. Decker objected, but I dismissed him out of hand. I had something to prove, that I could take on whatever was in that cloud and stop it. It was rash and bold decision making, which I felt were what I brought to the table as a captain.

We soon found a spaceship in the heart of the cloud, more massive than anything any of us had ever seen. It launched a probe that entered the bridge, a column of plasma energy. It attacked Ilia. She screamed, then disappeared. And then the probe was gone.

I could feel Decker's anger, but I couldn't meet his gaze. I'd just lost another crewman, and still knew nothing about how to stop this thing that was undoubtedly on its way to destroy Earth. My "rash and bold" decision making was causing deaths. I was failing, and for the first time I wondered if the mission would've gone better if I'd just left it to Decker.

✦

"Jim . . . I should have known."

Spock was lying on a diagnostic bed in sickbay. Something calling itself "V'Ger" was on the ship, and it had literally swallowed the *Enterprise* whole. Spock, against my orders, had left the ship and tried to make contact with this "V'Ger." He had mind-melded with something, and it had caused him neurological trauma. He was different, but not as cold as he had been when he returned to me.

"I saw V'Ger's home planet, a planet populated by living machines. Unbelievable technology. V'Ger has knowledge that spans this universe. And yet, with all this pure logic . . . V'Ger is barren, cold, no mystery, no beauty. I should have known." He then closed his eyes. I had no idea what the hell he was talking about. The mysterious spaceship had reached Earth, and I was no further along in stopping it than when we first encountered it. I shook Spock.

"Known? Known what? Spock, what should you have known?!" I was desperate, so lost. I'd been going through the motions of being a captain, but I'd done nothing to get us closer to completing the mission.

Spock opened his eyes and took my hand.

"This simple feeling," Spock said, "is beyond V'Ger's comprehension." And Spock smiled. Looking back, this was a pivotal moment in my friend's life. From this point on, he was no longer hiding his emotions; he found a way to integrate them into his life and character. He would later tell me that V'Ger showed him the *Kolinahr* was in itself illogical; knowledge of one's emotions provided answers.

But the more important moment for me was when he took my hand. I had my friend, my partner. I was no closer to finding the truth of how to get out of this situation, but with Spock returned to the fold, I had no doubts anymore. We'd beat this thing.

✦

"As much as you wanted the *Enterprise*, I want this!"

We were in the center of the strange ship, a concave amphitheater, pulsating with light and sound. The most advanced technological construction I had ever seen; a literal living machine. And in control of all of it, a 20th-century space probe called *Voyager*.

We had solved the puzzle. V'Ger was *Voyager*. This ancient NASA probe had disappeared into a wormhole and ended up on the other side of the Galaxy, where a planet of living machines had built an advanced ship for it to carry out its primitive programming to "learn all that is learnable." It then traveled the universe, amassing so much knowledge, the machine achieved consciousness itself. It had come back to Earth to find the "god" who created it, and join with it.

Decker was going to give it its wish. Branches of energy reached out to him from the floor, transforming him. I stared at this young man, whose life I'd changed. I'd taken him away from the woman he loved; I'd given him a ship then appropriated it out from under him, all for my own selfish reasons.

And I watched as he left our reality.

Decker was totally engulfed in energy; he was gone, and the energy started to spread, to engulf the entire spaceship. I was captivated, but Spock and McCoy pulled me away. We ran back to the *Enterprise*, as a torrent of light consumed the giant ship around us. In an explosion of energy, V'Ger's ship and the threat to Earth were gone, leaving only the *Enterprise*.

Back on the bridge, I looked around; the room was different, but the people were the same. I thought about Decker, who now existed on a higher plane; the knowledge of the universe was his. Despite what I'd done to him, he had gained something wonderful. And I had too. I had my ship back.

And of course the cliché is right: you can't go home again.

CHAPTER 9

"I DON'T THINK THEY'RE INTERESTED IN US, JIM," McCoy said.

Spock, McCoy, and I were in environment suits, standing at the edge of a pink and green "ocean," though it wasn't strictly water, more of an ooze of chemicals natural to this planet. Staring up at us from the ooze were three natives. They were all about three feet long, with blue skin that was like a flexible shell, no eyes that I could detect, and claws that resembled lobsters'. The liquid they were swimming in was abnormally hot, something on the order of 150 degrees centigrade. We all stood there, with the creatures vaguely clicking their claws. It was an unusual first contact.

We were about a year into my second five-year mission. Nogura, after my little bit of blackmail, had been in no rush to have me back in the Admiralty, and so, after some cursory congratulations for stopping V'Ger and saving the planet, he sent us out again. Once the technical issues of the refitted *Enterprise* were worked out, it became a very smooth-running ship. There were obvious advantages to having so much of my old crew back, as they could train the new crew in what I deemed priorities. We did a lot of what we'd always been good at: carried diplomats, resolved conflicts, and made first contacts.

We were on a routine mapping expedition when we detected something unexpected.

"The planet closest to the sun," Spock said, "has artificial satellites." The planet was not a Class-M world; it was much hotter than any celestial body we'd found life on before. But the artificial satellites indicated an advanced civilization.

"The planet has no cities on the surface. Its oceans are not water; they seem to be a swirling mixture of elements in a liquid state," Spock said. "I'm detecting abundant life-form readings beneath the surface." Though Starfleet didn't approve of a captain and a first officer being in a landing party, I was always nostalgic for the way we had done things during my first tour on the *Enterprise*. So I almost always went, and almost always took Spock and McCoy with me. As I stood face-to-face with some of the natives, however, I wasn't sure I was the best person for the job.

"These are the creatures I detected, Captain," Spock said. "There's over seven billion living in these oceans." Most of my first contacts were with humanoids. This usually made communication a little easier. In this case, these life-forms were unlike any I'd encountered, and I probably should've brought an expert in astrobiology. But at this stage I was still trying to recapture old glory, so I walked over to talk to them.

"I'm Captain James Kirk, of the *Starship Enterprise*," I said. "Representing the United Federation of Planets." The creatures continued to click their claws.

"I feel like this used to be easier," McCoy said, reading my mind. I was hoping the universal translator would work as it usually did, but we got no response. At least not initially. So Spock started to make adjustments on the translator in our communicators. It wasn't necessary.

"We understood you." The voice came out of our communicators. It was the creatures. "You have not observed the proper protocol." I couldn't tell which creature was speaking, so I decided it was the one whose claws had been clicking the most. I addressed it and asked what the proper protocol was.

"It violates *Legaran* protocol to ask," the creature said. Then, without another word, they all slipped under the ooze and were gone. *Legaran.* That must be the name they call themselves, or at least what the universal translator heard them call themselves.

I now was more determined to make contact with these creatures; they were clearly an advanced society. Spock pointed out that, with no knowledge of their customs, there was no clear way to proceed. But I didn't want to give up so easily. This was a fascinating discovery; I thought it was worth another shot.

"Let's go to them," I said, then called the *Enterprise* and asked for the new aqua shuttle. Scotty had successfully renovated one of our shuttlecraft to be able to effectively operate as a submarine. Sulu piloted the craft down to the surface; the three of us got on board and removed our environment suits.

"The natives may not react well to us invading their living environment," Spock said.

"I agree with Spock," McCoy said. "Let's get out of here."

"What happened to the hearty explorers I used to know?" I said.

"You're thinking of someone else," McCoy said. But we were going to go ahead. I told Sulu to first land on the ooze. The craft bobbed on the surface while Spock took readings. He served as navigator as Sulu piloted, we submerged, and they set a course toward the center of the population. As we moved deeper, I saw what appeared to be lights in the distance.

"Phosphorescence?" I said to Spock. He checked his scanner.

"No sir," he said, "electricity."

As we got closer, we saw the blue creatures moving in and out of openings in what at first appeared to be underwater caves in a cliffside. Upon further inspection, we saw that this "cliff" was in fact an artificial structure, one among many. It was a city, and it went on for miles. Thousands of the creatures swam about, engaged in various activities.

"Spock, are you picking up any transmissions?" I said. "We need to try to talk to them again."

"We can hear you," a voice said over our communication speaker. I turned to Spock.

"Were we transmitting?" Spock shook his head no. They could hear us; I wasn't sure how. I decided to take advantage of it. I told them we came in peace, and the voice responded and said they knew that, but that we had not observed protocol. This was frustrating, and I was single-minded about opening a dialogue. But it wasn't in the cards.

Sulu reported that several dozen of the creatures were closing in on the aqua shuttle.

"Take us out of here, Mr. Sulu . . ." But before Sulu could execute my order, the shuttle was suddenly jolted. Spock reported that about 40 of the creatures had latched on to our craft, pulling us down.

We were at a depth of 1,000 meters, and the shuttle could withstand 4,000. But that was in water. The liquid on this planet was a lot more dense. If these creatures brought us too deep, we'd be crushed. I spoke to the voice.

"If you just let us go, we will leave you alone," I said.

"You will leave us alone," the voice said.

"Depth now 2,000 meters," Sulu said.

"Killing us won't solve anything," I said. "And I don't want to have to hurt you by increasing my engine thrust."

"Depth now 2,500 meters," Sulu said, then checked the air pressure gauge. "Outer pressure 500 GSC and climbing." My eardrums started to hurt; the pressure was building. I went to the communications panel.

"Kirk to *Enterprise*," I said. All I got was static in response.

"I think we've been nice enough," McCoy said. I agreed. This trip had gone bad very quickly. Sulu tried to activate the engines, but they didn't work. The shuttle was going down, with no way to stop it. Just then, Spock detected tachyon emissions underneath us.[*]

On the viewscreen, directly below us, appeared some kind of pentagonal hole in the seafloor. There was a silvery glow in the center. The creatures were bringing us directly toward it.

"They're letting go of the shuttle," Spock said. "But it is too late . . ." Our momentum downward carried us into the hole. The shuttle shook violently, and then suddenly was still. The air pressure was back to normal. Sulu reported that outside pressure was now at zero, but we still had no engine power.

"Jim, look . . ." McCoy said.

Out of the view port, outer space and the *Enterprise* in orbit. The pentagonal hole was some kind of portal. The Legarans had sent us back to our ship, and Scotty tractored us on board. I suppose making contact with the

---

[*] **EDITOR'S NOTE:** Tachyons are particles that move faster than light.

Legarans was historic, and though I'd managed to do absolutely nothing, I take some pride in the fact that to this day, despite years of efforts, no Federation diplomat has managed to get in a room with them. But it was also the first sign that the Galaxy might be different, and not as easy for me as it used to be.

✦

"Sir, I'm picking up a group of strange readings," Chekov said from his security station. "Some kind of subspace displacement."

"Location?" I said.

"I can't pinpoint it," he said. "But it's definitely on the other side of the Klingon Neutral Zone." I got up out of my chair and went over to Spock at the science station. He wasn't detecting any ships, and I wondered whether the displacement was caused by cloaking devices.

"If so," Spock said, "in order for us to read the subspace displacement, it would have to be a large number of ships." Up to this point, the Klingons, as far as we knew, didn't use cloaking devices. But several years earlier, they had either shared or sold their ships and ship design to the Romulans. It made sense that, in trade, they had acquired the Romulans' cloaking technology.

I ordered Sulu to execute a course near where the readings were, but staying on our side of the zone. We hadn't had any specific trouble from the Klingons in a while, but if they had use of cloaking technology, they would have a tactical advantage, and they might decide to violate the treaty.

We reached the closest coordinates to the reading we could without crossing the Neutral Zone, and could detect that the displacements were following a straight course moving along the border but not crossing it. I ordered a parallel course at the same speed. If the ships were cloaked, I wanted them to know that we knew they were there. I had to admit the possibility of engaging the Klingons excited me. It was dangerous, but I was confident in my ability to deal with them.

After a few tense hours tracking the course of the displacements, Uhura turned to me. We were being hailed, but from an unknown source. I turned to Spock.

"I think we got their attention," I said. "Put them on, Uhura."

On the viewscreen, the stars were replaced by Kor. He was on the bridge of his ship. I hadn't seen him since our encounter on Organia. He looked somewhat older, had put on a little weight. His hair was longer and thicker, as the Klingons were now wearing it, and was mostly gray. He still looked dangerous, intimidating; he gave me his greasiest smile.

"Captain Kirk," he said.

"Commander Kor," I said.

"Oh, I wouldn't expect you to know this," he said, "but I'm a general now." He looked me over carefully, then gave me a look of insincere sympathy. "Sorry to see your superiors don't value you to the same degree."

I smiled and decided not to give in to this by explaining I'd already been an admiral. Instead I inquired about where he was calling from and told him that we weren't detecting a ship in the area. He said that it wasn't important where he was, then made an unusual pledge.

"Captain," he said, "you have my word of honor as a Klingon warrior that, wherever I am, it does not concern you or the Federation. I would encourage you to move away from the Neutral Zone, however, as it may provoke a reaction you do not intend." I looked at him. He was trying to tell me something. I signaled Uhura to cut off the transmission, and turned to Spock.

"Duplicity is not outside the Klingon code of behavior," he said. "But I do not think he's involved in an action against the Federation."

"I agree, sir," Sulu said. "He wouldn't have given himself away."

I decided that *we* might be giving him away. He was worried that, by tracking his course, we were calling attention to his position to whoever his intended target was. I had Spock plot a possible destination based on the course information we already had.

"It would seem, Captain," Spock said, "that they are headed for Romulus."

Were the Klingons starting a war with the Romulans? Is that what we'd stumbled onto? A surprise attack? It would make sense. The Organian Peace Treaty had tied the Klingons' hands as far as the Federation was concerned, and the policy of containment by Starfleet had worked. The Klingons needed resources, and the Romulans had a lot of valuable worlds.

I reopened communications and told Kor we were leaving the area. I then told Uhura to get Admiral Nogura on the line, and went to my quarters to talk to him in private.

✦

"We had intelligence that the Klingons were building new ships," Nogura said on the viewscreen. "This, however, is a complete surprise."

"Do you think this is a result of them straining their resources to keep up with our defenses on the border?" I said.

"Who knows?" he said. "And who cares? This doesn't concern us." I felt, however, that it did. I suggested that there was an opportunity here. The Klingons wouldn't reach Romulus for another 24 hours. They were about to engage in a war that could cost millions, or even billions, of lives. It seemed like this gave us leverage with both parties. But Nogura wasn't interested.

"It's a moot point," he said. "The Prime Directive says we can't interfere with the internal politics of another government." I could see from his expression that he was using this as a dodge, hiding behind principles to serve a less than noble end. I could also see he had no patience for my suggestions. The relationship between us had become very strained; what I'd done to get the *Enterprise* back had created a serious rift. But I still tried to do my job and pushed a little harder, suggesting he take it to the Federation Council, who might have success if they pursued a quiet and careful diplomacy that would serve the entire quadrant.

"I think what would serve the quadrant," he said, "is if they wiped each other out. The matter is closed. Nogura out." This was worrisome; Nogura had always had hawkish instincts, but sitting by and letting our enemies kill each other indicated a cold-bloodedness that I didn't expect. I had no love for the Klingons or the Romulans, but war didn't serve anyone. Yet there was nothing I could do about it.

I went about my work, and a few days later on the bridge, Uhura said she was receiving battle transmissions.

"They're Romulan, sir," she said. "Romulus is under attack."

Everyone on the bridge looked at me. My orders were clear; we couldn't interfere. And I didn't know what I would even do if we could. I could see, though, the crew expected me to do something.

"Very well," I said. "Inform Starfleet Command, and continue to monitor those frequencies. We'll continue on course to Starbase 10." I sat in my chair. There was a war going on, and we weren't invited. It was good news that the Federation wasn't involved, but it also gave me a sense of helplessness. I convinced myself I was angry that Starfleet was no longer the instrument of peace and civilization I believed it to be. In fact, upon reflection, I was craving action, but the Galaxy had changed. I wasn't sure I belonged out there anymore.

✦

"Mr. Chekov would like a transfer," Spock said. It was during our morning meeting.

"What? Why?"

"There is an opening on the *U.S.S. Reliant* that he would like to pursue."

I'd had Chekov as a member of the *Enterprise* crew for now almost ten years. He'd grown from an eager, hardworking navigator to a very capable head of security and weapons control. He'd received his promotions through the ranks from ensign to lieutenant commander at a little better than the average pace, so I couldn't begin to understand why he'd want to leave. Spock called for him, and he quickly arrived. The position he was seeking on *Reliant* was first officer, definitely a step up. I couldn't match it, but still wanted to make a pitch for him to stay. Maybe we could give him more responsibilities, different duties. But Chekov smiled and cut me off.

"Sir," he said, "please don't misunderstand me. I have cherished my time serving with you, but I feel that my career is standing still. I'm not embarrassed to admit to some ambition, and I think I am being honest when I say I will never be captain of this ship, or even first officer. There are too many people ahead of me." I was about to jump in and disagree with him, when I noticed Spock and the acknowledgment in his expression. And I had to accept the truth of what Chekov was saying.

For an ambitious officer, the *Enterprise* was a dead end job. I wasn't going anywhere, and as long as I was here, Spock was staying, Scotty wasn't leaving, and Sulu and Uhura were more senior than Chekov.

"Fair enough, Mr. Chekov," I said. "I'll approve the transfer."

It started me thinking about what I was accomplishing on the *Enterprise*. There were a lot of people aboard who were qualified to command. And I was keeping them all here, all to keep myself comfortable.

It turned out Chekov got off the *Enterprise* just in time.

✦

We finished our second five-year mission with a lot less fanfare than the first. On our way back to Earth, I did what I could for the crew. I felt both Spock and Sulu should make the captains' list and get ships of their own. I put Uhura and McCoy in for promotions and told them both that they were free to leave if they wanted to. I didn't quite know what was next for me, but I planned on staying with the *Enterprise*.

When we reached Earth, I was called into Nogura's office. Cartwright and Morrow were there. It might've been a friendly reunion, but Nogura got right to business.

"I'm giving Spock the *Enterprise*," he said. I could see the other two admirals avoiding eye contact with me. I wasn't sure what that meant.

"Sir, I'd still like to stay in command," I said.

"We need you here," Nogura said. "I'm making you fleet captain. Congratulations." Fleet captain. I remembered when they gave that rank to Pike, he said it was a desk job, one without influence. Nogura was mocking me and wasn't trying to hide it.

He was done with me; I'd played his game and lost. He'd used my five-year mission to keep me out of the way while he undoubtedly scrubbed any evidence of wrongdoing involving the incident on Dimorous. Now, he was sticking me at a desk, where I would stay for the remainder of my career, influencing nothing. I only saw one way out.

✦

"You resigned? You let him win?" I wasn't sure I'd ever seen McCoy this angry.

"Bones, I'd already lost," I said. We were at an outdoor cafe in the Embarcadero. Nogura, I found out, wasn't just putting me out to pasture; he wasn't accepting the transfers of any officers off the *Enterprise*. They would all have to stay there, or resign their commissions. He'd made Spock captain, which was the only way he could justify taking the ship away from me. Scotty's, Sulu's, and Uhura's careers would advance no further, at least as long as Nogura was in charge. He understood revenge; it pained me to admit that my political posturing had cost not just me but the people closest to me.

McCoy asked me what I was going to do. I was 43, there was plenty I could still do. I was going to start by taking over my uncle's farm. He scoffed at the prospect.

"You're not going to be happy on a farm."

"What are you talking about? I grew up on a farm, remember?"

"No you didn't," he said. "You grew up in outer space. I was there." I laughed, but it was a little joyless.

✦

I moved to the farm and life quickly got quiet. My parents visited a lot, with Sam's youngest sons, who were now rambunctious nine-year-olds. Peter had gone off to the academy, now the fourth generation in our family to make it. I spent a lot of time working in the fields like I did as a boy, then rode horses for recreation. I supposed I'd earned a vacation, and I took it.

But I was a little lost. I'd been in Starfleet since I was 17; I had not experienced adult life without the organization determining how I was going to spend every day.

I got restless on the farm pretty quickly and decided to travel. I acquired a shuttlecraft and took an extended tour of the Solar System, visiting sites I had never seen. But several months later I found myself in an environment suit exploring an impact crater on Jupiter's moon Ganymede, and all I could think was how bored I was. This wasn't exploration; it was tourism and couldn't match the excitement of discovering new worlds. So I went home.

I thought a lot about Carol and David, and made a small effort to track them down. Unfortunately, I couldn't find them; Carol was involved with some kind of confidential project, and my contacts couldn't (or wouldn't) tell me where she was.

I eventually found a rhythm. I did farm work, some teaching at the academy, and a little consulting to the ship builders on Utopia Planitia. Before I knew it, four years had passed. I knew I would need to find some kind of replacement for the discipline of the service, or I would slip into old age very quickly. One day while on a horseback ride, I inadvertently found it.

I saw another rider up on a hill. It was a woman. I rode up to her.

"I'm sorry," she said. "I'm a little lost. I hope I'm not trespassing." She was striking, tall and thin, with long brown hair and dark brown eyes to go with an olive complexion. She was also a fair amount younger than me.

"We like to share," I said. "I'm Jim Kirk."

"Antonia Slavotori," she said. She asked me to show her the way out of there. I asked if she'd mind joining me for lunch first. She smiled.

"I've already eaten," she said. "If you could just give me directions." She was shutting me down. I told her I would happily lead her out. I rode with her for a while.

She wasn't from Idaho, she was only visiting, buying a horse from one of my neighbors, who'd let her take it out for a ride. She lived somewhere in California, but withheld details of exactly where. As we rode together, I realized she had no idea who I was; that was unusual, as my exploits had gained me some notoriety. I somehow found this compelling, and I stayed with her far longer than I had to. When we reached the farm where she'd picked up the horse, I asked if I could see her again. Again, she smiled.

"Probably not," she said, and then rode off.

However, I was not deterred. She'd given me her name, and finding out more about her gave me a goal, albeit a short-term and lighthearted one. I took her as kind of a mission, and I decided to try to see her again. If she rejected me again, I would move on.

Her name was somewhat unusual, and the fact that she mentioned California made her easy to track down. I thought showing up at her home would be somewhat unnerving, but I saw that a designer with her name had a studio in somewhere called Lone Pine. About two weeks after I met her, I took a trip.

I beamed into the sleepy little town at the base of Mt. Whitney, beautiful, as even in April snow covered the nearby peaks. I found Antonia's studio attached to an ancient building called the Old Lone Pine Hotel. It was spartan and clean, with modern furniture that had a rustic touch. She sat at a drafting computer in the back, and when I walked in she looked up. It took her a minute to place me, and then she was incredulous.

"What the hell are you doing here?"

"I was interested in buying some furniture." She laughed. I asked her to show me her work. It wasn't really my area of expertise, but her designs intrigued me, and I was fascinated hearing her talk about her techniques and influences. After a while, I asked if she would finally join me for lunch.

"Look, Jim, I'm flattered," she said. "But I don't want to mislead you. I'm with someone." I felt like an idiot; for some reason, that had never occurred to me. I realized I'd given it everything I had, and decided to leave, but this time she stopped me. She invited me to join her and her boyfriend at their house for lunch. At this point, I figured why not.

She contacted her beau to let him know she was bringing company, then drove me up to a large cabin set up on the mountain. Set against the hillside, surrounded by trees, it was a lovely, peaceful setting. Her boyfriend met us at the door, with no shirt, holding the leash of a handsome Great Dane. I think he meant to present a picture that would mark his territory and intimidate me, but it really didn't work. I introduced myself, and once I said my name, his entire demeanor changed.

"Wait a second," he said. "You're Captain James Kirk!" This came as a surprise to both Antonia and me. Whatever slightly threatening persona he'd tried to affect was now history. He turned to her and sounded like a screeching teenager. "You didn't tell me you knew him!"

"I *don't* know him!" she said. But he wasn't interested in talking to her anymore.

"I'm sorry, I didn't introduce myself, Captain. Lieutenant Commander J. T. Esteban."

Esteban hurriedly ushered me in, leaving a bemused Antonia in his wake. I turned, and she and I shared a quiet laugh at the absurdity of it.

Three months later, Esteban had gotten a plum posting, so I bought his house. He also gave me the dog, whose name was Butler. Antonia, however, immediately moved out.

Four months after that, she moved back in.

She wasn't like the women I'd become involved with over the years. The "swagger" I tended to employ with other women didn't seem to interest her, and it took a long time before she would agree to see me romantically. She was 34 and had never gone into space; she paid no attention to Starfleet, and didn't seem interested in it. The only thing she found appealing about other worlds was the food that got exported to Earth. There was something about the relationship that reminded me of the one I had with Edith: I wasn't a starship captain to Antonia, I was just Jim.

We stayed in Lone Pine for almost two years together. I had lost touch with almost everyone at Starfleet, though Bones made a consistent effort to call. I thought I might marry Antonia; I didn't know whether I was truly in love with her the way I was with Edith or Carol, but I was very comfortable. Pursuing a romantic relationship over everything else was a new experience for me, and it gave my life the purpose it was lacking.

On a day in July, while Antonia was out at her studio, I was about to walk Butler, when I was surprised to see Harry Morrow walking up the path. He was wearing civilian clothes.

"Harry," I said. "I don't remember the last time I saw you out of uniform."

"I didn't want to draw attention," he said. "Admirals tend to attract junior officers." He was friendly but had a grave air about him. I took him back to the house and poured us some coffee while we engaged in a little small talk. Finally, he got to the point.

"Nogura is gone," Morrow said. "Resigned." I felt an unabashed pleasure at this news; Nogura had fouled my memories of serving in Starfleet. I asked what happened.

"Before the Organians forced peace on us," Morrow said, "Nogura was making contingency plans for an invasion of Klingon space." When I discovered the truth about the genetically engineered creatures on Dimorous, I thought it involved a possible invasion tactic. But I had also assumed that he'd gotten rid of all the evidence. Morrow confirmed that he had, but he made the mistake of trying to do it again. He'd moved a lot of Starfleet resources to the border with the Klingons, with the expressed purpose of pursuing his containment strategy, forcing them to spend and build to defend the border. But then Nogura started drawing up plans for an incursion.

"I took it over his head to the Federation Council," Morrow said. "They forced him to resign. I'm the new Starfleet commander."

"Congratulations," I said, but I wasn't sure it was good news for Morrow. Nogura had a lot of allies in the Admiralty: Cartwright, Smillie. I wondered how they felt about this. And I still didn't know what he was doing here.

"I didn't like what he did to you, Jim," Morrow said. "You're one of the best officers in the fleet, if not the best. We need you back."

The sad thing is, the minute I saw him on the path, this is what I was hoping he'd say.

✦

"Did you really think making me eggs was going to 'soften the blow'?" She was sitting in bed in an undershirt, her hair up, the breakfast tray in front of her. I'd made Ktarian eggs, her favorite, and brought it up to her. Then I told her I was going back to Starfleet.

"I guess that was kind of stupid," I said.

"I'm kind of relieved," she said. "I thought you were going to propose."

"You didn't want to marry me?" I was stunned.

"You're insulted I'd turn down a proposal you had no intention of making?"

"Well . . . yeah." We laughed. She often reminded me how "screwed up" I was where women were concerned, and this seemed more confirmation. I told her I was sorry to lose her.

"I'm not sure you ever had me," she said. "You're always a bit in outer space." She kissed me, then offered to share her eggs.

✦

Antonia moved into her studio; I left the house and got an apartment near Starfleet Headquarters. Morrow reinstated me as an admiral; I got a new uniform and began assembling my staff. Angela Martine, now a commander, became my chief of staff. Garrovick and Reilly also joined me; though they weren't friends necessarily, I felt at ease having old crew around who understood me.

Most of the people I thought of as friends were on the *Enterprise*, but it was off on a mission, so I threw myself into my work. The politics of the Admiralty were still just as uncomfortable to me, and I found myself going home to an empty apartment at night. The hollow feeling started to return. I began to examine my decision. Had it been too rash? Morrow had asked me to come back, and I'd thrown a happy life away with a beautiful woman for what?

One morning in my office, Martine gave me a tape. It was a project that needed a starship assigned to it for extended duty. I put the tape in the viewer. It was top secret, so I told Martine to leave. The computer scanned my retina as a security precaution, and as the recording began, I literally gasped.

"Project Genesis. A proposal to the Federation," Carol Marcus said. I hadn't seen her in over 20 years. I couldn't even listen to what she was saying, I was so lost in a reverie of memories. She was still so beautiful.

David. What had happened to David? I wanted to talk to her, to call her. She ended the proposal with "Thank you for your attention." And a little smile. I watched it three times just to see the smile.

I was overcome with a feeling of loss. There she was, everything I could've had. I caught my reflection in my glass desktop. For the first time I saw the lines on my face. I was old and alone.

CHAPTER 10

"WELL, MR. SAAVIK, ARE YOU GOING TO STAY WITH THE SINKING SHIP?"

Spock's trainee crew had made a mess of the Starfleet Academy simulator, which was not at all unusual. As I walked through the replica of the bridge, I remembered doing the same thing 30 years before. I still thought the *Kobayashi Maru* test was a load of crap, but, like every officer before me, I took perverse pleasure watching young cadets struggle with it.

The young officer Saavik was Vulcan but had more obvious emotional responses than I was used to seeing in her species. She didn't maintain her composure as confidently. And she complained that the test wasn't fair. She fell right into the trap I'd fallen into. I went on to tell her that a no-win situation was a possibility every commander might face, which is exactly what Commandant Barnett said to me when I put up a fuss. I actually imitated his condescending arrogance. I then strode out of the simulator, not quite sure what I had accomplished, except perhaps continuing a tradition I didn't believe in.

About ten months before, when the *Enterprise* had returned from its five-year mission, this time with Spock as captain, I'd had meetings with him and some of the crew. I wanted them to know I would do everything to help them in whatever career path they chose. The *Enterprise*, which was going to need another refit soon, had become a training vessel for Starfleet Academy, and I was surprised that Spock, Scotty, McCoy, and Uhura wanted to stay with the ship. The lighter duty of training cadets appealed to all of them. Sulu, however, had wanted his own ship for a while, so I put him on the captains' list. He decided to pursue the new ship *Excelsior*, which was still on the assembly line, and in the mean time joined his *Enterprise* friends in teaching as well. This group of cadets who'd just participated in the *Kobayashi Maru*, and were under Spock's tutelage, would be going on a training cruise, with support from some of the older officers. Out of a sense of nostalgia, I arranged to conduct the inspection.

As I exited the simulator, I was pleased to run into Spock. In the intervening years he'd become much more comfortable in his own skin; he balanced his human and Vulcan halves with much more ease and conveyed a kind of judicial wisdom. He was a pleasure for me to be around: he was captain to everyone else, but for me he fell right back into being a first officer.

We joked about what his trainees had done to the simulator, and he reminded me the only way I beat the test was by cheating. Before we parted, I took a moment to thank him for the present that he'd left in my office and I'd been carrying all day. A first edition of *A Tale of Two Cities* by Charles Dickens. I would take great pleasure in reading the book. Its themes of self-sacrifice and rebirth would end up having unique meaning for me. He went back to the ship to prepare for my inspection, and I went home. The ennui that had set in when I returned to Starfleet the previous year had not abated.

It was my 50th birthday. I decided to spend the evening alone, though Bones had other plans. He showed up uninvited, with a bottle of Romulan ale and a pair of reading spectacles to fix farsightedness. He didn't waste time getting to the crux of my problems. He told me the solution to my depression was getting back my command. I thought about it. I wasn't sure; I thought that my foray into space had shown me that my day was over. And I felt like I was lost in an endless cycle.

"What do you mean?" McCoy said.

"I go out in space, I get promoted, I give up the promotion and go back to a ship," I said. "I did that already. I can't do it again. I'll look like an idiot."

McCoy and I talked about the pursuit of happiness, and that some of us just didn't have the tools to achieve it.

"You're not going to find contentment outside of yourself," he said. "It's got to come from within." I then wondered why he thought I needed a command to make me happy. He said it was as close as I was going to get. And he was getting tired of taking orders from Spock.

We drank a few more glasses of Romulan ale, and McCoy staggered out. The intoxicating effects were a little hard to shake off the next morning.

"Admiral," Uhura said. "Are you all right?" She was in uniform, standing over my bed. I had arranged to travel with her, McCoy, and Sulu to the *Enterprise*. She gave me a warm smile; I wasn't sure how she'd gotten into my apartment, but when I checked the clock and saw how late it was, I was thankful she had.

We beamed up to the maintenance satellite, where we met Sulu. McCoy joined us, also looking a little worse for wear. Sulu piloted us over to the *Enterprise* in a travel pod. It was always nice to see my old ship from the outside. It was majestic, comforting.

We docked and entered through the port torpedo room, greeted by Spock, Saavik, and a phalanx of crew and cadets. This wasn't the first time I'd seen these trainees, but I still couldn't get over how young they were. They looked like children. But among the young faces standing at attention, an old one: Scotty, now gray, still with the bloodshot eyes, just like that first day I'd come on board, still enjoying his shore leave too much. I decided to talk with one cadet.

"Midshipman First Class Peter Preston, engineer's mate, sir!" He looked like he was 12. I couldn't imagine I was that young when I had served, and then I remembered myself sleeping under a staircase on the *Republic*, and smiled. Whatever ambivalence I had toward this inspection, it began as a paean to nostalgia. It would soon become a requiem.

✦

"Who the hell even knows about Genesis?" Morrow said. "It's a top secret project."

"It's not the first time that's happened, Harry," I said. I knew the Klingons and Romulans had extensive spy networks. And they'd all love to have it. The Genesis Project was a device that could theoretically reorganize inanimate matter on a subatomic level to create life on a planetary scale. It was Carol's project. I was very worried because she had just called me from her lab on the space station Regula I. We hadn't spoken in years, and she was angry. She was accusing me of "taking Genesis away." I didn't know what she was talking about, and the communication was quickly cut off. Someone was jamming it; she was in danger. I was worried, and I could see Morrow was worried too. The Genesis Project would be a powerful weapon; it would destroy all life on a world to make room for the new life it created.

"You've got to get a ship to Regula I right away," I said.

"Okay, get going," he said.

I hadn't meant me. I wanted to go; I was concerned about Carol, but I didn't have the support I needed. This ship and crew weren't cut out for it.

"You have to make do," Morrow said. "Except for some freighters and a science vessel, you're the only ship in the quadrant."

"But I'm going to spend the whole trip changing diapers." Morrow laughed, but he didn't care.

"Report progress. Morrow out."

I went to see Spock. I told him the situation and my concern that his crew would crumble at the first sign of trouble. They were kids. Spock, however, had faith in them. And he instinctually knew what I needed.

He gave me back the *Enterprise*. He could see that I wanted to take control of the situation, that I didn't want to be second-guessing him or anyone else. He made the right decision for me; I'm not sure it was the right decision for everybody else.

We soon ran into the *Reliant*. It cut into us with full phasers.

Reliant was the ship I'd assigned to assist Carol and her team in the search for a lifeless planet to test the Genesis Device. The last I'd heard it was several hundred light-years away; now it was intercepting us. That should have been my first clue that something was wrong; Morrow said the *Enterprise* was the only ship in the quadrant. If *Reliant* had been reassigned, it had come from the direction of Regula I. Morrow would've assigned it to investigate.

I had trouble believing a Federation starship would be an enemy, especially one where Chekov was the first officer. That was my mistake. They knocked out our shield generators and warp drive with their first shots.

The impulse engines came next. I hadn't been in a battle in years, and my instincts were slow. My crew consisted of a few adults trying to manage a screaming, crying nursery. A lot of people died in that attack; I felt responsible, and that was even before I saw who was firing at us.

The *Reliant* called for our surrender, and I had no choice. On the screen, a face I hadn't seen in 15 years. Long gray hair where it was jet black before, strange clothing, but it was him.

"Khan."

I couldn't believe it. I'd left Khan a hundred light-years away, but somehow he'd hijacked the *Reliant*. He said he wanted vengeance on me. At first I didn't know why. But I didn't see McGivers with him. I soon found out his wife was dead. He blamed me. And now everyone on the *Enterprise* was at risk. I offered myself in exchange for the crew.

"I'll agree to your terms if . . ." he said. "If in addition to yourself, you hand over all data and materials regarding the project called Genesis." Oh my god, how did he know about it? That weapon, in his hands. Had he already been to Regula I? Had he hurt Carol? David?

This was all my fault. I'd let this murderer live. I had to get us out of this. I remembered Garth at Axanar taking remote control of his enemy's weapons consoles. Federation ships had combination codes, but Khan might not know about it. It was all I had.

It worked; I lowered Khan's shields and damaged his ship so he had to withdraw. But I'd done nothing clever; my only advantage was I knew more about our ships than he did. As I watched the young cadet Peter Preston, whom I'd met only a couple of days before, die in sickbay, I realized it was no victory, and it would only get worse.

✦

We limped to Regula I, a lonely space station around a desolate asteroid. It was a chamber of horrors: bloody corpses hanging from the rafters; Carol's team had been tortured to death. Chekov and his commanding officer were locked up in a storage cabinet. They were not quite themselves after having been abused and forced to do Khan's bidding. More suffering caused by my hubris.

I had left Khan alive, and now he was leaving a trail of devastation across the Galaxy. I had to find Carol and David.

McCoy, Saavik, and I had beamed down into the Regulan asteroid with Terrell and Chekov. We found constructed tunnels, and we also found the Genesis Device. Carol had hidden it from Khan.

And then someone hit me in the back. He then jabbed a knife at me, but I easily disarmed him.

"Where's Dr. Marcus?" I asked. He was at least 30 years younger than I was, but he couldn't fight. I was going to hit him again, when he spoke:

"I'm Dr. Marcus!" I looked at him. Oh my god. He was a little baby the last time I saw him.

"Jim!" Carol came running into the tunnel. It was my family reunion. And I'd just greeted my son with a punch to the gut.

There was no time to catch up.

As I watched, Khan beamed Genesis up to his ship. The most evil man I ever met now had the greatest weapon man had ever created.

✦

"It's the Genesis wave," David said. Khan had set it off, and if we didn't get out of range, we'd be caught inside it, our lives wiped away by its life-creating effect.

We were on the bridge of the *Enterprise*. We'd defeated the *Reliant* in ship-to-ship combat in the Mutara Nebula. I had noticed that David came onto the bridge during the battle, and had allowed myself a moment of pride that my son was getting to see me in action. But it was short-lived. David was the one who recognized that the Genesis Device was going to detonate. He said we had only four minutes. We couldn't get away; we didn't have warp drive. We were going to die.

I don't know how I lost track of what happened next. We were only a few thousand kilometers away from *Reliant*, and then suddenly the cadet at the engineering station said we had warp power. I ordered Sulu to take us to light-speed, a second before the Genesis Device exploded.

We watched an amazing metamorphosis as it condensed all the matter in the Mutara Nebula into a new world. Khan was dead. I thought I'd won and cheated death for myself and the *Enterprise* once more.

I didn't know how Scotty had fixed the engines. Then McCoy called me from engineering. And then I noticed Spock wasn't in his chair.

I flew down there. I saw him in the reactor room, cut off from the rest of the engineering section, flooded with radiation. He was the reason we'd gotten our warp drive when we needed it. He had literally opened the warp reactor and repaired it *by hand*.

I hadn't cheated death, I was looking at it. The first officer who'd looked after me for so many years, my partner in so many adventures. He defined me with his friendship and loyalty; he taught me with his knowledge, honor, and dignity. And he sacrificed himself so that we, so that I, could survive.

He said goodbye, and I watched him die.

✦

We had a funeral, and I put his body in a torpedo casing. My best friend was dead, and I couldn't save him. I had experienced loss before. Gary, Edith, Sam, but this one seemed worse. He had been a part of my adult life like no one else. He himself had escaped death many times, and I assumed he would be immortal.

When I fired his coffin out to land on the new Genesis Planet, I cried, feeling selfish at what I'd lost.

The battle had wrecked the *Enterprise*, so while Scotty led the trainees in the needed repairs to get us home, I mourned. I finished the book Spock gave me. I read as the main character sacrificed himself for the greater good. It was as if Spock were speaking to me from the grave.

David came to see me. I was sad, but my son was reaching out to me. He was a brilliant young man, a little headstrong, certain in his point of view. Carol said he was a lot like me, but I didn't see it; I saw a man, whose life I hadn't been a part of, but who was welcoming me into it now. Maybe we could become friends. We spoke about Khan, who he was. David was a smart man; he seemed to understand Khan's ambition. I remembered when I was in school, talking to my professor John Gill about Khan, about how I admired him. And that conversation was a straight line to Spock's death; I admired Khan, and because of that he survived to try to kill us all. I'd been a fool; we so often hold up as heroes men who achieve great things, ignoring the sacrifices they force others to make in order to succeed.

David took what I said personally; he thought Genesis wasn't that kind of achievement. I smiled and nodded, and decided I wouldn't point out that we all almost died for it.

Scotty got us up and running, and we set out for Ceti Alpha V, where Khan had marooned the crew of the *Reliant*. It was an interesting voyage. Saavik and David started some kind of relationship, though the rest of us could only guess at exactly what was going on. McCoy went into seclusion; I'd wondered if the death of Spock had hit him harder than he wanted to let on.

And I had some time alone with Carol. She too was going through a difficult period of mourning. Khan had tortured and killed her entire staff. She spent a lot of her days reaching out to their families, and I could see it was taking a toll. In bereavement, we found some comfort together.

One night, we were sitting in my quarters, sharing a drink. She told me about David as a boy, as a young man, and the difficulties of raising him by herself.

"He was lucky, though," I said. "He always had his mother." After a while, I could see she had something she wanted to ask me, but was hesitating. I forced it out of her.

"Did you ever get married?" she said. I told her I hadn't, but she could tell that there was another story I wasn't sharing. She pressed, wanted me to tell her about this mystery woman. I realized I had never really talked about it with anyone.

"Her name was Edith Keeler . . ."

✦

We rescued the crew of the *Reliant*, all of whom survived, though they were in pretty rough shape, and took them all to Starbase 12. Carol had spent many years there, and she proceeded to set up a base of operations from which to coordinate the study of the Genesis Planet. She lobbied Starfleet Command to assign several science ships right away, but the Admiralty, for some reason, wasn't cooperating. I tried to intervene, but they said they couldn't spare any vessel. I volunteered the *Enterprise*, but Morrow pressed me on the damage that she had undergone, and I had to admit she needed more work before I could take her out again.

However, I had to help Carol and David. It was somehow related to Spock's death. They were helping to fill a hole, and I wouldn't give up. There was a new science vessel in orbit of Starbase 12, *U.S.S. Grissom*. It was finishing up some minor maintenance, and it turned out I knew its new captain. I decided to pay him a visit aboard his ship. I beamed up and walked onto the clean, bright bridge of the small vessel.

"Admiral Kirk," J. T. Esteban said, "great to see you again."

The *Grissom* was on a general patrol in this quadrant, but with Esteban's help, we were able to get it assigned to this project. I again was kind of proud that I could do something to impress my son.

The news on the *Enterprise*, however, wasn't so good.

"I cannot fix the damage without a spacedock," Scotty said. "She'll run at warp, but that's about all. I've got to get her home." The commanding officer of Starbase 12, Commodore Jim Corrigan, my old roommate from the academy, was very interested in my trainee crew.

"There's going to be a lot of ships coming through here needing replacements," Corrigan said. "It'd be a shame to make all those kids go all the way home just to come out here again." So I talked it over with Scotty, Sulu, and Uhura, who agreed we could run the ship to Earth with a skeleton crew, and I let the trainees be reassigned. I wanted to stay longer at Starbase 12, squeezing every bit of time I could with Carol and David, when Uhura came to see me in my quarters.

"Sulu was only supposed to be with us for three weeks," she said. "His ship is waiting for him back in Earth orbit." I'd forgotten. I was torn, but I had an obligation to him. I told her to prep the *Enterprise* to leave orbit immediately. I went to say goodbye to Carol.

She was in her office with David, going over some of the data on the Genesis Planet. David and Saavik would be going on to begin studying the new world, while Carol would stay behind on Starbase 12 to find more ships. I promised her I was coming back with a fixed *Enterprise* to help on this mission. She smiled.

"You'll forgive me if I take that with a grain of salt," she said. As sure as I was that I was coming back, I decided not to argue with her. We had reconnected after all these years, and now I wanted to be with her again. I knew it was what she wanted too. My promise was real; for the first time, I saw the future.

I then turned to David.

"It's been a pleasure, sir," he said. I shook his hand.

"Call me . . . Dad," I said. After a moment, we all laughed. It sounded ridiculous. "All right, don't call me that."

✦

"You left him on Genesis!" Spock's father, the Vulcan ambassador to the Federation, was in my apartment. I hadn't seen him in a long time, and he wasn't sounding logical. He was sounding angry.

I'd come home to a lot of bad news. The Genesis Project was a galactic controversy. No one was allowed to talk about it, and we were all going to be extensively debriefed. This meant Sulu wasn't getting his ship; they'd already given it to someone else. The *Enterprise* was going to be decommissioned, and I wasn't getting another ship, not until the Federation came up with a policy on Genesis. But the worst of it was Bones.

I found him in Spock's quarters on the *Enterprise*, babbling about having to go home to Vulcan. Spock's death had wrecked him; he had had some kind of nervous breakdown. I remember thinking that I had always taken McCoy's durability for granted: this reminded me he was only human.

And now Sarek, Spock's father, whom I'd first met almost 20 years before, was *shouting* at me. He said I hadn't carried out Spock's last wish. I didn't know what he was talking about. He asked to mind-meld with me.

Sarek's thoughts reached into my head, opening the door to memories I had no desire to relive. I was back in engineering; Spock was saying goodbye. And he was dead again. Sarek broke the meld.

"It is not here," Sarek said. He told me that Vulcans transferred their living spirit, called the *katra*, to someone or something when they died. But Spock hadn't been able to meld with me. And then I put it together.

It was Bones. It wasn't a nervous breakdown. Spock had melded with him, and somehow, McCoy had some bit of Spock in his brain. It was surreal, difficult to conceive, but Sarek's assuredness that this was true drove me to act. Sarek said I had to get Spock's body off of Genesis, and take it and McCoy to Mount Seleya on Vulcan. It was not going to be easy; Genesis was off-limits to everybody.

Morrow turned me down flat, so I went to my friends.

✦

"I've asked for transporter duty in Old City Station," Uhura said. It was the closest Starfleet transporter to the Starfleet security facility where McCoy was being kept. McCoy had gotten himself in trouble trying to hire a ship to take him to Genesis (clearly, on some level, he also knew what needed to be done), so we were going to have to break him out of prison. Uhura was a commander, and choosing this duty station would probably raise some red flags, but it would be too late before anyone noticed.

We were in my apartment: Scotty, Uhura, Sulu, and Chekov. Breaking McCoy out wasn't the biggest crime we were planning; we were also going to steal the *Enterprise*.

"There's at least two guards on McCoy at all times," Sulu said. "Visiting hours are over at 9 p.m., and the shift reduces to two people at 8:30." Sulu and I would be going in to rescue McCoy. We would then make our way to the Old City Station transporter room, and Uhura would beam us to the *Enterprise*, where Scotty and Chekov would be.

"Scotty," I said, "what about the *Enterprise*?"

"Chekov checked the automated systems this morning," Scotty said. "My new captain has been keeping me pretty busy on *Excelsior*." Scotty unhappily had been transferred to the new ship when we got back. But it would turn out to be our best bit of luck.

"Admiral," Uhura said, "if we do this, what guarantee do we have that it will help Dr. McCoy?"

"Or Mr. Spock?" Sulu said.

I realized at that moment that I'd been risking not just my life and career on Sarek's word, but theirs as well. I looked at my compatriots; they were willing to follow me without question, but I still owed them an explanation.

"I think the people on Vulcan will be able to help McCoy," I said, "but I'm taking it on Sarek's word that somehow Spock will rest easier. But I really don't know. You all have to make your own decision."

"We've learned a lot about Vulcan over the years through Spock," Scotty said. "It always seemed to me that his people had a little bit of magic."

"Nothing could ever stop him," Sulu said.

I looked over at Chekov. He was the only one not saying anything. He'd been first officer aboard the *Reliant* for a long time, and he'd lost his ship and his captain. I asked him for his opinion.

"Spock taught me how to be an officer," Chekov said, "how to be a man. I think it's worth the risk to try to get him to the Vulcan afterlife."

✦

"It is not I who will surrender, it is you!" The Klingon captain was calling my bluff, and I was out of moves.

We had stolen the *Enterprise*; Scotty had sabotaged the *Excelsior* so it couldn't follow us, and we'd gotten ourselves to Genesis. A Klingon bird-of-prey was waiting for us. It was small, but menacing, and the *Enterprise* was in no shape for a fight. We got in one good shot, but the Klingons knocked out our automation system. There were only five of us on board; there was no way to make repairs. We were dead in space. The Klingons had us. They'd destroyed the *Grissom*, and had hostages on the planet. They wanted the "secret of Genesis." They didn't seem to realize that their hostages, Saavik and David, were more likely to have it.

Saavik said someone else was with them. "A Vulcan scientist of your acquaintance," she said. *Vulcan scientist.* Spock. He was alive.

She also let me know something was wrong with the Genesis Planet, the thing the whole Galaxy was in an uproar about, but I didn't care. Spock was alive. Spock was *alive.*

I was going to get him back.

And then the Klingons killed David.

The Klingon commander, Kruge, wanted my ship, so the goddamn Klingon killed my son. I stood by on my dead ship on my dead bridge and couldn't do anything. My son, who I'd abandoned, who I'd only just gotten to know. Who was a wonderful, sweet, brilliant man. They killed him, because Kruge wanted me to surrender the *Enterprise.* He wanted to prove how serious he was about threatening the hostages. So I, in turn, showed him how serious I was.

I tricked most of the Klingon crew into boarding the *Enterprise,* and blew it up. McCoy, Scotty, Sulu, Chekov, and I watched from the surface of the Genesis Planet as it burned up in the atmosphere. I've thought back to this moment many times over the years. That ship meant a lot to me; the happiest moments of my life were when I was sitting on that bridge, and when I'd lost my command of it, I fought hard to get it back. How could I destroy it? Yes, Kruge was threatening to kill the others, and I had to stop him. But did I really have no other option? The *Enterprise* was a dead ship, with outdated technology. I could've erased every bit of computer information; the Klingons would've gotten nothing if I'd given to them. My career was already over; wasn't it worth our lives? I could've let myself be taken prisoner of the Klingons, trading myself for the hostages, and said I would tell them nothing if they didn't let them go. And my plan of beaming the Klingon crew onto the doomed *Enterprise* was a huge risk; Kruge could've immediately ordered the hostages killed.

The truth was, I wanted blood. And as soon as David died, all the emotions I'd invested in the *Enterprise* seemed hollow; it was a ship, a technological marvel, but still a piece of machinery. At that moment, it was nothing but a trophy to my accomplishments, and I purposely threw it away as penance for my son's death.

And now we didn't have much time—the planet we were on was breaking up. We found Spock; the energies that had created the Genesis Planet had regenerated him. It was, as Scotty said, a little bit of magic. His mind, however, was in McCoy's head, and if I could get them both to Vulcan, there was a real possibility we could get him back.

Nothing was going to stop me. I killed Kruge, and rescued Spock literally as the ground crumbled beneath my feet.

CHAPTER 11

THERE WAS NO COFFEE ON VULCAN.

The second day there, that was the least of my troubles, but I really wanted a cup of coffee. The Vulcans had strict rules about chemical stimulants, so none of their food replicators were programmed for it. Scotty found something on the Klingon ship called *raktajino*, but it really wasn't what I wanted. There was also no alcohol, which I thought was also going to be a problem.

When we had arrived on Vulcan, as I expected, its people were able to put whatever was in McCoy's head back into Spock's. He wasn't completely whole; he had some of his memory, but his mind would have to be retrained. Still, it was truly awe inspiring: he'd risen from the dead.

But it had come at a cost. We stole the *Enterprise*, Scotty sabotaged the *Excelsior*, I then destroyed the *Enterprise*, and we stole a Klingon ship after I killed most of its crew. Both the Federation and the Klingons wanted our heads on a platter (the Klingons, literally).

"We're intergalactic criminals," Chekov said.

"Scourges of the Galaxy," Sulu added. Now, we were on Vulcan, near Mount Seleya, at the edge of the Forge, the great tract of wasteland that was home to so much Vulcan history. I wasn't sure what to do next, so I asked Sarek if he could arrange for us to stay. Scotty, Chekov, Uhura, and Sulu could work on the bird-of-prey. If we could bring that ship home to

Starfleet, maybe it would do a little to smooth over the trouble we'd caused. Maybe.

But my real reason for wanting to stay was Spock. He still wasn't himself; they would have to retrain him. I wanted to see if he would come all the way back. It wouldn't make up for what I'd lost, but it might make my life easier.

But my first duty was I had to call Carol to tell her of David's death. She unleashed a rage that was frightening and justified. Her love and attachment to him was something I envied. She was also, like me, mad at herself.

And though David was investigating a planet that he helped create, the fact that he'd been killed in space by Klingons assigned responsibility for his death, in Carol's mind, to me. She knew it was irrational; she was grieving for her lost child. I wanted to grieve with her, but I could feel that there was no real chance at reconciliation. The Klingons were my mortal enemies, and they'd killed her son. Rational or not, she would always blame me for his death. I said I would be in touch with her soon, but I never spoke to her again.

✦

Sarek came to me on that second day. I assumed he was going to tell me we were going to be extradited immediately back to Earth; there were inviolable treaties guaranteeing that criminals could not find safe harbor on any Federation world. But Sarek said that was not the case, at least not right away. I was incredulous.

"Starfleet Commander Morrow's going to want my head on the chopping block," I said.

"Morrow is no longer the Starfleet Commander," he said. Morrow, it turns out, was another victim of my crimes. He was the one who brought me back into the Admiralty, and as his reward, I stole a ship, wrecked another one, and stirred up a mess with the Klingons. He resigned in disgrace. One more life I ruined.

"Who took his place?" I said.

"Admiral Cartwright," Sarek said. Cartwright had told Sarek that the Klingons were not yet aware that we'd stolen their bird-of-prey. There were a lot of secrets aboard her that would be tactically useful to Starfleet. Cartwright implied he would suggest to the Federation president we not be extradited. We may be tried in absentia, but with the help of the Vulcans my crew would find out all we could about the ship, before the Klingons tried to steal it back.

"Did he say we had a choice?" I said.

"He did not propose an alternative," Sarek said. Cartwright hated the Klingons more than I did, and was looking for any advantage. He was appealing to my sense of loyalty, and really offering nothing definite in return, though there was an implicit suggestion that it would help us at trial.

I decided, initially at least, that it was better than going home to immediate imprisonment.

"In the meantime," Sarek said, "my wife has invited you to join us for an evening meal." This came as a surprise, but I of course took him up on it.

Sarek maintained his home in the city of ShiKar, whose spires rose out of the surrounding rocks and sands like enchanted crystal. Their house was one level, bright, airy, and modern, filled with sculptures, paintings, and other works of art. Amanda met us at the door.

"Admiral, it is wonderful to see you," she said. Her warmth was infectious, and stood out to the aloofness of everyone else I'd been in contact with since arriving.

"Please call me Jim," I said. Sarek led us inside, and we sat down to a meal that, though vegetarian, was more human than Vulcan. It was a lovely supper. I discovered that Sarek had taken on opening diplomatic talks with the Legarans, the lobster-like species I had encountered several years before. I told him of our initial difficulties.

"You were ill-equipped to handle such a delicate first contact," Sarek said. "Humans lack the patience necessary to construct even a structure for diplomacy with this species." Amanda gave him an admonishing look, and I took a little umbrage at the insult; I'd made dozens of successful first contacts.

"How much patience would I need?"

"I estimate it will take seventy years before an agreement is reached to begin negotiations." I looked to see if he was joking, then remembered that

Spock was the only Vulcan who did that. I decided then, in this case, he was right, I did not have the patience.

When I got ready to leave for the evening, Amanda took my arm.

"You brought me back my son," she said. "I know what you lost, and I'm so, so sorry." In that moment, for the first time, I understood the wisdom of Vulcan society. I remembered David. The feelings of anger, despair, frustration invaded. I had no control of them, and I wished I had the discipline of a philosophy that would allow me not to feel.

Months passed and we worked on the Klingon ship, and I learned that though I had obviously spent a lot of time with Spock, that hadn't prepared me for life on Vulcan. For starters, there was no small talk. People only spoke for a specific purpose; if they didn't have one, they didn't speak. Initially, it was unnerving; it was like a planet of awkward silence. But over time I came to appreciate it. And eventually all the logic began to seep in, and some of my emotions seemed to fall away. I was "going native," and I think it helped me through a difficult period.

One day, we had a visitor at our camp. An elderly Vulcan woman in a hover chair floated toward me, escorted by several aides. Though she was much older, I recognized her immediately.

"You are not dead," T'Pau said.

"No ma'am," I said. I don't know how she heard that I was on the planet, but when she did, she obviously felt a need come see me. For what purpose, I couldn't even guess.

"You disrespected our traditions," T'Pau said.

"I did not mean to," I said. I suppose I could've blamed McCoy for what happened at Spock's wedding, but that didn't seem logical. "I apologize if that was the result."

"It was," T'Pau said. We stood in silence for a long moment. I knew there was nothing more to say. She then looked at me. "You have increased your weight. It is not healthful." She then turned and floated away with her entourage.

Did she come all that way to tell me I had gotten fat?

✦

"The Federation Council has finished their deliberations," Sarek said. It was about three months after we'd arrived, and upon hearing that the council was going to try us in absentia, Sarek had gone to Earth to speak in our defense. He was on the viewscreen of the Klingon bird-of-prey. McCoy and I spoke to him from the bridge, which Scotty and his team were almost finished refitting for human operation.

"You have all been found guilty of nine violations of Starfleet regulations," Sarek said, "which carry a combined penalty of sixteen years in a penal colony." I had no idea if our work on the Klingon vessel would gain us any leniency, or if that sentence had already taken that into account.

"In addition," Sarek went on, "the Klingons have threatened war if you are not executed."

"Everybody or just me?" I said.

"Just you," he said.

Even my time among the Vulcans had not tempered my rage against the Klingons. I was hoping to bump into them again. I could have easily killed some more.

Sarek asked what we intended to do. Prison waited for all of us. I suppose we could've taken the bird-of-prey and become pirates on the run.

But the truth was we wanted to go home, whatever the consequences. We couldn't hide on Vulcan forever.

On the day we left, Saavik came to see me. She was staying behind. The rumor was she was pregnant. I wondered whether it was David's, but it seemed inappropriate to ask.

"Sir, I have not had the opportunity to tell you about your son. David died most bravely. He saved Spock. He saved us all. I thought you should know." I nodded. I don't know if it was a comfort. He died a hero, but like many parents, I think I would've preferred if he'd been a coward and lived.

After Saavik left, Spock came on board. It was the first time I'd seen him since we'd been back. He had been undergoing a reeducation and seemed a kind of childlike version of himself. But he was just as brilliant and just as loyal. He was coming with us to offer testimony in our defense. We, and the entire population of Earth, were lucky he decided to do that.

✦

"Save yourselves . . . avoid the planet Earth at all costs." It was Federation president Hiram Roth, sending a planetary distress call. A mysterious probe had come into Earth orbit and had sent transmissions that were ionizing the atmosphere, blocking out the sun, and had caused all power systems to fail. We were in the bird-of-prey, approaching the Sol System, when we received the message. It was dire; Earth would die.

I had to do something, but it was hard for me to believe that we'd make a difference in our little alien ship, when all of Starfleet had been paralyzed. But we were the only ones who had Spock.

He listened to the probe's transmissions and determined that they were meant for something that lived underwater. The life-forms were trying to communicate with humpback whales, a species that had long been extinct on Earth.

If we got close to the probe, our power would fail too. So, the only way to talk to the probe was to find some humpback whales.

I told Spock to start computations for time warp. It had been almost 20 years since we'd attempted time travel in a ship. We were in a different kind of vessel, but the theory was the same. We would "slingshot" around Earth's sun, and it would send us back in time. I was on a mission to save my world.

✦

"Watch where you're going, you dumbass!"

San Francisco in the 1980s was a lot different than it was in the 2280s: loud, polluted, angry, but also intense, energetic, and more colorful. The person who called me a "dumbass" had almost just run me over with his automobile, yet somehow blamed me for it.

Spock had chosen the era based on accessibility of humpback whales as well as available power; the Klingon ship wasn't built for time travel, and going back in time had already weakened the reactor. So fixing the ship became part of our mission.

Finding the humpbacks ended up being relatively easy; they were at the Cetacean Institute outside the city. Spock and I went to investigate, while the others dealt with building a whale tank in the bird-of-prey and making sure our engines had the power necessary for the return trip.

Walking the streets of San Francisco with Spock brought back a lot of memories, especially of our trip to 1930. Stuck in the primitive past, we had a mission to save the future. It took me out of the darkness I'd experienced recently, and I had my best friend and companion back at my side.

And, just like in 1930, we met an angel who would help us.

Her name was Gillian Taylor. She was the guardian of the two whales in captivity at the Cetacean Institute. She was a guide and a scientist, young, pretty, and passionate about whales. The whales, named George and Gracie, were male and female, which fit in perfectly with our plan to repopulate them in the future. I assumed they were named for great leaders of the time, but I never found out.*

Spock and I had a lot more trouble seeming like we belonged in this era than we did in the 1930s. We looked out of place and a little incompetent. This ended up having the unintentional effect of gaining Gillian's sympathy.

She took me out to dinner for something called a "large mushroom with pepperoni." I also had a drink, which was remarkably similar to Tellarite beer.

During the meal, she revealed to me that she worried that the whales were going to be released into the ocean and be killed by whalers. I told her I could take the whales somewhere they would never be hunted.

"Where can you take them?" she asked. She was hopeful.

I was hinting around, and finally just came out and told her I was from the future. I somehow didn't worry that revealing it would change history. Given her reaction, I was right not to be concerned.

"Well, why didn't you tell me to begin with? Why all the coy disguises?"

---

*EDITOR'S NOTE: The whales appear to have been named for comedian George Burns and his partner and wife, Gracie Allen, although it is unclear what their relationship was to marine biology.

I didn't have to be concerned, because she clearly didn't believe me. I was frustrated because I needed her help to take the whales, and it initially didn't look like I was going to get it.

Later that night, I was back aboard the bird-of-prey. Gillian had dropped me off, with the food I'd ordered. It was in a square box and had an intoxicating smell. Spock and I opened it. There was a disc inside made of bread, with pieces of meat and vegetables mixed on top with cheese.

"This is a pizza," Spock said. I had heard of it. It looked delicious, but given what T'Pau had said to me, I decided to forgo it. Spock couldn't eat it because it had meat, so Scotty ate most of it.

I didn't know what we were going to do; without Gillian's help, I didn't think we'd find the whales.

The bird-of-prey sat in Golden Gate Park, but the cloaking device was activated, so it was transparent. Gillian was "banging" on the invisible hull the next morning. She must have seen me beam inside the night before, and this led her to begin to consider the possibility that we were telling the truth. She found herself in a quandary: believe someone she thought was crazy, or let her whales be hunted and killed. She decided on the former, and with her help, we rescued George and Gracie, beaming them into our ship to take to the 23rd century.

She didn't want to stay in her own time. And I didn't care. This time, I got to take the angel from the past home with me.

✦

"Because of certain mitigating circumstances, all charges but one are summarily dismissed," President Roth said. I stood with Spock, McCoy, Scotty, Uhura, Chekov, and Sulu in front of the Federation Council. The "mitigating circumstance" was that we saved the planet.

We dropped the whales off in San Francisco Bay, and they immediately started talking to the probe. And the probe left, just like that. And everything was fixed.

The remaining charge was disobeying orders, which they directed solely at me. They could kick me out of Starfleet for that. I thought of myself as a civilian again; I hadn't been able to make it work before, and now I was even older. I was scared at the prospect; the idea of prison seemed easier.

"James T. Kirk," Roth said. "It is the judgment of this council that you be reduced in rank to captain, and that as a consequence of your new rank, you be given the duties for which you have repeatedly demonstrated unswerving ability. The command of a starship." I smiled. I was completing the cycle again, going back to a ship after getting a promotion. Starfleet had decided to enable me.

I went to find Gillian. I was excited at the prospect of showing her my world. But I had barely said hello and she was already saying goodbye.

She was already assigned to a science vessel and was anxious to get started. She was a lot younger than I was; she really didn't need me in this world. She could make it on her own. She kissed me and ran off. I smiled and thought about Edith. I felt like I'd just rewritten some history: a young, selfless woman who saw the future but didn't belong to her time was now in a place where she could shine. A hole in me had filled.

I went back with my family. We went up to our new ship. The travel pod approached. It had been a *Constitution*-class ship called the *Ti-Ho*, but they had renamed it the *Enterprise*. We had come home for the last time.

CHAPTER 12

"I THINK YOU GOT DRUSILLA PREGNANT," McCoy said.

"There's no proof—" I said.

"Yes there is. We're looking at it," he said.

"Shhh!" said a stranger sitting behind us.

We were in a cinema, on Planet IV of System 892, watching people on the screen playing, well, *us*, the crew of the *Enterprise*. It was a strange experience; the actors on the screen vaguely resembled me, Spock, and McCoy. The movie got a lot of the details about Starfleet and the Federation right, which seemed impossible, Spock's doppelganger even had pointed ears and slanted eyebrows.

The world we were on was a startling example of Hodgkin's Law of Parallel Planet Development.[*]

We had originally visited the planet almost 30 years before and found a Roman Empire that had survived into the 20th century, finally struggling with the spread of Christianity. My landing party and I barely escaped with our lives, and the planet was marked "off-limits" by Starfleet. Enough time

---

[*]**EDITOR'S NOTE:** Hodgkin's Law of Parallel Planet Development was from a theory first proposed by the 21st-century biologist A. E. Hodgkin. He showed that if two planets had a similar biology, this could translate over time to similar societal developments. His theory was proven after his death when parallel humanoid societies were discovered across the Galaxy.

had passed, and it was determined by someone in the Admiralty (a young admiral named John Van Robbins whom I'd never met) that we should take another look at it to determine if there'd been any residual contamination from our visit.

We entered orbit and monitored their radio and television transmissions. Nothing seemed out of the ordinary. With knowledge of the society, I decided a landing party in disguise was worth the risk. McCoy, Chekov, and I donned clothing roughly corresponding to the Earth year 1990, and we beamed down to a midsize city.

Rome had not fallen, though the current emperor had allowed Christianity to flourish; it was already the dominant religion of the empire. We saw several examples of Christian churches nestled between homes and businesses, and religious iconography was prevalent. We gathered what information we could and were preparing to beam back to the ship, when McCoy noticed an advertisement on the side of a public transportation vehicle with an internal combustion engine that I believed was called a "bus." We barely got to read it before the bus pulled away from us, but among the images on it, there was a clear photo of a Vulcan. I turned to Chekov.

"Did you catch what it said?"

"'The Final Frontier,'" Chekov said. "It was a title."

"I think that's how they used to advertise movies," McCoy said.

"Contamination?" Chekov said.

"When we were here the last time, the government had a pretty tight lock on information," I said. Our mission to this planet back then was to find a missing merchant ship, the *S.S. Beagle*. The ship had been destroyed, but some of the crew of the *Beagle* had survived on the planet and had become part of the Roman society. The movie advertisement suggested we needed to do a little more research.

"Captain," Chekov said, "we might be able to find something in here." He indicated a bookstore, Cicero's Tomes. We went inside and quickly found a section on popular culture. McCoy pulled out a book on the topic.

"*The Making of 'The Final Frontier,'*" I said, reading the cover. The first chapter had a short biography of the filmmaker, whose name was Eugenio. He was born a slave, and from a very young age, his mother, whose name was Drusilla, had told him stories about his father.

"Uh-oh," McCoy said. He was reading over my shoulder. He recognized the name as well. Drusilla had been a slave to the proconsul who'd captured us on our first visit. She and I had been intimate.

"But it doesn't make any sense," I said. "It wasn't like I told her anything."

"I think we should go see the movie," Chekov said. So we did. (I also bought the book.) When we saw the movie, we noticed that a few people in the audience seemed to be wearing homemade Starfleet uniforms. McCoy had a theory about that.

"Those are fans," he said. "Dressing up like you."

Back on the *Enterprise*, we relayed what we found to Spock in the briefing room. The film had gotten a lot right about Starfleet and the Federation, and its portrayal of me, Spock, and McCoy was dead-on. Spock theorized that Drusilla must have been paying more attention when she served the three of us.

"I'm pretty sure she only served one of us," McCoy said, and I gave him an annoyed look. I still wasn't clear how they had gotten the details of Starfleet and the rest of the Galaxy.

"I think I know the answer to that," Chekov said. He had the book in front of him turned open to a page at the end. Under a title head called "Credits," there was a list of people who had been involved in the making of the film. Chekov had done some cross-checking in our data banks. Three of the names listed under "Consultants" matched the names of members of the crew of the *Beagle*

"So this slave, Eugenio," I said, "hearing some details from his mother, searches out the surviving members of the *Beagle*, and they fill in the rest."

"What was the nature of the film?" Spock said.

"This Eugenio was obviously using this film to say something about religion," Chekov said. "The *Enterprise* went on a mission to the center of the Galaxy to find God."

"That is not possible," Spock said. "The center of the Galaxy is a black hole."

"I thought you were going to say," McCoy said, "that there's no such thing as God."

"I have no evidence on that subject," Spock said, then brought up the question of whether this constituted a violation of the Prime Directive.

"It's just a movie, Spock," McCoy said. "I doubt it will come to anything."
I hoped McCoy was right.

✦

"Do you know Uhura's 54?" I said to McCoy. We were in my quarters enjoying a drink, as we were wont to do.

"The *Enterprise* now has the oldest senior officers of any ship in the fleet," McCoy said.

"How do you know that?"

"I looked it up," he said. "We've got three captains. Do we really need three captains?" Scotty had the rank of captain, along with Spock and myself. It was definitely a top-heavy ship, but no one wanted to leave. The last person who'd left was Sulu, who'd finally gotten command of the *Excelsior* three years before.

"We're doing our jobs, aren't we?" I said.

"Who's a little defensive?" he said, with a smirk.

I guess I was. We were on our last legs; our tour was over in four months, and the senior officers and much of the crew had decided to "stand down" and not seek reenlistment. It was just as well. In the last few months our missions had not been vital; we'd become a showpiece. I had a reputation that Starfleet used for security reasons. The Klingons still didn't like me, because they were also a little scared of me, which frankly pleased me. The work wasn't arduous, and the ship itself was a lot like us. They phased out the *Baton Rouge* class 40 years before, and now the *Constitution* class had seen her day. The *Excelsior*-class ships were taking over, and there was already one designated for the name "Enterprise" being assembled. They would be decommissioning this ship probably right after we walked off it.

The door chime rang. It was Spock.

"I request an extended leave of absence," Spock said. "I'm needed on Vulcan."

"Has it been seven years? You need to get someone pregnant?" McCoy said. He reached for the Saurian brandy but I grabbed the bottle first.

"I'm cutting you off," I said.

"When Vulcans reach a certain age, Doctor, they are spared the turbulence of the *Pon farr*," Spock said, then he turned back to me. "I have been requested to return."

I asked if everything was all right, and Spock said he didn't know; the reason he was being called back was something of a mystery. So I ordered the helm to set a course for Vulcan and told McCoy we would be down to two captains for a while.

"How will we survive?" he said with a chuckle.

We dropped Spock off at Vulcan and were then soon ordered to Earth. It looked like we would spend our last three months in dry dock. It was strange to think it was all coming to an end. I went back to my old apartment. It overlooked Starfleet Academy, and my mind often wandered back to those days. I felt a specific memory gnawing at me and decided I needed some closure.

On one of my leave days, I took a trip to the New Zealand Penal Settlement. Criminals from all over the planet lived and worked there, under guard, and were given carefully guided lives. It was punishment because it wasn't freedom, but it wasn't cruel either. I beamed into an administration building. The clerk behind a desk checked my security clearance and approved my request to visit an inmate. A guard took me out onto the grounds.

There were rolling green hills where inmates worked on a variety of building projects. The guard took me to a technical facility, where inside several men and women labored over an antique computer. One of them immediately recognized me.

Ben Finney was much older and thinner. When he saw me walk in, he immediately excused himself from the group, came over, and quietly said hello. He was not unfriendly, just reserved. I asked him if we could go for a walk. We took a stroll on the lush grounds.

"You'll be getting out soon," I said. "Do you have any plans?"

"Jamie and her wife live on Benecia; they've offered to let me live there with them." Ben's wife, Naomi, had passed away several years before. I didn't bring her up, but I gathered they had not stayed in touch.

"If there's anything you need," I said, "please let me know." Ben stopped.

"Jim," he said, "I appreciate you coming. I appreciate your forgiveness. I have a sickness, and it led me to hurt a lot of people. But I guess what I'm saying is, it would be easier if I didn't see you again."

"Okay," I said. "But I just wanted you to know, I don't think I would've been the person I've become without your help. I wanted to thank you."

Ben nodded. I think the pain of his own actions kept him from being able to embrace my appreciation. We shook hands and said goodbye.

I was glad I took the time to do it. My life as I knew it was about to come to an end.

A few weeks later, I was alone in the dark. I wasn't sure how long I'd been locked in the cell of the Klingon ship. There was no light, no bed, no toilet. Time would pass, I'd sleep for a while, then wake up in a panic, trying to find the walls, or a door, or a hatch. They didn't feed me or give me water. I was weak, disoriented. I sat in the dark, hungry, and I was sure that I was on my way to my execution. I had a lot of time to think about how I'd gotten there.

The chancellor of the Klingon High Council was dead. Apparently by two Starfleet soldiers who beamed aboard a Klingon ship from the *Enterprise* and shot him. We were escorting him to Earth for a historic peace conference. The Klingons had asked for the conference; they were desperate. Their moon, Praxis, had exploded. I remembered when I was part of the DSPS, Cartwright had done extensive studies on the Klingon Homeworld Qo'noS and its single natural satellite Praxis. Despite the widespread nature of the Klingon Empire, it was still highly centralized around their Homeworld; the overwhelming majority of the Klingon population lived there. The only moon, Praxis, had been discovered centuries ago, when the Klingons first went into space. Its rich mineral wealth had been considered a gift from the Klingon gods. According to the strategic studies I had read, without the moon providing energy, they would lose almost 80 percent of their available power.

This had been part of Nogura's plan all those years ago, one which Cartwright enthusiastically pursued: fortify our borders, forcing the Klingons to fortify theirs, spending capital we knew they didn't have. It looked like it had worked; now they didn't have the resources to combat this catastrophe. If they couldn't build air shelters for their population,

Qo'noS would be uninhabitable in less than 50 years, and most of the population dead well before then. When I heard this, I thought, our greatest enemy was about to be defeated. The Galaxy would be safe.

But I hadn't known about the peace mission. That was why Spock had been called home to Vulcan. His father had asked him to act as a special envoy, and he had begun negotiations with the Klingon leader Gorkon to dismantle the defenses on our borders and help the Klingons integrate into the Federation. And then Spock informed me at a meeting of the Admiralty that he had volunteered the *Enterprise* to bring Gorkon to Earth.

"There is an ancient Vulcan proverb: Only Nixon could go to China," Spock said, by way of explanation. I had no idea what that meant.*

I was furious. He knew how I felt about the Klingons, what they'd done to me, to David. I had no interest in helping them, or bringing them into Federation space.

"They're dying," Spock said.

"Let them die," I said. And I meant it. I wouldn't miss them, and, as far as I was concerned, neither would the Galaxy.

But then I met Gorkon.

We rendezvoused with his ship and had him over for dinner. He was a bit of a surprise. He didn't seem like the usual Klingon. A man about my age, he was cultured, civilized, and with a beard and manner that evoked the ancient American president Abraham Lincoln. Before we parted, he quietly said to me that our generation was going to have the hardest time living in a postwar society. His wisdom was lost on me at the time, but not now.

Less than an hour later he was dead. McCoy and I had beamed over to help, but the doctor was either too drunk or too inexperienced with Klingon anatomy or both to prevent Gorkon's death. We were placed under arrest,

---

*EDITOR'S NOTE: This is a well-known Vulcan proverb, but its origin is unclear. It derives from the events of 20th-century Earth, when President of the United States Richard Nixon opened diplomatic relations with Communist China. The meaning of the proverb refers to the fact that it was considered a political success because of Nixon's career history of being a virulent anti-Communist; as such, none of his opponents could accuse him of being "soft" on Communism. It is unclear, however, what Vulcan was a student of Earth history to the extent that they created a proverb. And it couldn't be "ancient," as the events it referred to were only 300 years old.

put into shackles, and shoved into these dark, separate cells. I knew I was being framed for the murder. And the problem was, I was a great suspect: I had means, motive, and opportunity.

Time passed. The darkness made me hallucinate. I thought I was beginning to see glowing orbs or bubbles, but then I'd put my hand in front of my face and it wouldn't block the light; it was true darkness. I began to think I was already dead; I had the urge to scream, just so I'd know I was still alive. But I wouldn't; I didn't want to give my jailers the satisfaction. I slammed my hand against the wall 'til it bled, then put it in my mouth. I could taste the blood. I was losing a sense of time and myself. Maybe the war had already started. Billions were dying because of me. They'd open the door and shoot me. There was no hope.

And then I felt it on my back. My thoughts were foggy. What was it, an insect? No, it didn't move. Then I remembered. Spock had put his hand on my shoulder before I left the bridge of the *Enterprise* for the Klingon ship. I thought he was uncharacteristically patting me on the back, wishing me good luck, but instead he had placed something there. I knew immediately what it was: a viridian patch. A little technological marvel that would allow the *Enterprise*'s sensors to locate me over 20 light-years away. As angry as I'd been at Spock for dragging me into this, he was still looking after me. I gently rubbed the patch. I smiled; it felt like he was in the room with me. He was going to save me.

Shortly thereafter, the door opened and light flooded in. I squinted as two guards grabbed me. I forced my eyes open in the glare and saw McCoy being dragged along with me.

"Bones," I said. "Are you all right?"

"Not at all," he said.

They brought us to the transporter and beamed us down to another prison. (We were on Qo'noS, but we didn't get a tour.) The guards threw us into a cell, this time together. This one at least had a toilet, and they gave us the leg of some dead Klingon animal, which we both tore apart. I was going to tell McCoy about the viridian patch, and then thought better of it; the cell could be bugged.

A few hours later, a younger Klingon, dressed in military robes, came in. He introduced himself as Colonel Worf, who'd been assigned to represent us at our trial.

"I am familiar with the facts of your case," he said, "but we should go over them to be certain nothing important was left out. First, why did you kill the chancellor?" (It reminded me of the famous example of the "loaded question" of ancient Earth, "Have you stopped beating your wife?") We were emphatic that we had not killed Gorkon. We went into great detail about what had happened from our point of view. Worf was another Klingon who surprised me; he believed us. He said he didn't think humans would carefully plan an assassination and then beam themselves into custody.

The trial was in a grand hall, with hundreds of Klingons yelling for our heads. The evidence was piled high against us, and my reputation for hating Klingons was well known. But in case the judge wasn't convinced, they played an excerpt from my log.

"I've never trusted Klingons, and I never will. I'll never forgive them for the death of my boy." I couldn't deny that those were my words. But I knew in that moment that it wasn't only the Klingons who were framing me. I'd recorded that a few days before; only a member of Starfleet, a crewman on my ship, could've gotten that log excerpt.

My own people were part of this. As angry as I was at the Klingons, it had blinded me to much closer enemies. And I had been an unintended coconspirator.

I had assumed Gorkon was lying, that he didn't want peace; I couldn't imagine a Klingon who'd seek the same things I did. And I would have let all them die rather than help. David's death festered, and I didn't want it to heal. It was easier to hate and blame. I understood the conspirators.

McCoy and I were of course found guilty, but due to Worf's spirited defense our death sentence was commuted to life imprisonment on Rura Penthe, the frozen prison planet in Klingon space. Thanks to the viridian patch, Spock was able to rescue us from there, and then we rooted out the conspirators.

Their leader was Cartwright.

I arrested him and put him in the brig on the *Enterprise*. I was personally going to take him back home to stand trial. I also wanted to talk to him. As we began our trip to Earth, I went to see him in his cell. He looked me straight in the eye; he was not sorry for what he'd done.

"I was trying to protect us," he said. He used the excuse men had relied on for centuries: war is necessary for security. I wanted details of the conspiracy. I knew it had involved several highly placed Klingons as well as the Romulan ambassador. All of them wanted the same thing: the same balance of power and the same borders that kept the Galaxy the way it was. Cartwright wouldn't give me too many details, and he apologized for having put me in prison. But he felt the consequences were too great.

"They're animals," he said. "We can't live with them." A few days before, I might have agreed with him. But now, I took great pleasure in pointing out something he'd missed.

"Lance, don't you see? You proved that we *can* live with them. You hate Klingons more than anyone, and yet your conspiracy proved that, when Klingons and humans have a common goal, they work together just fine."

I'll remember the look on his face for the rest of my life.

I went back to the bridge and looked around at my old friends. Spock, McCoy, Uhura, Chekov. We had all been brought to the brink of a holocaust that would've cost billions of lives, by a bunch of old men whose fear of death made them seek an unobtainable measure of security. Men like me, who'd grown up hating Klingons, and didn't know there was another choice. Men who'd gotten used to being the inner circle of a democracy's military, thinking they knew best, and depriving the rest of us of our right to make decisions. I'd seen it firsthand working with Nogura. And now, my contemporaries and I in the upper ranks at Starfleet had almost missed it. "The price of liberty," the American patriot Thomas Jefferson wrote, "is eternal vigilance." We needed the next generation to start keeping watch.

It was time for me to go.

We brought the *Enterprise* home, again. Or maybe the *Enterprise* brought us home, it's hard to know which. As we pulled into Earth orbit, we passed a space dry dock, where the next *Enterprise* sat, almost completed. This was truly the end of my era as captain of the starship; I didn't even know who would be taking over. I said goodbye to my friends, certain I would see them all again soon.

As I usually did after a long trip in space, I went back to Iowa. My father was there, and we sat on the porch on a pair of antique rocking chairs. Mom had taken off again to a conference, this time on Andoria. Dad was in his eighties; he was big and stocky, and still vital. He asked me what I was going to do now. I said I wasn't sure. I thought about the fact that I had nothing to come back to, no wife, no children, no home that I'd built myself. I looked over at my dad and saw myself, but also my opposite. He had all the things I didn't, and I had much of what he'd given up.

"Dad," I said, "did you regret giving up your career?" He took a long pause.

"I don't know," he said. "I made a decision. My dad was never home; I wanted you and Sam to know I would always be here. I don't know if it was a good choice, or the right choice; it was just my choice." We sat and talked a while longer, and then noticed a Starfleet officer walking up the path to our house. It was Peter, now in his thirties. Dad said he heard I was coming and decided to take a quick shore leave. He'd gotten a new assignment, commanding the *Starship Challenger*. I stood up to greet him, and he grabbed me in a hug.

"Great to see you, Uncle Jim," he said. I stood back and took in his new rank insignia.

"Great to see you too, Captain Kirk," I said.

✦

That was several months ago. When I announced my retirement from Starfleet, a historian at Memory Alpha contacted me. He requested if he could collaborate with me on my autobiography. With no other projects on the horizon, I agreed. I sit now, having finished it.

Tomorrow, they are christening that new *Enterprise*. I will be there, but there will be another captain in the command chair. I suppose the journey back through my memories has made me realize that perhaps I had retired too soon, because as long as I sat in that chair, I felt relevant. I have some regret that I could never figure out how to break the cycle of my life, finding relevancy in something besides Starfleet. I suppose that makes me like a lot of other people, who don't really know how to change.

My collaborator, upon reading an early draft, noted that he was surprised I didn't mention any of the commendations I received from Starfleet, and I had to examine that. I realized that the medals I have do remind me of my victories, and that's the problem. The Duke of Wellington said, "Nothing except a battle lost can be half so melancholy as a battle won." Too many people died for me to win those medals. And all those victories I suppose made it hard for me to connect, to foster relationships and a life. I just kept going back to being a captain. In that chair, I felt like I accomplished a lot; it felt like I helped more people than I hurt. I hope that's true.

Even as I sit here, this doesn't feel like an end. I realize 60 is not all that old. Starfleet may not want me, but maybe I can get a decommissioned ship. I could fill it with people like myself, who still want to help but have been mustered out. We could set our own missions, help where we can, try to stay out of trouble. But also get into some trouble.

I laugh. The cycle, it's starting again. I'm not finished with the Galaxy, not ready to walk away from command. I want more.

But then, who doesn't?

AFTERWORD

BY SPOCK OF VULCAN

JAMES T. KIRK WAS REPORTED KILLED IN ACTION shortly after completing this manuscript. He was aboard the new *Enterprise*, and helped save it from destruction. The report said he was blown out of the ship when the hull was ruptured. His body was never recovered.

But he is not dead.

I will justify that statement in a moment. First, I take fault with some of the logic in his manuscript. He wonders whether he helped more people than he hurt. But it is a matter of objective fact that due to his efforts, four major interspecies wars were avoided. The innocent billions whose lives were saved by his actions far outnumber those who fell by his hand. This does not even include all the discoveries the ships under his command made, which have gone on to improve the quality of life for all the citizens of the Galaxy.

He has many regrets about not having a family of his own. From my own perspective, James Kirk pushed me toward an acceptance of my humanity, and by extension, an acceptance of myself as a whole. I learned from him many things, especially how to joke, and always felt his watchful eye over me. I know that I was not the only crew member to feel this way. He was our father, and though it violates my philosophy to say so, we loved him for it. His children are the crew members who revered him and carry his legacy now to the limits of known space. His family lives on.

In addition, his work and accomplishments make him one of the greatest men who ever lived. That is objective fact; as a Vulcan, I am incapable of hyperbole.

But his story is not over, because, as I said earlier, he is not dead.

This is not the first time I have said this, and many individuals believe that I have no proof, and that I am indulging my human half's need for "wishful thinking."

But it is not. I know this logically; it is actually my Vulcan half that has the proof.

One of the effects of my people's ability to mind-meld is a permanent connection between the mind of the Vulcan initiating the meld and that of the subject. From moment to moment, I am only vaguely aware of these connections; our mental disciplines keep them compartmentalized and away from our daily thought processes.

But one thing we are always certain of is when a connection is lost when someone dies.

Over the years, I have experienced the death of the Horta on Janus IV, and of Dr. Simon Van Gelder, and of Gracie the whale. The experience was akin to a building at night with its windows lit. And then one light goes out. You know whose light it is; you feel them gone.

I had mind-melded with James T. Kirk on several instances over his lifetime. His light still burns. He lurks in the recesses of my mind. Sometimes, I try to focus on him, to try to determine where he is. I do not believe he knows, but I can sense his emotional state. Wherever he is, he is happy.

I do not believe in an afterlife, but I will let my human half indulge in some wishful thinking.

He will return.

ABOUT THE EDITOR

David A. Goodman was born in New Rochelle, New York. After graduating from the University of Chicago, he moved to Los Angeles in 1988 to write on the television sitcom *The Golden Girls*. Since then Goodman has written for over fifteen television series, including *Wings*, *Dream On*, *Star Trek: Enterprise*, and *Futurama* (for which he wrote the Nebula Award–nominated *Star Trek* homage "Where No Fan Has Gone Before"). But he is probably best known for his work on *Family Guy*, for which he served as head writer and executive producer for six years and over one hundred episodes. He is the author of *Star Trek Federation: The First 150 Years*. He lives in Pacific Palisades, California, with his family.

EDITOR GOODMAN'S ACKNOWLEDGMENTS

First and foremost, I'm incredibly indebted to Dave Rossi, who came up with the idea for this book, and who, along with John Van Citters, made me an author. Both also made huge contributions to the manuscript. Thanks also to Andre Bormanis who pointed out what really could have happened on Psi 2000, as well as giving me an indispensible email lecture on ion pods; Mike and Denise Okuda for all their work providing the timeline and then giving their permission for me to depart from it; Richard Doctorow for the Wellington quote; John Scalzi for writing "Redshirts"; Simon Ward, my editor at Titan; Rosanna Brockley at becker&mayer!; Russell Walks for his amazing illustrations; and endless appreciation to my editor at becker&mayer!, Dana Youlin, for her hard work, guidance, and considerable talent at both writing and intimidation.

To my friends Mark Altman, Chris Black, Adam-Troy Castro, Manny Coto, Howie Kaplan, Dan Milano, Peter Osterlund, Mike Sussman, and Austin Tichenor because they read my work; Seth MacFarlane, whose professional patronage allows me this sideline. Thanks to the writers and directors of the canon, especially Brannon Braga and Rick Berman for admitting me to the club; and to William Shatner, for obvious reasons. And to my two cousins Michael Kaufman and Mike Metlay, whose example jump-started this interest in me.

To my sisters Ann Goodman and Naomi Press, my brother Rafael, my nieces Julia and Emma, my nephews Josh and Steven, my sister-in-law Crystal, my brothers-in-law Steve Press and Jason Felson, my in-laws

Phyllis and Bill Lowe, and my father-in-law Fred Felson (who holds the record for buying copies of my last book to give as a gift). Thank you all for your love and support. To my mother, Brunhilde Goodman, for her inspirational life, and her guidance in mine. And finally to my delightful and astounding children Talia and Jacob, and my lovely and loving wife Wendy, who are probably only going to read the acknowledgments and that's okay.